GAME
MISCONDUCT

ALSO BY ARI BARAN

The Penalty Box Series

Game Misconduct
Delay of Game
Home Ice Advantage
Goaltender Interference

Game Misconduct contains descriptions of alcohol and drug use disorders, alcohol and drug usage, depression, under-negotiated kink, and discussion of a past sexual assault.

GAME *MISCONDUCT*

ARI BARAN

HARLEQUIN

HARLEQUIN®

Recycling programs for this product may not exist in your area.

ISBN-13: 978-1-335-00439-0

Game Misconduct

First published in 2023. This edition published in 2026.

For questions and comments about the quality of this book, please contact us at CustomerService@Harlequin.com.

® is a trademark of Harlequin Enterprises ULC.

Harlequin Enterprises ULC
22 Adelaide St. West, 41st Floor
Toronto, Ontario M5H 4E3, Canada
Harlequin.com

HarperCollins Publishers
Macken House, 39/40 Mayor Street Upper,
Dublin 1, D01 C9W8, Ireland
www.HarperCollins.com

Printed in U.S.A.
1 2 3 4 5 6 7 8 9 10 HDC 29 28 27 2

GAME
MISCONDUCT

I.
SUMMER

CHAPTER ONE

July

Summer in Philadelphia probably wasn't as hot as it might've been somewhere else, but it still felt like swimming through hot glue during the worst of it. The entire city smelled like baked brick and melting asphalt, sweat, and stale piss, and Michael Sato was alone and miserable.

The two things didn't connect, logically, but the smell certainly didn't help his mood.

He hadn't gone home for the offseason and he didn't regret it. His parents had asked. They had pleaded, actually. But he'd told them he had to keep training. After his mediocre-at-best season, he couldn't afford to slip one inch if he wanted to make the Philadelphia Constitution's roster this season.

And that was true, but it wasn't the whole truth. The half-truth had always been his modus operandi when it came to his parents. It was pretty much the only way they had ever let him leave Gardena, and it had worked for him for twenty-five years. It was also his modus operandi when it came to everyone else, if he was being honest with himself.

He'd spent most of his time during the summer lifting weights, eating an ungodly amount of grilled chicken breasts and salmon and protein shakes, trying to bulk up after the inevitable end-of-the-season *my body's eaten itself*, ignoring repeated calls from his mom and then texts asking how he was doing—which weren't his mom expressing concern about him so much as they were a trap to see *what* he was doing—and playing *Call of Duty* by himself for hours at a time until he passed out on the couch of his empty apartment. He'd spent a lot of time sadly jerking off, thinking of nothing in particular.

So yeah—he didn't regret not going home exactly, because that would've been bad for different reasons, but goddamn, he was fucking lonely.

He got along well with the guys on the team, but he didn't like…hang out with them outside of the season. That was partially his own fault, for being a secretive freak, but it was hard to feel comfortable around a bunch of dudes when you had so much to hide, when you had so much to lose. Really, his closest friend—*only* friend—was Bee.

But he didn't have Bee, because she was having the time of her life with her boyfriend this offseason, and Mike was…he just wanted to get fucked up, or fuck someone up, or maybe get fucked, or maybe all three at once. He felt like ripping his entire skin off and clawing out his eyes, Greek myth-style. If he sat in the apartment by himself for much longer, he was going to completely lose his mind. Like the inmates on the 567th episode of *Lockup*. Which he had watched, sequentially.

Or like, *despite all my rage, I am still just a rat in a cage*.

You know.

That shit.

That incredibly stupid shit, which his brain would not stop spewing at him whenever he slowed down long enough to let it.

It was that feeling, that restless fury, that had him wandering down from their shitty apartment at 17th and Arch and farther into Center City. He didn't really have anywhere he was going. He bought some falafel at Goldie and ate it as he walked. Licked tahini from his fingers. It wasn't in his diet plan, but that didn't matter. No one bothered him. The heat was oppressive and sweat dripped down his back by the time the sun set, so he decided to cool off and get something to drink.

One drink led to several drinks led to many drinks as he bar-hopped his way through Philly, all alone. It was a good city for it. A beer town; lots of options. If you wanted local beer and brewpubs, you could find it. If you wanted craft from anywhere else, you got it. If you wanted to chug Bud Light at a dive bar, Dirty Frank's or Oscar's or Drinker's had you covered.

He mostly just wanted to get fucked up and not talk to anyone.

He got recognized a few times anyway, signed some autographs and smiled awkwardly for pictures. It didn't happen to him nearly as much as it happened to Bee, and he didn't think it was even his face people knew so much as it was the muscles and the tattoos and the signature buzzed hair. *If I ever wanna go incognito*, he had thought once, *I can just grow it back in.*

He wasn't sure why, but he was still out near ten.

Mike's alcohol tolerance was decent enough that even though he was, objectively, wasted, no one could really tell. He shouldn't have walked the way that he did, but his ambling ramble took him down 13th Street and into the heart of the Gayborhood.

It was really a stupid idea. It wasn't like he could ever pick up here—no one really recognized him, but he couldn't risk ending up on Twitter or something in case someone did—but walking by some of the bars and seeing other dudes just not giving a shit about anything like that made him feel even more alone.

It had been a really long time since he'd hooked up with anyone. He'd done it a few times in his first year with the Cons, but only on the road, where it seemed less risky, where he definitely wasn't a household face. And now he was grounded for the summer, with nothing to do and no one to talk to. The silence of his and Bee's apartment weighed down on him until he gave in. He'd scrolled through some apps; his accounts were anonymous, of course, no pictures because even his abs were easily identifiable. But no one had even caught his eye. And even if they had, it wouldn't have been worth it anyway.

Shoulders hunched forward, he kept walking, and if he hadn't looked up at exactly the wrong moment, he would've missed it.

Someone lit a cigarette deep in the alley and the smell drew his attention like a siren's song. He'd quit. He was always quitting, because it was fucking hell for your game, and he was making healthy choices these days. There was a part of him that always craved it anyway. So he looked.

And then he kept looking.

The guy who lit the cigarette was a giant of a man, six and a half feet tall and burly as hell. Like he had muscle, but he wasn't cut like Zach Reed, one of the Cons' alternate captains, was cut. He was solid, a bit of meat to cushion him, like he came by all of his size and strength naturally. The kind of body Mike always found most attractive. Someone who could actually manhandle him, maybe, if he wanted it. Thick, wavy black hair hung in front of the guy's face, and when he flicked it out of the way with a jerk of his head, Mike realized two things. If you had asked him later which one he had realized first, he would not have been able to say.

The only thing he would admit to was that he recognized him.

Daniel Garcia, his archnemesis, the architect of most of his misery last year, his first in the league. Mike could still remember, clear as day, how nervous he'd been his first game, knowing he had to do something to prove he deserved to be in the lineup. He'd picked a fight with the biggest, meanest guy on the ice, and that happened to be Daniel Garcia. And Daniel Garcia had kicked his ass. Mike could still remember the fury burning under his skin, the unbearable humiliation. And the concussion. They'd dropped the gloves every game after that, too, and every single time, win or lose, it had only made Mike madder. The way Daniel Garcia always seemed to be *laughing* at him, the way Mike's rage and terror and desire and need to prove himself was just a joke to him.

He'd always fought back, always delighted in humiliating Mike when he could—maybe a mature, logical person would say that he hadn't needed to fight Daniel

Garcia to the point where one of his teeth had broken off on Mike's knuckles, but Mike was not a mature, logical person, and neither was Daniel Garcia. Daniel Garcia, here in Philadelphia, Mike's adopted hometown. Daniel *fucking* Garcia, that fucking asshole, because of course he would be here today.

If Mike hadn't been drinking for the last five hours, he would have turned on his heel and walked away. But he had been. And that horrible thing under his skin, the burning rage with no target, the thing that wanted to fight and fuck or fuck and fight, that thing was out in full force now. It was impossible to fight someone to bloodied faces and knuckles and concussions and broken teeth every time you met them and not feel the urge to do it again, even when you met them in different circumstances.

Wasn't it?

Didn't everyone have someone they needed to beat the shit out of, no matter where they were?

"Get the fuck out of my city" was the first thing he said to Daniel Garcia since the last game they'd played against each other, when Garcia had fought him to a draw and said, *gotta try harder than that, motherfucker, I let you have the last one.*

Garcia's head snapped up. He looked different off the ice, without his helmet and mouthguard and his pads. For a moment his expression was unguarded. Surprised. Mike could see the white scar that cut through his left eyebrow, his scruffy eight-o'clock shadow, the thick eyelashes around and the dark circles underneath his eyes. His nose had been broken a few times, at least one of them by Mike; it had healed crooked. His mouth was full and turned down at the corners. And then the moment passed and whatever he had looked like before, now his face set into the implacable mask of the rink.

"You can't kick me out of an entire city, Sato." He sounded amused and Mike wanted to smash his face in. Garcia was wearing stupid black sneakers and stupid khaki shorts and a stupid black tank top that showed off every muscle in his shoulders and chest and arms. "It's not yours."

Mike wanted—to *smash his face in.*

Instead he stepped forward, into the alley. He could feel his fists curling up, like they did when he was ready to throw down on the ice. He shouldn't be here, he shouldn't be talking to Garcia (*why is he here, why here, specifically*, his brain whispered). Garcia watched him approach, and dropped the cigarette on the ground, stubbed it out with his toe.

"Who says I can't? What the fuck are you even doing here, anyway?"

Garcia laughed. It might have been a nice laugh, except for the fact that Mike hated him, except for the fact that he sounded exhausted. There wasn't any humor in that noise. "None of your goddamn business, kid. Jesus Christ, leave me alone."

He stepped farther back into the alley, like he was trying to get away. But there was nowhere else to go.

Garcia was right: Mike should have left him alone. But he couldn't and he never had been able to. His pride and his fury couldn't let him. *Or*, the nasty part of his brain whispered, *your need for someone to* see *you?*

Almost like he was watching himself from outside of himself, he got right up in Garcia's face, close enough almost so their bodies touched. There was an inch of space in between them, but it felt like nothing. He had to look up at Garcia, something that had always annoyed the fuck out of him, but it didn't matter now. He'd knocked that asshole's teeth out before; they'd beat the shit out of each other every time they were in the same city. He could do it again.

He could do it here.

Garcia exhaled and Mike could smell his breath. Whiskey and cigarettes. He was close enough that he could see Garcia's eyes, pupils wide and dark. He was close enough that he could feel the space between them, electric.

"Oh, I got it," Mike said. "I see how it is. You're a tough guy on the ice, but you're a fucking coward off it."

"Sato—"

"No! You don't get to just fucking *show up* in *my city*—"

Mike threw the first punch. He always threw the first punch. Slightly hysterically, he was furious about the fact that to hit Garcia in the eye, he had to punch up, like he was throwing his hands in the air for a dance. It connected because Garcia didn't bother moving away. But then it was like something in him finally snapped, and the fight was on.

It was different throwing down when you weren't on skates. Balance was different. Height was different. Strategy was different. Mike had no real strategy except staying out of reach and throwing punches at whatever part of Garcia he could. Some of them connected. Some of them didn't. Mike was fast and quick; he knew it. Boxing jabs, in and out, light on his feet. Garcia didn't have any of that. He had brute force and fists that connected with the kind of reverberation Mike could feel. Knew there'd be bruises in the morning.

Fucking good.

Then Garcia landed a hit to the side of Mike's head that snapped his neck back, vision filled with stars, everything ringing. It was silent except for Mike's ragged breath and Garcia's slow exhale as he shook his hand out.

"Is that all you fucking got?" Mike demanded, when he managed to pull the shreds of his wits about him. He hoped that wasn't going to be a concussion.

It happened faster than Garcia should have been able to move. For such a big man, for such a deliberate, inexorable fighter, he was quicker than Mike had expected. The force of his entire body, shoulder first, a check without pads, slammed Mike against the brick wall. Knocked the wind out of him. His elbow pinned Mike's chest, digging in with such force that he almost couldn't breathe. Fifty pounds over Mike's 180, at least. He could feel his ribs creaking under it. Garcia's entire frame pressed against him, trapping him in place. Mike could feel him. Everything. Every ounce of weight, every contour of his muscle. His fingers slammed Mike's free wrist into the wall.

"No. It's not." Garcia's voice wasn't angry. There was something strange in it, though. Swallowed off in his throat. Mike looked up. Garcia's eyes were wide and dark and wild, and Mike had split his lip open again. Blood dribbled down it onto his black shirt. "Give it *up*, Sato. You lost."

"Yeah? Well, you can suck my dick," Mike said, strangled, because the weight on his chest was choking him, punchy because he was furious, hadn't been hurt nearly enough to feel any better about any of this. He struggled, squirming, his entire body vibrating against Garcia's.

Garcia looked back at him, measuring. And the pressure was gone, abruptly, as he got down on his knees right there in the deep shadows of the fucking alley. Like he wasn't wearing shorts, like the concrete wasn't digging into his skin.

Mike's mouth went dry and he felt kind of lightheaded, but that was probably because all of the blood had rushed downward. "What the fuck," he managed. This had to be the strangest thing that had ever happened to him. He half expected someone to jump out from behind a dumpster with a phone ready to film his reaction for a TikTok prank.

Garcia licked his bloody lip. "You said—what, are you fucking scared?"

"Jesus Christ," was the only response Mike could manage. This was insane. He fucking hated Garcia. He hated him. He *hated* him. But Garcia was looking up at him with those big dark eyes, half mocking, half measuring, face bloody and bruised, and Mike's dick was into it, the fucking traitor.

It twitched. Okay. Really into it.

It was so fucking stupid, so fucking risky, that Mike couldn't believe he hadn't just kicked Garcia in the chin and left. It was so fucking stupid, but Mike had done the stupid thing every single time he met Garcia on the ice before tonight, and it seemed like an alley didn't change one damn thing. Even if no one could see them from the street, it was risky, it was—

Garcia didn't say anything else, just reached forward and put his hand on Mike's belt. Looked up at him the entire time, unwavering. He had really long eyelashes. Mike still wanted to smash his face in, but he exhaled a shuddery breath and stood stock-still. Garcia smirked, like, *that's what I thought*, the cocky bastard. Mike looked down at the hands undoing his belt buckle. They were big hands, knuckles a mess of bloody cuts and scar tissue. Garcia opened Mike's shorts just wide enough that he could palm Mike's dick through the boxers and press down hard.

Mike's eyes screwed shut, his head smacked against the wall and he swore under his breath. It really had been that fucking long since someone else had touched him that even this brief contact, from Garcia of all people, could fuck him up that way. God, that was depressing.

When he chanced a look, Garcia was watching him still. Like they had all the time in the world, like they weren't in public. It felt like he'd been flayed open, everything exposed. He didn't like it.

"Are you—are you going to do it or what?"

Garcia didn't say anything, just leaned forward and tugged Mike's boxers down and took his entire length in his mouth, never looking away. Wet heat and suction, and a teasing press of his tongue against the slit. Immediately Mike knew he'd done it before. Like, going down on his knees in a fucking alley was the first clue and definitely a dead giveaway, but holy shit, Garcia knew what he was doing.

Any other thoughts he had, or was about to have, short-circuited completely when Garcia started to move his mouth. So Mike was drunk and horny and fucked up on adrenaline but he kind of lost control of his entire body, hips jerking forward as Garcia both took it, and then when Mike couldn't stop, viciously shoved him back against the wall, hard enough to bruise. Mike had to bite his lip to keep from making noises, although he was fucking whimpering anyway.

It was probably the meanest blowjob he'd ever gotten, but he wouldn't have expected anything less. Garcia would get him close, then scrape Mike's skin with his teeth and pull away, leaving him panting and cursing again. It seemed like it went on forever, but he was so fucking keyed up, it was probably only a minute or two before he could feel his toes curling and tried and failed to push Garcia's head to the side before he came.

Garcia didn't move.

Mike died for a couple of seconds there. Everything went blank.

"What the fuck," he gasped.

It was kind of a miracle he was still on his feet, honestly.

Garcia was still on his knees, wiping his mouth with the back of his hand, and Mike's dick was hanging like right the fuck out there, slowly softening. He looked down and saw with nasty satisfaction that Garcia was hard, just from sucking him off, just from watching him come. Just from swallowing.

Mike had thoughts about that, but his brain hadn't yet returned from the war, and every time he opened his mouth to say something, the only thing that would come out was, "What the *fuck*."

"That was a blowjob," Garcia said, finally. His voice was rough and gravelly because Mike had fucked his throat. "I know you've probably never had one before, Sato, but try to keep the fuck up."

"You—" Mike swallowed, then looked down. He

should probably be polite and…wave the white flag, at least temporarily. "Uhhh." He sounded like an idiot, but that was about the level his brain was operating at right now. "Uh. Did you want me to do something about that?"

Garcia looked down, like his own fucking erection was something he was just discovering, then hauled himself up to his feet. His knees were bloody too, abraded from the concrete and studded with little rocks from the ground, and Mike's dick gave a valiant little jump at the sight of them.

"Yeah, no. I'm good," Garcia said, and rolled his eyes like it wasn't a serious offer. Before Mike could say anything, he had turned and walked out of the alley, leaving Mike to try to shove his dick back into his boxers, buckle up his belt.

"What the *fuck is wrong with you*?" he yelled after Garcia's retreating back, but it was too late. He scrubbed his hand over his face, legs shaky.

He had definitely lost that one.

It was just Mike's luck that Bee came home before the bruises faded. Beatrice Morin, his best friend. Beatrice Morin, the first woman drafted in the league, a player whose sheer talent and bloody-minded determination had already proven wrong the people who'd said it was a publicity stunt by the worst team in the league.

The two of them had bonded early on in their rookie year, a Black woman and a Japanese-American guy forcing their way into a white league, long shots to make the team who'd managed to carve out a roster spot together. She'd spent the summer in Finland on her offseason crazy romantic-comedy grand gesture adventure with Sakari Mäkelä, the Cons' goalie.

Mike had spent the summer having a nervous breakdown and making stupid fucking choices.

She texted him from the airport, hello, just landed, be home in a few hours, hope all is well, because she was a hockey robot masquerading as a sixty-year-old woman. Mike looked at their apartment, which he had cleaned up in anticipation of her return, cleared it of the evidence of his depression summer, and thought it was probably mostly okay.

He looked at his eye and his cheekbone in the mirror and thought they were definitely not okay. Both of them were in the mid-bruise stage, purple and yellow and green, and every time he looked at his face, he thought about Garcia in the alley and kind of wanted to die a little.

Actually, the worst thing was remembering the dismissive way Garcia had said, *yeah, no, I'm good* and walked away. Mike still couldn't figure out if the insult or the unfinished business made him angrier—the implication that, once again, he wasn't *good enough.* In the end it was probably bullshit he was thinking about it still, anyway; it didn't matter.

Bee arrived with a suitcase full of clothes, all of which she had bought in Finland after showing up at the airport with only her passport and a crazy plan to tell Mäkelä she was sorry for breaking his heart and wanted to give their relationship a go after all and fuck whatever anyone else thought about it. Bee stood out no matter where she went, and it wasn't just because she was basically as famous as you could be in Philadelphia. She was tall and striking and usually wore an expression like she could see right through your damn soul.

Vacation and Mäkelä had clearly agreed with her, because she looked relaxed and happy, her entire face beaming, her brown skin tanned even darker, curly hair in slim braids tied up in a ponytail. She wore cutoff jean shorts and a Cons T-shirt, because she was exactly the kind of dork who wore jorts and team merchandise everywhere, and her face was bright and open when she shoved at the door with her shoulder.

But whatever she'd been about to say, she forgot when she saw him.

"Michael!"

She was the only person who called him Michael other than his parents and the only person he would ever let call him Michael, besides his parents, who did it entirely against his will no matter how many times he asked them not to.

"It looks worse than it is," he tried to reassure her, but she'd already dropped the suitcase and crossed the room to grab his head and turn it to get a better look at the injury. He winced as her fingers brushed his cheek.

"How did you even…? What *happened*?"

"I fell down," he told her, the age-old excuse that everyone could see through but no one would actually challenge.

She looked at him severely but asked only, "Who do I have to punch?" and he loved her for it.

He just loved her, period.

"Really, Bee, it was my fault. I was stupid." His traitor brain helpfully supplied several mental images of exactly how stupid he had been, like he needed that right now.

“I don’t think I believe you, Michael, but…”

“Thanks, Bee. Now tell me all the important shit.”

“Important shit?”

“Yeah. You know. How was *Finland*, how bad do reindeer smell, are Mäkelä’s parents as weird as he is, *that shit*.”

Bee laughed, and although he knew he wasn’t going to be able to hear the end of it, she let it drop, and that was all he could ask for.

The problem was that he couldn’t let it go. And it wasn’t like he could afford the distractions. He really was fighting for a spot on the team this year. Last year he’d done *okay*. He’d averaged about eleven minutes a game, which wasn’t awful for playing third pair or spending some time in the press box, but it wasn’t great by any metric. His advanced stats had been so abysmal he’d had them tacked to his bedroom wall for motivation. He’d won more fights than he’d lost, and he’d done his job during those fights. Namely: the dirty hits aimed at Zach Reed, the Cons’ star forward and alternate captain; Nate Singer, the Cons’ captain; and Bee had decreased.

But Mike wasn’t a standout; he’d only had three goals and four primary assists, a few more secondaries, and he wasn’t lighting any fires under anyone’s ass. He’d had some time on PK but not much. He’d never even gotten a glimpse of the power play. There were always going to be younger kids coming up, and although they weren’t generational players or even necessarily top-six guys, there were enough solid players in the farm system that he was replaceable. He was a grinder, sure, but even the skill players worked their asses off.

Everyone wanted the same thing, he just had to want it more.

If wanting guaranteed success, Mike would win the Defenseman of the Year award every season. As it was, he finished every day of training camp with his body aching, sweat dripping down his face, and Netty elbowing him in the back cheerfully and chirping him in his heavy accent.

Bee was home about half of the time. The other half she stayed over at Mäkelä's, which was an adjustment all on its own. It was fucking sad how much Mike had come to rely on her, even if he tried not to let her know, even if some of the guys who liked to live dangerously and had stupid, outdated ideas about things chirped Mäkelä constantly about his competition when they thought Bee wasn't around to hear it.

It wasn't even a satisfaction when they put out the roster and his spot was secure. He had a two-way contract, so they could send him down anytime they wanted to save the cap space and it wasn't like there was any danger of anyone picking him up off waivers. That was Mike's problem, really: no matter what measure of success he reached, he was never happy with it, feeling the edge like he was watching the pebbles tip off into the air before his weight launched him after them. For him, life had never been like it had for his siblings, who'd worked hard, but were, like, *another* professor, the founder of a stupidly successful tech startup that did something Mike didn't even fully understand, the head of a nonprofit that coordinated research and education on climate change. *They* didn't have to worry about slipping. Things came easily to them in a way they never did for Mike, and no one in his family would ever let him forget it, even when he did his best to avoid talking to them as much as he could get away with it.

It was in this self-loathing fog that he found himself watching Pittsburgh's first preseason game against the New York Liberty. He wasn't like Bee, who watched a truly staggering amount of hockey games in her spare time. Mike was content to rely on the team's pre-scouts and leave it at that.

This was just poking a bruise.

He had one eye on the TV, the other scrolling through different apps. If he mostly only looked up when number 21 was on the ice, that was his own business. It was weird, watching Garcia skate from the TV angles. Watching him skate when Mike wasn't on the ice waiting to fight him, he noticed a few things he'd never noticed before. Garcia skated slower than almost anyone else out there, that he favored his left side even though he shot right, that he always seemed to be where he needed to be to interrupt a play, but that he never pinched too far.

Mike frowned.

Garcia was barely on social media. His Snap was private. His Twitter was mostly bland RTs for shit like #bellletstalk and the Hockey Diversity Alliance; the last personal thing he'd posted was his broken teeth after he fought Mike last year. His Instagram wasn't much better. He'd shared his bloody mouth there, too, but there were two newer posts. One was in the gym, benching a pretty obscene amount of weight, muscles straining, every one of them standing out in sharp relief. Mike snorted, because bench was like one of the least useful lifts for hockey, and it was obviously just to show off.

In the other, Garcia balanced an admittedly adorable toddler on his knee, a girl with his big dark eyes and thick curly hair, wearing a child-sized Hornets jersey. *Mi sobrina favorita*, the caption read. He was smiling in the picture, a soft half smile, and he looked completely different from any other time Mike had seen him.

On TV, Garcia was fighting one of the Liberty's d-men, a guy closer to his size than Mike could ever hope to be. And Garcia was destroying him. It was barely a contest even though Garcia's heart didn't seem to be in it. He punched slow and steady, like he was bored. The Lib gave it his best but it was like swatting at the side of a mountain for all the good it did.

Mike looked down at his phone again. He took a deep breath. He shouldn't do it. There was no reason to do it. There was nothing to even hope for from doing it. But he couldn't stop thinking about it, no matter how hard he tried, on the nights he was home all alone with his thoughts. He clicked the little triangle, *very* fucking careful not to accidentally hit Follow, and typed in the message box,

you look slow as shit old man

you fighting in your sleep or what

It was a terrible fucking idea, but he sent it before he could second-guess himself, and after that, it was too late.

Maybe if he was lucky, Garcia wouldn't even see it.

Or maybe, his brain whispered nastily, *you'll get lucky and he will.*

II.
FALL

CHAPTER TWO

October

Danny was getting old.

Not *old* old; he was barely thirty-five. But definitely hockey old.

It took less and less to fuck up his body after a rough game, and it took longer and longer to recover. Danny stood in one of the cryotherapy tubes that the front office had invested in last year and felt his lungs expand in the push of below-freezing cold gas, blood rushing in his veins. It was better than an ice bath, but it didn't do much to force the ache from his hips or from his shoulders or any of the number of other small pains he lived with every day. Not in the long term.

It did allow him to get out of the CEC without limping too badly where other people could see him, though, so it was worth it.

The preseason grind was worse this year. He remembered a time when he'd looked forward to it, when it meant the year was going to start in earnest, when it meant more time on the ice. For as long as he could remember, Danny had loved hockey. Loved it more than anything, loved it more than anyone he'd ever been involved with. Loved it long after they left him. He still loved it, but now he just felt tired. Old and tired, even after a win. Felt like shit even after a good fight.

They'd lost tonight and that felt worse.

He said goodnight to Brian, the assistant equipment manager, hustled himself into his sweats, and took the slow walk out to his car. It was a beautiful fall night, the moon was a perfect crescent above him, and Danny looked at the yawning dark of the parking lot and thought, *okay.*

Some nights he'd just go for a drive for a few hours, doing loops around the city until he could barely keep his eyes open, before returning to the Victorian he'd bought in Highland Park. He'd been with the Hornets for two seasons, but it still didn't really feel like home. He had some furniture but not much else. Hadn't seen much of a need for it.

Tonight he went straight home, though, because they were playing the Cons tomorrow and he was definitely going to have to fight, and it was guaranteed to be a bad one. Some guys talked about the dread they felt before a game, knowing they had to throw down, psyching themselves up for it, but at this point in his life everything was one slow smear of exhaustion and numbness. Even when he knew he might get the shit kicked out of him, he didn't think about it at all beyond the peripheral awareness that his body was going to hurt later.

But it always hurt.

That was why he had Percocet. That was why he had alcohol.

He dropped his bag in the foyer and went into the kitchen without turning on the lights. He cracked open a beer, swallowed two Percs with it, went into the living room, and lowered his body gingerly down onto the couch. And when the beer was finished he opened another one. And another one. He watched some random cooking show in the background. When he looked up, Gordon Ramsay was yelling at people. Some of them cried. It took a half hour or so, but finally, the aches faded into the background, and he could exhale.

Danny cracked his fourth beer. Checked his phone. Sighed when he saw the notifications. After every preseason game he'd played, Sato had DM'd him with increasingly obnoxious insults. The first: you look slow as shit, old man, you fighting in your sleep or what. After a win: what the hell did you contribute anyway, i could skate fucking circles around you. After a particularly messy fight where Danny didn't have the full range of motion in his arm but had given it a go anyway: your niece could probably hit harder than you. Danny read every single message, but never responded.

What could he even have said?

He wasn't sure what to make of Sato. Wasn't sure what to make of himself anymore, if he was being honest. Wasn't sure why he had done what he had done that night in Philadelphia.

Sure, Sato was hot as shit, with his wiry muscles and his pouty mouth and the blackwork tattoos—a mix of woodcut style and American trad—disappearing under his clothing in a way that made Danny want to know how far down they went. If they had met in a different way he probably would have wanted to fuck Sato anyway.

But they hadn't, and he did.

He'd walked away from Sato. Away from that alley. Back to his sister, Araceli, and his family in that fucking restaurant, so claustrophobic and warm, so many questions about how he was doing and what he was doing and whether he was happy and making healthy decisions, he'd had to leave to clear his head. Left them gaping in his wake. Lied about the black eye and bloody lip and scraped knees when he'd finally gone back, unable to avoid them anymore. Knew they hadn't believed him when he'd said it was nothing. He'd seen their faces. They'd been worried about him. They were always worried about him. They were always worried he was making unhealthy decisions, worried he was shutting them out.

That was all Araceli. Healthy decisions. Being open and honest.

And that was all Danny, doing exactly the opposite, unable to help himself.

He didn't know how to tell them that there was nothing to worry about. He just had to make it through two more years, he'd retire, and it would be fine. He didn't know how to tell them his body was breaking down, but he couldn't give up the game, not just yet. He didn't know how to tell them that even though he couldn't give it up, he didn't love it the same way.

He didn't know how to tell them that he barely felt anything anymore.

He'd felt something in Philadelphia. He felt something now, looking at his inbox and every nasty thing Sato had ever written to him. He didn't know what that *was* yet, but it wasn't numb.

you talk a lot of shit for a guy who can't back it up, Danny said, and hit send.

Bee watched Mike with that disconcerting stare, the one that made you feel like she could see right through your fucking skin and into your guts. Mike wouldn't actually be surprised if she could. They were up later than they normally would have been on a game night, hanging out on the couch, his legs sprawled over her lap. Bee put on the latest Hornets' preseason game on demand in preparation for their game the next day. He had already seen it, but he wasn't going to tell *her* that. It was good to have her home again, and it meant more to him than he wanted to admit that they had the chance to actually spend some time together again.

He pretended not to watch while watching from the corner of his eye and still keeping half an eye on his notifications, and she watched until she'd noticed, and then started looking at him suspiciously.

"Why are you looking at me?" he asked, when it seemed like she wasn't going to stop on her own.

"You keep checking your phone."

He clicked the side button and locked it. "Yeah?"

Bee's eyebrows went up. They stared at each other, but he looked away first. "You never check your phone."

"Huh? I check my phone all the time."

Bee's eyebrows hadn't moved. "You never check your phone that often."

He gave her the patented Michael Sato glare, but it lost something, considering he couldn't even meet her eyes for longer than a minute, and she knew that he was more bark than bite, especially when it came to her. And he *was* waiting for a response to the last one, which was, can't back it up? guess you've got other teeth you don't need.

"I'm bored and I hate watching the Hornets play. Like in case you forgot, they're kind of our divisional rivals."

"They are, but..." Bee looked from the TV, where Garcia's fight against the Libs' d-man was playing, to Mike, phone tucked screen-down against his chest in self-defense. "You've been acting really oddly since I've been home."

He groaned. "I'm *fine*, Mom."

Bee said, "Hmm" in a way that did remind him disconcertingly of his mother. She went back to watching the game.

He waited until the clock ran down to two minutes left in the game before checking his phone again. Garcia hadn't responded but Mike wasn't really expecting him to. Garcia hadn't for most of the preseason; there was no reason he'd do it now. The brief message was the aberration. Bee looked at him again and frowned.

Mike locked his phone, untangled his legs, and said, "I'm gonna hit the hay. Big day tomorrow, eh?"

"Eh," Bee agreed, although she was still frowning at him in the glow of the television as he got up to go to his bedroom.

Mike felt off-balance the entire morning, like he had an electrical current running beneath his skin, and he could feel it whenever he stood still for too long. Morning skate went by too quickly, although apparently the fire under his ass impressed Coach, who clapped him on the back and said, "*That's* the kind of skating I like to see, Sato."

"Thanks, Coach."

Patrick Cote's full attention was almost as uneasy as Bee's. A lean man in his late forties, Cote had a, like, snooty bearing that seemed out of place on the ice, even though he had actually played professional hockey until he fucked up his knee. Hard to believe now, body wasted from years of just light weights in the gym, but he'd also been a fighter.

He knew what was up, in other words.

"And Sato."

"Yes, Coach."

"I don't want to see any funny business out there tonight."

"I don't know what you mean, Coach."

Coach looked at him with narrowed eyes, a small frown. "You know exactly what I mean. If you're going to fight, you fight clean. I don't want unnecessary penalties, I don't want any injuries, and I don't want a suspension before we even start the goddamn season."

Mike felt that itchy shock, the sting of disappointment, under his skin again. Why did everyone expect the worst of him? It was insulting, first Bee, and now Coach. Worse than insulting. It hurt all two of his feelings.

He might've fought on the ice, but he wasn't the kind of guy to argue with his boss, so he said, "Yes, Coach. I'll keep it clean."

"See that you do." Coach was still frowning. "I know you had a rough first game, but that was last season, and at this point, Sato, it's time to let bygones be bygones."

"Umm," Mike said. It wasn't a bygone and he couldn't let it be, but there was no explaining that to Coach. He couldn't explain it to himself, even. Something about Garcia's face just brought out the worst in him. Something about an entire season's worth of petty grudge moments building up brought out the worst in him.

He tried to keep his expression as neutral as possible, but Coach must have seen something in it he didn't like anyway because he shook his head and said,

"Dismissed, Sato." He sounded disappointed, but Mike didn't have time to worry about that.

He stripped quickly in the locker room so he could shower, not really looking to get hassled by any of his teammates today. The room atmosphere was about as perfect as you could ask for, especially compared to the Grizzlies—Columbus' minor-league feeder—where he'd spent a few seasons before getting traded to the Cons. In Philly, a lot of the players were friends. He was friends with some of them. They had that thing every hockey analyst talked about: chemistry. But sometimes the guys just liked to give each other shit, and sometimes it just made him feel even worse than he already did.

He wasn't nervous exactly, but he knew something was going to happen, he just didn't know what. Fighting was one thing, but this was something else.

Garcia had changed all of the rules and everything was all fucking mixed up in his head now. Pain and pleasure; crossed wires. Or maybe it had been mixed up before but he didn't have to look at it. Somehow Garcia had seen something in him, figured it out, even if he'd done it inadvertently. And Mike had never had to deal with any of this on the ice before. Had always kept hockey and sex pretty firmly separate, except for clandestine teenaged fumbling in juniors, and even then, it hadn't been an issue. It was with teammates and he hadn't felt strongly about any of it, or any of them.

That was the problem.

He felt really fucking strongly about Garcia.

He hated him and he shouldn't have let him go down on his knees like that. Shouldn't have thought sex wouldn't change things. That's what had fucked everything up. Well, it didn't matter, it wasn't going to happen again, and he wasn't going to even chirp anymore, even if he did want to throw Garcia off his game. Everything from now on was gonna be strictly hockey.

"Sato, what the hell? You've been in the shower like fifteen minutes, come *on*," Sean Elliott said. He was one of the fourth-line grinders, with a shock of ginger hair and a face like an overexcited poodle.

"Jesus Christ," Mike said, because he hadn't realized he'd been standing under the water that long. "Gimme a second."

"He thinking about his fight," Andrey Kuznetzov told Elliott, grinning as he walked out of the other stall toward them. He was, of course, completely naked, because Netty didn't give a shit about anything, let alone modesty. He didn't really need to: a big man with sleek black hair and a gray shine like a seal's, coal-dark eyes, and a strong jaw, always in on some joke you were too stupid to figure out. "You gonna fight tonight, Misha? We play Hornets, course you gonna fight."

Mike could feel his mouth twisting down. Exactly what he'd wanted to avoid, especially when he was naked too. Not that it was embarrassing, exactly, but it felt vulnerable and exposed. Especially when the only parts of him that weren't covered in black ink were his dick and balls, and a little bit of spare real estate in the crease where his leg met his torso; the back of one hand.

"I dunno, Netty. Coach told me I had to keep it clean tonight."

"Never stopped you before." Netty was always smiling, the gap in his teeth on display. He stuck his tongue into it, mocking. Not malicious, but definitely mocking. The pink tip wriggled obscenely.

"Yeah, well, I'm not trying to ride the bench this whole season," Mike muttered, as he pulled on his pants and shirt and beat a hasty retreat. You weren't going to win fighting with someone who never got offended and was pathologically determined to have fun no matter the cost. He'd learned that a long time ago. If you couldn't fight and couldn't win, you had to leave.

He was going to fight Garcia tonight, in the last game of the preseason, but he had to keep his shit together.

He had to keep it aboveboard.

Danny stood in front of his stall in the visitors' locker room and took a breath. His only pregame ritual was silence. Silence where he gathered his thoughts, assessed the parts of his body that would be giving him the most trouble and how to avoid putting more stress on them, silence where he thought about the guy he'd have to fight and the best way to fight him. It usually worked. Calmed him down. Helped him get through the game with his usual tunnel vision. But today he found himself unable to focus and scrubbed his hand over his face.

"Dude, you good?" Landry asked.

"Fine," Danny said, without thinking. *Fine. Fine. I'm fine. Fine, I'm fine, I'm fine.* Strangely, today, it wasn't even his hip that was giving him trouble. Wasn't his hands. Wasn't his knees.

"You look like you're miles away, man."

Danny shrugged, turned away from the stall to face Matthew Landry. He was still a kid; constantly fighting to prove otherwise. Sato's age, twenty-three or twenty-four. He reminded Danny of a leashed junkyard dog. Vicious to outsiders and almost desperate for approval from the team. Not that it made Danny feel any better about some of the shit that came out of his mouth on the ice. Just something to keep in the back of his head: that Landry couldn't be trusted. Teammates came and went, and so did he. It wasn't worth getting into it if it wasn't aimed at him directly.

No one had ever been able to say that Danny Garcia was a problem in the locker room.

"Happens when you get old."

Landry laughed and slapped him on the back. "Well, kick his ass out there tonight anyway, old man."

"Yeah," Danny agreed, without rancor and without warmth.

It would be the first time he'd seen Sato in person since the last time he'd been in Philadelphia. Where he usually felt tired, now he felt uneasy, mulling over how this was going to work on the ice. He knew Sato would go for him, because Sato always did, no matter if Danny'd been instigating the game before or not. It had been that way since their first game. Danny had embarrassed Sato badly, knocked him to the ice and put him out of commission for three games. He thought about Sato messaging him *guess you've got other teeth you don't need* and half smiled to himself, hearing it in Sato's low-pitched drawl.

Christ, that kid was a grade-A asshole.

A grade-A asshole who liked to run his mouth but made helpless noises Danny couldn't get out of his head months later.

Danny considered various other ways he could get Sato to shut the fuck up and shook his head. Not the thoughts to have before the game. He squared his shoulders and tried to get himself back into the right state of mind, thoughts void, emotions erased. And he followed the rest of his team out into the tunnel and onto the ice.

Playing the Cons this season was like playing a different team. They'd had the trappings the season before, but it hadn't been enough to get over the hump. Their GM had made a bit of a stir when he'd traded Kyle Hill, a former second overall pick, who'd had a disappointing rookie season but definitely still had time to grow. They'd shed deadweight like Jonathan Bouchard, who'd needed Player Assistance and an early LTIR-ment more than he'd needed a contract extension. They'd made the playoffs for the first time in half a decade and it was obvious they wanted more. He'd watched some of their preseason games, particularly keeping his eye on Sato.

It was funny: for someone who clearly had the potential to play a decent two-way game, who had the speed and strength, Sato certainly seemed afraid to play the way he could have. And Danny, who felt the loss of that kind of ability every time his hip ached when a storm rolled in, every time he pushed himself too hard on the ice and paid for it later, could appreciate the humor in the situation. They were both at the bottom of the lineup, although for very different reasons. And it didn't matter at all. Their coaches deployed them for the same thing.

As the lines changed and Danny swung himself over the boards onto the ice, he tensed for a confrontation he knew was inevitable.

* * *

Mike knew that what he was doing was stupid. He was playing farther into the o-zone than he usually ever played, and more often, and it was solely because Danny Garcia moved too slowly and never came too far over the blue line. There was no other way for a confrontation. He knew, as he was doing it, skating literal circles around Garcia, chirping him, poking at him with his stick. Not close enough for a slashing or hooking penalty but close enough to be a pest. He knew it was obnoxious. He knew, worse than that, that it was obvious.

But somehow, he couldn't stop.

"So I *can* skate circles around you," he said, as he flew by Garcia and with a clever hook of his stick stole the puck from him. The linesman didn't even see.

He could see Bee watching him from the bench. But he couldn't spare much of a thought for her. As they fought along the boards, he dug his shoulder into Garcia's chest, gasped a few muttered curse words before they pulled apart and Elliott drove the puck to the net and snapped in the Cons' first goal of the game.

Garcia didn't react much beyond looking at him, even though Mike knew he was a regular trash talker on the ice. He just didn't want to give Mike the satisfaction. Their eyes met, briefly, as he shoved Mike into the boards and Mike choked out, "Fucking clumsy-ass piece of shit." Mike couldn't parse the expression on Garcia's face. Except his stomach did a flip and he suddenly felt like any fucking six-year-old on the schoolyard, pulling pigtails.

Back on the bench a few minutes later, he watched the action, chewing on his mouthguard and frowning in intense concentration at the back-and-forth. The Cons were playing a strong offensive game today, led by Bee and the first line, but the Hornets' goalie had gotten lucky and the bounces weren't going their way. One of Reed's shots had gone off the post. Mike chewed harder, like if he could bite through the plastic, he'd crack the secret of widening their lead.

Then he looked at the opposing bench and saw Garcia watching him again, staring at the guard hanging crooked out of his mouth. Jesus, he probably looked like a fucking idiot. He shoved it back over his teeth and glared at Garcia, and to his surprise, that asshole smiled. It was a barely there kind of grin, flashing across his face in an instant, replaced by nothing. If Mike hadn't been staring at him, he never would've seen it. His stomach did that flip again, and he resolved that the next time they were on the ice together, it was going to go down.

He had his chance five minutes later. Singer had scored a fucking beauty of a goal, Jakub Černý took a stupid penalty shortly thereafter, and Mike was out to kill the penalty. Garcia never got power play time, usually, but there he was, out on the ice. So that could only mean one thing. And when Mike saw Garcia heading for Antti Salonen, one of the Cons' A's, he muttered *fuck no you don't* under his breath.

The trick to checking guys who were bigger than him—which was, he hated to admit, a lot of them—was the speed and angle. He used geometry and physics to his advantage to shoulder Garcia out of the way. Even the impact felt heavy. Meaningful. Garcia was big. Like…*big.* But Mike had caught him unawares and while he didn't lose his balance, exactly, he staggered sideways, and Sally skated on, unmolested.

Garcia glared at him, and Mike's dick twitched in his fucking cup. Jesus Christ. He immediately dropped his gloves, like if he fought, maybe the stupid fucking parts of his body with a mind of their own would all shut the fuck up. He stood there glaring back, and Garcia looked him up and down, like at first he wasn't gonna drop too. For a split second Mike wondered whether this was just business, whether Garcia hated him as much as—

But then he did, and it was on.

Mike squared up to grab Garcia's jersey, but Garcia had other ideas about how this was going to go. He skated forward, shoulder down, and before Mike could react to the weird-ass start to a fight, Garcia slammed into him, full body, and they were falling to the ice. Mike had to fight to try to pull his weight so that he fell on top. It wasn't how the fights usually went. It also wasn't a fight he could easily win. Garcia outweighed him by fifty pounds and was over half a foot taller.

Everything happened fast. Couldn't have been more than a few seconds. He landed on the ice with Garcia's body on top of his. The impact hurt, both under him, and Garcia's pads pressing against his. The sudden jolt of 230 pounds of muscle slamming him into an equally unforgiving surface, Garcia's elbows digging into his chest. His knee between Mike's legs. Garcia's head was very close to his and Mike looked up into his eyes. The long lashes framing them. The sweat dripping from his hair into Mike's face.

"Is that what you wanted?" Garcia whispered in his ear, and Mike was suddenly, painfully hard.

The linesmen separated them before he could answer. Garcia gave him another look before he skated off to the penalty box, and Mike thought, for a second, maybe he was punching above his weight class after all. The thought only made him angrier. But then again, so did the inconvenient fucking erection that refused to subside, even as he limped his way to the box himself.

Fucking *Garcia.*

"Why did you fight the way you fought today?" asked Sophia Dawsey, the *Post-Gazette* reporter assigned to the Hornets' beat.

Danny didn't usually get trapped in the media scrum, particularly after a loss, mostly because no one was interested in what he had to say. They would come looking for him if he had a particularly violent fight—they'd been all over it when Sato broke his tooth; when Danny'd accidentally concussed the Jersey goalie. Otherwise, they focused on the stars, like Henri Jean-Phillipe Lévesque and Semyon Artyomov, or the guys with big personalities who gave good quotes, like Landry or Mitch Sorenson. This fight had not been a flashy one. He hadn't even thrown a punch, just wrestled Sato to the ice and left him there.

And yet Dawsey had sought him out, trapped him in the hallway before he could make it into the dressing room, and was looking expectantly up at him. Not for the first time, he cursed the weirdly casual scrum that Pittsburgh allowed.

"I don't know what you mean," Danny said, though he knew exactly what she meant.

"You didn't throw a punch. You took Sato right down to the ice."

Danny dug his teeth into his lower lip and looked right and left for anyone to rescue him, but the other Hornets were either answering questions of their own or had already made their own escapes. Whatever he said was going to be taken the wrong way by almost everyone. Sato especially. Dawsey was still looking at him with that reporter-eye he didn't like to see. He could have pushed around her, but he didn't do shit like that. It was bad enough being called a goon on the ice, let alone off it. Danny was always conscious of his size; of the space he took up.

"I've fought him before. I don't need to fight him again," he said finally, shrugging. "Seemed better for both of us to end it quickly."

"I note that you've actually fought Sato in every game you've played against—"

"Excuse me, Ms. Dawsey, I need to go." Danny side-stepped her.

For a moment she looked as though she was about to try to follow him down the hall. She had that determined face that made him think—but she didn't, and Danny, shoulders hunched, fast-walked into the dressing room. He breathed a sigh of relief. He was tired; his entire body sore from the aborted fight and from getting stuck out against the Cons' first line multiple times in the third period and then getting trapped on an almost two-minute shift without a change. There was a hotel room a bus ride or a twenty-minute walk away. Percs and alcohol waiting for him. And after that the possibility of sleep.

He thought about that in the shower. Whether it would be worth it to walk, stretch out his legs farther before he made it back, or try to hurry and catch the bus with the rest of the team. It was always a bad atmosphere after a loss. Lévesque was a perfectionist in all things and took it hard. Sometimes Danny didn't want to spend the entire ride talking about what they'd done wrong and what they needed to improve. That was what morning skate was for.

After a game all he wanted was to not think.

He was walking out of the arena when his phone buzzed in his pocket. His sister Araceli's image flashed on his lock screen. He'd recently updated the picture; she was holding Josie and smiling. He declined the call and slid the phone back into his pocket, anticipating an annoyed voice mail he'd listen and not respond to in the morning. He kept them on the phone with their transcriptions, reminders of all the ways he'd disappointed her and his parents.

The stadium where Philadelphia's basketball and hockey teams played their games was part of a massive complex that housed the Franklin, the football field, the baseball stadium, and a building that was mostly bars and restaurants. It was all hemmed in by what seemed like miles of parking lot, all steadily emptying. Its boundary on one side was Broad Street and I-95 on the other. The streaky headlights of a traffic jam ran up Broad and into the city and the other way as fans tried to get back onto the interstate.

He started the long trudge across the lot, illuminated by floodlights. There was always the chance a fan might recognize him and start something, but Danny didn't care. It had been such a shitshow of a game that he thought maybe the cool night air might clear his head.

It didn't.

He was still the same asshole who'd knocked a guy over rather than fight him or decline, just to humiliate him at a home game. He was the same asshole who wouldn't talk to his fucking sister, because he was afraid of what she'd say to him; because he was afraid she'd noticed the prescriptions and the drinking. He shoved his hands into his coat pockets and for a moment he felt a loneliness so intense it hit him like a punch to the solar plexus.

It passed. It always did.

No one recognized him, and he was glad of it. He left through the open gates, nodding absently to the guard in the booth, and started the long walk into the dark. The wide sidewalks of Broad Street gave way to narrower crosswalks that zigzagged under the overpass. He could hear the noise of horns in the distance; cars still moved at a snail's pace onto 95.

He kept walking.

The Navy Yard was a strange area of the city. It wasn't exactly a neighborhood: it was mostly industrial sites, corporate offices, and actual government buildings. They'd built a hotel there, but with that one exception, almost everything was closed by ten p.m. and it was relatively deserted except for traffic to and from the stadiums, the occasional late-night runner, and flocks of aggressive geese. The hotel wasn't far into it. All the buildings sat in the midst of long green fields, the older brick and stone, the newer glass and metal.

Footsteps behind him, a hand grabbing his shoulder. Danny whirled, tensed to fight, and didn't relax after that. Sato. He was wearing his street clothes, all black. Beat-up black leather jacket. Black skinny jeans, ripped at the knees; a hoodie with a band logo Danny couldn't even begin to recognize. His hair had started to grow in just long enough that you could probably get your fingers into it if you really tried. He didn't look surprised or worried when he saw Danny's stance. Just those dark brown, almost black eyes boring into him.

He could feel them like a hook in his stomach.

"Why the fuck wouldn't you fight me for real?"

Danny just looked at him. At first, he couldn't say anything. He was so tired. All he wanted was sleep. He knew he should walk away, but Sato pulled him like a magnet. A planet orbiting against his will. He couldn't walk away, not yet.

"Your ribs'll tell you it was real tomorrow," he said finally.

Sato's lip curled up. "Some bruises. What-fucking-ever, dude, I've cracked my ribs before, some bruises ain't shit. Why didn't you *fight me*?"

He moved forward and Danny moved back. It wasn't a retreat. They continued that dance, like neither of them knew what they were doing. But Danny knew exactly where Sato was maneuvering him. And he knew Sato knew why he was doing it. Around the back of the hotel, toward an area fenced in high concrete and wooden doors that must have held generators. One of the doors was open.

He had no illusions about what was going to happen next. He could not look away from Sato's face. Could not look away from the black ink tattoos that curved around his neck, thought about putting his hand there and closing his fingers against Sato's skin.

Then they were over the threshold into the little fenced-off generator yard, and Sato shoved him hard against the concrete. Danny let him. It felt reassuringly solid behind his shoulder blades.

"Why didn't you fight me?"

"It was easier," Danny said, honestly. "I don't need to fight you when I can just take you down."

Something complicated happened with Sato's face. Rage and disgust and arousal flickered across it, chasing each other. Then he was just glaring. "I fucking hate you, you know that?"

Danny knew that. He didn't answer, just extended his hand into the space between them and pressed it hard against Sato's chest, his ribs, his heart. Where he knew there were probably bruises already, the color rising without making a show until the next day. Sato hissed at the contact but didn't pull away. Danny pressed again. He knew it had to hurt. He watched Sato's face, his eyes. He couldn't have looked away if he wanted to.

"I wasn't going to do this," Sato was saying, and he sounded angry, *so* fucking angry, "I *wasn't*—I fucking hate you, this is supposed to be about hockey, this is supposed to—"

Danny dug his fingers into the bone and muscle, and Sato made a strangled noise halfway between a gasp and a moan. Danny thought he could listen to him make that noise for hours without getting tired of it. More than that, maybe.

"This is…this is supposed to…"

The blows came as a surprise, though they shouldn't have. Sato's hand knocked Danny's away and his elbow slammed into Danny's throat. Gasping, Danny let him do it. It hurt, of course. He could feel Sato's bony elbows catching him in tender places that had deep-layered bruises already, feel Sato's fists against his bone. It didn't matter. He didn't move to cover his face, didn't move to fight back, not yet. The blows jolted feeling back into his body. Sharp pains against the dull background ache he always felt.

It was a gift he was offering Sato. Danny could take it. Could take whatever he had to give.

When he'd had enough, though, he extended his hand and did what he'd wanted to do earlier. Grabbed Sato by the throat, tightened his fingers, framing the black ink hands on Sato's neck. Sato never stopped fighting, although whenever the kid struggled or tried to knock Danny's hands away, he just tightened his grip again, slow and inexorable. He could feel Sato swallow hard, Adam's apple pressing against his fingers. See him lick his dry lips, desperately. Meet his hot, furious eyes, so close now.

"Is that what you wanted?" Danny asked, for the second time that night, and Sato, his voice croaking, said, *"No."*

Danny let go and Sato gasped for air. They were so close Danny could feel his breath on his lips. Sato stepped back, rubbing his throat, wheezing a little. The generators' low hum almost drowned it out, but Danny felt like he would have been able to hear the smallest noise Sato made anywhere, through anything.

"What did you want?"

That complicated dance across Sato's face again. Danny wondered if he even knew what he wanted. He didn't think so, somehow.

Sato licked his lips again and said, "I *owe* you," and went down on his knees. "I don't like owing anyone anything. Especially assholes like you."

"What if *I* don't want this?" Danny said. It was a lie. It was obvious he wanted it. He could feel the frisson of desire spark along his spine. The electric burn of it, cutting through the dull haze of his days and nights. Feel his dick straining against his pants. It was dumb as hell, again, with the shaded windows of the hotel looking down over them, scrubby little trees that didn't provide any cover at all, and he didn't *care*. It was dark enough and he wanted—

"You do," Sato said. "You definitely fucking do." So cocky and sure of himself, and Danny was helpless in the face of it.

Not that he could say anything, his mouth had gone so dry. He probably looked stupid as hell, his eyes wild, fixed on Sato and the promise of his mouth. Danny swallowed hard and unbuckled his belt. Sato watched him do it. His face was unreadable, but he didn't pull away, didn't stand. Just watched as Danny slowly and deliberately exposed himself, exhaled when he saw.

"God," Sato muttered, half to himself, reaching out to take Danny in hand.

Danny looked down at the tattooed fingers wrapped around him. Sato's hands, like the rest of him, were covered in black ink, except for some of the skin on the back of his left hand. The knuckles on that hand said *S I C K*. He forgot to look at the rest of them when Sato slid his dry, calloused hand up, when he leaned forward and took Danny in his mouth.

Sato gave head exactly the way he played. Aggressive, like this was a contest to be won. Too rough, but somehow Danny was already breathless. As Sato worked his mouth lower down the shaft, he moved his hands to Danny's thighs, his fingers digging painfully into the muscle. Into the yellow-green bruise left behind when Danny had blocked a shot a few games ago. Danny couldn't focus on either sensation: the pain in his legs or the hot, slick pleasure of Sato's tongue and the vacuum of his mouth. Before he could think about what he was doing, he had his fingers around the back of Sato's head, over his barely there hair, pulling him forward.

Sato choked but didn't pull away. His eyes watered.

"Fuck," Danny groaned. "Goddamn, fuck, your *mouth.*"

Sato wrenched himself and his mouth away and said, a little snottily, "That's the general fucking idea, Garcia, try to keep up."

Danny didn't know whether to laugh or not, so he settled for slapping him, a hand sharp against his right cheek. Not as hard as he could have but nowhere near easy either, and he was rewarded by Sato's eyes widening and the kid shutting himself up, practically choking in his haste to suck Danny down again. It wasn't like Danny could relax into the sensation because that wasn't the way things were with them. It was on the wrong side of too many teeth, a little too hard, almost painful. It was one of the best things he'd ever felt in his life, right behind the first time he'd been seriously injured and the Percs had taken the pain away. It was only a supreme act of self-control that he wasn't babbling more idiotic things, that he wasn't begging Sato to keep going, to take it deeper, not to stop.

It was too much. Sato's hand tugging at his balls, the suction of his mouth, the picture of him, on his knees but still looking up with his eyes open and furious, like he was daring Danny to say anything. Danny wrapped his fingers in Sato's hair again and closed his eyes and that was the end.

He was still shivering a minute later, hauling Sato up to his feet.

For a minute, those big dark eyes were wide and uncertain, like he didn't know what to expect. Like he wasn't sure if they were going to fight again. Maybe they were. But when Danny spat in his hand, shoved it down Sato's jeans, and grabbed his erection, his head fell forward against Danny's chest. Hit it hard, almost like a headbutt, except it felt like a surrender. Sato said, *"Ah,"* his hands fumbling with his belt. Freeing Danny's hands to move.

Sato kept his head down and resting on Danny's chest, like he couldn't bear to look at him while Danny's fingers were in such an intimate spot, gripping him so tightly. There were still a few inches of space between their bodies, and Danny jerked him off angrily, because this was Sato's idea, because Sato couldn't leave him alone, because he didn't want Sato to leave him alone. His other hand pressed against Sato's chest, digging in. Sato was making those noises again; the whimpering fucking groans that almost had Danny's spent dick trying to make a repeat performance.

But Sato was so keyed up by it—by fighting Danny, by going down on him—that he didn't last long. Sato laughed, a choked-off little groan, and pressed his entire body up against Danny's. Sato's teeth dug into his shoulder as he came, spurting hot on the exposed strip of Danny's stomach.

Jesus Christ, what a mess.

They stood like that for a second, Sato shaking against him, before he came to his senses and pulled away. He looked like someone had fucked him up. Like someone had fucked him. Swollen lips and hair in disarray, a red mark on the side of his face where Danny had hit him, his fathomless dark eyes huge. A beautiful mess.

"I—" he started, his voice rough. "This was a fucking mistake. Jesus Christ. I—" And before Danny could reply, he was fumbling with his pants and trying to beat a retreat all at the same time.

Danny watched him go. His stomach felt cold and sticky. It *was* a mistake. And strangely, it was the best he'd felt all week, even if he also felt like someone had slammed him in the head with a sledgehammer. That was Sato in a nutshell.

Danny looked down at his stomach and sighed. Prepared for the walk of shame back to a hotel he hadn't even slept in yet.

And the rest of the night, alone.

It was a good thing Bee had gone home with Mäkelä after the game, because that way, Mike had the apartment to share with himself and his nervous breakdown. He *wanted* to break every dish in the goddamn house.

He didn't.

He went into the bathroom and stared at his face in the mirror for a long time. His hair had been getting a little long for his liking in the preseason—he normally kept it buzzed or completely shaved—but he'd been toying with the idea of leaving it alone and letting it grow in more. Now whenever he looked at it all he could think about, all he could feel, was Garcia's fingers in it, yanking him to his feet.

It took him about ten minutes to buzz it all off again and wipe out the sink. He could still taste Garcia, so he brushed his teeth until the only thing left was mint.

It didn't help. He could still feel Garcia's hands on his dick, the muscle of Garcia's chest against his forehead.

What the fuck was wrong with him? His brain kept replaying everything. Going down on his knees. He didn't know why the fuck he'd done that. Why he'd said that. Like: he didn't like owing people, it was true. But Garcia was an asshole and Mike didn't have to…

It had been really fucking good, and that was worse. He felt like he was going to rip his entire fucking skin off and he didn't know why.

He'd fucked guys before. He'd fucked guys he hadn't particularly liked before. He didn't understand why fucking Garcia made him feel like this. He couldn't explain it.

Even thinking about doing it again was crazy. Garcia was an asshole, he was a Hornet, they were barely ever even in the same city.

He didn't ever want to do it again.

He wanted to do it again.

He couldn't do it again.

Well: he could fight Garcia. But he absolutely was not going to fuck him. This was *it*. Except Garcia, because he was a fucking asshole, hadn't even let Mike even the score. He was still up by one and Mike had just let it happen because he had no self-control, because he was, what? Because he was *lonely*?

Mike walked naked into the kitchen and looked at the bar shelf. There was enough whiskey left to get extremely drunk but not enough whiskey left that getting extremely drunk wouldn't finish it off. That was fine. Bee wouldn't miss it. He drank the whiskey straight from the bottle, then set it carefully down on the counter. The taste of alcohol and toothpaste made him want to throw up, but he felt like shit anyway, so that was nothing goddamn new, at least.

He went into his room to sleep all of it off.

Mike woke up a few hours later. Motion sickness lurched in his stomach, behind his eyes. He closed them, counted to three. The room was still spinning. He rolled over and fumbled for his phone.

In the morning he felt a nausea that had nothing to do with drinking. He'd typed stop one upping me bc now i ducking owe u again asshole. Garcia had read it but hadn't responded. Mike couldn't remember typing it, but it was there, in black and white. Jesus Christ. He felt like puking again, but this time, it was humiliation. At least they didn't have a game today. With the regular season starting that week, they were on their own to work out as they saw fit.

Mike, hungover and miserable, made his way to the boxing gym. Maybe letting someone beat the shit out of him or beating the shit out of someone would make him feel better. It usually did. Mike was on the lower end for light-heavyweight, but he fought cruiserweights or heavyweights pretty regularly. Just like on the ice, it felt right. Felt like the thing to do. It started off a good fight. He got in a few decent punches before Arjun Sharma jabbed him in the ribs, right where the bruises were deepest.

It took Mike's breath away. The kind of pain you felt in your stomach, like you were going to vomit.

And then Sharma blocked a punch on his gloves, deflected Mike's arm, and stepped back. "Bro."

"What? Come on, come *on*, try and hit me again. We're not fucking done, dude."

"Your head isn't in this at all. And your chest is all fucked up. Doesn't feel right, man."

Mike looked down. They sparred shirtless and even though a good portion of his chest was covered by black ink, the ugly purple-and-blue bruise spreading across his rib cage was visible through some of it, like a spectacularly ugly watercolor tattoo.

"It looks worse than it is," he lied.

"I'm not doing it, bro."

And that was that. Mike spent the rest of his time at the gym slamming his fists into a punching bag until sweat ran down his back and the pounding headache had settled into a dull ache behind his eyes. On his walk back to the apartment, his phone vibrated in his pocket.

Stop making it easy for me then, Garcia had responded.

tell that to your face, motherfucker, Mike wrote back immediately, too tired to be creative, too angry to let it go.

I'm serious, though.

That was new. Mike stared at the message box and the first time Garcia hadn't let him stew with the little *SEEN* mocking him at the bottom.

yeah well we beat your asses last time and we'll do it again.

You guys got lucky, but I didn't mean the team. I meant you.

well you can fuck right off

Creative. But I mean, it's not hard to one-up a guy who's too fucking scared to play to his potential.

wtf. Mike paused for a second, then said, just to be clear here are we talking abt bjs or hockey.

You figure it out.

Mike stared at his phone and realized, belatedly, that he'd started walking out into traffic against the light. He backpedaled and stared again. This was the longest conversation he'd had with Garcia since this whole thing had started and he didn't know what to make of it. What the fuck did Garcia mean, he wasn't playing up to his potential? That was like… That was a really good blowjob, if he had to judge. It was part of the rules he hadn't entirely articulated but knew instinctively. It had to be better than what Garcia had done to him.

He had to *win.*

He'd put a lot of thought into it.

He was so unsettled that he never answered.

Mike had gotten used to playing third pair or sitting in the press box. It wasn't a bad thing, really. Every team needed bodies. His job was to go on the ice mostly rested and shut down the opposing team's checking line or their stars, who had probably played more minutes and by now were flagging. His job was to use his body as a shield and a weapon. He wasn't supposed to be on the ice for fancy footwork or strategy. He was a solid space-filler, a shot-blocker, a fighter. It didn't matter that he'd always been the lowest man on the depth chart, that he'd never so much as *sniffed* the starting lineup. That was how it had always been, and he'd adapted.

Sometimes when he watched Bee on the ice he felt a pull of envy deep in his chest. They played different positions, with different responsibilities, and she was so much more talented. Watching her acceleration was like watching someone in a different universe. Her stick handling was ridiculous. He loved to watch her take another team apart, but the shittiest part of him was so fucking jealous.

It wasn't that he didn't love her and look up to her and all of that shit. But hockey was something he'd wanted, the *only* thing he'd wanted, since he could remember wanting anything. Knowing that even though he'd made it this far, it wasn't good enough? That was fucking hard. Watching Bee just drove it all home. Even when they lost, she was just…on another level. Bee and to a lesser extent, Reed and Singer. All of them were.

There was a reason they were the first line.

"Third pair up!" Coach snapped, and Mike swung into action.

The things Mike was good at on the ice were: he had stamina, he didn't let pain stop him from trying to get to his goal, he could check or fight guys who were a lot bigger than he was, and he had a wicked slapshot from the point. He was a solid six or seven. He did what he'd been traded to do. Wasn't that good enough?

As he hustled his ass down the boards to battle the puck away from a Justice forward in the corner, the words echoed in his head: *a guy who's too fucking scared to live up to his potential.* He didn't need this kind of distraction. The forward managed to hold on to the puck so Mike hit him. The impact jarred his pads against the rib bruises, but he ignored it. The guy picked himself up off the ice, but by the time he did, Mike had gotten a neat pass to Parsons, who sauced it up to Netty, who skated it out of their zone.

He was fine at what he did.

Garcia was trying to get into his head.

It was just Mike's fucking luck that it was working.

The shift ended and Mike was back on the bench.

"What wrong, Misha?" Netty asked, knuckling his glove against Mike's helmet. "Look like you gonna murder something."

Mike shook his head wordlessly. There wasn't a whole lot of time to talk on the bench; even when they weren't skating, they had to be alert for the lines changing again. It was always chaotic, always noisy, with guys going and coming over the boards as Coach called the shots.

Netty rapped his helmet again and said, "Misha."

"Am I playing my best game?"

Netty was always smiling, always joking, that it was a little disconcerting to see the sudden shrewd gleam in his eyes. "Who ever play best game?" he asked, the jester's grin back in place again.

"That doesn't answer anything, dude."

"Then that your answer."

Before Mike could ask him what the hell he meant by that, Coach called a change, and both Netty and Mike were back on the ice. He didn't forget about the conversation, exactly, but by that time, he sure as hell had other shit he had to worry about.

Danny knew he should have felt better about the end of the week. They hadn't just won, they'd crushed the

Monument at home, which almost made up for losing to the Cons. Danny had fought Marek, one of the fourth-line wingers. A decisive win. Marek was bigger than most, six-four and probably 225, but it hadn't mattered in the end. Danny's major strengths were his reach, which he'd used to his advantage even against Marek, and the fact that you could hit him one time, ten times, it didn't usually matter. He had a rapidly darkening eye socket to show for it today, but he'd dropped the guy to the ice, so he would count it as a win.

He'd given that interview calmly. Politely. Ignored the flashes going off, because reporters always liked to take pictures of the aftermath. In most of the shots you could find of him on the league's official website or HornsBurgh or *The Athletic*, he was bruised, bloodied, sporting stitches, or punching some other hapless asshole in the face.

"Some of the guys are gonna get drinks after we get out of here," Landry said, as they toweled off the shower. "You gonna come for once?"

Danny thought about it. He rationed his social outings with the team because too much was too much, and he was always tired. But if he didn't go at all he'd get traded again and the press release would be some bullshit reason about how he was a problem in the locker room or something even more absurd, like he liked going to museums too much. It was early in the season, so he had more of an opportunity to make it up later.

He was going to drink either way. He was going to feel alone either way.

"Sure," Danny said easily.

"Hell yeah, bro!" Landry said, and went in for a fist bump that Danny responded to slightly too late.

It wasn't that his teammates were bad guys. Lévesque was kind of a prick without meaning to be, Artyomov was completely full of himself while completely meaning to be, and Landry was *really* young, but the rest of them were just like any hockey team he'd ever played on. The problem, as always, was Danny. As he got older, he just didn't enjoy the things he used to enjoy. Or enjoy things, period. Sometimes hanging out at a bar for a few hours listening to the guys shoot the shit, chirp each other, and pick up was just too much.

The group of nine ended up at a sports bar with air hockey tables—Landry and Riley Girard, the Hornets' baby defenseman, were embroiled in a bitter tournament that had been going on since last year's dev camp—and they still let you smoke inside. Danny didn't do it often anymore, only when his nerves were really shot and Percs weren't an option, but it was kind of comforting to smell it.

It was always a careful dance when he did this, though. Some guys were partiers, that was true, but Danny was always careful that people didn't know how much he drank. He was never as bad as Zach Reed had been in his Montreal heyday—he had never ended up as a meme of the day or the main character on Twitter, and no one he hadn't sent it to had ever seen his dick on the internet, that's for sure—but there was a difference between being a partier and what Danny did. He didn't usually do hard liquor when he was out, and he usually stuck with the same beer so if you weren't watching him too carefully it looked like he was nursing it all night.

It was a lot of work sometimes. But it did the job.

"Brooooo, come kick Gears' ass for me while I get a

refill," Landry demanded, gesturing to the air hockey table he was monopolizing.

Danny, who was drunk but not as drunk as he wanted to be, said mildly, "I'm good."

"You're so fucking boring," Landry complained, and punctuated his sentence by punching Danny in the arm.

Danny looked down at Landry's fist, then up at his face, and raised his eyebrows.

"Fiiiine," Landry muttered, and sulked away to the bar for a refill.

Danny looked around him to make sure no one was watching him too closely and took out his phone. He read, again, the message exchange he had going with Sato. It was pretty much the most he'd talked to anyone since longer than he wanted to think about it. It was just easy to get a rise out of him, and there was no pressure like there was talking to Araceli or his parents, or any of his exes. Sato already hated him, so there was almost nothing he could do to ruin things like he had years ago with Lauren, the woman he'd thought he was going to marry.

Danny might have hated him to start out, because Sato made his life so unnecessarily difficult, but the more they interacted, the more he wasn't so sure. Strangely, it comforted him to know that somewhere out there, someone was thinking about him that angrily, that intensely. Someone who still wanted to touch him after seeing even a part of what he really was. Someone who still needed to touch him even when he desperately seemed not to want to.

are we talking about bjs or hockey, Sato had written, and Danny frowned. It really wasn't the best place for that kind of shit. He knew it was probably a bad idea, but he closed the app and opened Snapchat instead. Sato had the same username there, so it was easy to find him. Before he could talk himself out of it, Danny added him and then went back to drinking.

Around one a.m., when he was absolutely as drunk as he wanted to be, the ache around his eye fading to background noise even though the aches in his hip and knee stood in sharp relief, his phone buzzed. Sato had added him back and sent him a chat.

are you fucking serious

This is practical.

oh yeah you're mr practicality

You may not give a shit, but I don't want to talk about bjs on insta

so you wanna talk about them here? kinda desperate don't you think 😛

I just don't want it to be an issue in the future

Sato snapped him instead. Danny looked up again before he opened it, but no one else from the team was watching him. He opened it. That was a mistake, because for even the brief amount of time he was able to view it, the image burned itself into his retinas like he'd stared at the sun for too long.

It was taken with the front camera, Sato with the middle finger of his right hand raised. The background was a beige wall and a dark headboard. Close enough to see Sato's hand and the lower portion of his face, his lips curled in a sneer. Close enough to see that he was shirtless. It was late; he'd probably been sleeping. Behind the hand, Danny could see, slightly out of focus, the wiry muscle of his shoulders and chest. And a brief, tantalizing glimpse of what the tattoos looked like after they normally disappeared under his shirt.

It was all black work, a mix of traditional and newer styles, some of it clearly larger pieces, but all connected with fillers. Danny could only catch brief images in the time he had to look: *H O M E* on his right fingers, *HEART IN HAND* scrolling across his collarbone, a dagger dripping blood, a crown, a wolf's head.

It was a lot.

Danny thought about learning each one of those tattoos by heart. About putting his teeth into them.

Then it was gone.

Danny, his mouth dry, really needed another drink before answering.

"Who're you texting?" Girard demanded, plunking himself down into the booth next to Danny.

"Uh…no one."

Gears had ears that stuck out like an elf's, a broad smile with crooked teeth, and freckles. He was a sweet, enthusiastic kid, and Danny contemplated shoving him off the bench and onto the floor.

"Do you have a *girl* you're not telling us about? *You?* The monk?"

Danny winced. The press and opposing teams might call him the Goon, but in the locker room, his seeming austerity had gotten him tagged with that unfortunate nickname. Jesus Christ, the monk. "Yeah, it's your mom," he replied easily and without rancor.

"Oooh, shot to the heart," Gears said, and pushed a beer toward him. "Aw, man, I'm just kidding, but you really gotta come and play some hockey with Landry and me. I'm gonna murder him if I gotta keep that fucking tournament going one day longer."

"You go. I'll be right there."

Danny looked down.

if i knew that was what it took to shut you up, i would've done that sooner, Sato had written.

I'm out with my teammates.

no shit? and yet...? speaking of desperate

Fuck off, I already know what it takes to shut you up. A slap to the face and a cock in your mouth.

There was no answer and Danny frowned. Maybe he had taken it too far. He didn't want to think about that, so he went and played air hockey. Won a round, lost a round. He was really drunker than he thought he had been. Slaps on the back from Gears and Landry, room a pleasant blur of teammates and bar patrons and smoke, phone an unpleasant weight in his pocket, a reminder. He half walked, half swayed his way back to the booth and checked his phone again.

Sato had sent him nine middle-finger-raised emojis.

Danny smiled. Cute, but I liked the other one better.

FUCK. YOU.

"Stop texting Gears' mom and come play another round," Landry groused, appearing at Danny's shoulder so suddenly he dropped his phone on the table.

"Yeah, yeah, coming."

He thought about Sato, alone in his bed, probably furious and definitely thinking about him, and forced the smile down. Maybe there was something to be said for team bonding activities after all.

Bee punched him in the chin and Mike said, *"Fuck."*

She let her gloves drop. "Oh marde, I'm sorry, Michael."

"Dude, it's fine. Don't apologize. I got you in the eye earlier."

"You did." She knuckled her eye socket with the round end of the boxing glove. "I'm going to have a black eye, probably."

"Sorry."

"I don't care. I'll look tough like you," she said, teasing.

His mouth twisted a little as he tried to frown rather than smile. "That's not a *good* thing."

"Also not a good thing—what's going on with you, mon chum? I almost never get a hit on you."

She had put her gloves up again and they circled the ring. It was always good when Bee came with him to the gym, because he liked fighting her. She didn't go easy on him when he was bruised, not like *some* dudes he could name and shame. Also he liked to think he had something to do with her growth from uncontrolled punching to a more strategic terminator. She didn't really fight much on the ice anymore; Coach had put a stop to that. Even without the intervention, Bee didn't have to fight much on the ice anymore. Everyone knew she could handle herself, and everyone knew that even if they thought she couldn't, either she'd fuck them up, or Mike would.

Also, she didn't complain when he punched her in the stomach or the face. And she'd punch *him* in the stomach or the face.

Mike didn't answer right away. He took several test jabs at her, but she danced back easily enough. He hadn't been really trying to hit her. "Nothing's up."

"Mmm," Bee said, taking the offensive.

He led her around the ring, letting her wear herself out. Blocked the occasional punch she threw his way, harder than he had to, probably. That was the problem when people got into relationships, they suddenly got real fucking concerned about whether their friends were happy, whether they were lonely, whether they were taken care of. He wasn't sure if that was really what Bee was doing but he sure as hell hoped it wasn't. He didn't mind her mother-henning him occasionally because he did the same thing to her. But this…

He threw a right hook and smacked her on the arm as she tried to step back and protect her face; she swore.

The problem was this wasn't anything he could talk about with Bee. Like, they'd shared a lot. She knew about all of the fighting he'd had to do as a kid, because other players saw the name on the jersey and how small he was, and figured he'd be easy prey. He was the first one she'd come to about problems she was having with one of their teammates, Kyle Hill, who didn't like that he'd lost his spot on the first line to a woman. But there were limits.

Like Mike couldn't just come up to her and say, *I*

keep fucking a guy I hate and I don't want to do it but god, he's so *hot.* That was an awkward enough conversation on its own, but Mike just couldn't get over the hurdle, even with Bee, of actually telling the truth. He'd been keeping it quiet for so long that even with his best friend, a woman who knew him better than his own siblings, it seemed impossible. It had been a secret for over half his life. Sometimes he could barely even think the word.

As soon as he'd realized certain things about himself, he'd figured out that if he wanted hockey, he wasn't going to be able to be open about it. It was bad enough being one of the only not-white kids at the rink. It was bad enough being smaller than everyone else at the rink. He didn't want to be the only gay kid at the rink too. It was a pretty shitty way to live, and it weighed down on him sometimes, but he didn't know any other way to make it work, not when he'd wanted to play hockey more than anything else. It was so ingrained at this point it was a habit.

And now here he was, letting his best friend beat the shit out of him in a bighearted attempt to cheer him up and he couldn't even tell her why he was in such a bad fucking mood.

"You know you can tell me anything," Bee said, as she faked him out and punched him in the stomach. "I'm not going to be an asshole about it."

"I know," he wheezed, the breath knocked out of him. She gave him a minute to recover, and then he was back in the game, throwing a flurry of jabs up and down, trying by sheer volume to get past her guard. "If there was anything to tell you, I would." He was a liar and a shitty friend, but there were some things he just couldn't let go. There were some things that were practically muscle memory at this point, no matter how much they hurt.

She punched him in the face and his nose started bleeding.

Mike smiled. It felt like the right thing.

When they showed up to practice later that morning, Mike's nose had stopped bleeding, but they both sported cuts and scrapes and fresh bruises. Coach took one look at them and inhaled sharply. He wasn't the kind of guy to scream, but his quiet disapproval felt almost as bad. "Morin, Sato, what the *fuck* are you doing?"

"I am training," Bee said promptly, before Mike could answer.

"Training."

"We box together."

"Neither of you are taking any hits to the head," Coach said with the kind of level flatness that was the equivalent of spittle flying from the mouth of another kind of man. "Especially you, Morin. If you want to box, fine, but no more fucking hits to the head."

"Yes, Coach," they chorused, like guilty schoolkids.

Mike probably pushed himself too hard during practice, particularly after an hour of letting Bee knock him around in the ring, but it was a good kind of sore. They were playing the Carolina Oaks later that night, and he and Bee went back to the apartment to sleep before the game. In his room, he stripped down to his boxers, ready to try to close his eyes.

Instead, he checked his phone.

He hadn't really known what to think when Garcia had added him on Snapchat. Garcia never actually messaged him first, but what Mike had gotten was a continuous thread of chirps and nastier insults. And some shit he'd angrily jerked off about, more than once, which was a whole 'nother problem. The Hornets had lost to Arizona, which had given him a shitload of things to needle Garcia about. The conversation wasn't always constant; he'd have somewhere to be, or Garcia would, but they'd pick it right back up again later on.

He didn't want to think too much about that. He didn't want to think too much about the fact that he looked forward to seeing whether Garcia had written something, looked forward to it even more when he was around to respond in real time. It was just easier to shit on him when he was actually there, that was all. He liked knowing if he was getting under Garcia's skin.

The latest response was just a snap of Garcia's face staring straight at the camera. His expression was so deadpan and completely unamused that Mike laughed before he caught himself doing it. He scowled at his phone.

you look about as energetic as you did on the ice, bro. no wonder fuckin arizona handed it to you guys

Don't you have a game you should be preparing for?

i'd rather give you shit than sleep right now, i guess

With that attitude...

what???

I'm just saying, this conversation could go the other way and I'm not gonna let you forget it if it does.

Mike glared at his phone again. He really, really didn't like when Garcia was right. But he also didn't want the conversation to end. For whatever reason.

whatfuckingever, tbh, like i give a fuck about your opinion. And then on a whim, tilted his head to the side to take a picture of the dark red, early-stage bruise Bee had left on his jaw. It was large and splotchy, and it ached. His teeth had rattled when she'd done it. He added the caption—not from you—and before he could think too much about that, he sent it.

There was a long pause, before Garcia said, So who's punching you that's not me?

nah

Who?

lmaoooo are you jealous?

You do have a very punchable face, so I guess shit happens

dude, you ARE jealous, this is hilarious

Garcia snapped him instead, and Mike realized with dizzy excitement he was playing a game with rules that changed by the minute and in a way he could never predict. Garcia in his bed. He must have been holding the phone in his left hand. Mike's eyes were drawn down the shot. He had a glimpse of Garcia's muscled chest, the trail of hair that led down to his boxer briefs and massive thighs. His right hand palmed his cock, and

Mike could see the outline of it through the fabric, and he swore to god, his mouth fucking watered.

He stared at the picture until it vanished. Then he stared at his screen. It was like a fucking dog and a bell response; he could feel himself getting hard thinking about it. Thinking about Garcia.

fuck you, he wrote, before his head thumped against the pillow. He felt hot and prickly, but he didn't touch himself. He didn't want to give Garcia the satisfaction of being able to get to him like this, but god, he wanted…

Rather fuck you, actually, Garcia wrote back, and Mike actually groaned, alone in his room.

god i fucking hate you

Yeah you do, but you're still so fucking easy for me, huh? what does that say about you?

Before Mike could think of a reply, he got another snap. Garcia's knees raised a little, his hand under the fabric now. Mike stared at it, stared at the way the muscles in his thighs flexed. Something in his brain short-circuited. It was one thing to do this hurried and quick where anyone could have walked in on them. The first time it had happened he'd almost been too surprised to enjoy it. And the second time was in the dark, and he was fucked up from the game, and he'd only looked at Garcia's face, murdering him a million times in his head while he took Garcia apart with his tongue. Both times he'd only been able to see a glimpse of skin.

This was the first time he'd been able to actually look at Garcia's nearly naked body, the first time he'd been able to imagine all of the things he'd do to it if he had the space, the time. All he could think about was straddling one of Garcia's thighs and just rutting into it, like a teenager.

He needed to touch himself—it was, like, kind of a situation—but he couldn't. His breath sounded harsh in his own ears, his skin prickling with awareness of his own near nakedness. He'd jerked off thinking about Garcia before, but this was different. This was…this was like he was alone, but Garcia was almost there in the room with him.

Time ticked by and Mike wanted. He wanted, he wanted.

Like watching someone else's fingers moving, Mike swiped the button to start a video call through the app, his stomach somewhere up in the area where his throat should normally be. He didn't know if Garcia would answer.

Mike was kidding himself, because he did, like, immediately.

He looked into Garcia's eyes, dark and hooded and lazy, exactly like he'd just been jerking himself off for the last few minutes. Or longer, because Mike didn't even know what he'd been doing before they started this. A thin sheen of sweat on his forehead, his neck. If Mike was there, he could like. Lick his throat and taste it. Press his fingers in until Garcia gasped against them. Mike had no idea what he looked like, but it felt like he'd completely lost his mind. So however he looked, it probably wasn't anywhere near as in control as he needed to be.

"Hi," he said stupidly.

"Hey," Garcia said, like he hadn't started this whole thing by sending Mike what was basically a dick pic, even if he'd covered it, barely. He had a stupid sexy voice, huskier with arousal, and Mike thought furiously that if he could shove his cock right in there and punish him for that casual "hey" he absolutely would. He would a *million fucking times.*

"I—" he choked. He couldn't finish the sentence. He was so turned on and so mad about it he could barely think of a word. Let alone multiple words. Let alone in a coherent order.

Garcia was still holding the phone so Mike could only see his face and the spread of his shoulders. He was propped up against the pillows on his bed, a gray blanket and pillowcases. He licked his lips and Mike's eyes followed his tongue. "You can ask for what you want, you know."

"I…"

"What do you want, Mike?" Garcia's voice was dangerously even, and the use of his name like that wasn't fucking fair. "I'm not going to give you anything unless you tell me."

He could hang up. He could hang up, and he could jerk off alone like he'd been doing since the game against the Hornets, and Garcia could go fuck himself. Well, Garcia was already fucking himself, that was the fucking problem. Mike couldn't hang up. He needed…he didn't know what he needed, but it was burning him up from the inside.

What *did* he want?

"I… Jesus fucking Christ, I hate you."

"I know you do, babe, but if you want something, you gotta tell me."

The words were mocking, but Garcia wasn't smiling. His eyes were dark and intent. Mike hadn't touched himself since the whole thing had started, and when Garcia said *babe* his dick gave a little jump in his boxers, straining against the fabric, a wet patch forming. He didn't know how it was possible that Garcia could do this to him, when they weren't even in the same city, when they weren't even touching. Just his voice and his eyes and his mouth. They hadn't even said that much, and Mike felt almost nauseous, he wanted so much.

He didn't know how the fuck Garcia did this to him.

"God…fuck. I need—I want—" His voice cracked, but he was too frustrated, too focused, to even be embarrassed about it. All of the things he wanted couldn't be done. Not right now, maybe not ever. "I want to fuck you, god, I need to fucking like—I wanna see you come, I *need*—"

"Shit, you're hot when you're desperate," Garcia muttered. He bit his lip again, like he hadn't meant to say that, and there was a rustling as his body shifted. Mike stared at the ripple of muscle in his shoulders.

Then Garcia moved the hand holding the phone and propped it up against a pillow so Mike could see he'd shoved his boxers down just far enough to expose himself, hard and straining, in his other hand. Fuck, he had a nice dick, long and thick, and Mike could have wept thinking about all of the things he wanted to do to Garcia. To have Garcia do to him. Jesus fucking Christ, he thought he could handle this, but he couldn't. He was out of his depth; he was going to die. He could feel it, hot and furious.

"What do you want?" Garcia asked him again, and a noise like a whine escaped Mike's mouth.

"Move your fucking *hand*," he managed. He sounded like he was choking.

"Yeah," Garcia said on the exhale, and his hand slid up and down. Mike strained to hear every sound, every hitch in his breath. "Don't touch yourself yet. Not until I'm done. I wanna watch you too."

"Fuck you, I do what I want," Mike said, which was a lie, because he moved his hand out of his boxers and clenched it in a fist at his side. "Come on, come *on*, I wanna *see it*."

Garcia's breath came faster as he jerked himself off, and Mike stared at him doing it, like a starving beggar alone at an all-you-can-eat. He didn't know where to look first because there was so much to look at. The way the muscles on Garcia's abdomen moved as he strained up. Those fucking *thighs*. And, of course, his big hands, fingers curled around his dick, thumb stroking over the head.

If you had asked Mike a few hours earlier about the sexiest thing he'd ever seen in his life, he couldn't have answered. But if you asked him now, at least under the influence of a truth serum or something, he would have to say it was a guy jerking himself off on camera while Mike watched, a guy he hated and wouldn't hesitate to punch in the face again.

He couldn't even say anything, he was so wound up, watching. Every muscle in his body was straining up, like if he just twisted himself into enough knots, he could somehow teleport himself to Pittsburgh, shove Garcia down into the bed and fuck him up. The only saving grace in this situation was that Garcia seemed like he was just as undone by it all as Mike was. His hand had sped up and Mike could hear the sound of skin on skin, the occasional soft groan that escaped. It just made him think that if he was there, if he was fucking Garcia, he'd make him be noisy, he'd fucking tear the sounds right out of him.

Later.

Another time.

Not now.

He couldn't do it now. He was so hard it actually hurt. His free hand white-knuckled at his side. He couldn't even muster up the energy for anger, he was so consumed with watching, with needing.

"What do you want?" Garcia gasped, like every word hurt him.

"I…come on, come, please, please, I—I can't—"

"God, babe, you have to *tell* me, you have to ask—"

"I want to see you come, I want to—*please*—"

And with another soft gasp that sounded like he'd been punched in the gut, Garcia came, and Mike had the weird pleasure of watching it, the white spurts against the shadowed skin of his belly, the way his body trembled. The noise that came out of Mike's mouth was like he'd come himself.

When Garcia picked up the phone again, Mike could finally see his face. The flush in his cheeks, the huge pupils, mouth hanging open, stupid. God, he looked like he'd been taken apart, and Mike wanted that. Wanted *him*.

"Can I—" he managed to choke.

"It's all you now," Garcia said lazily. "Take off your boxers, though. I want to see you. I want to see everything."

Mike kicked off his underwear before he could even think about it, too eager to argue. Set the phone down so Garcia could watch him do it, see all of him. The tattoos covered most of his belly and thighs with some small gaps. It felt even more obscene that way, knowing everything that *wasn't* tattooed was highlighted. He knew he was making noises, embarrassing noises, but he couldn't control them. His hand flexed open and shut in the air over his dick, but he didn't touch it. Couldn't touch it.

"Jesus Christ," Garcia said. He didn't sound lazy anymore.

"God, please, please, please," Mike groaned. "Please, fuck, I gotta come, you're *killing me*—"

"Touch yourself. Go on, babe, go on."

He almost sobbed when he wrapped his hand around himself, when he started to move it. It was dry, which usually would have been a little uncomfortable, but he was so fucking turned on that he could just use the moisture from the beads of precome because he was literally five seconds away from embarrassing himself. It took all of his concentration to keep from coming and still jerk himself off at the same time, so he almost didn't realize Garcia was still talking him through it, not as urgently as he'd done before, but low and filthy and encouraging.

"That's it, just like that, come on, think about my hands on you, I'd fucking destroy you, I'd—"

Mike came so hard that his whole body bowed as he accidentally knocked the phone over and smacked himself in the face with one flailing hand. The noise he made sounded inhuman, not like him. He shivered and shivered and shivered again, and by the time he got his shit together to pick up the phone, his dick was still making sad attempts to keep coming, even when there was nothing left to give.

Garcia was staring at him when he finally got up the

courage to look. "Jesus Christ," he said after a moment. "You're something else, kid."

Mike, too fucked up to even bother snapping at him, made an inarticulate noise and closed his eyes.

Garcia laughed, sleepy and satisfied and strangely warm, and said, "Go to sleep, you stupid motherfucker. You got a game tonight."

"Oh, fuck," Mike said, "god, you…" and before he could embarrass himself further, he hung up.

These days Danny had a love-hate relationship with exercise. There was a certain dumb sense of accomplishment in hitting and exceeding numerical goals, or at least there used to be. Now it just felt as rote and mechanical as everything else. Even though he didn't have to work out the same way during the season, he still pushed his way through rounds on the bike or sets in the gym even when most days his body was screaming at him. At the end, though, he was mostly just aware that this, like the rest of his life, was a means to an end. He lifted weights. He was stronger than anyone else on the ice. He would drag his way through the next two years, or until his body gave out on him, whichever came first.

It was a Saturday morning and he lay on his back on the bench, staring up at the bar above him. His back was slick with sweat and his muscles ached in a good way that would probably be a bad way in a couple of hours. It took him a minute to get himself together before he hauled himself up to unrack the plates and limp back to the lockers.

His phone was ringing, and he was worn out enough

that he wasn't really thinking about it. He answered automatically, half expecting it to be Mike.

"What the hell," Araceli said.

"Hi, Araceli."

"What the *hell*, you actually picked up?"

Danny leaned against the shelf of lockers, resting his head against the cool metal. "Sorry. I've been busy."

Araceli made the *hmm* noise he imagined she probably used on her patients. It was just his extremely bad luck that his older sister was a therapist. "So, look, Danny, I just want to know if you're okay."

"I'm fine," he said automatically.

"None of us have talked to you since—since that dinner."

The guilt that was always with him prickled under his skin, lurched in his stomach. "I know. I promise I'll call more often."

"No, buddy, don't make promises you're not going to keep. You don't even have to call, just pick *up*. Mom and Dad are really worried about you."

"Well, they don't need to be. I'm just playing hockey."

Araceli paused. She always did that; tried to think of the best way to phrase a question or an accusation, and he hated it because he knew she was going to start picking apart everything he said in response, even the things he didn't say. Even if she didn't do it maliciously. He wished Araceli wouldn't try to be a shrink at him, but it was like sometimes, she couldn't turn it off. He wouldn't have answered more often even if she could, but he lived with the eternal sick fear that something he'd tell her would set everything in a clearer view than she already saw it.

Already saw him.

"That kid who broke your tooth last year is still at it, I see."

Danny thought about Mike's elbow slamming into his throat the last time in Philly and about Mike jerking off desperately, losing his shit so completely that he smacked himself in the face when he came. They hadn't talked much since then. Mike seemed either angry or embarrassed or both, which was to be expected. Danny was giving him some space.

He pressed the side of his face harder against the metal locker. "Uhh…yeah. But it's fine. We don't play them that often. And I got a new bridge already."

"Danny."

"It's fine. I'm fine."

"I just hate watching you get *hurt*."

"I don't get hurt that bad."

"Danny—"

"I know you're my sister, but this is my job. I'm a tough guy. I can take it."

"But should you?"

"Celi, I don't really wanna talk about this right now."

"Fine. We will literally never talk about it, because you will never want to talk about it."

"How's Josie?"

She sighed, long and deep. He knew she was mad at him, because she was always mad at him these days, and she was right to be. He knew that she didn't want to tell him about her daughter, about his favorite and only niece, unless he assuaged some of her fears first. But she wasn't a vindictive asshole. She was a better person than Danny. She had never given up on him. Not yet anyway.

"She's good. She's got your height, I think. She's in

the ninety-eighth percentile right now. And she asks about you all the time."

He couldn't do it. If he thought too much about Josie's giggly little laugh and the way she liked to sit on his foot and let him walk her around the room like he was her own personal taxi service, the way she called him tío Danny in her tiny piping voice, he was going to break completely. "Uh…tell her I love her and I'll see her soon, okay? I, uh, I have to go."

"Sure," Araceli said, resigned. "Sure you do. Bye, Danny. I love you, hermanito."

"Love you too, Celi."

He felt like a complete piece of shit, driving home from the gym. He was an asshole who couldn't even talk to a family who loved him, a family he loved more than anything or anyone. A family who worried about him. That was what he couldn't deal with. The worry; the pity. If he told them the truth they'd feel sorry for him. And if they felt sorry for him—

He was driving faster than he should have been driving, he realized, when the brakes squealed a little pulling into his driveway. What Danny really wanted was to get fucked up and not think about it, but he couldn't even do that because he had a game tonight.

Instead, he poured himself a single shot of whiskey. Beer before a game was a bad idea. He swallowed two Percs with it. That took the edge off enough that even if he was pacing around the house, he didn't feel as manic about it as he had before, and nothing hurt. He never had the attention span for books or TV anymore, unless it was in the background and he was just staring at it. He ended up in the kitchen again, halfheartedly scrambling some eggs and chopped-up sausage while he scrolled through his phone.

Danny found himself looking Mike up on Instagram and browsing through his feed. He was pretty active, posting a few times a week. Some of his grid was stupidly arty shots of little-known parts of Philadelphia or whatever city he happened to be in, some of it was pictures of his teammates with mocking captions. There was a lot of Morin: Morin making faces, Morin smiling at the camera, Morin in boxing gloves, a sports bra, and shorts, Morin shaving Mike's head for him while Mike took a photo of them in the mirror and grimaced with comical exaggeration. There were some selfies: Mike frowning, Mike sneering, Mike and his bloody nose at the boxing gym. He had posted updates every time he got a new tattoo, although as far as Danny could tell, the only space he had still available was the back of his left hand.

Well. And his dick.

Danny's eggs were burnt and browned, but he dumped the whole mess out into a plate and ate them anyway. The house was so fucking quiet and empty and not for the first time he wondered why the hell he'd bothered buying an entire home when a studio apartment probably would have suited him just fine.

He looked down at the phone again and opened Snapchat.

Hey.

He put the phone down on the counter and went to wash the dishes. When he came back, Mike had written, hey, asshole. Danny caught himself smiling, which was dumb as hell, considering.

What's up?

shoveling endless fucking chicken breasts into my gullet. gotta keep my weight up we can't all be giants like you

Is that a compliment? Be still my heart.

it was an observation but if you're that starved for compliments idk what to tell u bro. kinda pathetic. There was another pause, then Mike added, wyd?

Danny thought about what to say, but none of the options were good. I don't know, he typed finally. It wasn't good either, but it was true.

listen i know you're old as balls but u really don't know wyd?

I know what it means, I meant I don't know what I'm doing

Mike was silent for a while. rn or like in general.

It felt like too much. Both what Danny'd said, and what he could see himself saying. So he turned his phone off, dry-swallowed another pill, and went upstairs to sleep before he had to get ready for the game.

Mike got knocked out of the usual warm-up elimination soccer round early and spent the rest of his pregame routine down the hall, throwing a spare ball against the wall and catching it as it bounced back toward him. He scowled at the ball and threw it again, harder. He still felt like beating the shit out of something or someone, which was the right kind of energy to have before a game, even if it was only against Florida.

There was a lot of shit going on in his head and he didn't like it. There was always shit going on in his head, but sometimes it was louder than others. If he could punch the wall without breaking his hand he would. He thought about something he'd seen on a documentary about enforcers on Netflix, an interview with Dave Tremblay, a guy Mike had actually fought down in the minors before his retirement. Tremblay was telling the camera about how he'd wrap chains around his hands and punch a tree to get the calluses layered on his knuckles faster.

Maybe Mike should do that.

Maybe that would make him feel more in control of his stupid head.

Of his stupid life.

"Mike," someone said behind him.

Startled, he missed the ball bouncing back. It thumped into his shoulder, dropped to the floor. Rolled away. Mike turned and looked Nate Singer, the captain of the Cons, in the eye. "Yeah?"

"Just wanted to check in with you, see how you're doing." Singer was a big guy, almost as big as Garcia. But where Garcia was almost 240 pounds of asshole, Singer was basically just a tall as fuck golden retriever. He even had the sandy blond hair and dumb, friendly smile. He turned it on Mike now, and even though Mike hated people except Bee being fucking *nice* to him, he had to fight the reflex to smile back. Singer just had that effect on people.

"Uh...why?"

"Checking in on all my guys this season," Singer said. It wasn't convincing. Like sure, Singer might've only been a year or so older than him. But there was a reason all the rookies and young guns called him Dad. Mike could *feel* the fatherly concern. Singer was worried about him. Jesus Christ, had everyone circulated a memo or something?

"I didn't do anything," Mike said. "I stopped letting Bee punch me in the face."

Singer winced. "I know you did. But—Mike, I just wanted to check in. Make sure you're feeling okay, make sure you're going into the season in the right mindset."

Mike looked at him, like if he looked at him long enough, bland enough, it would satisfy him.

Singer plowed on through it, like he had a predetermined point in the conversation he needed to reach, and he was going to get there whether Mike helped him or not. "So, uh, if there's anything you've got going on in your personal life that's, ah, affecting your play, or your general well-being, I just want you to know that we're here for you, me and everyone else, and also if you, um…well, what Coach said, the other day. That was pretty not cool, uh, generally, pretty much the opposite of cool, I really don't want you to get head injuries. Like, I don't want anyone on the team to get head injuries. But I particularly want *you* to know you shouldn't get head injuries. And that you're not expendable."

Mike stared at him. It was probably the longest speech he'd ever heard from Singer, who tried so fucking hard to be motivational, but who squeezed out words like he was embarrassed anyone would bother looking at him. What Coach had said… Mike was so used to hearing things like that, he hadn't even remembered it after he'd gone out on the ice. Singer continued staring at him, blue eyes so earnest, so concerned.

"Seriously, Cap, it's not even a thing."

"Okay, well, I'm here for you, buddy," Singer said, and patted him dadishly on the shoulder. "Good talk."

Mike said, "Oh my fucking god," but Singer was already walking across the long hall to the dressing room doorway, where Reed was waiting for him.

He was still in a foul mood as he dressed for the game. Singer had meant well and in a weird way Mike was like, touched, or something, something stupid like that, that he'd at least identified something that might have been a legitimate issue.

Knowing people thought there was something wrong was infuriating, *humiliating.* Especially when there was absolutely nothing wrong, when it was just that he was fucking distracted at the worst possible times by the thought of Garcia's dark eyes and long eyelashes, by the image of Garcia naked burned behind his eyelids, the way he couldn't stop thinking about *I don't know what I'm doing*, the way he hadn't even answered when Mike had tried to figure it out, like.

It probably wasn't normal to extrapolate what someone was feeling just from text when you didn't even talk all that often, but everyone was worrying about Mike, and he just had the feeling that Garcia was the one who was really fucking sad.

Which was a good thing, because he hated Garcia. Garcia deserved to be sad.

Mike was trying to be more strategic about his fights, but when he beat the shit out of the Barracudas' biggest forward, he felt like probably if anyone knew what was going on inside of his head, they wouldn't blame him for it. They won 5–2 and Mike got his first goal of the season, but he was starting to realize that he could beat the shit out of someone different every night and he wasn't going to make himself feel any better that way.

Mike couldn't get it out of his head.

Garcia was sad.

It bothered the shit out of him. He was furious that he was thinking about it; furious that it bothered him. He didn't know why it'd gotten under his skin like that in a way that the actually embarrassing thing—Garcia making him come so hard he'd punched himself in his own damn face—hadn't. It wasn't even that it bothered him, actually. It was just that Garcia was an asshole who deserved to be sad, but that didn't mean Mike didn't want to know why.

And it wasn't like he could just ask.

He scowled at the buckwheat pancakes Mäkelä was making for the three of them while Bee was in the shower. Mäkelä wore a pair of athletic shorts and nothing else, and his sandy blond hair was sleep-messy, but he didn't seem self-conscious about any of it at all. There was no reason for him to be.

Mäkelä was kind of an enigma. Clearly, Bee saw something special in him, and so Mike was predisposed to like him. Also, generally, he was a good dude. Mike sure as fuck didn't understand him, though, and he wasn't sure if that had more to do with the fact that Mäkelä was a goalie or the fact that he was Finnish. He was a weird guy, but he made good fucking pancakes. Mike probably would have appreciated them more if he'd been in a better mood.

He did appreciate that Mäkelä, unlike almost everyone else in his life, wasn't trying to pry. In fact, he just acted like Mike wasn't there. Which normally Mike really would have appreciated. However. He considered that maybe Mäkelä had some kind of goalie wisdom. Bee, who otherwise had excellent taste in associates, put up with him on a regular basis so like…maybe there was something there. Maybe Mike could pick his brains about the entire Garcia situation without, like, actually going into detail about the Garcia situation.

"Mäkelä?"

"Yes, Michael."

Mike wrinkled his nose: he'd have to explain to the goalie that just because Bee did it, didn't mean *he* could. But he had more pressing concerns. "You like… *know* people, and stuff."

Mäkelä turned those ice-chip eyes on him and flipped a pancake without looking at the pan. "I know a lot about reindeer."

"Ha, ha. I mean your goalie wisdom. You understand people. You can get in their heads, right?"

"So you have a question about people, is what I gather."

"Well…a person, really."

"Oh?"

"It's not anything—"

Mäkelä looked at him over the kitchen counter and said, very seriously, "Michael, I'm here for you, but you don't have to tell me anything you don't want to tell me."

Mike half choked, because apparently he was collecting dads this week, then took a long drink of his coffee to try to cover it up. Mäkelä also made really good coffee. It was a big deal in Finland or something. Bee was lucky as fuck, really. For all she'd tried to make things complicated she had figured it out in the end, and her boyfriend was the kind of guy who'd make excellent coffee for her in the morning.

"I mean just…what do you do when there's someone you're like…not dating…kind of…talking to? But not really…talking to…" Mäkelä was waiting for him to go on, so patiently that Mike's entire body almost withered and died in protest. "Like, a person you're, you're fucking, I mean…you have fucked…or you want to fuck…"

"Is this a conjugation lesson?" Mäkelä asked, with an utter gravity that would have been mocking, if it wasn't for the crinkle at the corners of his eyes. "Because I'm basically fluent in English, and I know that one."

Mike put his head down in his hands.

"I'm sorry," Mäkelä said, "this is serious."

"But like—the person you want to fuck—like—what do you do when there's something, you know, going on with them and you don't know what it is?"

"Well…have you tried asking?"

"It's not like that."

"You can't ask?"

"It's not really that kind of…thing."

"If you can't ask them…are you sure this person even really likes you very much?"

"They definitely don't like me that much," Mike said, glaring at his pancakes. "I don't like them that much either. That's kind of the point. Of this whole thing."

"So…let me get this straight, for my own reference. This person, who you are not dating, but who you have fucked, or want to fuck—I'm still not entirely clear on that part and please do not clarify for me, I don't actually need to know—who doesn't like you very much, has something…going on? And you want to know what it is?"

"Yes?"

"Are you sure it's really your business?"

"Of course it's my—" Mike started, then looked up. Mäkelä was right. It wasn't his business. Did he want it to be his business? "You're right. It's not my business."

Mäkelä was looking at him again and Mike made a silent, thankful prayer for the Nordic stoicism that didn't allow space for pity on Mäkelä's face. "Have another pancake," Mäkelä said finally, at the same time that Bee emerged from her bedroom.

She looked at Mike, she looked at Mäkelä, and back at Mike. "What did I miss?" she asked suspiciously.

"Nothing, mussukka," Mäkelä said, and leaned over to kiss her on the cheek, and she leaned into his shoulder. It wasn't, like, overwhelming PDA or anything, but it was the kind of sweet gesture that let you know that Mäkelä was hers, that she loved him. "Sit down and have some coffee."

Mike sawed at his pancakes a little harder than he probably needed to and thought about how that kind of a relationship was probably pretty boring after a while. Always liking someone, always being affectionate with someone, hanging out with the same person all the time. What did you even talk about after a year? How great it was being in love? Gross.

And because it wasn't his business, he absolutely did not think about Garcia.

It was an off day and Danny spent most of the morning sitting on his porch, trying and failing to read a book.

It was some kind of fantasy novel about nuns who were also assassins and he'd been reading the first fifty pages over and over again, losing interest, and then having to read it again because he'd forgotten what was going on. At least the weather was nice. He could sit there in a sweater, no coat necessary.

what did you mean when you said i wasn't playing up to my potential? Mike asked, on Snapchat. And then: u weren't actually talking about bjs, were u.

I was talking about hockey.

but what did you MEAN

I meant you have what it takes to be better than you are, and you're not doing it.

i'm good! like i'm in the fucking major league good

Yeah, but don't you want to be great?

lmao buddy idk what the fuck you're smoking, but we all want things we can't have

Danny thought about Mike's mouth, smiling or sneering or furious, thought about what it would be like to kiss him instead of just blowing him in an alley, and said, yeah.

so what the fuck

He thought about the best way to phrase it. Something that wouldn't come off too strong. Something that would convey… Fuck it. He initiated a voice call, even though he didn't know where Mike was, what he was doing. The Cons weren't playing today either, but it was a calculated gamble.

"What the fuck?" Mike snapped when he picked up.

The tension in his shoulders he hadn't realized was there released and Danny sagged down a little in the chair. "Hi."

"You can't just fucking *call* me," Mike said, and Danny could hear the scowl in his voice. He could also hear the faint tremble, the uncertainty, that underpinned all of Mike's bravado.

"You didn't have to pick up." He put the book down on his lap and stared out at the street. His neighbor, an ornery old man who complained about Danny's lawn no matter what he did, was out front raking leaves but wasn't watching him. "Bad time?"

There was a long pause that said more than any excuse he might have made, and Danny knew the truth: Mike wanted to talk to him, but he didn't want to admit it. He wondered how much of the hatred was genuine, how much of it was just Mike's personality, and how much of it was for show at this point. If they were ever in the same place more than a night at a time, Danny thought, he could figure it out, he could chip away at Mike's spiky exterior. He realized it was probably not normal to want to know everything about someone so fucking badly, but he was starting to admit to himself that the Mike thing was more than a problem and was now a full-blown situation.

"Is there ever a good time?" Mike grumbled, so put upon that Danny had to bite down a laugh. "But seriously, I want to know why the fuck you'd even say something like that to me in the first place."

"Why wouldn't I?"

"Because I'm the last man on the fucking depth chart, dude, always have been, always will be."

"I don't think so."

"Oh, fucking thanks, Coach, so glad I have your fucking encouragement."

"Easy, kid," Danny said, and he heard Mike's sharp little intake of breath. He filed that one away as both *interesting* and as *something to explore later.* "Look, I'm not trying to be an asshole about this. I've—watched you play."

"You've seen me fight and you were pretty busy for most of that."

He didn't want to admit that he'd watched Mike's games, that he'd analyzed them, that he'd spent the time just…wanting to know him. Know how he played, know things about him from how he played. Somehow, he suspected that it wouldn't be taken well, but he'd put himself out there before, and Mike had more than surprised him, so. Danny took the plunge.

"No. I've watched your games. Like, ones you haven't played against me." He had shocked Mike into silence, maybe, but he pressed doggedly on. "And I think—I think you have potential that you aren't using. You're fast; you're strong. You have good ice sense. You're not an idiot—"

"Oh, *thanks*—"

"Let me finish."

"Fuck you," Mike said. There was a weird panic threading the words, and Danny wished like hell he could see his face. Just to figure out what was going on with him.

"I was going to say, you have everything you need to be on the second pair at *least*. Why are you wasting your potential brawling all the time?"

"Daniel 'the Goon' Garcia telling *me* not to fight."

"It's *Daniel*," he said, annoyed, correcting Mike's pronunciation. Even now, everyone still defaulted to the English pronunciation. "Or Danny, if you absolutely can't manage that. But I'm just—it's really fucking frustrating watching you throw it away."

"Garcia," Mike said pointedly, "if I had what it took to be anything but a goon, don't you think someone besides you would have fucking told me by now?"

"Maybe. Maybe not."

Mike's voice cracked when he answered, too high, almost shrill. "Do you think I haven't been fucking trying? Do you think I don't want to be here more than I want *anything* fucking else in my life? What the fuck do you think I was doing in the A for four fucking years, just fucking around?"

"No, that's not what I—"

"You fucking asshole, how dare—"

"Mike, *stop*."

Silence again. Then Mike said, very carefully, "I'm going to hang up now, and you can go fuck yourself."

The call dropped, and Danny looked up to see Mr. Thomas staring at him, rake frozen in his hands.

He closed the book and went inside.

The phone call pissed Mike off like nothing else he could remember. It pissed him off almost as much as Garcia humiliating him during his first game in the show, kicking his ass so badly that Mike ended up missing three games in concussion protocol. Because of course the two worst things he could remember involved that fucking asshole. It pissed him off so much he didn't talk to Garcia for two whole days.

How fucking dare Garcia tell him he wasn't fucking playing to his potential? If Mike could play better, he would have killed himself to do it, literally, figuratively, anything, and the fact that Garcia just assumed he was, what? Being lazy? Coasting? Mike could have punched him in his smug goddamn face. If Mike was capable of being something other than third pair at best and 7D press box filler at worst, wouldn't Coach have realized it and worked with him to make it happen?

He was in Boston, and they had a game tonight, so he couldn't even go to the boxing gym and try to bait people into punching him, couldn't even slam his fists into the heavy bag and imagine it was Garcia's face. Nothing helped. He did push-ups in his hotel room until his arms hurt, he did sit-ups until he felt like he was going to puke, and then he did jumping jacks until he did throw up.

He was furious, so why did he also feel like he was going to cry? Mike couldn't remember the last time he'd done that. Maybe not ever. But it felt fucking awful, like Garcia had somehow stripped off his skin and left him vulnerable to the cold air. Every aching piece of him. It was like Luke Skywalker getting the proton torpedoes into that one fucking thermal exhaust port. Somehow Garcia, whether he realized it or not, had found the one thing that just destroyed him.

Mike tried to channel the energy into the game. He killed it on PK, keeping the Beacons from evening up the score on three separate opportunities—blocking a shot, sending a guy straight into the boards, and picking the puck on a pretty slick takeaway—but he still felt itchy under his skin, kinda nauseous. In the third period he picked a fight with Gardiner, one of their wingers, who just happened to be about six and a half feet tall. It was a nasty fight, one of those brawls where you were just out there slugging away and no one wanted to give in and finally the refs had to put an end to it. By that time Mike was bleeding from the forehead and the mouth, but Gardiner looked a hell of a lot worse after Mike had gotten a hold of his jersey, yanked him off-balance, and slammed his fist into several key parts of Gardiner's face before he could get it together again.

Mike ended the game in the penalty box, licking salty blood off his lip and wishing it was Garcia he'd been able to punch in the face. He could see Bee out on the ice, shooting him worried looks, but he ignored her. This wasn't anything she could help him with. She couldn't help him and Singer couldn't help him. This was something he had to come to terms with himself.

The penalty box was where he belonged. The press box was where he belonged. Garcia was *wrong*. Mike wouldn't have wasted the first six years of his professional career if he could have done any better. The feeling bubbled up in his chest again, like he was just going to go completely nuts, lose it right out there where everyone could see him. What exactly was going to come out of his mouth, he didn't fucking know.

After the game he didn't bother sticking around for the meal. He needed to get so fucking drunk he stopped thinking about this. What he really needed to do was fuck Garcia out of his system, but that was a bad idea in a hockey town like Boston, where even if he didn't go to a gay bar or try to pick up on Grindr, someone would probably recognize him. He settled for the next best thing, which was going to a bar not too far from the hotel and buying himself shots until he was well on his way to wasted and then a good way past it.

"Rough night?" asked the bartender, a handsome woman with her hair shaved just as close as his. She had neck tattoos, too. She looked sympathetically at the gash on his lip, which burned every time alcohol touched it.

"Nah, I won a fight and a hockey game," he slurred back at her. "It was actually a pretty good night. Really, I'm doing like…great. Really good."

She looked at him. Skeptical. "*You're* doing really good?"

"I'm doing fucking great," Mike told her, slamming his fist on the counter. "I'm doing like…way better than that fucking asshole even *knows*."

"Ohhhh. Bad breakup, huh? That's rough."

"What? No, no, I'm not da—no, no. I'm not dating anyone to break up with. I'd have way better taste than that. Like…way better taste. I wouldn't…"

Her mouth twitched, and Mike swore to god if she laughed at him, he was going to cry. Instead, she said, "Well, whatever's going on, tomorrow's going to be better, you know."

"Yeah. It always is, right? And I'll uhh, take another one of, one of those."

"Hmm," she said, and turned around. When she returned, instead of a drink, she gently pushed the check toward him. "We're not allowed to serve visibly intoxicated patrons."

"You're a bar," Mike said, affronted, "that's your job."

"Our job is to *get* you intoxicated, but then we have to stop. And I'm going to cut you off."

"Fuck."

"I can get you a glass of water, though?" she asked brightly.

"No, uh, no. Thanks. Thank you."

Mike left her a 150% tip and stumbled out of the door and into the street. It was supposed to be a chilly night and he didn't really have a coat, but he didn't feel the cold. He'd made a good choice going somewhere close by, because suddenly even the few blocks seemed kind of daunting and going to sleep like an extremely good idea. What did not seem like a good idea was taking out his phone and voice calling Garcia, but he did it anyway.

"You," he said, when Garcia picked up, "are fucking *wrong* about me."

There was a pause. "Have you been drinking?"

"*No.* Yes. A little. Did you see me play tonight because then you like, you *know* that's what I'm good at doing."

"I didn't mean—I didn't mean to insult you. I meant it. I was being sincere. I think you could be—really good."

"Well, I fucking *can't*, buddy, so keep your, your advice to yourself and your stupid fucking thighs."

"Hey, Mike."

"What."

"Do me a favor and stay on the line with me until you get back to the hotel, all right?"

He was suddenly furious. "Fuck you! I'm not a fucking kid, I can take care of myself."

"Yeah, but you kind of like it when I tell you what to do, don't you? So stay on the line."

Fuck. He was way too drunk to get it up, but his dick was making a half-hearted effort anyway as he trudged the block toward the hotel. "I see—I see what you're doing, you *fuck*."

"Uh-huh," Garcia said placatingly. "Keep walking, kid. So you kicked Gardiner's ass tonight, I saw."

"You *did* watch me."

"Not live. We played tonight too."

"You record my games?"

"They're all on ESPN anyway, and you're not in my blackout area. Gotta keep up with the competition."

"You fucking *dork*."

"Yeah, yeah. He really got you in the mouth, though, didn't he?"

"Bet you're jeaaaalousss."

"Hmm."

"Bet you wanna lick the blood off."

"That would be—no."

"Yeah, but I bet you wanna, because you're just as fucked up as me."

"How far away from the hotel are you?"

"Just a block but…"

"Okay. Keep walking."

"I'd let you."

"What?"

"I'd let you. Lick the blood off."

"Jesus Christ."

"Not so fucking smooth now are you. You sexy fucking *asshole*."

"How much did you *drink*?"

"Enough. I'd let you…"

"Okay. Okay. Jesus. Keep walking."

"Would you?"

"Would I what?"

"Lick it off. I'd let you bite me there. Right where it fucking hurts. I bet you'd like *that*."

"Mike…fuck."

"I know. Keep walking." He groaned. Squinted up at the lights of the hotel's entrance and valet parking area. It was *so* far. "I'm at the hotel. And also, you know, I fucking hate you."

"I know, Mike."

"I hate you and I *really* wanna fuck you, I wanna fuck you up, like—Jesus fuck, I wanna make you feel as shitty as I feel right now. I…"

"Shhh, babe, just get through the door, all right?"

Mike did what he was told, although it was taking a lot of effort to take his attention away from the conversation and smile at the front desk agent. "Hello!" he said, and then realized he sounded extremely shitfaced. He *was* extremely shitfaced. "I'm really drunk, sorry," he apologized, and he could hear Danny's husky gasp of a laugh over the phone. "You, shut up. No, no, not you," he said hastily, when the guy looked up at him, offended. "You're fine."

Somehow, he made his way down the hall to the elevator, checked his door key for the room number. Sixth floor.

"You still there?"

"*Yes.* I was just in the elevator, I'm not an idiot. And now I'm in the room. Any other *orders*, Your Highness?"

"Maybe drink some water and sleep it off, huh?"

"You know, I was drinking so I could fucking forget you, and I fucking *can't*."

"I…look, Mike, maybe we should talk about this when you're sober."

"Fuck," Mike said, and belly-flopped on the hotel bed, on top of the comforter. "I fucking hate when you're right. It makes me like fucking madder than anything. It makes me wanna—"

Danny exhaled sharply. "You're good, yeah? So I'm going to hang up now, okay?"

"Fine."

"Night."

"G'night, Danny," Mike slurred, and knocked out before he could hear whatever Danny said in response.

Danny opened his eyes around six in the morning. The ceiling of his bedroom was white. He'd spent a lot of time looking at it and had all of the cracks and spidering sections of paint memorized. At some point he needed to repaint it, along with most of the house. It had never really seemed like a pressing priority when he was only in there maybe half of the year at best. And the cracks gave him something to look at while his brain was slowly recalibrating itself. Some days it took longer than others.

Today was one of those days. He was a little hungover, but probably nowhere near as bad as Mike. Danny closed his eyes again. He was a shit excuse for a person, but he had some morals, so he knew he'd done the right thing making sure he got Mike back to the hotel and not taking advantage of the situation.

But he'd dreamed about it, about Mike's voice, slurred but full of heat and promise, *I'd let you bite me there. Right where it fucking hurts*, about doing that, about the way Mike kept telling Danny how much he hated him but still liked being told what to do. It was a lot. He was hungover, sure, but part of it was just the fact that talking to Mike sometimes felt like having a sledgehammer taken to the side of his head.

Not always in a bad way.

Danny folded his arms over his chest and thought about all of the things he needed to do that day—groceries, cooking, yard work, making it to the CEC for a home game, sleeping early because they were going on the road tomorrow—and thought about Mike again. He was starting to piece together what was going on. It was…it was pretty fucked up, actually. It was one thing to be in Danny's position, unable to play the way he wanted to because of old injuries, because his body simply couldn't handle it.

It was another thing entirely to have someone like Mike, the raw clay there for sculpting, and the coaches were just apparently too fucking stupid to see it. No wonder he'd been so upset. Danny knew exactly what he'd been getting into, knew what he was capable of. He'd had literal years to get used to the idea that he wasn't going to win the Defenseman of the Year award or even move up the lineup anytime soon, anytime ever. He'd known pretty much as soon as the doctors told him the broken hip could be career ending. It probably should have been, he just hadn't let it.

He was very aware of his body's limitations and his play style had adapted to hide them. At this point there wasn't anything he could do about it. Even surgeries could only do so much.

Mike had probably gotten used to that idea too, except he didn't have the fucked-up hip or knee or any of the other shit Danny had to balance every day. What Danny didn't understand was why no one had figured this out before him, why no one had thought it worthwhile to put in the investment into developing Mike as a player. Pure enforcers were on their way out of the league and even someone like Danny, who had some skill and good hockey IQ, even if his body couldn't keep up, even if everyone mostly knew him for his fists, wasn't going to be able to stick around much longer.

But it was like everyone had looked at Mike's play style, at his size, at the bad habits he'd developed all the way back to juniors to compensate for the fact that he was on the smaller side, and completely written him off.

Danny stared up at the ceiling and entertained a completely insane idea.

He was going to *make* Mike a better player. Somehow, he was going to mold him into the kind of d-man Danny couldn't be. Mike was still young, only twenty-five, and if Danny had managed to play for ten years after that, then Mike still had the chance to make a real career for himself. He couldn't fix his own broken body, he couldn't change the past, but he could do something for Mike's future.

If Mike would let him.

He'd just have to recalibrate how he approached things.

How's your head, he asked.

none of your fucking business. There was a pause. it's fucked.

Told you to drink some water, buddy.

ughhh. There was a longer pause. so uh, abt last night. if i said anything fucked up i'm sorry. don't remember a lot of it.

First compliments and now apologies? If you're not careful I'm going to think you actually like me

i'm serious!!!! did i say anything fucked up

You were fine, Danny said, which was a necessary lie.

i uh…don't know if i believe u but ok.

Look. Mike. About the other stuff.

you don't have to. fuck, hang on

"Look," Mike said, when Danny answered the call. "I lost my shit, I know, it's fucking stupid, you didn't mean anything by it." His voice was raspy and scratchy, and he spoke very slowly, like every word hurt him. Danny imagined it was probably a pretty epic hangover.

Danny gnawed on his lower lip. "Well, I didn't mean anything insulting by it. But I did mean it."

There was a long exhale on the other end of the line and Danny could almost feel Mike's breath against his ear. "So did I. I'm not *good*, Garcia. Like, I guess I was good enough to get here. *Eventually.* But that's about it. I'm not as good as I want to be."

"You could be. It's not your fault your coaches—"

"Yes, it is, I don't know why you—"

"Mike, you're the most fucking stubborn, annoying asshole I've ever had the misfortune to know, so why the fuck do you think I'd waste my time even trying if I didn't see something in you?" The words were harsh, but he kept his voice gentle, and he could hear Mike swallow hard again.

"I don't know. You're trying to get in my head, fuck me up," Mike said, and laughed. It wasn't a real laugh. There was a wobble in it. He sounded, again, like he was going to cry, but at least he wasn't hanging up. Progress, of a strange kind. "It's working, by the way. You motherfucker."

"Dude, I'm serious. You… I know you want it. So why are you afraid to try?"

"You really fucking have to ask? If I try and…"

If I try and fail. He knew. Oh, Danny knew. And it was time to play dirty and hit low. "What, are you scared?"

"I'm not—I'm not scared of *anything*."

"I think you are."

"Fuck you!"

"So prove me wrong."

"Ugh, I don't want to even think about this right now. My head feels like a fucking elephant stepped on it."

"Drink some water."

"Bossy," Mike grumbled, but there was a rustle of sheets and the creak of bedsprings as he got up. Danny wondered if he was wearing clothes, if he was just in his boxers, if his lip had scabbed over. There was the sound of a tap running, and Mike said, "Fuck, I have to get my shit together or I'm gonna miss the plane. Bye."

"Yeah."

"I—Gar—bye."

"Yeah, you said that."

"Jesus. I'm *going*."

Mike tried not to think about the conversation he'd had with Garcia. It drummed in the back of his head any time he had a minute's downtime. He still felt sick when he thought about it. What if Garcia was right? What if the key to being better had been with Mike the entire time and he'd wasted it? Why the fuck had Garcia—a guy who probably didn't even like him very much because fuck knew Mike had spent a lot of time being a complete asshole to him—seen something in him that none of his coaches, in the twenty-one years he'd been playing hockey, had seen before?

He couldn't afford to hope that Garcia was right, because if he wasn't, it was going to crush him.

This was why it was better to know your place and do your fucking job. Then you were never disappointed when the inevitable things happened. He was a stupid fuck, that was for sure.

It was in this mindset that Halloween and Netty and Reed's annual costume party blowout bash snuck up on him.

Mike wasn't entirely sure how he'd gotten roped into doing a group costume, but Netty and Reed had gotten Singer in last year, and they'd bullied the rest of the team into joining in this year. The theme, unfortunately, was superheroes. Mike had picked the *Guardians of the Galaxy* superhero he thought would require the least work. He'd basically owned Drax's pants already. He'd only had to shave his head completely instead of buzzing it, and smear himself with gray body paint. It was sort of cheating to just let his own tattoos peek through, but even if he tried to copy the red, it probably wouldn't have shown up over all of the black ink. It was chilly, and he was shirtless, but that was fine. He just had to try not to get the paint on the car seat, or, like. Anything else.

Mäkelä drove Mike and Bee to Reed's town house, which he had purchased a month ago and hadn't finished furnishing, so it was ideal for a party. It was, Mike had realized with some amusement but zero surprise, right around the corner from Singer's place. The two of them, Singer and Reed, were really fucking weird about each other. And they lived out of each other's pockets anyway, so almost no one on the team had blinked an eye when Reed bought it. Like: of course they'd live around the corner from each other even though they were attached at the hip anyway.

Mäkelä and Bee had done a couple's costume, kind of. He was Thor, post eye-gouging. Because he was driving, he had the eyepatch flipped up in his hair, but the fake blood he'd caked around the eye socket was horrifying anyway. Bee was Valkyrie. She looked completely badass in the white-and-gray armor, but it wasn't too far off from how she looked on the ice anyway.

"This is stupid," Mike grumbled, as they walked from the parked car to Reed's house, trying not to cross his arms over his chest and smear the paint.

"You look very frightening," Bee said.

"I *feel* really fucking *cold*," he said, because his nipples were trying to retract their way into his body.

"This is like summer weather," Mäkelä said, flipping the eyepatch down. It was even more brutal because the way he said it was so friendly.

Mike sighed; he could probably learn a lot about chirping from Mäkelä. Instead, he knocked on Reed's door and left a little smear of gray on it. Yeah, the costume was definitely not one of his better ideas.

Reed answered, Netty at his side, and Bee startled everyone by making a sudden, choked noise of laughter when she saw them. Reed was the Winter Soldier, long hair and metal arm and eyeliner and everything, but Netty…had unzipped his black leather catsuit down to his belly button, exposing his hairy chest and stomach.

"Is good costume, right?" Netty asked, cheerful as always.

"It's—wow, it's something," Bee gasped.

"I tried to talk him out of it," Reed said, sounding more than a little rueful, "but he insisted."

"Had to be three." Netty shrugged, gesturing to his costume and Reed's. "Captain America, the Winter Soldier, and the Black Widow."

"Well, if you don't care about the circulation to your balls, that's not our problem," Mike said, thinking about how uncomfortable those pants looked. "Jesus Christ, will you let us in? It's fucking cold out here."

"Welcome to my humble abode," Reed said, and stepped aside.

The house was kind of empty, though. Instead of dining room furniture, Reed had a ping-pong table covered in red Solo cups. The living room had one large couch and an entertainment station with video game consoles, but the rest of it was folding chairs. Because it was Reed, he knew a million people in the city and he'd invited guests who weren't on the team, so there were crowds sitting and chatting on almost every available surface, including the floor. He saw a Batman cape and cowl and a woman he was pretty sure was an Instagram influencer in a Wonder Woman leotard. Even worse, Elliott had some pretty intense Joker makeup.

Mike left Mäkelä and Bee with Reed and Netty and went to find something to drink.

Singer leaned against the wall in the kitchen, away from the crowd, flicking his thumb against his phone screen as he scrolled. The costume was a reference to an in-joke Reed had made their first season together, but also, it fit, completely without irony, even if he'd grown out the beard and gone the *Infinity War* tragic Cap route. It was a good look on him. Singer glanced up and smiled when he saw Mike there.

"Hey, buddy," he said. His cheeks were pink. Apparently, everyone had gotten started before they'd gotten there. And like fine, so had Mike, but he was gray, so no one could see how red he got when he was drinking. "Nice costume."

Mike shrugged. "It was easy. I'm probably gonna get paint all over everything here, though."

"Well, it's easy to clean," Singer said, looking at the long marble counters, hardwood floors, packed bodies, and very little else. "I told him he should get some actual furniture before he had people over, but he said why buy it if it'll just get trashed."

"He has a point."

"So how are you doing, Mike? You've been tearing it up at practice recently."

"Yeah, I… I'm fine. I've been…trying some new shit, I guess."

"Yeah?"

"Um. I need a drink, Cap. I'll see you around."

He could feel Singer's intent gaze on his back as

he walked away and poured himself a Jack and Coke that was mostly Jack, but he was nowhere near drunk enough to even begin trying to explain to the captain what Garcia had said. How would he even explain it? *Oh, yeah, I've been talking to some guy on the Hornets about my game and he's really trying to get me to play up to my potential.*

Singer would probably laugh him out of the fucking house.

Speaking of Garcia, the Hornets were playing in Vegas. The game had started at ten p.m. Mike's time, so he was keeping an eye on the score. Not that he wanted them to win. The Cons and the Hornets were jockeying for the top two spots in the Metropolitan division and obviously he wanted them to lose. But if he wanted to keep an eye on what Danny was doing that was his own business.

They were nearing the end of the first period and the Aces were up one. He kind of wished he could just watch the game, see whether Danny showed any of the fucking initiative and talent he'd apparently seen in Mike. Instead, he obsessively refreshed Twitter to see whether anyone had uploaded relevant clips. There was one of Danny rolling one of the Vegas forwards against the boards, which was a really good look on him. He realized what he was doing immediately after thinking it, scowled, and put the phone away.

The rest of the party went by in a blur of faces around him, beer pong with Netty, who was nearly unbeatable, against Reed and Singer, trying to avoid being pulled in to dance with anyone on the team. No one on the Cons could dance—Bee and Sally excluded—and neither could he. His only experience was youthful flailing in Portland mosh pits and he didn't think anyone here would appreciate that. The charms of accidentally being kicked in the face by someone's combat boot as they crowd-surfed by would definitely be lost on them. Reed's taste in music was terrible and Mike had to beg Netty to take over the playlist so he didn't have to listen to country anymore. Even Russian EDM was preferable. Drinks were pressed into his hand, and he drank them.

The Hornets won their game. No one tried to fight Danny, so Mike messaged him, guess your ugly face finally scared 'em away, not really expecting a response, since they were probably in postgame media scrum and the showers and cooldown by now.

By the time he checked his phone again it was maybe a half hour later, he had wriggled his way out from under Netty's arm, leaving a streak of gray behind him, and Danny had written, well, you like it.

He thought about Danny's face. His broken nose, the little white scar on his eyebrow. His big dark eyes, the way they got even darker when he was turned on. The way his full mouth moved when he smiled. It was a really good face, and Mike was a fucking liar.

Nah, he said.

wyd? Danny asked, and Mike caught himself laughing at the callback. Then scowled at the phone. This was bad. This was really bad.

Halloween party, he said, and sent a snap of his torso, still half covered in gray paint, gradually being rubbed away when people touched him. On the shoulders, on the arms, brushing against him while they danced. It annoyed him. They weren't the right hands.

What the hell are you supposed to be?

drax the destroyer, dude, are you so old you don't know superheroes

You mostly look like you're melting.

ok, the paint was a bad idea. it's cold

I'm sure no one's complaining.

compliments? you're gonna make me think you like me

Mike.

????

nvm. Wait, is this a theme party?

And just like that, Mike was distracted from whatever Danny had been on the verge of saying.

It had been a rough game. Danny hadn't had to fight anyone, but he hadn't stretched long enough or carefully enough beforehand, maybe, or maybe his body was just breaking down again. Either way, everything hurt and his muscles were screaming in protest as he sat through the postgame shit. No interviews. He barely even noticed what he was eating, just shoveled it down and got the hell out of there, avoiding Landry's puppy dog eyes because some of the guys were going out for Halloween.

Halloween in Vegas didn't really have the same kind

of appeal it might've had for him if he'd been fifteen years younger.

"I'm old," he'd said to Landry, "and everything hurts. I'm going back to the hotel."

"Dude, you're not *that* old, stop saying that, and it's not every day you get to spend Halloween in Vegas, right? I bet the costumes and the chicks are gonna be nuts. Come onnnnn, Garcia."

"I really don't need to see any costumes," he'd mumbled, and made his escape.

The hotel was barely a two-minute walk from the arena, which was good, because walking any farther was going to hurt like hell. His phone vibrated as he was walking and it was, unsurprisingly, Mike. The only person who regularly talked to him anymore.

By the time he thought to ask if it was a theme party, he was back at the hotel, stripped down to his boxers, supplementing painkillers with a drink from the minibar, which was probably not the best way to end the evening, but fuck it. It was a holiday for parties, and his—Mike—was on the other side of the country, half-naked and covered in body paint, and Danny was alone, avoiding a team full of children.

Mike had said, *dude, it's all comic book shit, at least for the team*, and then he'd started going around the house and sending snaps of different Cons, guys Danny didn't know very well, but Mike seemed very fond of.

this is what netty's like all the time, he'd typed over a picture of an extremely large Russian guy in a black leather catsuit and red wig, striking a pose for the phone camera as he puffed out his hairy chest.

captain america is his actual nickname, over a

picture of the Cons' captain in the Cap's gear. He was giving an impressive side-eye to a guy dressed as Raoul Duke—he apparently hadn't gotten the theme memo, or he just didn't give a shit. Danny recognized him under the shades. Jamie Ayer, one of Montreal's d-men: right, the Royal had been in Newark that night. In between them was Reed, arms slung over their shoulders, beaming in a very un-Winter Soldierly manner.

The pictures kept coming. bee, the goat, he'd captioned Beatrice Morin, wearing white-and-gray armor and pointing her sword at Mike; mäkelä, he's the goalie, so basically an alien. A stocky blond guy with sharp pointed features, a little shorter than Morin, staring solemnly, one-eyed, at the camera.

Some of these costumes are fuckin terrible.

they're not bad except for jammer, idk what he's supposed to be, but he looks like a complete douche

It's from Fear and Loathing in Las Vegas.

what?

Jfc Mike have you ever read a book in your life?

nah, too busy playing hockey

For fuck's sake. And anyway, I meant YOUR costume is fuckin terrible.

ok point taken, it's bad. sue me

You're being awfully agreeable. Drunk enough, eh?

i could tell you to go fuck yourself if it'd make you feel more at home

Sure.

go fuck yourself

Again: I'd rather fuck you.

didn't know you were into dudes who look like they're melting

Danny thought about typing, *I'm into you*, but he knew that wouldn't have gone over well and he was enjoying the chance to actually talk to Mike, to get a glimpse of what he was like with people he didn't hate. What he was like when he wasn't interacting with Danny. He sighed and poured himself another drink. guess I'm into some weird shit.

yeah, i figured that one out when you got down on your knees in an alley for me, bro

He frowned at the phone. Do you really want to start this now?

start what

Mike.

yeah, yeah.

Mike sent another snap of himself, flipping Danny the bird. In the interim more of the gray paint had been smeared away, and Danny felt a brief, bizarre moment of caveman jealousy at all of the people who could touch him, who were clearly touching him, when he couldn't. When Mike probably wouldn't have even let him. Or maybe he would have, if there wasn't an entire continent between them.

You need to work on your chirps.

Instead of a response, another picture of his middle finger, his hand positioned in front of a lower portion of his torso. Danny stared at the shot until it vanished, at the lines of Mike's abs and hips, the V leading down to the ridiculous pants and belt. He stared at the tattoos there, a fucking Doré woodcut, Jacob wrestling with the angel across his stomach, which was both the most appropriate thing he could think of for Mike, and also surprising from a guy who'd claimed to have never read a book in his life.

What Danny wanted was the time to pore over every single piece of ink on Mike's body and figure out why he'd picked them, which would take more than the minute he had before the photograph vanished.

He knew what Mike was doing. He was trying to bait Danny into something, and on another day, Danny might have given in immediately, because Mike clearly wanted him, wanted whatever weird shit they had going between them. Tonight, though, something about the sadness of it all, the sheer hopelessness of this entire fucking endeavor, weighed on him. Sure, he could get off. It would probably be good; it would definitely be good. Mike was hot as fuck and together they were something combustible. He had a brief mental image of Mike jerking himself off, getting gray paint all over himself, streaks where his hands had been, streaks where Danny's hands should have been.

And then it would be over, and Mike would either lose it because he'd said too much, or passed out, and Danny would be alone in his hotel room again. As much as he wanted it, the problem was he wanted it too much. The problem was he wanted things he couldn't have. There was a moment where he almost considered telling Mike, *I gotta go*, and it would have been better for both of them in the long run. But he was a piece of shit, and he couldn't.

You're such a fucking brat, he said, instead.

you like it, Mike responded, like it was a taunt. It was, more than he would ever actually know. you like me.

It was a bad idea, but that had always been his unfortunate tendency. Once, when he was six years old, he'd stood too close to the plancha at the diner. *Don't do it, Danny*, his mother had said, when she saw him staring, fascinated by the way the heat rose off of the iron, smacked him in the face. *It's hot, be careful.* He'd slammed his fingers down on the hot metal and dealt with the burns for almost two weeks.

He'd never learned either.

You are a pain in my fucking ass. Find a bathroom or something.

yeah. this fucking house is the worst, there are people everywhere.

I bet you get off on that, huh. Someone hearing just how fucking desperate you are.

jesus fuck, give me a second, im still trying to find a door i can lock

"Okay," Mike said, after Danny answered his call. He sounded breathless already, more than a little drunk, but nowhere near as smashed as he'd been the other night. "I found a bathroom. But I gotta be *quiet*."

"Hah. You've never been quiet in your fucking life, I bet."

"I can keep it down!"

"Mhm."

"I *can*."

"I'll tell you what, if you can't, you're gonna have to do some practice drills for me."

"Daniel fucking Garcia," and Danny was pleased to hear he'd gotten the pronunciation right this time, "are you trying to bribe me into your fucking insane idea with phone sex?"

"Seems like it's working, so I wouldn't say *trying*."

"I fucking hate you."

"So is that a yes or a no? Because I can hang up, Mike."

There was a long pause and a shaky breath out. "Yes. It's always fucking yes with you, you asshole."

Danny tucked the phone between his ear and his shoulder and slid his hand down his boxers. The whole situation was definitely getting into shame-boner territory. He was only half-hard, stymied by the contrast of the melancholy he'd felt earlier and the animal need he felt now.

"You have to be quiet." His voice sounded funny, not like him. Too rough already. That fucking *kid*. He could hear a sharp breath in, but nothing else. It wasn't enough. "Tell me what you're doing."

Mike made a noise that wasn't quite a giggle, a nervous bark of laughter, which he swallowed quickly. "Jesus, this is weird. I'm, uh. Hand in my pants. I'm—" There was a brief moment of just a breath; a little sigh. His voice was low, not quite a whisper, but close. Danny could imagine how it would sound in person, in his ear. God, he was so fucked. "I'm touching myself, okay?"

Danny moved his own hand up his dick, thumbed the head and slid it down again. A full-body shudder ran over him. Doing this with Mike was like the shivery head rush you got with really good IV painkillers. He didn't want to go too fast, lose this opportunity, but he knew they couldn't stretch it out as long as he wanted to either. "When you do it think about how I'd do it. How I'd touch you."

"Fuck."

"You know how."

"Fuck, you did it like you were fucking angry with me and—and your hands are so fucking big, I couldn't—I hate you, it's not *fair*—"

"My hands are big? That's what you're going with?"

"Fuck you, they *are*, I like it—"

"Shh, keep your voice down, or I—"

"You're not going to win this one, Danny, fuck you."

"I got you off so fast because you just—god, you just need it so badly, you're so fucking—"

"Fuck, fuck," Mike was muttering to himself, like a curse or a prayer.

"Tell me—"

"I'm trying to pretend it's you," he said, his voice a little higher, ragged. "I'm—faster now. I can't—"

"Do you?"

"Do I what?"

"Need me to get you off, need *me*—"

"Why do you think I—fuck, Danny, I haven't felt like this, not ever…" He breathed out again, almost a sob, choking it down in his throat.

Danny thought about his dick in Mike's mouth and how it would sound if he shoved it in hard. Probably like that. "Like *what*."

"I don't know," Mike whisper-shouted. He sounded desperately turned on and furious and Danny loved it. "I don't know how to, how to say it, you just, you fuck me up."

"I would," Danny said. It was a promise. More. "I would, I *would* fuck you up, I'd *make* you—" Mike made one of those whimpering noises again, and Danny's hand sped up as he said, "Shh, shh, you have to be quiet, remember? I don't think you're winning this one."

There was a noise on the other end of the line, another choking sob. "Fu-u-u-ck."

"Are you close?" He could feel it, prickling over his entire body. "You have to be quiet, babe. You have to—"

Mike wasn't being quiet. Oh, he was trying, but he was a fucking mess, and Danny couldn't see it but fuck he could hear it. He had reduced Mike to a whimpering, groaning incoherency, and he could hear a noise like Mike had smacked his head on the wall. Danny loved that about him, that he was a guy who by necessity had to have control of his body to do well at his job, but Danny could strip that from him so easily. He couldn't even answer, he was that worked up, and he made a noise like Danny'd slapped him when he came.

Hearing that tipped Danny over. It took him a minute to recover, still shuddering with how good it felt, how guilty he felt. But: demonstrably, Mike had lost that bet.

"I'll send you the drills tomorrow," Danny said, still a little breathless, and Mike groaned.

"Fuck, I hoped you'd forgotten about that."

"Not a fucking chance, buddy."

"Oh, fuck, I gotta go," Mike said, sounding momentarily panicked.

And then the line was dead and Danny was left alone, in the dark, as he should have been.

I want he started to type, but stopped and deleted it.

CHAPTER THREE

November

Mike was not thinking about Reed's face—horrified and impressed—when he'd slunk out of the bathroom, leaving a smear of gray paint behind on Reed's brand-new wall. He hadn't even been able to say anything about it because it was clear enough what he'd been up to. It had been a stupid fucking idea, but he had zero self-control when it came to Danny. He'd mumbled an apology and beat a hasty retreat into the crowd.

Luckily, Reed had been either too embarrassed or too understanding to say anything, or practices would have been unbearable after that. There were, like, hockey bros. And then there were hockey bros who knew what you sounded like when you were coming your brains out and if he'd had the choice, he definitely would not have put Reed into that category. Ever, under any circumstance.

For one thing, Singer probably would've murdered him.

And it wasn't like Danny had given him any time to actually recover. True to his word, he'd messaged Mike in the morning, give me your email address. Mike had thought about refusing, but a bet was a bet, and he'd lost. So he gave Danny his Gmail and right away received a list of files with names like *St. Cloud* and *horseshoe skating drills* and *offensive blue line support* and for a minute Mike stared at his email and thought about catching a flight to Pittsburgh, tracking down Danny to wherever he lived, and murdering him.

this is shit i learned in juniors

Yeah, and when's the last time you did them, really did them, for hours on end until you can't fucking do them anymore?

Mike thought about it. Probably the last time he'd done drills that hard *was* in juniors, or maybe peewees. The closest he'd come was when he was trying to make the team but even then, it was mostly general conditioning. Skating, strength, boxing, and Muay Thai to make himself more useful in the role that Coach had brought him onto the team to perform. Not precision work. And generally, he was only ever on the ice for the shorter practices and morning skates they always had during the season.

"So how many of these do you want me to do?" he asked Danny, early in the morning. Bee was at Mäkelä's, or he wouldn't have risked calling in the apartment. Not after the Reed catastrophe.

"Pick one or two per day, and do them until you can't anymore," Danny said in the tone of voice that Mike had come to associate with sex, and it was kind of embarrassing that his dick perked up at the sound of it. Like. Maybe there were worse ways to try to improve your game, but still. "I'm talking hours."

"Which ones?"

"We're gonna work our way through all of them, so whatever you want to start with, it doesn't make a difference."

"Danny—" It slipped out before he could stop it, and then it was too late. He was sober, and he'd used the nickname, and he couldn't take it back. He was never going to live that one down. "All of them?"

"You want to improve, right? You're going to work your way through all of them, and then you're going to do it again, until you get it right."

There was no hint of any of the warmth or humor Mike thought he could pick out of his voice sometimes. It was all business, and a little cruel, like if he didn't squash Mike's ego a bit, he knew Mike wasn't going to do it. He was right about that, which sucked, but those were the breaks. Too bad he needed that for motivation and found it boner-inducing.

"And then what?"

"We'll talk about your game later, but I want you to start working on just forcing this shit into your muscle memory first. You've developed a lot of bad habits that we need to break."

The longer he talked, the more Mike felt that vicious little animal stirring, the one that reared out when he wanted things too much. The nasty urge to destroy anything good in his life before it could destroy him. "Remind me again why I'm doing *anything* you tell me? Last time I looked we were basically on the same lineup depth, dude. Same level. Same shit, except you're a hell of a lot older than me. The fuck do you know?"

Danny was silent for a minute, and Mike could feel the chill across the phone line. Glacial. At first Mike thought he might hang up. Instead, he said very evenly, "You're young and you've got full use of all your limbs. Maybe you can actually appreciate that for a fucking change, all right, instead of pissing it away. Do the drills, and then we'll talk."

He hung up.

The fact that Mike knew he had crossed some kind of a line didn't make it any easier, knowing he'd fucked up and really upset Danny. In a way that any other charged interaction hadn't. Mike looked down at his phone and frowned. For all he'd been stalking Danny's social media, he hadn't really read anything else about him. He googled it now.

And read.

And read.

Danny had grown up in Detroit, and his parents, José Luis and Verónica, owned a diner. There was a picture of it in the Wikipedia article. It was a Detroit institution. It had been there since the 1930s, in continuous use. Danny played Tier II junior hockey, been drafted like 150 spots higher than Mike anyway, and got a single season in the minors before being called up. There had been some stuff about how promising he was, how underrated he'd been during draft scouting, how his size combined with his speed and his ice sense meant great things for Chicago. He was a defenseman who had the potential to do it all: a great two-way game. He'd just needed some time to gain experience and mature as a player.

In his first full season with the Boilermen, Danny had been hit from behind by a guy on the Royal and landed badly, and then a teammate had tripped over him, too. He'd broken his hip and his leg. *After surgery,*

Garcia was never able to return to the same level of play he had achieved before this potentially career-ending injury, the article said, then listed all the times Danny had been injured. He'd had surgery on the same knee three times in total, the other one twice, his shoulder once, a shitload of concussions. He'd been traded or claimed on waivers, and then the results were mostly articles about what a goon he was and how it was a shame he'd never been able to live up to his earlier promise.

Mike felt like the worst kind of asshole in the entire fucking world.

To try to distract himself he read about Danny's family. His parents had emigrated from a city called Torreón in the early 1980s and lived in Detroit since then, but Danny's sister was a therapist in Philadelphia.

Well, that explained a lot.

He found Araceli Garcia's Insta, and maybe he creeped on it a little. She was a tall woman, strongly resembled her brother except for the fact that her nose had never been broken. If Danny hadn't played hockey he probably would have had a nose like that, long and proud, only a little natural bump at the bridge. But they had the same firm mouth and chin, the same stubborn jaw, the same dark eyes and long eyelashes. Her curly hair was threaded with gray, and in most of the pictures she was holding her daughter, an adorable toddler, or laughing with her husband, a distinguished-looking professor type with smooth brown skin, a twitchy mouth, and eyes that fucking twinkled.

It occurred to him that Danny was, like, a real person, with a real history, not just a sexy voice on the other end of the telephone or a guy he wanted to punch in the face in person. It was a weird fucking feeling, and he wasn't sure if he liked it. It was unsettling, to know shit wasn't the way you thought it was.

Mike closed the window and called Bee, who picked up on like the second or third ring.

"Michael? Is everything all right?"

"No—I mean, yeah, everything's fine, why would you think everything isn't—"

"You just don't usually *call*."

Jesus Christ, he was an asshole. "Can I ask a favor?"

"Of course," Bee said without hesitation, "what is it?" and he loved her so fucking much his chest was going to split open.

"Will you." He hesitated. "Will you come to the rink with me on our off days? And do some drills?"

"Drills?"

"I have to do a lot of skating. I'm trying to, um, improve my play."

"Of course I'll be there. Just give me the time and day."

"I was gonna start this morning. If you're free."

"I'll have Sakari drop me off. I wouldn't miss it for the world."

"I owe you, Bee. Anything."

"Mon chum, you know I'd never cash in on it."

True to her word, Bee met him at the Cons' Skate Zone in Voorhees, and together they dressed and went out on the ice while Mäkelä sat in the stands, his legs thrown over the arm of a chair, headphones in as he zoned out, staring up at the ceiling and thinking whatever weird little goalie thoughts kept him occupied.

It was also strange, being there on a day when the rest of the team wasn't. Because the rink administrators knew them, they didn't have any trouble getting out on the ice before the public skate. But he knew he was going to end up working through it—or around it, given what he remembered of public skates from his childhood—and after it.

"So what brought this on?" Bee asked as they skated out for warm-ups.

"I, uh, I wanted to get better. And I'm not going to get better unless I practice. Unless I change the way I'm doing things."

He was stunned when she hugged him so hard she almost boarded him, the force of her body pushing him down the ice. Bee was about four inches taller than he was, and they were right at the same weight.

"Michael!" she crowed, delighted.

"Bee, what the hell?"

"I'm so happy, I can't believe you're finally doing it!"

He pulled out of her embrace, already on the defensive. "What do you mean, finally?"

"I've always known you could do this, it's just, it is good to see you *do* it."

"And you—you never said anything?" Mike couldn't help the sick swoop of his stomach. It wasn't just Danny? Bee had known?

"Michael," she said, grabbing his shoulder pads. "I've always known you had talent and I've always hoped you'd use it. But your friendship is more important to me than that. I was afraid I'd lose that. Us. Is that selfish of me?"

"I don't know what the fuck to say," he said, because he didn't.

"If I'd told you that I thought you weren't playing the way you could, would you have listened to me? Instead of telling me to fuck off, instead of things being wrong after that? You're very proud."

He knew how he'd reacted to hearing it from Danny, and he honestly didn't know how he would have reacted to hearing it from Bee. He'd known her longer and trusted her more, but he'd lived with bone-deep weariness and fury about what he wanted and what he was capable of, like, forever. Maybe their friendship wouldn't have survived. She was looking at him, her brown eyes warm, her face open. She never would have been able to look at him like that their first season together, when she had a pole up her ass a mile long and felt that any emotion was a show of weakness and someone would take advantage.

And now she was looking at him with love. She loved him too.

If she could change, he could at least try to be kind of honest about how he would have treated her then.

"No. You're probably fucking right," Mike said, and looked down at his skates. "Jesus fucking Christ, I've been fucking up my life."

"Stop being dramatic, Michael. You're only twenty-five, you've still got time."

Mike bit back the urge to say, *you and Danny, you motherfuckers*, but Bee didn't know about Danny, and he couldn't tell her. He'd been keeping these secrets for so long that even now that he had a guy he was talking to regularly, even with his best friend, it still felt too risky to open his damn mouth.

He didn't like having all of these emotions all at once. It was a lot easier to feel angry, or maybe horny, but as they went out onto the ice, he felt shame and embarrassment and frustration that he couldn't tell her what the tipping point for this had been, couldn't tell her that he was doing it for himself but also for a guy on a rival team, couldn't tell her where he'd been and who he'd been talking to at all hours of the night for the last two months.

One day at a time.

"All right," he said, "so the first one simulates a breakaway—"

"Just tell me where I need to be," she said, and gently headbutted him with her helmet.

He'd picked out two exercises for today. One was a basic agility drill, which he was planning to do when Bee took a break, and the other one was basically infinite variations on Bee trying to get close to the crease while he tried to stop her. As they were running through the motions, he realized how little he actually thought about what he was doing on the ice. He reacted a lot but he didn't plan anything. The drill instructions had extras in them, like *try to think about your skates as being extra sticks* and *only keep one hand on the stick when you poke check* and, like, Mike knew that these were things he should have been thinking about when he was playing. But mostly when he was out on the ice, he was using his body like a battering ram, or he was fighting.

It was kind of sobering and kind of humiliating.

How had he even gotten this far?

It was because he was good at what Coach used him for. Being a pest, throwing himself into a fray, running a physical game. But when he compared himself to Bouchard, when he'd still been around, or Novotný or Lindberg and Graham, there was no comparison. He'd let Parsons guide his game his rookie year because they were a pair and Parsons had longevity with the team but… Jesus.

Mike threw himself into the drills and skated until he was sweating bullets. Bee didn't even seem particularly fussed as she wheeled and dodged around him. It wasn't ideal. Half of their movements were scripted, and the other half he could guess himself, because he knew her, and he knew the way she played. *Translate that*, the internalized Danny-voice said, and Mike almost bit his tongue in horror.

"You okay?" Bee asked him.

"I just realized something," he said. He skated over to the side of the rink where they'd lined up their water bottles and gulped some of it down.

"What?"

"I've just been thinking about this all wrong, I guess."

Bee was staring again, like she didn't even know him. "I don't know what's gotten into you, buddy, but I like it."

"You don't have to stick around for the agility stuff," he mumbled, unable to meet her eyes. "I know you probably have shit to do."

Bee did them anyway. It was like old times at development camp, pounding the ice together and dodging around the public skaters. That was tough on its own. Bee was kind of a local hero at this point, and constantly getting stopped by little girls and little boys, and not-so-little girls and boys, for autographs and pictures. No one really bothered him, but it was probably because Mike was looking murderous and feeling murderous, the more he could feel the burn of his muscles and his lungs.

It was good.

He didn't want to be bothered anyway.

Danny saw the fruits of his experiment early. Mike sent him a link to some random woman's Twitter: she'd been at the rink for the public skate and taken a video of Mike and Bee running Danny's drills. That was a surprise, since Morin wasn't the kind of player who needed extra practice, but also wasn't really a surprise, when he remembered she and Mike lived together and had been practically joined at the hip since their first year on the Cons.

It was, admittedly, a pretty cute video. The girl had captured the two of them staring each other down, mock-serious, before Morin tried to weave around Mike and he controlled the space she was able to take up, herding her away from the crease. Toward the end of it they'd exploded in mock-shoving, gloves on the ice, like little kids or overly energetic puppies.

There was another video of Mike without Morin, doing the horseshoe drill around obstacles that proved to be mostly the general public wobbling on shitty rental skates. He was—this was what Danny had wanted to see. Mike's speed and agility, without the constraint of feeling like he needed to constantly board the forwards, constantly fight them.

Danny would have smiled, but he was still pissed off. Not that he'd expected an apology, but Mike had cut him deeper than he'd probably realized. Nothing like having your failures casually thrown in your face by a guy you wanted but couldn't have.

Mike had been doing the drills, clearly, but Danny didn't really feel like talking to him very much.

He'd pushed himself at the game against the Cougars—his most recent team before they'd traded him at the deadline for a conditional seventh-round draft pick—harder than he should have. He'd followed his own damn advice and focused on playing as technical a game as he could, and it had paid off with a three-point night, two primary assists and one secondary. He couldn't skate, but he could still fucking clear the puck. And it wasn't like the Cougars were actually any fucking *good*; it was just like he had to do something because it was Detroit.

He hated coming home for games. He knew his parents were out there in the crowd somewhere, and he hated when they watched him play these days. It was one thing if they were at home, but another if they were there, in person, seeing his body break down. He hated that he still felt like he couldn't actually talk to them, hated that he didn't feel like he could find them in the crowd afterward and give them a hug, hated everything about it. It was easier to avoid them, but that didn't mean he liked it or didn't miss them.

His dad, especially, gave really good hugs. He was almost as tall as Danny, all barrel torso and chicken legs, and his arms were just as strong and enveloping as they'd been when Danny was a kid.

They wouldn't have been very proud if they knew anything about his life right now.

"Hell yeah, bro!" Landry said, holding up his fist and eagerly waiting for Danny to fist-bump him back. "Garcia with the *assist*. We make a good team, huh?"

Danny wondered if there was a prayer for god to save you from overeager children who needed your attention, but instead of trying to find it, he raised his fist and touched it to Landry's. The kid's eyes widened and he ducked his head to hide the grin, and Danny sighed. Inaudibly. He wasn't a monster, and he'd promised Marty, his old coach on the Boilermen, that one day he'd pay it forward. "Nice goal, kid."

Landry was floating by the time they made it out of the dressing room and into the postgame meal. He wasn't a bad kid, just...didn't think about the shit that came out of his mouth on the ice. Maybe. Danny caught Lévesque watching him and he wished he had a drink instead of the chewy Detroit-style pizza the team had had delivered to the Cougars' visiting room.

He'd been on teams where the captains had nicknames, but he couldn't imagine referring to Lévesque with one. There was something too serious about his face and his general everything. People usually referred to him with all three of his names, like two wasn't enough to show the full respect. Sometimes they'd have to include his title too. Henri Jean-Philippe Lévesque, the captain of the Hornets.

"Yeah?" Danny said, when he saw Lévesque was still looking at him. He took a big bite of his pizza and chewed. Wasn't hungry but he needed to make a point.

"You were different on the ice today," Lévesque said, with his vaguely French and very flat affect. It wasn't a question.

Danny took another bite of his pizza. "Yeah?"

"You don't usually play with that much attention to detail."

"I'm an enforcer," Danny said, wiping grease from his fingers onto an already-crumpled paper napkin. He felt like he was channeling Mike, except it wasn't really a good look on a dude who was closer to forty than twenty. Most people probably wouldn't have thought it was a good look on Mike, either, even though Danny liked it very much. Still. Something about Lévesque and his know-it-all arrogance and perfectionism brought it out in him. "I'm not really on the ice to pay attention to the forwards unless I'm fighting them."

Lévesque had slightly dead-looking shark's eyes, a brown so deep it was practically black, and Danny didn't particularly like meeting them. "Hmm."

"Going somewhere with this, Cap?"

"You should keep it up. Landry looks up to you, for whatever reason."

Danny exhaled through his nose, short and sharp. Landry had bad taste in potential mentors, and worse taste in the way he chose to speak on the ice. "Sure, Cap," he said, so bland that even Lévesque must have suspected what was up.

Lévesque's thick eyebrows shot up, but he didn't say anything.

Sure, Cap, that's me. Inspiring the youth, helping people improve their game, doing good in the 'Burgh. If he thought about it too long, he had the urge to laugh. Or maybe puke.

Araceli texted him as he sat on the bus with the rest of the team on the way back to the hotel. You're not going to stop by and say hello, are you?

I can't, Celi. We fly out early tomorrow and I'm wiped.

Yeah, okay.

Sorry.

Mom and Dad were just asking about you, that's all.

What'd you tell them?

What could I tell them? I don't know what you get up to, and I don't know why you won't talk to us. I'm not even at home.

Danny rested his head against the cool glass window and wished, for a minute, that he could just scoop out his brain like it was melted ice cream and drop it in the trash can. His parents deserved a better son than him, but he was the only one they had. Gears had passed out next to him, his head drooping to rest on Danny's shoulder. Danny shifted the phone to his left hand, so he wouldn't wake him, even though it was awkward typing.

You don't have to tell them anything.

Yes, I do! They're fucking worried, Danny!

I don't know what to tell you. I'm fine. Nothing's falling apart.

They're not worried about your knees and hips, asshole.

I know.

Well...it was a good game anyway. Three points, huh?

Why is everyone so goddamn surprised?

Fastest you've moved in a while. Someone light a fire under your ass?

Coach mostly leaves me alone. And I haven't dated anyone since Lauren.

This was, technically, not untrue. Araceli knew about him. He'd come out to her a long time ago, back when she was still effectively his hockey mom, and he'd been fourteen and hormonal and really fucking confused. But he didn't know how he would even begin explaining Mike and their whole thing to her. It was definitely easier not to. And it wasn't like Danny was talking to him right now, anyway.

Yeah, well, maybe you should.

That's not very therapist-y of you.

I can wear more than one hat. You don't pay your goddamn bills anyway.

I love you, Celi.

Love you too, hermanito. Sleep well, okay? And please think about talking to them.

I will.

He wouldn't.

He had a bunch of unread messages from Mike, but he locked the phone and slipped it back into his pocket. Gears' mouth was pressed against Danny's shoulder, his breath warm and humid against it, and Danny closed his eyes too. He was exhausted, in too many ways.

Mike was in a shitty mood, which wasn't anything new. He was usually in a shitty mood, he just usually hid it better.

Currently the problem was that he hadn't really realized how much he talked to Danny until Danny wasn't talking to him anymore. The apartment seemed really fucking quiet now that Bee was over at Mäkelä's a good portion of the time. Before, it hadn't mattered, because he'd been busy bothering Danny whenever any kind of stupid thought popped into his head, knowing he'd respond eventually. He'd been alone, but he hadn't really been *alone*.

Mike messaged Danny a few times about the drills and his progress, but Danny'd just read them and let it go, and Mike was starting to feel something that was like…the closest way he could think of to describe it was like being stir-crazy, like he was actually locked in his apartment with nothing to do. He wasn't, of course. He could leave whenever he wanted to.

He was still traveling for games and he was still going to optional skates and he was still killing himself running through Danny's drills in the spare time that was left after all of that was over. Mike was busier than he'd ever been, and he was playing better than he'd ever been. It was a grind, because he wasn't getting the kind of minutes he'd need to show off the tighter skating and the way he was trying to pay attention to what was going on, to think strategically about how he was approaching the other team's forwards and the empty ice. Even if Coach didn't notice, Mike did.

It was hard not to notice when you were playing the best fucking hockey of your entire life.

Like, he scored two more goals over the next two weeks, bringing his season total to three, which was the most goals he'd scored in such a short period in his entire professional hockey career. And he couldn't even tell Danny about it. Well, he'd told him, but Mike was at the point of getting ghosted where it felt pathetic to keep trying, rolling over and showing his belly like a dog. Just begging, please, pay attention to me, look at me.

He'd just gotten used to having someone to talk to. Someone who could make him laugh when he felt shitty. Someone who gave him shit and pushed him and forced him to be better. And now he didn't have that, and he felt like he was going to crawl out of his skin.

He threw himself into working out even though he shouldn't have. He benched. He did dead lifts. He did squats. He pushed himself past his one-rep maxes and kept going. It was one of those months where he was having more than one emotion at the same time for more than one day and that alone kind of made him furious. Except this time, he couldn't even be mad at Danny, because it definitely was not Danny's fault. So that just left being furious at himself, which he was good at doing. But even being good at beating yourself up didn't make the whole situation easier to deal with.

He sat in his empty apartment when he got home from games or practices or the gym and did more push-ups or pull-ups or whatever the hell hurt worse that day. At least it got his mind off of the situation, which was rapidly going from bad to pathetic. He jerked off, but it wasn't, like, well. He came, eventually, but it didn't feel good. He just kept thinking about the times he'd jerked off listening to Danny talking him through it and even when he was coming, he felt fucking like. Not sad. He wasn't *sad*. He felt something. Several things. All the time, unceasing.

He didn't know how to fix it. It would've been one thing if they lived in the same place and he could just show up at Danny's house and, like, make things better. Except the only way he could think of doing it was offering to blow him. But you couldn't use your mouth to make things better if you weren't anywhere near the other person, ever. And he didn't know what to say to someone who wouldn't answer him, and he didn't know what to do when he'd fucked up so badly, except keep working so hard it hurt. Which felt good, and again, like the right thing to happen. The worst part wasn't even that he didn't know how to fix it, it was that he had to admit to himself that he…he didn't hate Danny.

Not much. Not at all.

It felt bad, admitting that.

"You okay, buddy?" Singer asked him after practice one day.

He'd sort of herded Mike off to the side of the rink, using his sheer size to steer him away from the rest of the team as they trooped back toward the dressing rooms. It was a move that reminded him so much of Danny that he bit his lip. He could see Bee looking over her shoulder at them, worried, but when Mäkelä put his hand on her shoulder, she let him lead her away.

"I'm fine," he said, automatically. "Uh, why?"

"You've been killing it during the games, but you just—you don't look good, Mike."

"Thanks," Mike said, sour. "Real nice, Cap."

Singer's blue eyes were painfully earnest. "I wasn't *insulting* you, Mike, I'm worried about you." He reached out and knuckled his smelly glove against Mike's face.

Mike spluttered in protest, unable to keep the wounded disbelief from his voice. "Did you just *face wash* me?"

"I want you to take it seriously, and you're not gonna, apparently. What's going on? Let me *help*."

Mike thought about telling him to get his own house in order first. Singer'd been grumpy as fuck since Reed had started bringing around his girlfriend, a smiley college athlete with long legs, blond hair, perfectly tanned skin, and a 4.0 GPA. But he couldn't bring himself to be that much of an asshole. Not again.

Instead, he said, "I'm not sure if you can help me with this one, Cap."

"At least let me try? You really…look…yeah."

Mike tried to rub his face on his shoulder, scrub the smell away with the fabric of his practice jersey. It didn't work. "Umm. It's personal stuff, okay?"

Singer was still watching him with that implacable, steady gaze, boxing Mike in with his body, and he wasn't going anywhere. The words tasted sour in his mouth, like he was puking up bile.

"I, uh—I said something pretty shitty to, uh, a friend. Like the kind of thing you can't take back. And I've tried talking to, uh, my friend, and it's just not working. And it just…"

"Your friend." Singer's jaw worked briefly, like he

was trying to think about how to phrase it, and Mike suddenly had a brief moment of panic, like he'd said too much, exposed too much. "You tried apologizing and your friend won't accept your apology?"

Mike stared at him.

Singer, eyes narrowed a little suspiciously, said, "What?"

"Say that again?"

"You tried…apologizing…and your friend won't accept your apology?"

Mike stared at him. And stared again. "Cap, I…"

"You didn't apologize, did you," Singer said, resigned.

Mike swore, and pushed around him.

Danny wasn't sure how to feel.

At first, Mike had given him some space and didn't say anything. Then he tried to act like nothing had happened and the messages came as fast and as many as they usually did, except Danny didn't answer them, so the one-sided conversation eventually petered out. And then Mike just stopped, except occasionally sending one sentence here or there. scored a goal tonight, it'd say, or. that was a damn good fight. Danny didn't answer those either.

At first Danny had been hurt; angry, even. Now he just felt numb. It felt like he'd been before Mike barreled his way into Danny's life, except maybe with more alcohol and more team involvement.

And also somehow worse, because he missed talking to Mike, really. He missed *Mike*. He didn't realize how little he smiled on a day-to-day basis until Mike wasn't around to drag it out of him. That was a pathetic thought, but the absence of that mercurial presence really highlighted how empty his life had become over the last few years. When he felt this shitty about someone he'd only really known a few months. Sure, it had been a year or two he'd known him, granted, but it was only recently that Mike had done more than knock his teeth out.

After a while, Mike stopped messaging him, and that was better, too. Better that Danny didn't have to look at it and talk himself out of answering. It wasn't even that he was angry anymore, it was just…the whole thing with Mike. It was stupid; it was better to just let things end in their natural course. He couldn't offer Mike anything and he'd been fucking nuts to think he could.

He concentrated instead on the team. His actual team. They didn't have *that* many rookies, but a bunch of the guys were twenty-five or under and for whatever reason they'd latched onto him as like. Not a mentor, exactly, because what could he show them except what not to do? Maybe that was enough. He ended up spending a lot of time with Gears, especially, because he was also a defenseman. They didn't always play on the same pair because they were both right shots, but if he had to have an adopted hockey child, there were worse guys than Gears, who worked his ass off and kept his head down. Marty would be proud, Danny thought, aware of the irony of it all.

Lévesque watched it all with his cool black eyes and Danny shrugged off the stares whenever he noticed. Some captains he'd worked with got weirdly protective at any suspicion someone else might be interfering with the team, but for all that he was a weird-as-fuck perfectionist, Lévesque seemed genuinely invested in making everyone better and didn't mind when Danny spent time with the rookies.

There was only so much he could do with Landry, though.

That situation came to a head on the road in Toronto. It was the third period and Danny was on the ice for a penalty kill. He was exhausted. He couldn't think of anything except the hotel room, longingly, and a drink—whiskey, maybe. Enough painkillers to quiet his throbbing knee and let him sleep. He pushed through it, mucking and grinding along the boards, keeping the puck away from Blomquist's crease.

Then he heard Landry chirping Wolf, one of Toronto's d-men. He wasn't being particularly quiet about it, because Landry never did anything quietly on the ice. It started off with the usual shit. *I'll be there all night, you fuckin' duster.* Or more vicious, considering Wolf had been called up only this season, *Enjoy the game, you stupid fuck, you'll be back in the A before you know it.* Danny tuned it out the way he usually did.

He used to say shit like that himself, because it was easier to start fights when the other guy was pissed off. But as he got older, the less he saw the point in it. It was just extra effort. If he needed to fight, it was easier to cut out the middleman.

When Landry saw that he wasn't getting a rise out of Wolf, he switched it up. Foul shit about Wolf's mom, then on to the personal, the emasculating, the things Danny had heard him say before but had bitten his tongue every time. *You fucking pussy, you sure as fuck don't got any balls, you fucking fa—*

Danny wasn't sure when he'd started moving, but he was pushing off the line and shoving his way in between Landry and Wolf, which wasn't hard because neither of them were particularly big and Landry had that rangy look like he was still growing. He saw Wolf's eyes widen in surprise when it happened, but he was moving too fast to stop, too pissed off to shut his goddamn mouth and stop himself from doing something potentially really stupid.

But he was getting older, and he only had two years left if his body didn't give out on him before then, and he kind of didn't give a fuck anymore.

"Cut it out," he said to Landry. His voice was very flat and very even. Like talking to a naughty child.

"What the fuck, Garcia?" Landry spluttered, caught off guard, almost losing his balance when Danny's weight pushed him away from Wolf.

Danny's hands curled into fists in his gloves, but he kept them on. He felt that cold, sick fury that was nothing like what he felt when he fought Mike. He'd just felt like shit the entire week, everything piling up on him. And then Landry had said one stupid thing, probably without even thinking about it. And that thing was the last straw. One last little piece of straw on his back. The crowd was going nuts, like they were half expecting him to drop gloves against his own teammate, like they were clamoring for it. No one could hear what had been said on the ice. None of them were mic'd.

He knew, though.

He knew, and Landry knew. Wolf knew.

"Cut it out," he said again. His voice sounded like it was someone else's. Cold and grim.

One of the linesmen, confused, had blown a whistle. Play had stopped around them. The rest of the team was watching, the forwards skating in from the other end of the ice. Lévesque, on the bench, looked like he was about to go over the boards and pull them apart, and the only thing stopping him was a too-many-men call. It was hard to tell if he was angry or not. Nothing ever showed in his face.

"What the fuck do you care?" Landry sounded wounded. Like Danny had hurt *his* feelings. "It's just chirping, I'm just trying to get a rise out of him. You do it all the fucking time."

"Say shit like that where I can hear you again and I will fucking drop them," Danny said quietly, only for Landry's ears. Pushed his glove against Landry's chest. It was almost gentle, given what he'd felt. Even given the kind of hell he'd previously unleashed on Mike for less provocation. "Go on and say it again then, buddy."

Landry was staring at him like he'd never seen him before. But that was fine, because he probably fucking hadn't.

Danny did two minutes for roughing, which he took without complaint. He could see himself on the Jumbotron, and he looked like…well, he looked like a guy who'd completely run out of any kind of fucks to give. His face was still red and sweaty from exertion and fury. But his expression was blank. For once, he looked exactly like he felt. Toronto won the game by a single goal scored while the Hornets were shorthanded and Coach, understandably, lost his shit. Danny listened silently to the tirade without expression.

He'd fucked up, sure. He would have done it all over again exactly the same way.

Landry was watching him, still wounded, still like he was trying to figure something out but couldn't quite put his finger on it. Danny didn't give a fuck what Landry thought about him.

He was never in the mood to talk to the press afterward, but he was especially not eager to talk to Sophia Dawsey tonight. She had homed in on him like he was the magnetic north, her soft brown eyes eager. "*Danny*, can you tell us what all of that was about, on the ice?"

"No."

She wasn't put off. "I know you and Matt Landry play very similar games, for all you have different positions—did he say something that went over the line—"

"I don't have anything to tell you."

"Well, that's fine. I'll go ask Matt, then."

"Do that," Danny said, and hauled his aching bones into the locker room. He wondered whether Landry would say anything. Or Wolf. That would be just his luck.

He went home and got drunk. The quiet, efficient drunk of being alone with whiskey.

Mike tried to call him, and Danny declined. Mike must have been watching the game, and probably saw all of that mess on the ice, and Danny didn't want to explain.

danny would you pick up? we gotta talk

Actually, we don't.

yes we do, you stupid asshole

For a minute he stared at the message and a laugh escaped before he could stop it, kind of wild, kind of despairing.

Mike was still typing. look, no, i'm sorry, that's not what i meant to say at all. danny, please?

Danny's mind turned the word over. *Please. Please, please.*

This time when he called, Danny picked up. "I don't really want to talk, Mike."

"Have you been dr—never mind. Danny, I'm *sorry*."

"You're what?"

"I'm sorry, what I said was fucked up, it was wrong, *I* was wrong, I was an asshole, I'm fucking sorry, all right?" Mike sounded distressed. His voice had that ragged edge of exhaustion that Danny felt too, except he sounded like it *really* mattered what Danny said to him next.

Danny stared at the wall. "Okay."

"I didn't know, and it was just, it was a fucked-up thing to say, and I—I didn't mean it. I'm really sorry. I read about your—about *you* and I'm—"

"I accept your apology."

"You—you still sound upset."

"Mike. I've had a couple weeks to think about this and we haven't—can you give me some time? I…"

"I mean, yeah, but Danny—"

"Mike, I don't want to do this right now," Danny said, and ended the call.

Mike started typing something in the message window but stopped. Danny looked at the phone until he was sure that Mike wasn't going to say anything else, and then went to lie down. In the morning he saw Mike had said, i really miss talking to you, is that weird? Danny didn't answer. He got up, got dressed, and went to practice, and he only thought about Mike when he wasn't moving.

III.
WINTER

CHAPTER FOUR

December

Mike tried not to think about it too much, but it wasn't fucking easy. He kept working on the drills, running through them like Danny had said. Sometimes he'd skate with Bee, who somehow had the energy to keep up with him despite posting more minutes per game than almost anyone except for Reed and Mäkelä, and sometimes he'd do it on his own. It was exhausting, how much he was working, and he was a wreck at the end of every day, sleeping like the goddamn dead, consistently starving because he was burning so many calories. He force-fed himself more protein shakes in addition to the insane amount of food he already put away.

After that last conversation he stopped trying to update Danny on his progress. Maybe he was still watching Mike's games, seeing the improvement there. Maybe not.

Toward the end of November, before Thanksgiving, he actually bought a car so he could get to the rink and back more easily instead of just bumming rides from Mäkelä or Singer. He got to know the rink workers, who were kind of confused by how often he was there. Usually players didn't skate as much as he did now, because they tried to conserve their energy for the games. Eventually they got used to his presence and even started joking around with him if he missed a day here or there, that they were gonna let Coach know.

Mike had just looked at them and said, *not funny.*

Coach eventually pulled him aside after a morning skate. "I hear you've been at the rink."

Mike wasn't sure where this was going, so he just nodded.

Coach stared back at him like he was waiting for him to crack and explain. But that wasn't going to happen, because both Mike's father and mother were teachers, high school and college, respectively. He was extremely used to being stared down disapprovingly. He usually won because the staring contests required you to give a shit about what the other person thought about you, or at least, to know there was some kind of immediate consequence if you didn't start talking like, right then.

Coach was giving it a good try, but he was no Dr. Sylvia Sato, who didn't even need consequences. As much as Mike hated to admit it, he had always cared what she thought. Coach might've held the keys to his professional future, but he was a distant second to Mike's mom.

Finally, Coach said, "You want to tell me why, son?"

Mike shrugged. He didn't, really. He felt like he was fifteen again, anxious and resentful and fighting anything he could get his fists against. But no matter how much you wanted to, you couldn't punch your coach, the same way you couldn't *make* your parents proud of you. He said, "Extra practice."

"You're not getting enough practice *at* practice?"

"Not really."

"You wanted to say something to me about that, then?"

Mike weighed his thoughts and his words. He was really fucking tired. He didn't want to say anything that would fuck up his spot on the team, which was why he hadn't said anything before. He hadn't talked to Danny in a week, and he was thinking about how Danny had sounded on the phone the last time they spoke. Completely checked out and drunk and empty and that maybe something Mike had said had made him feel like that. He shouldn't say anything that would fuck up his place on the team.

What came out of his mouth was, "Why would I? You don't think I can do it anyway."

"Excuse me?"

"You don't think I'm worth the extra practice." As he was saying it, he could feel the pit of his stomach drop out, but he couldn't stop the words once they'd started. This was always how shit went with him when he let his feelings get the better of him. This was why it was better not to have them. "I mean. It's cool. I get it. You picked me up because you needed a guy who'd drop 'em. That's me. I fight. I'm a warm body on the blue line. You wanted to be hard to play against. But I'm not worth the extra time. Not like Bee or Reed are worth it."

"Son, I—"

"Come on," Mike said. He was really tired. "I'm not your *son*, Coach. I know why I'm here. I just thought maybe if I worked hard enough, I could be better. But I didn't think you'd listen."

Coach stared at him like he'd never heard Mike

speak before. It wasn't like he talked a lot at practices or during pre-skates or anything. It wasn't like he had anything anyone wanted to hear. So it wasn't surprising. Finally, Coach said, "You should have brought your concerns to me. I would have listened."

Mike stared back at him. "Okay."

"If what the rink personnel tell me is the case, you're doing too much. From now on you can work with Smithy if you feel like you need extra work."

"Okay," Mike said, already running through the rinks he knew of in Philly, some of them run by parks and rec, most of them open to the public. It wouldn't be the best option for what he wanted to do because he wouldn't get any ice time to himself, but if he had to make it work, he'd make it fucking work.

"And you *will not* do more on your own," Coach said severely.

"Sure," Mike agreed, because he had no problem lying.

Coach looked at him like he wasn't sure what planet Mike came from. "You *will not do more on your own.*"

He didn't actually end up having to do it on his own, because once Coach put in the word, Smith, the d-man's assistant coach, started him on a more regular regimen. One that didn't have him passing out as soon as he got home because his body needed sleep so fucking badly. It wasn't anywhere near as intense as what he'd been doing, but he figured if things started backsliding, there were other rinks in the city he could sneak into.

That was where he was in the week leading up to their next game against the Hornets on December 1. He felt like he was definitely capable of showing Danny on the ice the progress he'd made. But not sure what that would mean, in the end. He knew something was going to happen because it always did whenever he and Danny were in the same city. Even when Mike thought he'd hated him there was something irresistible, something combustible about it. They were going to fight or they were going to fuck or they were going to do both. Or the fighting *was* both. Somehow, he knew that even if Danny was upset with him nothing would change.

Or he wanted to believe that.

He was gonna fight Danny, but whether Danny fought back, that was another question.

He was so fucking jittery leading up to the game that Bee actually took him by the shoulders before they left the apartment and dug her fingers in. "Michael—what is going *on* with you?"

He squirmed out of her hold, guilt twisting his stomach along with nerves. It was harder and harder not to tell her the truth. Finally, he said, "I'm going to fight Garcia tonight."

"You don't *have* to. Isn't that what all of this extra work has been for?"

"That's not really related."

"Oh, it's not?"

"I have to fight *him*."

Bee looked at him levelly and he wondered whether she knew. She was kind of socially awkward and more than a little oblivious, but she *got* people sometimes, like the same level of weird, intense study she brought to the game translated well to figuring out shit she shouldn't have been able to guess. It was Russian roulette whether she'd completely miss the entire thing or see right the fuck through you.

"You don't have to fight him."

"I want to, though," he said, which was as close as he could get to telling her.

"Are you going to have a grudge against him for that first game for the rest of your *career*?" She didn't sound angry with him, just worried, which was how she always sounded recently.

"It's not even like that anymore," he said, trying to reassure her.

"Uh-huh," she said, looking at him like he was crazy. "And how isn't it? Every time you're on the ice together, you fight him."

It's foreplay, he thought, but what he said was, "Uh, it's just, it just is."

She was unconvinced, but let it go, because they were going to be late if they didn't get out the door immediately.

At the arena, he was knocked off-balance by the fact that Coach had listed him above Parsons on the daily lines. Parsons stared at the board, a frown twisting his mouth, but didn't say anything to Mike. That was just fine with him. He didn't know what he was going to say, anyway. *Sorry you fucked my game the last two years and I'm finally fixing it* wouldn't have soothed any ruffled feathers even though it was the fucking truth.

It was a dirty, physical game right from the start. The Hornets were still smarting from the last loss to the Cons, and they were both battling for number one in the division. Singer and Lévesque looked grim as players who didn't usually take penalties started racking them up for stupid, sloppy things. Hooking, slashing, roughing. Bee almost dropped gloves with Landry for the second time in their careers when he slammed into her slightly too late, but the linesmen separated them and shipped him off to the bin before she could manage it.

The first few shifts Mike skated, Danny wasn't even on the ice, so he kept his head down and tried to play as clean as he could. Landry was unusually silent, considering Mike's memories of him jawing at Bee after Garcia had knocked Mike down on the ice, but he put it out of his head and focused on grinding the game out. The score was still 0–0 at the end of the first period, and despite the bullshit, he knew they were playing damn well.

On the bench, he looked sideways to the visitors' side. Sometimes Danny watched him. He looked tired, with dark circles under his eyes and a beard that had grown out to fill in his chin and jaw like another shadow, and Mike had the sudden, intense urge to slap him in the fucking face and tuck him into bed. He shook his head to clear that particular idiot thought away and tried to keep his attention on Coach's instructions.

He didn't get the chance until the second period, when he saw Danny going over the boards at the same time Mike was already out.

"Are we gonna do this, huh?" he demanded.

Danny just looked at him, flat and emotionless, before he turned away and skated off and Mike felt the insane desire to apologize again, right there on the ice. He was really fucking losing it. Instead of doing that, he skated after Danny and did the only other thing he could think of to do, which was to annoy him into fighting. Mike was normally pretty good at being a pest, at annoying Danny, but today it wasn't really working. Everything he tried, Danny just turned the other way.

So Mike did the only thing he could, which was to take a run at the Hornets' captain. Lévesque seemed stunned that someone had actually knocked him down, even though he'd been playing the puck. Almost no one tried to hit him anymore, because Danny and the rest of the team would destroy them. The Pittsburgh fans in the crowd saw it and screamed, and Danny saw it and immediately pushed his way through the scrum and shot Mike a look that was half *are you really doing this, you fucking asshole*, and half smolder.

Mike could live with that.

The gloves dropped and they circled each other, and Mike said, "Hi," a little more brightly than he probably should have given the circumstances. He was so fucking happy, honestly, and he wasn't even going to think about that and the whys behind it right now.

Danny threw the first punch and said, as Mike dodged, "You are *such* an asshole."

"Yeah, but it worked, didn't it?"

Mike had Danny's jersey in his hands now, which meant Danny could reach his, and they were doing the slow circle around the ice, testing strength, before the blows fell again. It was a particular kind of balance, holding a guy's jersey and trying to skate, to grapple for a hold, and then to punch. The balance you needed to throw a hit was almost opposite from skating. Mike was used to it by now.

Danny might've been bigger and stronger, but Mike was still pretty damn capable for his size, and he'd learned where to take advantage of Danny's bad knee.

It wasn't as unbalanced a fight as it had been before. He still got punched in the face, of course, because Danny's arms were just longer, and he was still bleeding as it went on, but he gave as good as he got, and he stayed stubbornly on his feet.

At some point Danny knocked Mike's helmet off and then lost his own.

Everything narrowed down to him, just his fists and his body and the pain sparking behind Mike's eyes.

He chanced a look up into Danny's sweaty face, bright red and eyes shining, thought, *god, you're fucking beautiful*, and tried to ram Danny hard enough to knock him down. And Danny let him, or Mike had got him at just the right angle to throw him off. Everything happened very fast after that.

They tumbled, and as Mike landed hard on top of him, Danny murmured in his ear, "Room 516."

"What?" Mike said, confused. Blood dripped from his nose into Danny's face.

"My hotel room. After the game." And Danny threw him off like he weighed almost nothing, flipped him over, and slammed him down on the ice so hard his jaw rattled.

"What the fuck?" He was confused as hell, but he couldn't help the idiot smile that was splitting his face, a grin that probably made him look completely insane, completely out of character for both him and the situation in general. The entire fight and the fact that he'd just gotten the wind knocked out of him.

"What the *fuck*," he repeated, because this wasn't fucking fair. His head was a mess, and it wasn't because he'd been punched in it. They'd barely talked for so long and Mike had tried so hard and, like, of course, letting Danny punch him in the face fixed things. He should have known.

Danny only raised his eyebrows as the linesman skated him away to the box, and Mike hauled himself to his feet, and realized he was going to have to fucking play the rest of the game thinking about this.

He swore under his breath, but he was still fucking grinning, and he couldn't stop.

They lost the game, but Mike didn't even give a shit. His stomach churned with nerves and nausea and anticipation and Danny saying *Room 516 after the game* echoing in his head. He felt like he could peel his entire skin off.

He wasn't entirely sure how he got through the postgame shit. The reporters were in his face about the fight, and like always lately, someone was asking him about why he fought Danny, whether he knew they'd fought every game they'd played against each other. Mike had mumbled something about how guys like him and Danny needed to look out for the stars and obviously he'd hit Lévesque pretty hard, which was true but probably more diplomatic than they'd expected, and tried to duck out of there as quickly as possible.

Mike was one of the last ones in the shower, and he looked down at himself, half-judgmental, seeing what Danny would see. He wasn't bad-looking. He had some muscle. He wasn't as big as a lot of guys, but he was strong. He might have been constantly bruised or stitched up, but it was hard to see most of the time, hidden under the ink. Blocked shots did a number on you and so did getting thrown into the ice by giants.

And maybe getting thrown around later. He wasn't

even trying to convince himself he wasn't going to go. It was just a matter of how quickly he went. Or how desperate he wanted to look.

Who was he kidding? As soon as he got dressed, he was going to walk back down to the Navy Yard, trying to look as inconspicuous as possible. Part of him realized it was a stupid fucking idea anyway—what if he got recognized in the lobby?—but finally he settled for throwing on his winter leather jacket and a hoodie under it. He flipped the hood up and hoped no one would look too hard at the tattoos of hands gripping his throat, distinctive and recognizable.

Thank fuck he hadn't been dumb enough to start tattooing his face when he was a teen. He'd almost done it, once, but the guy doing stick and pokes in a Portland basement in exchange for weed had realized Mike was fifteen and suddenly developed some fucking scruples.

He was still buzzing with nervous anticipation when he slouched through the lobby of the hotel, when he leaned against the wall in the elevator as it went up. Luckily it was late enough that although there were some people hanging around at the bar, they were the kinds of people who were focused mostly on drinks.

Mike knocked quietly at the door of Room 516. There was a pause, and the door opened, and he looked up at Danny—all six foot five of him—and his mouth went dry. Like, sure, Danny was hot: he was a *big* guy, a presence, all thick slabs of muscle and strength held in check. But Mike had never noticed the thick white scars poking out from the hem of his boxers or messing up his knee or any of the other injuries he'd collected from a lifetime of taking a beating. He'd never noticed the way Danny collected bruises the same way Mike did, dark splotchy purple and yellow under his skin. He'd never noticed the way Danny's eyes looked when it hit him that it was Mike, that he'd actually come—like he could ever not come—like a light turning on in a dark room.

Like Mike meant something.

His first instinct had been to make a smart-ass remark, to make a joke of the whole thing, but instead he found himself lunging forward, up onto the tips of his toes, and smashing his mouth against Danny's.

It wasn't much like a kiss. At least not at first. What Mike did was attack Danny's mouth, their teeth clacking together painfully, ringing in his skull. What Mike did was grab him by the beard and yank him down, his fingers digging into Danny's jaw so he couldn't pull away, even if he'd wanted to. What Mike did was bite his lower lip until Danny gasped and opened his mouth and let Mike lick the blood off it and the taste of whiskey out of it, their lips clashing, just like any other fight on the ice.

And Danny kissed him back just as ruthlessly, despite the sutures on Mike's mouth.

It took him a minute before he realized the door hadn't closed behind him and he was a fucking idiot, and he was—he was *kissing* Danny. Kissing him, like some kind of dumb teenager, his hands on either side of Danny's face. Even though Mike had never really kissed anyone much when he was a teenager. Jesus fucking Christ, Danny fucked him up.

Mike pulled away, breath ragged, and kicked the door shut. Kicked his boots off too, because he wasn't a fucking monster. Took a minute to orient himself. It was just like any other hotel room, two queen beds, one of which had Danny's bags and shit spread all over it, the other one rumpled, like he'd been lying in it, waiting for Mike. There was a glass with probably whiskey in it on the end table, half-full, and a bunch of Danny's other shit piled behind it. And Danny himself, already stripped down to his boxer briefs while Mike was still in his coat and hoodie and clothes.

Danny, all hot eyes and strangely melancholy smile, a smile Mike wanted—*needed*—to change.

"Jesus," Mike said at the same time that Danny exhaled and said, "Wow."

Mike took another step forward and said, "Are you—are we actually—"

"I need this," Danny said, simply, like it was an explanation, and Mike thought, *I need you*, although he was suddenly furious that he'd bared everything, every feeling he had, every embarrassing fucking weakness, and Danny had just let him dangle on the end of the line like it was nothing.

Somehow he was moving like he was on the ice, his entire body and weight crashing into Danny's. Then they were on the floor and Danny was moving with him like he wasn't even a little surprised, like Mike's 180 pounds on top of him wasn't anything. It probably wasn't. It was probably exactly what he wanted.

Danny wasn't even trying to throw him off, he was just trying to unzip Mike's hoodie and get him out of his clothes. Okay, fine. Mike could work with that. It got frantic quickly, Danny muttering, "Why do you wear these fucking *jeans*, Jesus Christ," as Mike tried to wriggle out of them and Danny pressed clumsy, biting kisses against Mike's chest, shoulders, whatever he could reach. By the time Mike was mostly naked, he was still on top of Danny, and Danny was staring up with an unreadable expression, so intent that if Mike was a different kind of person he might have felt shy, weirdly exposed.

Instead he was just so fucking hard, like every piece of his body was tense and straining, needing.

He very deliberately reached out and pressed his fingers against a deep purple bruise on Danny's collarbone, dug them in until Danny made a noise of pain that sounded more like a groan of pleasure. His eyes closed, and Mike stared down furiously at the long eyelashes fanned out there, at the flush on his cheeks, and felt like he could just—just destroy him, destroy everything, so he didn't have to think about the way Danny made him feel.

He ground his knee into Danny's sternum, sharp bone against bone.

"You little *asshole*," Danny gasped, and threw him off, and then they were wrestling in earnest.

It was one thing to fight bigger guys on the ice and it was another thing to fight them in close quarters like this, constrained by furniture and Danny with the size advantage. There were a few times that he just flat-out trapped Mike under his suffocating weight. Except what he didn't count on was that Mike was quick and Mike was vicious, and all he had to do was wriggle enough space to get a knee in or his elbow up, and the tables turned quickly enough.

It was fighting, but he could feel Danny's cock, hard and hot and pressed into the line of his hip. It was more than fighting. For a second, he stopped struggling, relaxed under Danny's weight on his torso, let Danny prop himself up far enough that he could look down at Mike stretched out underneath him.

"I'm going to learn every one of these," Danny muttered, and Mike realized he was looking at the tattoos on Mike's chest and his shoulders and his neck. "Every single fucking one."

"You're going to need more time than this."

He'd tried to say it cutting, like an insult. It came out weird and shaky and kind of needy. He was breathing hard, from the wrestling, from the chance to have Danny so close to him for so long. It was…it wasn't what he was used to, and he was suddenly angry again, at Danny, at himself. And he threw himself back into the fight and used the element of surprise to twist Danny off and throw him hard on the carpet.

They were probably making a shitload of noise, but Mike couldn't fucking care. Scrambled on top of Danny's big body, grabbed his wrists and slammed them down on the rough hotel carpet, like he was proving a point. What point even he didn't know. Danny stared back up at him, eyebrows raised like, *are you done*, and Mike leaned down before he could stop himself and kissed him again. He could feel Danny's pulse under his fingers. Feel his dick straining against Mike's. Feel the way his chest heaved as he lurched up into Mike's mouth, restrained enough to leave Mike there, but not enough to be patient. Jesus, just the sounds he was making, these quiet, desperate gasps every time Mike kissed him or pressed his weight against a bruise.

"Danny," Mike said helplessly. Helpless against the vortex of violence and tenderness in his chest. Like he didn't know if he wanted to keep fighting Danny or kissing him, like he didn't know if he had to make that choice at all.

"What do you want, Mike?" Danny mumbled into his mouth, ages later, because they had to stop every now and then for air.

He couldn't answer. Frozen. He wanted everything. Danny under him, Danny over him, Danny inside of him, Danny around him. Somehow it was just. It was overwhelming, it was embarrassing, because Danny *knew what he wanted*, and he still couldn't fucking say it.

"Mike," Danny said, again, and his voice was so fucking gentle that Mike could have killed him, if his hands weren't still occupied holding Danny's arms down. There would be bruises on his wrists tomorrow, probably, and Mike thought about him in the locker room, someone seeing them, and felt a weird kind of possessive pride. *He'd* done that.

Danny twisted one of his wrists out of Mike's hold, his hand going up to trace the line of Mike's spine, the knobs of his vertebrae where it bowed as Mike leaned over him. "C'mon, babe. Tell me."

He couldn't help shivering, the touch and the words cutting right through him. "I want to fuck you," he said, the words tumbling out all at once before he could stop them.

Danny looked up at him again with that small half smile tilting his mouth up and said, "You only had to ask."

"God, I hate you," Mike said reflexively, out of habit, and flinched.

Either Danny didn't notice or didn't care. "I got one request, though. Let's move this to the bed, huh?"

"Why?" Mike asked before he could stop himself. Danny's fingers were curled around Mike's dick and his brain was short-circuiting. "You too old to fuck on the floor?"

"Jesus Christ, you little shit," Danny said, tightening his grip, his voice weirdly fond considering. "*Yes*, I am."

"Oh. Well. Okay."

Mike scrambled backward and got up, and there was an awkward moment as Danny hauled himself up too and Mike could hear a pop and a crack in either his back or his knee. Danny stumbled and winced. Mike was about to say something, not a chirp, an expression of *concern*, he wasn't entirely an asshole, but then Danny shoved him hard, and he fell onto the bed with a yelp of surprise, too startled to pull Danny down with him. It didn't matter. The bed dipped almost immediately under his weight, and Mike was grabbing at him, reflexively, until he was crouched over Mike.

"You can fuck me," Danny said, his body bracketing Mike in, "but if you want something you have to tell me."

"What?" Mike asked, stopping abruptly. His dick, which had been almost painfully hard the entire time, twitched and flagged.

"You heard me," Danny said. Like it was an entirely reasonable request. "Just tell me what you want. Tell me what you're going to do. I want to hear you *say* it. Otherwise I'm going to do what *I* want to do."

"You're really fucking weird, dude," Mike mumbled. He could feel his face flushing, thinking about Danny doing anything he wanted, thinking of all the shit he wanted to do to Danny, thinking about having to say it out *loud*. He wanted so many things and he didn't entirely trust himself. It was so uncomfortable. He wasn't a virgin or anything. He'd had sex before, obviously, but it was never like this, and he didn't… he didn't know what to do. He could just refuse, but he didn't want to risk this. He wanted it too much. Wanted Danny too much. "Uh. Get off of me. I…I want to—I want…"

"Mike."

"I want to like—I want to leave marks. On you. *Okay?*"

Danny's eyes were dark and intent and Mike shivered again when he said, "Okay."

When he was lying down, Mike just stared at him for a minute, all of him, not quite believing that it was really happening. Before he could psych himself out too much he bent down and set his mouth against Danny's collarbone, against the bruises there. It was a kiss, first, until he could feel Danny relax, and then he dug his teeth in hard and sucked, rewarded by an answering shudder that was definitely not relaxed.

He did it again, and again, hunting for the sensitive parts of Danny's body. Digging his teeth in until he could feel Danny's breath go out like *hah ah ah.* Everything was so sensitive. Nipples, obviously. Neck, yes. The curve of his ass, after Mike forced his leg up. His hip, right over the worst of the scars. Surprisingly, yes. Inside his thigh. Mike could lick and bite into any part of Danny's body, and Danny groaned and shuddered and kept himself very still despite everything, despite the fact that his cock was leaking on his stomach, painting it with sticky streaks.

Danny's eyes were screwed shut, and so Mike thought he could get away with teasing a finger inside of him, but the minute he tried it, Danny slapped him in the face so hard and so suddenly that Mike's head rocked back. He shouldn't have been so into it but it was just like every other fight they'd had on the ice, except now he was able to get what he really wanted. Would be able to get what he really wanted. Somehow Danny had just known—

"Jesus," he gasped, dick jumping. Oh, *Jesus.*

"What did I tell you?"

"I have to—I have to say it."

"And?"

"I didn't say it."

Danny was a picture, his body marked up with dark hickeys, his hair sticking up in all directions, sweating and trembling, and still staring at Mike like he would fuck him up if he didn't listen. Which he could. Mike's face stung and he was shivering now, as he licked his lips, tonguing the stitches there.

"And?"

"I want. I want to put my fingers—inside of you. I—want to fuck you with my fingers."

Danny nodded and waved his hand vaguely at the end table, where Mike noticed lube and condoms for the first time, next to the whiskey. He was going to make a joke about how Danny had been waiting for him, how Danny had really expected a lot, but he couldn't joke now. Everything felt weird and loaded and heavy. Both his dick and his head felt, like, hot and throbbing, dumb, moving only on instinct.

Mike fumbled clumsily, slicking his fingers up, but Danny's hitch of breath when he slid them in, probably rougher than he should have, was worth the humiliation of having to ask. Of knowing that Danny was watching him, everything he did, his eyes hooded but open. And then it was just satisfying, watching Danny watching him, watching the way he reacted when Mike crooked his fingers up, trying to find a rhythm that felt good, watching the way he shoved back down on Mike's hand, watching the way he twisted and swore when Mike slapped his thigh with his other hand, hard enough to make a cracking noise of skin-on-skin. Before he could do it again, Danny's hand was around his throat, warm fingers flat against the inked ones. No one had ever touched him like that before and he swallowed hard against their weight.

"What did I tell you?" he asked again, his fingers pressing in, like Mike wasn't doing anything to him at all.

Mike took his hand out of Danny's *ass* and was secretly kind of pleased when Danny made a wounded noise, even though his hand didn't loosen one bit.

"I have to *tell* you," Mike said, voice choked a little. He could feel his Adam's apple bob against Danny's relentless pressure, could barely talk or breathe, and he wondered if it was possible to be so turned on that you like. Astral projected or something. He didn't entirely feel like he was in his body still. He was light-headed and grinning, stupid, loopy.

"You are *such* a brat," Danny said, and pulled him down by the neck into a kiss. Things got messy and frantic again as they rutted against each other and Danny's tongue took him apart piece by piece and Mike panted, "I need to touch you, your dick, I need to touch your dick," and Danny said, his fingers still resting on Mike's throat, "Yes, fucking do it," and reared up into Mike's grip.

Mike wasn't even touching himself, couldn't even think about touching himself right now, he was so focused on Danny, on Danny's body, Danny's eyes. "God," he mumbled into Danny's mouth. "God, I'm not going to—I need to fuck you, Danny, I need to do it *now*, you *need* to let me up, I—god, *god*—"

"Yes," Danny said, and let go long enough for Mike to fumble with the condom packet and roll it down, slick himself again. He could barely manage it with the way his hands were shaking so badly. But he did. He took a minute to look down at Danny, so thoroughly fucked up that Mike's dick twitched again. Danny on his back, knees raised, his dick straining against his stomach, his eyes dark and his mouth swollen.

Mike pushed himself in, all at once, past the initial resistance of Danny's body, knowing it was rough, knowing it was too fast, but Danny didn't seem to mind, closed his eyes, breath going out in an *oof* noise. It felt. It felt like nothing Mike could remember. He'd fucked other guys before, but this was different.

"Danny, Danny, I need to—I need to move."

"Yes," he breathed into Mike's mouth, and so Mike did.

It took them a few awkward seconds to get the rhythm, but then Danny made another noise, one of those ragged, completely uncontrolled groans, and Mike knew he had it, and he thrust harder, faster, as Danny rose to meet him. Maybe it was just that he didn't have to worry about hurting Danny, knowing Danny could take whatever he had to give. Knowing that Danny liked it just the way he did.

Or maybe it was just that Mike was completely losing his mind, moving on instinct, his hands braced on the headboard as his hips ground into Danny's body. Maybe the shock of pleasure sparking up his spine, the way it felt to be inside of Danny, warm and tight, had made him lose it.

Danny's head was thrown back on the pillow, his eyes screwed shut, his hair damp with sweat and his teeth digging into his lip, and Mike thought, *I'm making him look like that, me, he looks like that for me*, and he said, "I'm going to jerk you off," and Danny said, "Ah, ah, ah—yes, yes, okay, Jesus, Mike, fuck *me*," and Mike figured that was good enough.

It didn't last long after that. He wanted to, but he couldn't control himself, and Danny couldn't either, apparently. He came in Mike's hand with a noise like he was dying, come splattered on his abs, and Mike tried to stretch it out as long as he could, his hand still moving, but the way Danny shuddered, oversensitive and tortured, tipped him over the edge.

It seemed like he came for a really long time, shuddering, murmuring Danny's name into his skin. He pulled out and half flopped, half fell on top of Danny's sweaty, sticky body, and buried his face in Danny's neck, mouth pressed against it. He didn't say anything, because he didn't trust himself to speak. Danny's big hand splayed on his back, briefly, fingers stretched between his shoulder blades, and Mike could feel his entire body settling itself under the weight.

"Ugh, get up, or you're gonna regret it," Danny said finally, and Mike, with reluctance, pulled himself away and stumbled toward the bathroom to take care of the condom and wipe the worst of the mess off his stomach.

When he went back into the room, he saw that Danny had passed out. Mike just stood there staring at him for a minute. For such a strong guy, he looked strangely vulnerable like that, naked and splayed out where Mike had left him, his eyes shut and a small smile on his face. Mike's chest did a little jump like his dick did sometimes. Like being horny except with…weird feelings.

Like Mike wanted to get back in the bed with him and wake him up and kiss him until he got hard again.

Jesus, this was a strange fucking year.

Mike didn't have the heart to wake him, so he cleaned him up as best he could without disturbing him, then went to the little table to take the whiskey and dump it out. That was when he saw two things that made him pause. One, an orange prescription bottle, for oxycodone acetaminophen, which he knew was Percocet. Two, Danny's phone, and saw the little banner alerts pop up. *Celi.* Whatever she had to say she was saying in quick succession.

Are you going to come home for the holidays?

Mom and Dad are asking. You still haven't called.

Mike stared at the phone, stared at Danny, and wondered what would happen if he stayed the night. But he definitely couldn't do that. He frowned at the phone and the medication and the drink, and finally settled for pouring the whiskey down the sink. He couldn't do anything about the pills.

It was concerning. It wasn't his business to be concerned.

He got dressed and he left. He looked over his shoulder one last time before he closed the door, at Danny in the bed, and he tried not to think too much about anything.

Danny woke up alone to the sound of his alarm, which didn't surprise him at all but still felt kind of like a disappointment. The first thing he noticed was that Mike had made an attempt to clean him up, which was not what he'd expected. It was a surprisingly sweet gesture for Mike.

He limped his way in the bathroom to survey the damage, which was extensive and almost comical. Mike had left absolutely no doubt about what Danny had been doing. There were mouth-shaped hickeys, dark and splotchy, all over his body. The imprints of Mike's fingers on his wrists and hips. It was ostentatious, childish almost, and he was definitely too old to be going around looking like he'd been mauled by an overexcited werewolf. But he couldn't say no when Mike actually gave in and asked for things, desperately, like he was going to die if he couldn't.

He was sore in places he wasn't often sore these days. That was good. He was sore in places he was usually sore, and that wasn't. The play-fighting on the floor had done a number on his knees, even if in the end it was more than worth it. He was going to have to take a couple of pills if he wanted to get through the game.

He looked at the bruises in the bathroom mirror, then at his face. He still looked exhausted but he felt—better. The glass he'd used earlier was on the side of the sink, empty, but he couldn't tell if Mike had finished it off or poured it out. The team was leaving for another road game, anyway, so it wasn't like he could have drunk it anyway.

As he was waiting at the airport, he saw that Mike had snapped him a picture of his mouth, chin, and neck. It was hard to see under the black-and-gray ink, but the skin under the tattoos was purple and bruised. from you, Mike had captioned it, and Danny could see the quirk of his lips. Not the usual smirk: something wry and inviting. Danny smiled to himself, stupid and fond, and took a screenshot.

lmao, Mike said immediately, and Danny responded, shut up.

Artyomov looked over and said, "Got girl, Garcia?"

Danny composed himself, forced the smile down, and shrugged. "Something like that."

"If y'all make a *your mom* joke at me, I'm gonna throw down," Gears mumbled, his face buried in a steaming-hot cup of coffee. "It's too damn early for that."

Danny patted him on the shoulder, sympathetically, because there were definitely going to be *your mom* jokes in the future now that he'd said something. Showing weakness in front of hockey players was asking for trouble.

Distracted, Danny glanced back down at his phone and thought about what he wanted to say to Mike, but somehow, any words he could think of seemed inadequate. Instead, he said, this was good, see you next game? and let the rest of it speak for itself.

He dozed on the plane to Tampa, very much feeling how late he'd stayed up and what he'd done, knees and back screaming at him, but it wouldn't matter. With medicated numbness he'd be able to get through the game physically, anyway. Mentally...well. He was distracted but maybe not surprisingly in a better mood than he'd been in for a while. Particularly because when they landed, he saw that Mike had written back, fuck yeah.

The contented mood didn't last all that long. There was no hiding what Mike had done to him, and when they were dressing for the game and Danny was completely naked, Gears noticed.

He let out a whoop that was half scream of horror and half howling laughter. "Oh my god, Garcia, what the *hell*."

Danny looked down at his torso, and back up at Gears, and grinned a little sheepishly. He could only shrug: there was no explanation or excuse he could give that would sound convincing. It could only ever be what it was.

Gears was still staring at him like this was a revelation, both impressed and terrified. The rest of the team was staring too, or snickering, or both. It was a locker room: you saw everything. And it wasn't like no one had ever come in with scratches on their back before, or even hickeys on their necks or other places, but this was…well, it was Mike. So it went without saying that it was a lot. Danny got it. It was embarrassing, and everyone knew, and that was probably exactly what Mike had been going for.

Gears was saying, "Seriously, man, you're like a monk, you *never* bring a girl around, but you're like… oh my god, your chest? Your *ass*? What the *hell*."

"Gears, when you're old enough to date, one day in the distant future, you'll, uh, learn, maybe."

"I'm twenty years old!" Gears insisted, "I'm twenty, I've dated girls before, and that's—that's fucked *up*, man, holy shit."

"Why you look at his ass?" Artyomov demanded.

"Well, it's right there! And it's—dude! *Look* at it!"

Across the locker room, Landry watched him with narrowed eyes. He was hockey-handsome, with the kind of small-town Canadian face that Danny had gotten so used to seeing in the league. He was usually grinning, but he wasn't smiling now. He watched Danny like something that hadn't made sense was adding up. Danny met his eyes across the circle and held his gaze. It was a dare: *go on, you want to say something to me?*

But Landry didn't have the courage to say it, or maybe he just had the sense not to screw things up irreparably for both of them. He looked away first, and Danny went back to dressing for the game, although he'd filed it away in the back of his head. Not only could Landry not really be trusted, but he had probably guessed. And it was anyone's best guess what he would do with that information.

Maybe Landry would surprise him.

Danny snorted as he put his helmet on. No one really surprised him anymore.

What also didn't surprise him was falling back into the easy grind of playing games, working out, occasionally hanging out in crowded rooms with his teammates in hotels across the country, and trying not to think too much about one night out of his entire year. It was hard not to think about it, though, when Mike started doing things like giving Danny his phone number instead of just using the voice call function, or FaceTiming instead of using Snapchat, and Danny could see him in his apartment on a steady computer camera instead.

It definitely made phone sex easier, but sometimes they didn't even screw around, Danny just watched Mike going about his night. Playing *Call of Duty*, watching YouTube clips of the teams he'd be playing, cooking dinner, or they talked about random shit. Danny hadn't told him about the first, big injury in any detail, not yet. It was still hard to talk about it at all, even years later, even with how often Araceli told him he should really talk to a therapist who wasn't her. But he told Mike about getting traded, the last time, from Detroit. How disappointed he'd been. Told him about Josie and how much he missed her when he was on the road.

Didn't tell him about why he rarely saw her.

And Mike made him laugh until his stomach hurt with stories about the band he'd had with two of his teammates on the Harriers. "I was sixteen, I was super into hardcore, and I wanted to be Mike Maxymuik, and they just wanted to play, like, My Chemical Romance covers," Mike said sheepishly. "So I'd just, uh, play my own shit in the background while they did their thing. We sucked, dude. Majorly sucked."

"What did you play?"

"Are you serious? Drums! Maxymuik was your first clue."

"Like I'm supposed to know who that is?"

"Ugh, of course you don't know Cursed."

"What was your band called?"

"Uhhh..."

"You don't want to tell me?"

"I do, but give me a break, I was only sixteen. It's pretty bad."

"What was it?"

"Uh. Suicide Pass."

Danny just shook his head, and Mike sighed and made Danny promise to listen to some albums. Not *his* albums, which Mike swore had never been recorded. Just albums Mike liked. He wasn't sure if he'd actually do it, because he was getting the idea that they had no overlap in their music taste, but it was kind of cute that Mike had wanted him to listen. The whole thing felt weirdly normal. Despite the fact that they were often a country away, despite how they had started this thing in the first place.

He caught himself feeling good, which was dangerous.

Except it wasn't like he could let himself enjoy it too much. He knew why it was so easy. Mike didn't know the worst of the shit going on in his head, with his body. Mike wasn't *worried* about him. It was an easy thing, but if it got deeper than that, if Mike started looking at him with the kind of worried eyes that Araceli always had these days, Danny wouldn't be able to handle it. That would be the end of things.

The only reason it worked was that Mike just let him be, and they were both kind of assholes, and…and that was it. He didn't deserve people worrying about him like that, and for now, it was a relief to be with someone who wasn't.

And if Mike had an easy talent for making him smile, well. That was a bonus, wasn't it?

It was a night when Mike wasn't around and Danny didn't have a game, and he was lying on the couch nursing a drink and staring at the television as it spewed out Netflix documentary episodes without actually registering what was going on. That was how he usually spent those kinds of evenings, cradled in the fuzzy embrace of alcohol and narcotics, no pain in his body and no pain in his head.

There was a noise from outside. A crash and a rattle of metal and glass on the pavement.

At first, he didn't think twice about it. There were raccoons sometimes, and they could get into anything. Sometimes they got into the garbage cans. There was another crash, and this time, Danny hauled himself to his feet to check outside and figure out what to do if it *was* raccoons. The last thing he needed was a rabies shot.

It was almost midnight, so overcast that the only light was the diffused gold of streetlamps. The little path that led from the driveway to his kitchen door was strewn with garbage; one of the cans had been knocked over and the lid had popped off. He could hear rustling from within and sighed. It didn't really sound large enough to be a raccoon, but he wasn't in the fucking mood to pick up all of the trash tonight.

He crouched down in front of the can and used his phone flashlight to peer inside. Glowing green eyes stared back at him, and the filthy, scraggly orange cat hissed. It had either knocked over the can or something larger had knocked it over, and the cat had decided to take advantage.

"Hey, buddy," Danny said, extending his fingers toward it.

The cat was a kitten, really; it couldn't have weighed more than two pounds. It lunged forward and dug its tiny needle-pointed teeth into his hand, which, well, Danny couldn't blame it. He let the cat attack him, scratching and biting, until it abruptly decided either that he wasn't a threat or that it was bored of such an undignified display. Instead, the kitten turned away from him and began licking its own ass, and Danny found himself laughing, in the dark, trying to pull a cat out of the garbage.

It had been a strange enough year, that was for sure.

The kitten bit his hand the entire walk back to the house and scratched him viciously while he tried to figure out where it could sleep. It probably had fleas and other parasites, but he had the free day tomorrow to find a vet and get it treated. Or drop it off at a shelter or rescue, which was probably the more sensible thing to do.

The cat glared at him, and Danny said to it, "You've got a long way to go before you can really hurt me, buddy."

He ran his thumb over the kitten's skull. It howled with fury.

Once it had worn itself out attempting to rip him to shreds while he washed it in the bathtub, the cat slept on his chest on the couch, and he just had to hope for the best.

Mike wasn't an idiot, and even he could sense that things had changed after the last game. It wasn't that it was bad, exactly. Some of it was actually really fucking good. It was just *weird.* The more he talked to Danny without the pretense that every single conversation was a fight, the more he found that he just really liked talking to him. Danny was—really smart, and funny, and thoughtful, and all of that was wrapped up in the kind of reserved exterior that made Mike feel like he was constantly tugging on Danny's shirt, trying to get his attention, trying to get any reaction he could. Needing it.

He'd started like. Not quite keeping a running tally of the times Danny smiled at something Mike said or did, but it was pretty fucked up, the kind of shit he'd started thinking about, and that was one of them. Fucking *smiles.*

The problem was that it was pretty hard to get Danny to smile. Every time he did, it was reluctant, like he felt bad about doing it. Somehow Mike got the idea that he didn't do it often. That sadness that had bothered him before was still there, just distracted. Mike was a distraction. So was the hellcat that Danny had literally found in the garbage, a cat that still didn't have a name but was already extremely spoiled, with a cat sitter who came to feed him and keep him company for a few hours a day whenever Danny was on the road.

But the sadness never wavered.

He thought about asking sometimes, but he got the sense that Danny wouldn't tell him anything. Like, it probably wasn't his business anyway, but he wanted it to be? He thought about the fact that Danny was almost always drinking when he was at home, or in hotels, or when he'd come home from the occasional night out with the rest of the team. He thought about the fact that Danny never really seemed drunk, but once Mike started keeping an eye on how often the glass was refilled, and how Danny tried to do it casually, half-hidden when he thought Mike wasn't looking, it bothered him.

One night he was in Calgary and Bee had already left to go hang out with Mäkelä, so he FaceTimed Danny to catch up. Danny was in San Jose, so the time difference made it awkward, and Mike really should have tried to sleep anyway. He'd wanted to see Danny first. They caught up about the games: the Cons had won and the Hornets had lost. Neither of them had fought. Mike had scored a goal, which brought his season total up to seven, a career high.

"You've been doing so well, buddy," Danny said, with a kind of possessive pride. He had a glass cradled in his hand and Mike tried not to look at it.

"Haven't been doing your drills," Mike said, pressing his fingers against a new bruise on his thigh. It hurt, but not that bad. It wasn't too deep. "Coach found out and made me stop. But I've been working with the coaching staff."

"As long as you're working. We can talk about some of the other stuff during the day, if you want. The mental stuff."

"Yeah."

"What's wrong?"

Mike gnawed on his lip. He knew he wasn't great at hiding what he felt, but this was new ground. This wasn't just trying to figure out his feelings, it was trying to figure out someone else's. "Are you…you know…like…good?"

"Am I good?"

"Yeah, I mean. Like your hip, your knee. And shit." Maybe that was too much?

Danny looked at him with the kind of blank expression that he hated seeing. Danny should always be smiling, because he had a great fucking smile. Danny had the kind of eyes that crinkled shut when he was really happy, before he realized he was doing it and looked a little ashamed. Danny shouldn't look so empty like that, Mike thought, furious, unable to do anything about it.

"I'm fine," Danny said, and then, "Look, let's talk about moving the puck, huh?"

Mike frowned. "Let's talk about you."

Danny was silent for what seemed like a long time but was probably only a minute or so. "I don't want to," he said, finally. He wouldn't look Mike in the eyes.

"But you want me to talk to you about me, like, all the time? And about what I want," Mike said. It didn't really seem fair, even though he was kind of getting the impression that Danny had a lot more going on inside his head than Mike usually did. "Is that usually how this shit goes? What if I want to talk about you?"

"I don't know. It's been a while since I talked to someone like this. Hey, Mike, I have to go. The cat needs to be fed."

"That fucking cat," Mike muttered, but Danny had already closed the window, and his screen was silent. Mike might have been getting used to having feelings, even if he couldn't always put them into words, but this felt distinctly bad.

Still, he didn't have time to indulge the bad feelings. Even though the coaching staff weren't anywhere near as intense about stuff as Danny had been while kicking Mike's ass into gear, it was still a lot of extra work on top of the extreme amount of work he already had to do in order to keep in shape. And that wasn't even counting the games. But he kept turning it over and over in his head. What he should do, could do. It was a weird shift from hating Danny to worrying about his drinking habits and his sadness, but Mike was trying to roll with things now. Fighting it hadn't gotten him anything much except a long stretch of being miserable alone.

It was in that spirit that he slouched back to his apartment after optional skate. He hadn't even taken the car, just the subway, and he was crossing JFK Boulevard when he looked up and realized that the woman waiting at the crosswalk for the light to change looked really familiar. She was wearing black leggings and a huge black parka, the kind of coat that you wore to go, like, serious mountain climbing in the snow. She was as tall as he was, but her curly hair was swept up in a high bun, and she wore high-heeled combat boots, adding a few inches to her height. When she turned and he caught a glimpse of her face, he knew for sure.

He had been aware Danny's sister lived in Philly, but he hadn't really expected to see her here. It was a small city in the sense that you could walk across the entirety of Center City in like half an hour, but he didn't know where she worked or where she lived. It was definitely her, though, and he had a moment's agonized indecision trying to figure out whether he should approach. In the end, like always, it seemed like his body acted without his brain, and he was walking forward to catch up with her as she entered the intersection.

"Dr. Garcia?" he said, and she turned. People moved and flowed around them. It was rush hour, and people in suits fled Center City like rats from a sinking ship.

He was struck again by how much she looked like Danny. And then again by the look she gave him, like if he tried anything she was going to reel back and punch him in the face. That also reminded him of Danny. Well. That wasn't surprising. As far as she knew he was just a tattooed stranger who'd stopped her in the middle of an intersection.

"What do you want?" she asked. Behind her, the crossing light had flipped from white to orange. She didn't ask who he was or how he knew who she was, and Mike realized she'd recognized him. From her expression, she felt pretty much the same about him as he'd feel about some dog shit on the bottom of his shoe.

"Can I talk to you?" Mike's mouth was dry and his stomach was doing those loopy jumps that it had done the day of the draft. He hadn't thought this plan through at all.

Araceli Garcia turned on her heel and kept walking. She said, over her shoulder, "No, and I particularly don't want to do it in the middle of traffic, Sato."

Mike followed her obediently; once they were safely over the curb on the other side, she turned to look at him again, regal and withering. "I really do want to talk to you, um, about your brother—"

"I don't see what you could possibly have to say to me." Her voice was low and husky but sharper with rage. "Unless it's to apologize for going after him on the ice like that, for *hurting him like that*, and somehow, I don't think that's what you're planning to do."

Mike's mouth opened and closed. He could feel the gears grinding to a halt in his head. The need to tell her was there but he didn't know how to say it, and for a minute he regretted everything in his life that had led him to be, like, the kind of person who desperately wanted to make things better for someone who was kind of important to him, but whose family probably hated him. Definitely hated him. And for a good reason. It was really fucked up. His face must have been doing something he didn't know it was doing, because Araceli's expression softened, minutely, as she waited for him.

"Please," Mike swallowed. The words ground themselves out against his will. "I *am* sorry for the tooth thing—but it's not like that anymore."

"Oh?"

It took him several false starts to the sentence before he managed, "Danny is—"

"Danny?" Araceli repeated, her eyebrows shooting up, then apparently made her decision in a snap second. It was the kind of decisiveness that Mike admired. "Well then. I think you'd better come and have a cup of coffee with me. We can go back to my office, if you'd feel more comfortable speaking to me there."

"Uh, okay. Sure. I mean. We can."

He followed her back across the street like he was walking in a dream, or maybe a nightmare. This was exactly his nightmare, both talking about things he was feeling and someone figuring out things about him he had always been more comfortable keeping secret. The feeling of exposure and of humiliation of someone knowing what was going on in his head, someone he'd never even met before. He was doing this impossible thing for Danny, he told himself, as he followed Araceli into the lobby of the huge building at the corner of Eighteenth and JFK and tried to ignore the panic twisting his stomach. Of fucking course Danny's sister worked like two blocks away from his apartment.

"Hey," Araceli said, when they were in the elevator, "take a deep breath, okay? It's okay. We're just going to have a chat."

"It's not really okay," Mike mumbled, catching himself

running his hand over his skull. He was sweating a little, and not because the building was warm.

It was a small office with a waiting room and a few doors that branched away from it. She gestured to him to go into the one with her name on it, while she slipped off her parka and went to make him a cup of coffee at the mini Keurig they had set up against one wall.

"How do you take your coffee, Sato?"

"It's just Mike. And, uh, black, please."

He went into the room and looked around at it, at all of the psychology books she had on the shelves, at the plants that covered every surface. The room was relatively devoid of anything personal about her, and it had the kind of bland comforting air that Mike had instinctively hated the one time his parents had tried to drag him to see a shrink in middle school.

He didn't know where to sit. There were three chairs arranged in a kind of a half circle, and another chair behind Araceli's desk. In the end he took the chair closest to the door. He could feel his heart beating a billion fucking times a minute, and knew his leg was jiggling up and down, but he couldn't stop it even when he tried.

Luckily Araceli didn't say anything about it when she came back in, just handed him his cup of coffee and sat down in the chair that was opposite his, giving him a little space with the third chair in between them. He curled his hands around the hot cup and chewed on his lip and waited for her to start, but she just watched him, studying his face. This wasn't a standoff he could win because he'd started this.

"Dr. Garcia, I—"

"You can call me Araceli," she said, the corner of her mouth tilting up, "you're not one of my patients."

"Right. Right. I'm Mike, then. Because like, um, Mr. Sato is my dad." He drank the coffee, a too-large gulp that burned his tongue, and looked down at his boots and tried to think of how to say this. There were so many *ums* punctuating the words that he felt, for a second, like he was back in school in Portland, sweating in front of the class and trying to give a book report on a topic that he understood about halfway. "I'm sorry to have, like, scared you or whatever, I know what it looks like on the ice and I'm sorry, you probably hate watching that shit. I didn't mean to hurt him like that, I just…"

"Hey," Araceli said again, over the rim of her own coffee cup. "Mike, it's okay. Take a deep breath. I'm not going to do whatever you think I'm going to do."

"I know, it's just… I'm really fucking bad with this shit, okay?"

She raised her eyebrows. "Give yourself some credit, please. You approached me, you came here voluntarily, that's more than many people would do, I think. Just calm down. Okay? You have all the time you need."

Mike took another hasty gulp of the coffee. "I'm worried about him," he said, finally. "Okay? I'm really worried about him and I thought maybe you should know. I…"

Araceli was looking at him again, and he couldn't tell if her expression was surprise or pity. "May I ask—why?"

Mike's ears burned and he knew his face was probably bright fucking red. Or making some kind of expression he couldn't control. He was going to throw up, or pass out, or, or just, like, scream and run out of the room. He wasn't going to be able to do this; he was going to chicken out like he always did when he thought about telling Bee. Strangely, he thought about Danny's hand on his back, the way he'd said, *c'mon, babe, just tell me*, and tried to use that to calm himself down. He had to say something, even if he exposed things.

"Danny's really like…kind of important to me? We've been talking a lot this season."

"Okay," Araceli said, and her voice was so even, so comfortingly nonreactive, that Mike wanted to fucking cry. He'd basically *said it* and the world hadn't ended. "I did mean why are you worried about him, but thank you for telling me, Mike. Danny doesn't tell me very much about his life anymore."

"You and like everyone fucking else," Mike said sourly, and he'd evidently surprised Araceli into a short barking laugh.

"I'm sorry, this situation is just—I don't know you very well, but the way you said that is just—you could have pulled the words out of my own head. In exactly that tone."

He found himself smiling back at her, a little shaky. "Yeah, well." He chewed on his lip again, tried to slow his bouncing knee. "I *am* worried about him. He drinks a *lot*. And I know he tries to hide it, but I notice. And he's taking some serious painkillers, which isn't, like, completely unusual for guys like us—you get wrecked on the ice sometimes and that shit's fucking painful to play on—but… I don't know, I don't think he's had any major injuries recently so…"

Araceli was still watching, waiting, and Mike tried to gather all of his scattered thoughts together, all of his worries about Danny, into something resembling coherence.

"Either he's got something chronic and he *shouldn't* be playing through it, or the pills aren't really necessary, and that's worse. Or both. But either way, it's bad. You read about guys all the time with problems and…he's playing fine, it's not like he's fucking up his career or anything, but he's so fucking *sad* all of the time and I don't want—I can make him smile but he's *always* fucking sad and I—and I—"

Mike had to stop. He felt overwhelmed by the effort of forcing the words out, by talking this much about such real things, and his hands shook so badly he couldn't even lift the coffee mug to drink it.

"I just want him to be okay," he mumbled, finally, unable to look Araceli in the eyes. Instead, he focused on his boots. If he stared at them long enough, things would be okay. "And I don't know how to make him okay. And I thought maybe you'd know. So, uh. That's why I'm here."

She was quiet for a long time and Mike started to get worried she was angry about it, but when he chanced a look at her, her eyes were like—she wasn't crying, but she was definitely almost close to it, and he hastily said, "Oh shit, I'm sorry, I fucked this up again, I didn't mean—"

"No," Araceli said firmly, and put her hand on his knee. "You didn't fuck anything up. I *love* my brother, our whole family does, but he doesn't let us in very often. I'm just happy he has someone in his life that cares. Even if I will murder you if you break his teeth again."

"That's fair," Mike said, and swallowed hard. He awkwardly patted her hand until she took it away again. "I'd let you murder me."

"As to your question… I suspected some of this; I didn't know all of it. And I don't know what to do. I don't know if there's much we *can* do, until he wants to make a change. I've just been trying—and you can try—to make him know you're there for him. Things are so much harder in isolation, you know?"

Mike thought about basically his entire life in comparison to the last six months of it. "Yeah."

Araceli looked at him again, and smiled, suddenly. "So, Mike. What are you doing for the holiday break?"

Danny was back in Pittsburgh for the next week, a few home games before he had to go on the road. The cat was steadfastly pretending not to be happy to see him. Except he was doing a piss-poor job of it, so instead of actually ignoring Danny, he prowled around the perimeter of any room that Danny happened to be in but hissed if Danny came too close. Then he'd follow Danny again if he went into another room. The cat was an angry idiot with a bad habit of fighting shadow monsters no one else could see and tripping over his own paws, which he hadn't entirely grown into yet, and Danny thought he was perfect. He just couldn't come up with a name that fit.

He made himself dinner, but it was basically the same meal he made himself every day he was home by himself, which was a rotating protein cooked in the pan and then popped in the oven, brown rice in a rice cooker because he burned it every time otherwise, and a vegetable on the side. Today it was chicken breasts and kale. When he'd cared more about food beyond needing to put calories back in his body, he'd put an effort into spices and seasoning and switching up techniques, but now it just seemed like a waste of time. He mostly ate it standing up in the kitchen before moving back into the living room anyway.

The cat jumped up on the counter and glared at him, and Danny relented and gave him a little piece of chicken he'd pinched off. The cat seemed to like that, so Danny gave him another one. The cat slunk forward and rubbed himself against Danny's hand, and he laughed.

"Oh, now you want to hang out? I guess the secret was people food the whole time."

The cat stared at him, completely unimpressed, so Danny gave him one more piece. "Okay, I have to eat the rest of this, buddy."

The cat batted at his hands, begging with strident meows. It wasn't until Danny realized the cat had started answering to *buddy* that he had inadvertently given him a name, and a horrible name. Appropriate for a hockey player's pet, he supposed.

Mike called him a little later so he turned off the TV to answer. Danny wasn't too drunk yet and since that awkward conversation a few weeks ago he'd been careful to watch the way he talked when they were on the phone or when they were video chatting.

"Hey, Mike."

"Hi," Mike plowed on immediately, like if he didn't, he wasn't going to be able to say it, "so what are you doing for the holiday break?"

Danny blinked. The holiday break was three days long, December 24 through 26. In prior years, especially when he was playing for the Cougars, he'd gone home to his parents' house. The last few seasons he'd spent it alone, at home. "I was just going to stay here, I guess. Why?"

"Well…" Mike sounded uncertain in a way he usually didn't, in a way that got Danny's hackles up.

"Mike."

"I know, I know. Look, dude, don't be mad at me and don't hang up, okay?"

Alarm bells, clanging in his head. "Why would I be mad at you?"

"I, uh, ran into your sister the other day."

Danny's mind went completely blank. It felt exactly like taking a hit to the head, like he was prone on the ice while the rest of him tried to catch up. He couldn't say anything.

"*Seriously*, please don't be mad at me, but would you come visit me for the holidays? Bee and Mäkelä are going to be at Cap's house for the team party and then Mäkelä's apartment, and your sister said they're not going home to Detroit, it's just going to be her and Chris and the baby, and you could like—it's only an hour and a half for the flight, you could stay with me, we could leave if it was too much, but I just thought that for a little bit, we could—"

"Mike?"

"I didn't mean to, but she was just right there and I had to—please, Danny, would you?"

Two things were happening in Danny's head. One of them was a cold kind of fury and panic that this was how it had unfolded, that the two sides of his life had intersected in a way he couldn't control, and the other thing was how stupidly proud he was of Mike for actually wanting something and asking for it, something so big, something so potentially awful for both of them.

He couldn't even be really angry, not at Mike, anyway. Mike had tried, in his own clumsy way, to do something good for Danny.

Danny's fury was mostly at himself. Because he still was terrified of seeing his sister, because the idea of staying with Mike for a few nights was something he wanted more than he should have. Something he wanted so much he almost said no on reflex because it scared the shit out of him.

Jesus, he was a mess.

"Danny? Say something."

He thought a lot of things. First: how the hell had Mike pulled this off? When had he even managed to track Celi down? It felt, a little, like a collision of his two worlds, claustrophobic and terrifying.

Second: what the hell was he going to do? He wanted to go; he didn't want to go. It would be easy to use this as an excuse—to see Mike—and it would be easy to try to talk him out of it once he got there. Or he could man up and just get it over with. Maybe if he saw Celi and Chris they'd tell his parents he was okay, and everyone would let up and leave him the fuck alone to finish out his seasons the best way he could. Maybe it would…maybe it would be a good thing?

"I—this is just a lot at once, Mike."

"I know, I just didn't know how to tell you when it happened."

"Well. You certainly told me now."

"Yeah, well. Hey, you know, your sister's pretty cool. Hard to tell how you're related, like, at all."

"I know you're trying to distract me with insults, you little shit, and it's not going to work."

"Can't blame me for trying. So will you? Come?"

"I'll—I'll come."

"*Why the fuck not*—I didn't—shit, sorry, I was just expecting you to say no. I mean, awesome."

"I can always change my mind," Danny said. His heart was still pounding and his undershirt stuck sweaty to his back.

"No! Don't do that. Buy your ticket *now*."

"Huh, you really miss me," he said, trying to make a joke out of it.

"Yeah, I fucking do, so the fuck what?" Mike said, like he was spoiling for a fight, and Danny felt his chest constrict. When he'd run into Mike in that alley all the way back in July he never would have…

"Mike…you didn't have to do all this."

"Yeah, I did. And you're gonna come, and you're gonna like it. So fuck you."

"Wow. So romantic. Sweep me off my feet, why don't you."

"What, you want flowers or something?" Mike asked, although he was teasing now. The kind of flirtatious drawl that Danny liked so much and found so hard to resist.

"Sure. Buy me flowers, buy me dinner, the whole nine yards."

Mike snorted, but Danny could hear the smile in his voice. "Okay, well. I probably shouldn't pick you up at the airport, just in case, but I'll text you my address. Araceli said they have dinner on Christmas Eve, and we have a game in New York the night before, but I'll be home late if you wanna come Monday night instead?"

"We don't have a game so…okay."

"If you back out on me now, Daniel Garcia, I'm going to come to Pittsburgh and *murder you.*"

"You don't know where I live."

"I'll find you. I'll track you down."

"Very frightening, Mike. I'm shaking over here."

"Yeah, yeah, fuck off."

"Hmm."

"Okay, I gotta go, Bee's coming back today and I haven't seen her outside of work in forfuckingever."

"Have fun, kid."

"I will. Bye."

Danny did buy the ticket. He chose the latest non-stop flight he could find, figuring he'd kill some time in the city until Mike got back from New York, and maybe a little optimistically, a nine p.m. flight home on the 26th. That would give him more time if he needed it, and he wouldn't have to rush.

The day crept up on him. He packed his bags in the morning, feeling strange about the whole thing. He didn't know what it would be like, spending so much time with Mike in person, even though they admittedly talked quite a lot now. He was more apprehensive about seeing Celi, whether she'd say something he couldn't handle hearing.

Somehow he got through the flight, helped along by free drinks, and then he was in the Philadelphia airport, wondering what the fuck he was doing but still feeling strangely hopeful about the holiday. It was only seven, so Mike would just be going on the ice about now. He texted Mike, I know you won't see this in time, but I just landed. I'm going to go get dinner or something. Good luck. He had until midnight, at least.

Danny took a cab into the city, which was a weird

experience. Usually he was on a team bus during this stretch of the ride. The driver tried to chat with him, even though he didn't recognize him, thankfully, but Danny wasn't really in the mood. He tried to be polite but curt and shrink into himself. Not easy to do when your knees were bumping against the back of the passenger seat.

The night was cold and brisk. Mike lived in the city center area, but there wasn't much near his apartment building. Danny walked around the streets immediately near it and eventually wound up at a bar called City Tap House, because he wanted to see if he could catch Mike's game while he was eating dinner and having a drink.

He always watched Mike's games, usually on replay because he was either playing that night or they were playing against each other. But he watched every single one, mostly in the privacy of his own home. It was a different experience watching it in Philly, in a bar with fans. They cheered when the Cons scored, they booed and cursed the Liberty any time they scored or prevented a scoring chance, and they completely *lost their shit* when Mike hit one of the opposing forwards so hard he went right through the glass.

Danny grinned at the TV, like, *that's my boy*, but of course he couldn't say anything, so he just ate his dinner in silence and tried not to look too dopey. He thought he saw one of the younger guys at the bar wearing a Morin jersey glance his way occasionally, but he wasn't sure if he was being recognized or checked out. It was an ambiguous look. Either way, Danny looked down at his miso-glazed salmon, which he wasn't even enjoying very much, and steadfastly didn't say anything or catch that guy's eye again.

Mike hadn't gotten a penalty; it was a clean if brutal hit. Despite the glass incident, the Cons played a tight game, and they won with two goals to spare. The first line of Morin, Reed, and Singer was really a beautiful thing to watch, the way each one of them moved like they knew exactly where to expect the other two. They were going to be interesting to face in the playoffs, that was for sure. As of right now, it looked like it wouldn't be until the second round. Even better was watching Mike during the postgame interviews, stripped down to pads and Under Armour, sweaty and red-faced in a way that just reminded Danny of sex now.

Finally, Mike texted, we're about to board, home in a few hours.

Don't worry about me, I found a place to hang out. Also. Through the glass, huh?

you were watching me? course you were, you fucking dork

Danny sent a nerd face emoji then added, It was pretty hot.

perv. see you soon.

Danny slid his phone back into his pocket and ordered another beer while he waited. He passed the time, half listening to the conversations around him, half watching the LA/Ottawa game on the TV. Around one thirty in the morning, Mike said, hey i'm back at my place come up whenever yr ready.

Danny exhaled. Be right over.

He settled his tab, left a generous tip because the bartender hadn't hassled him about hanging out there until it was almost time to close, and walked the half a block with his small bag to Mike's apartment building. Stood in front of it for a moment, wondering what the hell he was doing, what the hell he hoped to get out of it. He wondered what Mike actually thought about him, whether he saw Danny the way Danny saw himself sometimes, the worst times late at night. A washed-up wreck of a man trying to relive his youth with a guy a decade younger. When you looked at it that way, it was kind of pathetic, and he definitely couldn't handle Mike's pity.

But he was already here. He'd paid for the ticket. He'd come this far, and Mike was quite literally waiting for him.

He went in.

Mike opened the door and Danny just stared at him for a minute because it was just really good to see him. He was wearing a ratty black band T-shirt with its sleeves cut off and his boxers and nothing else, and he looked almost nervous at first. Individually, all of Mike's features were striking, but together, with the tattoos and lean muscle and intensity of his eyes, Danny felt almost overwhelmed just looking at him. His hair was in the growing-in stage again and Danny thought about pulling it.

"Hey," Mike said, and leaned around him to shut the door. "Welcome to my humble abode." Before Danny could do or say anything else, though, Mike pushed him against the door and got down on his knees.

"Mike, what—"

"What does it look like, dumbass? Take 'em down."

Danny, who had dropped his bag when Mike pushed him, looked down helplessly. Mike looked back up at him, but it was so different from the last time they'd done this. It was a challenge, but he wasn't angry, just eager. His lips were parted—

"Come *on*, Danny, drop it." Danny's hands were moving, pushing the waist of his pants down, and Mike bit his lip, watching him, and murmured, "Dude, I've been thinking about this since like…the last game, at least."

"Yeah?"

"I'll show you," Mike said, "exactly what I've been thinking about," and blew him against the door.

Danny came with his hands gripping Mike's head, because the hair wasn't quite long enough to pull after all, his fingers digging against the bone of Mike's skull, and said, "Jesus Christ, what was that for?"

Mike, still on his knees, wiped his mouth on his shirt collar and looked up at him. "Thank you. For coming."

"Mike, you, uh, didn't have to blow me as a *thank-you*."

"Well, I wanted to. And anyway, now we're even."

"Even? Do I…want to know?"

Mike accepted his hand and let Danny haul him to his feet, but he looked a little sheepish. "When we first started doing…this… I uh, was keeping track. So you wouldn't win. And, uh, you were still ahead by one. Now we're even."

Danny stared at him, not sure whether he wanted to

laugh or shake him. "Mike, you are a beautiful fucking fool, you know that?"

Mike's nose wrinkled in disgust. "Beautiful? Handsome. Hot. *Devastating*, thank you. Also, I got you flowers."

Danny noticed, for the first time, that there were indeed flowers on top of Mike's travel bag, still unpacked. It was an assorted bouquet in a Trader Joe's wrapper, the blooms a little wilted because they hadn't been put in water in time. He felt like what he imagined being at sea must feel. Unmoored, like everything had gone topsy-turvy, and he was unable to get his footing. He knew Mike but he was starting to realize he didn't really know Mike at all. Danny was completely bemused.

"You got me flowers?"

"Yeah. You know, like you said. Flowers, dinner, the whole nine yards. I missed the dinner, but… Got a fucking problem with that, Garcia?"

"Mike, I…"

"Dude, you don't have to say anything, okay? I'm just glad you're here."

Danny, on reflex, gathered him into his arms and Mike went willingly enough, his head resting on Danny's coat for a minute before he pulled back. "But let's just sleep, okay? I'm still fucking wiped from that game, and we got a big day tomorrow."

"Okay," Danny agreed, because he didn't want to think about the big day tomorrow.

He followed Mike toward the bedroom, glancing around the apartment as he did. It was the sort of nondescript, bland decoration that he suspected meant it had come pre-furnished, which he wanted to ask about later. There were signs people lived here, of course.

There was an Xbox with games strewn about, some pots and pans in the drying rack. But it was devoid of decoration or any of the things that Danny typically associated with Mike. It made him almost sad.

Getting into bed was both awkward and surprisingly not. He hadn't been sure how Mike would handle it, but he did it as matter-of-factly as he did anything else. Stripped the shirt off, threw it in the corner, pulled the blankets back, and flopped down on the mattress and waited for Danny to undress. There was enough space for both of them, but it had been a long time since he'd actually slept with anyone, and he suspected that it was possible Mike never had. But once they were both lying down, Mike immediately shoved his leg in between Danny's and pushed himself as close as he could get, and Danny relaxed.

"Can't believe you left your hell beast," Mike murmured into his chest.

"I have a cat sitter!"

"Mhm," Mike said, and yawned. "All right. I *gotta* sleep. My alarm's set for ten. That okay?"

"That's fine," Danny said. His hand was on Mike's back, tracing over the lines of muscle that shifted beneath the skin as he tried to get comfortable. Eventually Danny had to pull back because his arm was falling asleep and turned over on his other side. His hip and knee ached a little, but he didn't want to get up and wake Mike, who, still sleeping, had plastered himself against Danny's back like a barnacle. He fell asleep like that, slightly too warm, but more content than he had been in a while.

Danny woke up, disoriented and a little panicked. It took him a minute to realize that he was awake because sun was streaming through the window at an unfamiliar angle, and that the weird feeling at his back was Mike, still asleep, his erection sandwiched between his stomach and Danny's ass. And Danny remembered the entire crazy plan Mike had forced him into and felt, at once, terror and a kind of overwhelming warmth.

He shifted out of Mike's grip and propped himself up on his arm to look down. At some point during the night Mike had kicked the blankets off and his entire body was exposed. Mike moved in his sleep again, his arm thrown over his face, his mouth slack. His lower lip was full and completely healed for once, and Danny thought about biting it. Instead he sat up and looked at the entire stretch of Mike's chest and ribs and abs, the tattoos that had always fascinated him. They were clearly not planned in any kind of overall order, but the way that he'd added ink in similar styles and had gotten some larger cohesive pieces and connected them with filler just worked. It was a very Mike kind of chaos, and Danny traced his hand over one of them, the wolf with a dagger through its head.

Mike opened his eyes when Danny touched him. They were bleary and unfocused, and his voice was rough with sleep. "What time is it?"

"Eight, but…" Danny leaned forward and slid his hand along the line of Mike's dick, palming him over the fabric of his boxers.

"Oh," Mike said, more a sigh than a word. It felt unbearably, uncharacteristically soft for Mike. Then, when Danny shifted so he could get his fingers under the hem, *"Oh."*

Danny hadn't come all the way from Pittsburgh to give him a hand job, although it was kind of nice to watch him pushing up into Danny's hands, his eyes closed. Still sleepy, relaxed in a bone-deep way he never seemed to be out of bed. He looked down at Mike with a weird, fierce fondness, and then let go of his dick, ignored Mike's noise of protest, and pulled his boxers down. It bobbed free, and Danny stared again at the contrast between the small amount of skin Mike still had bare and the tattoos where they started below the dark hair that thatched his groin.

"Fuck," Mike mumbled, when Danny took him in hand again, his thumb pressed against the head. "Danny, come on."

Danny didn't know what he wanted to do first. They had all day for once, and maybe if he distracted Mike long enough, thoroughly enough, he could get out of—no, that wasn't what he should be thinking about. Not now. He leaned over Mike, whose eyes were open now, watching him warily, and said, "I'm going to blow you and we're not going to be even today."

"No?" Mike asked, his voice jumping a little higher.

Danny didn't answer, just leaned forward and pressed one hand hard against Mike's hip, kept the other on his dick. Mike was squirming a little, with anticipation, but he stilled when Danny said, "Shh, stop moving, stay still," and slid his lips around Mike's dick.

"Danny," he groaned, and he was already trembling when Danny started to move.

Danny's mouth and eyes and head were full of him. He couldn't see anything else, couldn't think about anything else. He wanted—needed—to make this something that Mike would remember, no matter what happened after, no matter how far Mike would run when he inevitably figured out what the fuck was going on with Danny's life. He needed Mike to think of him one day when he wasn't there anymore, because that was inevitable, needed him to feel Danny's hands on him like a brand.

Mike's hand twisted in Danny's hair. "Danny, you okay?"

Danny pulled away. "What? I'm fine."

Mike, on his back, frowned up at him. "For a minute you just looked—I don't know."

"You're the only person I've ever known who'd argue while getting a blowjob."

"Well…you know me."

"Yes," Danny said, full of that horrible, melancholy fondness again, "I do." And he went back down.

By the time he was finished, Mike was a groaning, panting mess, incapable of coherency, and he probably would have punched himself thrashing around if Danny hadn't grabbed both of his wrists in an iron grip and held them down against the mattress. As it was, he almost choked Danny when he came, thrusting up with a sobbing cry, his entire body struggling mindlessly against the weight of Danny's hands and knees pinning his arms and legs down.

Danny wiped the spit from his mouth and chin and watched Mike trying to recover from it, mouth slack and fists clenching and chest heaving, and thought, *goddamn*.

"Here, let me," Mike said, reaching for Danny's dick.

"No," Danny said, catching his hand, "that's not how this is gonna go today."

Mike's eyes were so dark and so warm and he stretched his thumb forward to rub it against Danny's forearm where it still gripped his wrist. "How's—how's it gonna go?"

Danny didn't answer him immediately, just took the time to enjoy looking at him.

"Danny—how's it gonna *go*?"

"Impatient," Danny said, teasing. "That's not gonna work for you."

How it went was Danny shoved Mike over onto his stomach, his face pressed into the pillows, and just didn't do anything to him. He left his hand on Mike's lower back, pressing him down just enough to indicate he should stay. The silence in the room was loaded and although Mike hadn't said anything, he was tense and almost screaming with nerves. But he wasn't moving, and Danny pressed his thumb down harder.

"Danny, what are you…"

"Shh," he said, distracted, thinking about all of the ways he wanted to touch Mike, all of the things he could do to him now that he had the time and the space. At first, he just looked.

Mike was on the small side for a defenseman, probably twenty-five pounds below average, but the muscle he'd worked so hard to pack on was impressive, and so were his surprisingly broad shoulders. There wasn't an ounce of extra body fat and with every small movement, Danny could study the shift of muscle beneath his skin. He knew exactly what Mike could do on the ice despite his size.

He ran his hand down Mike's back again, tracing the line from shoulder blades to his waist to his ass, which was also tattooed as part of a larger piece that went up his lower back and wrapped around the side of his ribs, a knight fighting a lion that had dragged him down from his horse, mauling him with his claws.

"Danny…"

In response Danny slapped him hard enough on the ass that the sound of his hand almost echoed in the room. Mike made a choked-off noise of surprise, but didn't cry out and didn't pull away, so Danny hit him again on the back of his thigh. Mike's breath hissed out but still, he didn't move.

So Danny kept hitting him, keeping his hands moving at first, arousal roiling in his stomach at the way Mike tensed in on himself every time, absorbing the shock of it, instead of pulling away. Danny started searching for the places he'd been bruised during games and targeting them specifically, three times, four times, over and over, until Mike, who had his head buried half under the pillow, took a great, heaving breath and exhaled with a whimper, like the noises had been dragged from him involuntarily.

Danny soothed his hand over a bruise on Mike's shoulder blade before he hit it even harder, the blow falling with all the force he could muster, and Mike cried out, his entire body rocking up like he didn't know if he was trying to get away or lean into the touch.

"Jesus, Danny," he managed, shivering every time Danny touched him, whether it was to stroke him or slap him. "God—please—"

"Please what? Should I stop?"

"No, no."

"What do you want, Mike? Is it too much?"

"No. No. It's not—I—I—keep doing it."

"You are *so* good," Danny breathed, so painfully

hard but unwilling to do anything about that yet. He was sitting on Mike's legs now, both holding him down and giving himself a way to lean over his entire body. Danny leaned forward and dug his teeth into Mike's back and kept hitting him until he was sobbing into the pillow, unable to stop moving, squirming away and toward Danny's hands.

Getting Mike to the point where he was completely out of his head, not thinking about the noises he was making or what he was doing, was overwhelming enough on its own, and the worst part of Danny was singing in his head *push it push him break him*. Maybe he wasn't as in control of the situation as he thought he'd been.

His hands stilled on Mike's back, and Mike craned his head around to look at him.

He was panting, his face flushed and his eyes glassy and unfocused. "Why—come on, Danny, please, Jesus."

Danny's chest felt like it was going to burst. It was just… Mike was so much. Mike meant so much, and he didn't know what to do with that. He just wanted Mike to feel the same way he felt, overwhelmed and hopeful and hopeless all at once, a joy so intense it sometimes felt the same as sorrow.

"Mike, I—" He needed to say it, and he couldn't say it, not now. Instead Danny leaned forward and kissed him, awkward angle and all, a clash of mouths as desperate as the first time Mike had greeted him in the hotel room.

Mike went with it, bemused but easy, went with it when Danny pulled away and pushed him back down. He was tense again like he was expecting Danny to hit him, but Danny had other ideas, leaned forward and spread Mike's cheeks and pressed his tongue against him. Mike's entire body spasmed again, surprised and oversensitive, but as Danny teased him first and licked him open once he'd relaxed, his initial shock gave way to pliancy.

"—what the fuck—oh, Jesus, fuck, Danny, *what*, the—shit, shit, shit *fuck*," Mike managed, after what seemed like a very long time, each word half laughing, half groaning, shaking so much that Danny had to pin his arms down with one hand again. "Oh my god, oh my god, ohhh my—" When Danny pressed a finger in, and his tongue around it, Mike sounded like he was choking. "Jesus, stop, stop, stop, it's too much, it's too much, I'm going to come if you—I can't—"

Danny pulled his head up, and his voice didn't sound anything like him, deep and rough and full of shivery longing. "You can if you want, but I'm *not* finished," and Mike made another one of those whimpering noises.

"God, please, please, then fuck me, fuck me, you have to—"

"That's what you want?"

"Yes," Mike said, and his voice cracked when Danny dipped his head down again. "Yes, yes, please, Jesus, I fucking hate you, fuck's *sake*, Danny, you're going to kill me—"

Danny felt light-headed, almost, hearing it, knowing it. Feeling exactly how much Mike wanted him, and exactly how difficult it was to hold himself together even to beg for that and needing him the same way. "Okay, babe," he said, then paused. "Uh—"

"The bureau, the bureau, top drawer, shit, come on, hurry the fuck up—" Mike said, rolling over onto his back and propping himself up on his elbow as he watched Danny hunt for the condoms.

As soon as he found them, as soon as he was back on the bed, kneeling, Mike surprised the shit out of him by lunging up to kiss him. Danny managed, "Are you—"

"I don't *fucking* care, come *on*, I need—"

And Danny gave in, his hands fumbling with the condom packet and then the condom while Mike's hands traced the muscles in his arms, his chest, his back; Mike's tongue fucked his mouth; Mike's eagerness and desperation and longing like an electric shock over his skin. Danny pulled back long enough to say, "How do you—"

"I don't care, however you want, please just *do it*—"

Danny pushed him over again, then hooked his arm under Mike's torso and pulled him up onto his knees. Mike, who normally fought everything, went with it, trembling, and Danny found that strangely, he was shaking too, had to grip his dick briefly to keep himself even. He started steadily, pushing into Mike with unbearable care, his eyes slipping shut at the feeling of Mike's body struggling to accommodate him. He went slowly, so slowly, torturing Mike and himself with the drawn-out friction, wanting nothing more than to fuck him into the mattress, not allowing himself to do it yet.

Mike started trying to move, to shove himself back onto Danny's cock, and Danny was swamped with a feeling of tenderness toward him. Toward his demanding, frustrating Mike. But that wasn't how he wanted this to go, and so he brought the flat of his hand down hard between Mike's shoulder blades, the force of the blow knocking him off his elbows and pushing his face down into the bed.

"Jesus Christ," he moaned, and Danny could feel him, clenching tight.

"Behave yourself," Danny said, although his voice was uneven and shaky. "I'll give it to you, but we're doing it at my pace."

Mike panted into the mattress, shaking his head.

"Yes," Danny said, even though Mike hadn't said anything.

And he started to move, still agonizingly slow, so slow it was almost painful for him. Mike shook underneath him, almost silent now, but when Danny leaned over, he could hear Mike whispering, *please, please, please, please*, and he said, "It's okay, babe," and pressed his mouth against the same place he'd slapped. He never wanted this to end and he knew it had to.

Danny pulled himself up far enough that he could flatten his hand against Mike's back and start fucking him in earnest, harder and harder, until the bed shook and Mike wasn't even making noise anymore, just had his hands fisted in the blankets, biting his lip bloody. Danny felt every movement of his body, every breath Mike could barely get out, labored and completely fucked up, and felt himself trembling on the livewire edge of an orgasm he didn't want to give in to yet.

But then Mike thrashed underneath him, his whole body bowing, and Danny realized he'd come without Danny touching his dick, and that did it. He lost himself in the feeling as it dragged up his spine in an almost painful release, his hands still struggling to keep Mike still, before he just ended up collapsing on top of him.

It seemed like a long time before Mike said, "Jesus, you're heavy," his voice hoarse from begging.

"Hmm," Danny said, disinclined to move.

"I'm still like—my whole fucking body is vibrating," Mike said, "shit, this is fucking *weird*," then started trying to wriggle out from underneath him, to push at Danny's shoulders. "Get off of me, asshole."

With anyone else it might have ruined the moment, but Mike said *asshole* in the same tone of voice Danny used when he said *I love you* and for a minute, he thought, *god, I'm going to fuck it up, I can't fuck it up.* What he said was, "Okay, okay."

"Shit," Mike said, again, and he started laughing, a sort of hysterical giggle. "You really fuck me up, Danny."

"That's the general idea," Danny replied, pressing his lips against Mike's shoulder. He couldn't help smiling, warm and fond, even though he knew he should rein it in.

They spent most of the rest of the morning in bed, until around noon Mike staggered out of the bedroom complaining, "Dude, I don't know how you're still—and you're *old*—I have to *eat* something, okay?"

They passed the remainder of the afternoon eating delivery pho and watching *Goon* on Netflix, at least until Mike glanced at his phone and said, "We should get cleaned up to go, right?"

Danny, who had been dreading this, said, "Yes."

They showered together, didn't fool around—"I couldn't get it up even if I wanted to, dude," Mike groaned when Danny tried—and then there was no getting out of it.

It was time to get ready to see his family.

Danny had agonized over what to wear, not wanting to seem as though he was trying too hard to look normal, not wanting to seem like he was a depressed slob who spent most of his time at home alone on the couch, his body aching. In the end he'd settled on something completely nondescript. Khaki trousers and a blue, gold and tan Fair Isle sweater, brown leather dress shoes, and hoped for the best. He discovered, not surprisingly, that Mike didn't own many clothes that weren't Under Armour, band T-shirts, skinny jeans, black oversize sweaters, or leather jackets. He had a single pair of dress shoes, but they looked like the kind of thing an awkward teenager would buy for a prom.

"How many leather jackets do you *need*?" Danny asked, bemused.

"I wear all of them, fuck you," Mike said, then looked mournfully in his drawer. "I guess I could wear my ugly sweater from last year..."

It was, indeed, an ugly sweater. It was knitted and stylized with the Cons' red, white, and blue logo, and it looked completely, incongruously out of character on Mike, but it was that or black and more black. In the end, that and a pair of jeans that weren't ripped yet had to do.

Mike drove and Danny tried not to fidget in the passenger seat. He really wished he'd thought to have a drink at Mike's before they left, just to calm his nerves, but he didn't want to ask Mike for that. That would be another kind of exposure he couldn't handle today. So his fingers tapped on the armrest and he chewed on his lip.

Mike, making a left-hand turn, glanced sideways at him. "Dude, it's gonna be fine, okay?"

"I know," Danny answered, curt and clipped.

Mike reached over and put a hand on his knee. "Really. And if it's not, I'll take you home, okay?"

He hadn't noticed what he'd said, but Danny did, and he stilled, slid his own hand on top of Mike's. "Okay."

Chris and Celi lived in Mt. Airy, a residential neighborhood filled with Victorian twin homes constructed of brick and stone. They had bought the house a few years ago and spent the entire time they lived there renovating it, and it was homey and warm, everything Danny's wreck of a house wasn't. They'd landscaped the front lawn. He was pretty sure they'd never found any cats in their garbage can. Josie had a little swing set in the backyard and they had a vegetable garden on the sunny side of the house. They'd decorated for the holiday, strings of multicolored lights, some hung neatly, some messily at about the level a two-year-old could reach.

Mike parked outside and looked sideways at him. "You good?"

"No," Danny said, because it was easier to be honest. He felt the yawning void inside of him, and he didn't like it.

Impulsively, Mike leaned across the center console and kissed him. It was brief, barely anything but a press of Mike's mouth against his—they were almost in public, after all—and pulled away. "You will be."

It wasn't fair, Danny thought as he followed Mike up the stone path to the door, holding the bag with Josie's present in it. It wasn't fair that Mike was such an asshole sometimes but was instinctively so kind. He was thinking how fucked up he was going to be when this was inevitably over, but then Celi opened the door and Josie, dressed in reindeer pajamas, came barreling out barefoot and shrieking, *"Tío Danny! Tío Danny!"*

He knelt down and dropped the bag to catch her in his arms, and his knee cracked. He winced in pain but kept his balance and hauled her up into a bear hug. She had grown so much since he'd last seen her, but she was still the same affectionate, silly Josie, patting his beard with inquisitive hands. "Your face!" she said, delighted. "So fuzzy."

"Te quiero mucho," he murmured into her hair.

"Te quiero," she assured him.

Danny finally looked up and saw that Celi and Chris were standing there too, and his stomach dropped. This was the moment he'd been worried about. Someone who would hold him accountable for the shitty way he'd acted this year. But Celi, gray at her temples and laugh lines at the corners of her eyes, just stepped forward and hugged him and Josie both.

"Danny—god, it's so good to see you."

His throat was suddenly full of a lump that made it hard to speak, and he could feel the corners of his eyes burning. "It's good to see you too."

"Does everyone want to come in from the cold?" Chris asked dryly. "Touching as this is, we do have the whole house for your tender reunions."

"Chris," Celi said into Danny's shoulder, "I can and will make you sorry."

"Not on Christmas you won't," he said, his voice full of holiday cheer.

They did follow him in, though, and Danny set Josie down. She clung to his leg as they tried to make their greetings in the hall. "Ah—Celi, Chris, this is my—this is—this is Mike."

Mike, who'd been hanging back behind him and had picked up the bag, came forward and shook both Chris and Celi's hands. He looked uncomfortable, a little awkward, but he behaved himself, engaging in small talk with Chris ("so I understand you also play hockey, Mike?"), who picked Josie up so she couldn't follow while Celi led Danny into the kitchen.

The lump was back in his throat again, because it smelled exactly like their parents' house on Nochebuena, the heady mélange of meat and spice that promised special treats like tamales and pozole and menudo in addition to a turkey, stuffing, and potatoes. Their parents had always hosted friends and family in the city and anyone within driving distance, unable to stop cooking even when it was the one vacation they took all year, and the house had always been packed, too loud, too warm, almost humid from so many bodies, and Celi and Danny had looked forward to it every year. Just smelling it now almost broke him, knowing that she had put in all of this work just for the five of them. Just for him, really. Instead he pulled her into a hug and tried not to cry.

"Danny," she said again, patting his back, "it's okay. We love you, hermanito."

"I'm fucking sorry, Celi, the last few years have—the last few years—it's been—Jesus, I'm sorry. This isn't the time."

"Whenever you want to talk is the time," Celi said, into his chest.

"I—not now. But—thank you—for—for not giving up on me."

She pulled back, and looked at him, fierce and loving. "I would never give up on you."

He couldn't help laughing. "One of these days I'm gonna be too much even for you."

"No such thing, bro," Celi said, and poked him in the stomach. "Although I gotta say, the self-pity doesn't look good on you. Mike, though…?"

Danny surprised himself, feeling his face heat a little. "Uh, yeah. He's, uh, really great."

"He is," Celi agreed, surprising him again.

"You were ready to kill him a few weeks ago."

"Well, that was when I only knew him from the games. He has a good heart," Celi said, leaning against the counter, her arms crossed over her chest.

"He does," Danny said, glancing back in the direction of the living room. Mike was still talking to Chris, but he kept looking over at the kitchen door, trying to see how Danny was doing, and he felt that pain in his chest again. "He really does."

"Come on, let's get some of this food on the table, huh?"

The dinner wasn't as awkward as he'd thought it was going to be. Mike didn't seem like he'd be the chattiest person when he didn't know people, but he was making a valiant effort to keep the conversation going whenever Danny flagged, particularly when he felt like things were getting too close to home. It helped that the food was really good: Celi had always been better at the cooking portion of helping at the diner than he had, and she'd clearly taken the time to perfect the recipes their mother always wanted both of them to learn. And they had beer, and that helped too, although he tried to limit his drinking when Celi looked at him. He knew she knew.

"So," Chris said, after a while, "how did you meet Danny, Mike?"

Mike choked on the pozole and said, "Well, uh, I guess you could say we met during my first game with the Cons? I was trying to pick a fight and Danny, uh, kind of kicked my ass."

"You gave it a good effort," Danny said.

Mike sighed. "No, dude, you definitely kicked my ass."

"So you just kept fighting each other?"

"He had something to prove," Danny said, unable to keep the fondness from his voice.

"But, uh, we started talking online this year, I guess, and we've—we're friends, now, I guess. And Danny's really helped me improve my game, really, he's been a better coach to me than my actual coach."

Chris's eyebrows went up, but he said, "Well, we always knew Danny had a good sense for the game. But it's pretty big of you to help someone that broke your tooth like that, man."

"He, ah, didn't mean to," Danny said, although he knew it sounded like a lame excuse. Mike had absolutely meant to, but Danny didn't mind. He'd do it all over again if he had to. "That's just how the game goes sometimes."

The conversation flowed easily enough after that. Chris's job had been frustrating: with Xfinity expanding and hiring, the HR department had been insanely busy. Josie had been suspended from preschool for repeated biting incidents and being unable to follow the behavior plan they'd written up for her, but had won over the teachers again by hugging all of them and saying *I sorry* when she'd returned. It felt weirdly natural to have Mike here with his family, like he fit right in. At some point during the dinner Josie decided she wanted to sit on Mike's lap, fascinated with the tattoos peeking out from beneath his sweater. He let her.

"Drawings?" she asked.

"Yes, but they don't come off," Mike told her. "They're called tattoos."

"Why?" She sounded impressed, though.

"I like them, and I wanted them forever."

"You color them?"

"I like black," Mike said, and patted her on her chubby arm.

"They need color," Josie said, frowning.

Before it was time for buñuelos and coffee, Danny helped Celi and Chris clear the table while Mike took Josie into the living room to play and keep her away from their feet. Danny was washing the dishes when Chris said, "So how long has this been a thing?"

"Uhh..." Danny really didn't want to say July, because he knew Araceli would put two and two together, and the less he thought of that awful dinner, one of his true low points, the better. He still broke out in a cold sweat when he thought about his parents watching hopefully as Celi had started talking about how concerned they were. What a horror and a relief it had been to just get up and leave them all behind. "October, I guess?"

Saying it like that, things sounded probably as though they were moving too fast. But Mike had been a part of his life, for better or worse, since that first game in October last season. When Danny had almost knocked Mike out cold and started something neither of them knew would happen.

Chris's eyebrows went up again. "October, wow. He seems, uh…pretty smitten."

"Chris," Celi said, warning. "Stop teasing him."

"Sorry, sorry, I can't help it. It's, uh, it's sweet."

Danny looked down at the sink, embarrassed but also weirdly, strangely pleased, and said nothing. He was mostly just relieved that no one had said anything about his long absence, and if they hadn't exactly picked up like nothing had happened, neither of them was rubbing his nose in it. He knew he'd fucked up but for now, it was just nice to be here, near them.

"Hey," he said, drying his hands on the towel and shoving an envelope at them, "I got you guys a present."

"Danny, you didn't have to—"

"Well, I know, but take it, okay?"

It was a set of gift certificates to different restaurants in the city. He'd picked Mike's brain for trendy places that a couple of forty-somethings would enjoy on their nights off from toddler-wrangling and chosen a week's worth of them. The gift for Josie, which she wouldn't open until the morning, was a tabletop easel appropriate for toddlers, and brand-new sets of markers and crayons and acrylic paint.

"Well, thank you," Celi said, a little severely.

"I'm not trying to buy my way out of this," he muttered. "It's just Christmas and I wanted to do something nice for you."

"Thank you," Chris said, and patted him on the shoulder.

By the time the worst of the mess was cleaned up and Celi had started frying up the buñuelos, Danny went back out into the living room and saw that Mike had rolled up his sweater sleeves and was letting Josie color in his tattoos with the markers. Josie bent over him in intense concentration, her tongue sticking out as she worked. Mike's forearms were a riot of color, yellows and reds and oranges all bleeding into each other and into the negative and gray space of his tattoos. She'd drawn a huge ladybug in the blank space on his left hand.

When he saw Danny watching, Mike grinned. "Everyone always asks me if they're finished. Guess they are now, huh?"

I love you, Danny thought, and said, "Well, until you take a shower, anyway. Josie, what a good job you did," and he sat down on the floor next to them, the weight on his shoulders lighter than it had been in a long time.

Mike wasn't sure what he'd been expecting when he'd invited Danny to stay for the holidays. He'd done it the same way he did a lot of things in his life, which was to act on instinct and worry about the consequences later. It turned out to be one of the better decisions he'd made that way but also he'd been embarrassingly wrong about several things, though he couldn't really muster up the energy to be angry about it.

The first thing he'd been wrong about was that it wasn't awkward at all hanging out with Danny's family. Okay, wrong: it had been a little awkward at first, especially because he wasn't at all used to dealing with babies, but they were really *nice*. There was none of the out-of-place feeling he hated so much when he went home to his own parents and siblings, the way he couldn't talk to them about anything he was actually interested in, none of the desperate longing for approval that he never truly received. Celi and Chris were just really, genuinely nice, incredibly welcoming, and hadn't made him feel weird or out of place, especially considering their first impression of Mike had been him knocking out Danny's teeth.

The second thing he'd been wrong about was his worry that maybe having Danny staying at his place for so long would be uncomfortable, or that they'd get bored of talking to each other for so long. Instead it turned out that the more time he spent with Danny it was like the more Mike needed his attention and the more he wanted to talk to him and find out things about him and know him, which was kind of actually terrifying. Mike didn't want to think about that one or what it meant for too long.

The third thing he'd been wrong about was the drinking and drug shit. Mike watched him like a hawk the whole time, but Danny only drank when Mike did, and not to excess. He was still taking the pills, but the prescription was a legit prescription, so. Mike couldn't really say shit about that, even though he was still so fucking worried. It was just that he'd been prepared for something worse, and he hadn't seen it.

The fourth thing he'd been wrong about was sex.

Like obviously when you invited a guy you'd been fucking to crash at your place for three days, sex was on the table. Mike had been looking forward to that, because, like, of course he was, he was only fucking human. He thought he'd known what he was getting into, thought he'd been prepared for it. But once he'd done it, once he had Danny in his bed (*and on the couch and in the kitchen and in the bathroom and—*) and all of the time in the world, he'd realized exactly how out of his fucking depth he was when it came to sex and exactly how far Danny had him outclassed. That first morning had just been the beginning. Part of him was a little shocked at the way Danny seemed so consistently ready to go and how often they were fucking, but part of him smugly thought, *he's like that because of* me, *he wants it so often because it's* me.

On Christmas morning he was lying in his bed, a sweaty, fucked-out mess, body bruised and limp, his brain still not entirely able to connect words in actual sentences. Danny, next to him, had his eyes closed and a big dumb grin on his face that Mike couldn't even make fun of because his was probably a million times worse.

The sex was really, really good.

Mike rolled over on his side and pressed his face into Danny's shoulder, boneless and exhausted and still riding on an endorphin high. He'd already come like three times that morning and he wasn't sure if he could get it up again even if he'd wanted to. Except he kind of did want to because apparently he had it just as bad as Danny did.

"Hell of a Christmas present, dude," he mumbled into Danny's skin.

Danny, also unable to form sentences, exhaled a noise that was almost a laugh, and allowed Mike to run his hand over Danny's stomach and thighs while he appreciated the contrast between his black ink and Danny's skin. Danny didn't open his eyes, but his face had the kind of serene blankness that Mike knew was good. That look meant he wasn't thinking about injuries or hockey or anything except Mike, and that screaming possessive demon in Mike's head said, *good, good, that's the way it should be.*

But he was thinking about it again and the words came out before he could stop them, like fucking and getting fucked until he forgot his own name for a few seconds and had cut the brain/mouth controls he had kept firmly in place for years and years. "It's just—like—dude, I—never thought sex could be like—"

What the fuck, his brain was screaming at his mouth, *shut the fuck up, you fucking moron.* He managed to stop it, but it was too late.

Danny's eyes opened. He was looking at Mike, rolled over so half of his body trapped Mike against the bed. "Why not?"

"I dunno, dude," Mike said, squirming. "I dunno."

Danny's hand on his cheek, fingers tracing the line of his jaw. "Tell me," he said. It was a command, but in a gentle kind of way that made Mike's stomach turn itself inside out, because he was apparently that much of a fucking idiot when it came to Danny now.

"Tell you what?"

"Why you didn't think sex could be like this. Is that what you were going to say?"

Mike squirmed again, not quite trying to push Danny away. It was hard to do it when the rest of his body instinctively melted into Danny's hands. This was the kind of shit that made him uncomfortable. No, it was worse than that. It was fucking terrifying, talking about something so real.

"Come on, babe," Danny said. His voice was low and rough from exhaustion and his thumb was gentle against one of the bruises he'd left on Mike's throat last night, stroking, then pressing in just enough that Mike could feel the dull ache. "You can tell me."

Mike had his eyes screwed shut, unable to look him

in the eye. Kind of fucked up that Danny had seen him naked every way you could see someone naked, had his dick in Mike's mouth and ass and the other way around, had slapped him around until Mike begged for more, made him lose control of himself so badly that he'd actually cried, kissed the tears off of his face after. And this was still the most cut-open and embarrassed Mike could remember being.

"Babe," Danny said again, his voice like a caress, and Mike choked out, "It's just—it's never been like—"

He had to stop.

"Hey. Come on, open your eyes."

It was almost painful to do it, but he tried. He looked up. Danny, his face shadowed with a few days' worth of beard growth and his eyes warm and intent, was watching him with the kind of expression that Mike couldn't entirely decipher but whatever was in there made his stomach do that flip again. Made his heart feel like Danny could hear it beating, it was so loud.

"It's just…dude, okay, so. I had just barely turned seventeen when I got fucked the first time, okay?" Danny didn't say anything, but his hand hadn't moved from Mike's cheek, and Mike turned his face into Danny's palm so he didn't have to look. "It was at some shitty house show and I was so wasted I could barely stand because that's the only way I could, like, do anything back then, and—and he was a lot older than me, and it was—it was—"

"Hey," Danny said, and his voice was so fucking soft Mike was frozen between the twin urges to shove him out of the bed and push his head into Danny's chest so he didn't have to look him in the eye. "It's okay. It's okay, Mike."

"It wasn't great," he said finally. It wasn't exactly true, or at least, it wasn't an accurate way to put it. It had been worse than wasn't great. It had kind of hurt. No, it *had* hurt. He'd felt like…humiliated, but not in a good way, except he shouldn't have, because he'd wanted it, right?

At the time he hadn't thought about it much, because he'd been a dumb kid full of bravado and the inability to admit he might've made a stupid decision, even though it hadn't really felt like a decision at all so much as something that had just happened to him. Because he was a tough guy, he should have been able to fucking handle it, but he—couldn't. He couldn't handle it.

He'd felt the sharp, sour shame that accompanied most of his sexual escapades at that age, had still been vaguely relieved to get it over with, because that was always going to be the first time, and no matter how bad it was, it could never be worse. He'd woken up in the morning on the floor, found some of his clothes, and made the walk of shame back to his billet, grimy and sore and hungover. He'd mostly put it out of his head after that. It wasn't until he'd had some distance and a chance to think about it that it had felt—

"It really wasn't great, and afterward…" Mike had to stop and collect himself for a second. He couldn't think of the words to explain to Danny the way it had felt. "Even when it hasn't been painful like that, it's always been a secret because of the hockey shit, you know? I've been rushed. Or drunk. I've never fucked someone I ever wanted to hang out with again or fucked someone more than once, I've never gotten to know anyone—no one's ever tried to make it *good* for me—you just—you know what I want, it's never felt like this. I've never *needed*—"

He couldn't go on and Danny didn't make him, just leaned forward and kissed him. His mouth was hot and wet and Mike's opened eagerly under his tongue, without even thinking about it.

That was something else he'd never really done as a kid or even as an adult. Hadn't really thought of it as anything worth pursuing. But kissing Danny was like… his brain went into overdrive trying to come up with words for it and failed because he wasn't good at trying to describe things he felt. It made his stomach burn and his toes curl and his entire body melt into Danny's, and he couldn't even care that it felt like Danny could see right through him, just by putting his tongue in Mike's mouth.

Danny pulled away, and when Mike opened his eyes again, he saw that Danny had pushed himself up on one arm and was looking down at him again with that Danny Look. The one that made him feel weird and shy and like he wanted to crawl out of his own skin all at the same time. But this time he couldn't look away.

"Fuck me," Mike said, because it was easier than saying any of the other things that were kicking around in his head and it was almost what he wanted to say anyway.

Danny made a noise that was half a laugh and half a groan and fell back down on top of him, his weight more comforting than it should have been. "I think we gotta wait for a bit, babe."

Mike wrinkled his nose. "A'ight, old man."

"I think I'm acquitting myself pretty well," Danny said, like he knew exactly why Mike was saying it and didn't care. "Didn't hear any complaints from you earlier."

He couldn't help the shiver that moved over his shoulders when he thought about it, knew Danny could feel it, knew Danny knew he was right. "Fuck you," he said, into Danny's mouth, because Danny was kissing him again.

They spent most of the rest of the day like that, a seamless shift from the everyday shit: taking a shower, because holy fuck he was disgusting, to talking to making out to realizing they were ravenously hungry and ordering takeout to fucking again. In the evening Mike was flopped on the couch with his head in Danny's lap while Danny had his legs propped up on the coffee table. He was sort of but not really watching a movie because he was distracted by the way Danny's fingers were combing absently through his hair, by the little shiver of pleasure that zipped up his spine every time Danny's fingernails scratched along his skull.

It took him a minute to realize that the warmth that he was feeling in his chest and his stomach and the way he didn't feel fidgety at all was because he was happy, like really fucking happy, in a way he could barely remember ever feeling, and that thought made him tense up, suddenly self-conscious.

Of course Danny felt it.

"Mike?"

"I—sorry, I was just thinking about stuff."

"Yeah?"

Mike dug his teeth into his lip because he felt embarrassed about it, didn't want to say anything. Like: it seemed really weird to say, *you make me really happy*, just out of nowhere.

Instead, he said, "Um, thanks for taking me to meet your family. I'm glad you took me, but also… that they knew we're—" They weren't dating, and *fucking* seemed like the wrong word too, wasn't enough to describe the shit knocking itself around Mike's head. "You weren't worried?"

Danny shrugged and Mike was kind of glad they weren't looking at each other. His fingers didn't stop moving, thumb stroking over Mike's temple. "I came out to Celi when I was fourteen. My parents figured it out when I was sixteen. Bisexuality was never really a big deal for them, you know? They were always more concerned I was dating good people. I knew once they met you it'd be fine."

"Your sister was the first person I ever…you know." What Mike didn't say was: *dating? Really?* What Mike didn't say was: *I did it for you* or *I'm still really fucking worried about you, dude*. What Mike didn't say was: *I don't think my parents would be that chill* or *they might be okay but honestly I'm too scared to find out*.

Danny didn't say anything but his fingers tightened around Mike's head, where his hand was resting. "I'm uh… I'm glad you told her. I'm glad you made me fly out here."

Mike's chest was doing that thing where it felt like his ribs were going to split open with the force of the feelings he could not put into words. It was too much, especially knowing he only had another day of Danny being here before it was over. "Yeah, well. Fuck you."

He couldn't see Danny's face, but he could hear the smile in his voice. "Okay, babe."

"Yeah?"

Danny turned off the TV, and that was the only answer Mike needed.

On Thursday morning, Danny packed up his shit fairly early in the morning but let Mike talk him into spending most of the rest of the day in and out of bed because apparently Mike turned him into the worst version of his teenaged self. A hair-trigger erection and a refractory period that was frankly almost obscene. He was sore and exhausted and his hips and back and knee were screaming at him by the end of the long break, but it was like both of them knew this would be the last opportunity like this they'd have for who knew how long.

He had to make the most of it.

He had made the most of it.

He needed to catch a cab to the airport. It was seven thirty, and he really needed to get going. But every attempt he made to head for the door Mike would catch him by the wrist, ask something like, *you sure you remembered your phone charger* and they'd end up making out for another fifteen minutes, which was rapidly adding up to minutes he didn't have. He was incapable of saying no to Mike, though, and so when Mike got down on his knees and blew him one last time, he just let it happen, eyes closed and fingers tangled in Mike's hair, finally long enough to pull.

After Danny came, Mike lurched to his feet and pressed him against the door, mouth warm and salty, still tasting not unpleasantly of come, kissing him even while Danny was trying to shove his dick back in his pants, and Danny thought with a kind of sharp, horrible melancholy, *goddamn, I love you.*

Eventually, reluctantly, he disentangled himself and

said, "Mike, babe, I really gotta *go*," and Mike had relented, his face red. The way he'd needed it, needed Danny, even when he was embarrassed by the things he wanted. God, it was really fucking hard to leave him.

Danny was aware that he was a fucking idiot, but he couldn't really help it. Not when Mike was Mike. Not when Danny loved him, not when this was the absolute worst time in his life to fall in love with anybody, especially someone like Mike. Someone who needed careful handling and stability, someone who needed things Danny wasn't going to be capable of giving him in the long run. Someone whose halting, awkward trust Danny sure as fuck didn't deserve.

Mike didn't drop him off at the airport, because there was still the risk of someone seeing them, the kind of attention neither of them wanted, so the goodbye at Mike's door was the last time Danny saw him. Danny looked over his shoulder as he went down the hall of Mike's apartment building, and saw him standing in the doorway, leaning against the doorframe. His arms were crossed over his chest, and his dark eyes bored into Danny's back, and Danny was overwhelmed with everything that had happened to him that weekend, and looked away because if he didn't, he wasn't going to make his flight.

He was going to go back in there, get down on his knees, and do something fucking stupid.

He didn't do anything stupid.

It wasn't until he was going through security that he realized how little he'd had to drink that entire weekend, because he'd been so busy with Mike, because he'd been scared shitless that if he told Mike how much he'd wanted to drink, Mike would try to pry into the parts of his life that were best kept a secret. His hands were shaking a little. He couldn't tell if it was emotion or something else.

Danny got extremely drunk on the plane back to Pittsburgh, even though it was only an hour and a half. It was too fucking much. Every time he closed his eyes he couldn't sleep, he just thought about Mike, Mike letting Josie color all over his arms, Mike's face when he'd said *it's never felt like, I've never needed*, Mike facedown on the bed, sweating and gasping, Mike smiling into Danny's mouth, Mike begging him for relief. It was too fucking much. The only thing that alcohol made a little easier was that even though he still remembered all of those things, they were dulled around the edges and he didn't care quite as much.

Danny ignored the silent, judgmental gaze of the cab driver in the rearview mirror, because he was really obviously wasted. Had smacked his head on the top of the door, trying to get into the car, had badly misjudged the distance and his balance.

Instead of saying anything or looking up, he checked his phone. Araceli had texted, it was really good to see you, tell Mike it was nice to get to know him, ok? And Mike had asked, hey did u land ok? Danny scrubbed his hand over his eyes and thought again how he didn't fucking deserve any of this. Not when he was drunk as fuck in a cab at midnight on a goddamn Thursday. He made himself write back to both of them: to Araceli, thanks, I missed you, and he liked meeting you too, and to Mike, cabbing it home.

wish you were here ☹, Mike responded almost immediately, and Danny's entire body winced into itself with the urge to just get even more fucked up so he didn't have to think about it.

He'd hired a cat sitter for Buddy, because three days was too long to leave a kitten alone, so it wasn't like he was by himself the whole time. Still, when he stumbled through the door Buddy hissed at him from the corners of the foyer, followed him from room to room, so he'd know exactly how mad he was that Danny had left, and eventually, gave up on being mad once Danny had swallowed a few pills, poured himself another generous drink, and flopped down on the couch. Buddy jumped up onto his chest, and together, they watched a few episodes of a baking contest, only half paying attention, while he smoothed one thumb over Buddy's tiny skull and thought about the way he'd soothed Mike with almost exactly the same motion.

I wish I was there too, he did not text Mike back, although he thought it, over and over again, until he fell asleep.

Danny woke on the couch in the morning to find that he had six missed calls, four voice mails, and twenty-three text messages. Most of them were from the Hornets' coaching staff, first from Beranek, the assistant coach who worked with the defensemen, and then from the head coach himself. It was one p.m. on a game day, and he'd missed morning skate.

Fuck, fuck, fuck, fuck, fuck, fuck, he thought, because he was a fucking idiot who'd drank away his feelings and forgot to set his fucking phone alarm like a rank *fucking* amateur. He already knew what the voice mails were going to be about, so he didn't bother listening to them. Morning skate wasn't optional these days, and even if it had been he still would have missed video, so he was definitely going to be scratched from the game that night.

Danny had been scratched more than a few times in his sixteen-year career, but it was mostly when he was recovering from surgery and technically could have played but had been pressured into not playing and ultimately, it had been the right decision. He couldn't risk aggravating old injuries on top of old injuries. He hadn't liked it, but he'd accepted it. This was—this was different. He could feel the humiliation of it, sharp even through the dull throbbing headache. This was Coach telling him he needed to get his shit together, or he was gonna find himself waived or traded again.

He thought he'd been better at hiding it. He thought he'd been keeping it together. It was like seeing Mike and his family again had split open something inside of him, some rotten thing he'd been able to hide away before. This was why he had fucking avoided it, avoided *them*.

He was drunk at the game, too. Fucked up enough that he couldn't feel the humiliation of sitting in the press box in his suit any longer, fucked up enough that it didn't matter that everyone knew exactly why he was there.

The Hornets won without him, and he mostly just concentrated on walking in a straight line. Concentrated on avoiding Gears' disappointed face and Landry's expressionless mouth and worried eyes. Concentrated on getting back to his house.

Mike called him four times and Danny declined them until he finally got up the courage to pick up on the fifth.

"Danny, I saw you in the stands, what the fuck happened, are you okay?"

Danny didn't want to tell him even though Mike probably already knew. "I…missed practice this morning."

"*What?* Why?"

"Slept through my alarm," Danny managed to grind out.

"You—what the fuck, Danny, I'm sorry, I shouldn't have—"

"What, *you* shouldn't—"

"I didn't even think," Mike was saying, and he sounded so panicked that Danny wished he were there to gather Mike into his arms. He wanted to throw himself off a cliff. "I just wanted to see you, I didn't even think it might've been too much and you'd be—"

"Mike," Danny cut him off, an almost horrified laugh bubbling up from his chest. "Mike, it wasn't your fault, babe, this was all me."

"Danny, what the fuck? You *slept through a morning skate*? You seemed fine? Dude, what the fuck is going on with you?"

Danny closed his eyes and leaned against the refrigerator. The metal was cool against his flushed cheek. He had three pills in his hand. He lifted his hand. He swallowed the pills. "I…" *I have a problem.* And that was the first step, right, even while he knew he was waiting for the pleasant, numb tingle that would wash over his skin very shortly. Even while he was waiting to be able to not care that he did. "I don't know, Mike."

"Can you let me—would you tell me? Please? I told you about losing my—" Mike swallowed, suddenly. "Danny, that was really fucking hard for me, can you at least fucking tell me why the fuck you missed a skate? I'm kinda really fucking worried about you, dude."

"I was drunk," Danny said, finally. "I was drunk, and I forgot to set my alarm, and I slept through it."

Mike was very quiet on the other end of the line at first. "Danny…"

"Mike, can you not—can you not say anything else. Just right now."

"Danny—babe—" It was the first time Mike had used the term of endearment that came so easily to Danny, and it cut right through him. "Are you *okay*?"

Danny hadn't taken his head away from the fridge. He thought about all of the things he could say. He was so tired. "No."

"Can I do anything?"

Just love me anyway, Danny thought, but said, "I'm going to be more careful from now on. It's not going to happen again."

"Danny—"

"Mike, I really, really don't want to talk about this now," Danny said, painfully self-conscious about the way the words were thick and a little slurred.

There was a long pause. "Okay. But, Danny—I—"

"What, Mike?"

"I just want you to be okay. Okay?"

The fridge was warming under his sweaty forehead. "I'm going to try to be, Mike."

"Okay," Mike said, but he sounded so uncertain, so unlike himself, that Danny knew he was just going to get fucked up about it as soon as he hung up.

"Mike, I…"

"Yeah?"

I love you, he thought, *I love you, I fucking love you,* but he said, "Don't worry about me, okay?"

"Right," Mike said, "sure, who was worrying," and hung up.

Danny got fucked up about it, but this time, he set his phone alarm.

On the morning of New Year's Eve, Mike wasn't even upset that they had a game on New Year's Day. He was on a plane to Nashville while Danny was on a flight to Minnesota. Tomorrow the Cons were playing in Dallas, so it was unlikely there was going to be any kind of crazy party like there'd been last year. He'd been working so hard at practice and during games, playing solid minutes on the third pairing and had even a few games as a second pairing with Lindy when Graham had been out with a concussion. With all of that, these days, alcohol hit him like a sledgehammer, and he felt like shit in the morning.

Of course, he kind of felt like shit anyway.

He'd been thinking about Danny pretty much constantly, but they hadn't talked about it. In fact, they'd barely talked at all. It wasn't that Mike didn't have a lot of things to say because he sure as fuck did, but he didn't think Danny would listen.

That was the fucked-up thing. He'd gotten used to keeping secrets, even from Bee. But they were the kind of secrets Mike had always kept: dumb shit like hookups he'd regretted, exactly how sad he was on a day-to-day basis, the jealousy he was ashamed of feeling when he thought about her All-Star Games and Rookie of the Year award, the usual. Bigger secrets, like the one he'd still never been able to say out loud.

Even compared to that, this felt bigger and more complicated than he could describe.

For the first time he wanted to tell her. Almost felt like he needed to tell her. It was eating at him, not knowing what to do, not being able to ask anyone for advice. And it wasn't like Bee was really gonna be able to help with that because fuck knew it had taken her an entire year to figure out her shit with Mäkelä, but at least she would probably have like. Listened sympathetically. He'd gotten used to Danny doing that, but he couldn't tell *Danny* how upset the situation was making him.

What the hell did people do when they had feelings? Did talking about it help? Did people actually do that? Or did everyone just walk around like they were going to crawl out of their own skin, all the time?

"Michael," Bee said, her voice low. The plane was always pretty noisy unless it was a red-eye home, but she knew him. She sat with Mäkelä sometimes, but she sat with Mike just as often. "Are you okay?"

He knew he was looking at her funny, but he had no idea what his face looked like. It was just one of those moments he knew he couldn't control whatever was happening there. "I'm having a really weird year."

"It's almost over."

"I can't really see it getting any less weird anytime soon."

Bee glanced around, scoping out the scene. Netty was in the front of the plane noogieing Singer's head while Reed laughed at them, and some of the other nosier Cons weren't paying attention. "Do you want to talk about it, Michael?" she asked, her brown eyes so warm and sincere that he almost gave in and told her right then and there.

"Uhh…maybe…but not, uh, here."

"Whenever you want to, mon chum."

"Thanks, Bee. Really."

She patted him on the knee, and said, again, like a threat, "Whenever you want."

He wasn't fighting as much these days, but it was almost a relief when they were on the ice in Nashville and that rat Kovalenko slashed him in the back of the head and he had an excuse to beat the shit out of someone. His ears were ringing, but he whirled immediately to drop gloves and punch the helmet fucking right off that fucker's head.

It was different fighting guys who weren't Danny. He was furious, but he could focus in a way he couldn't otherwise. Kovalenko wasn't much taller than Mike, although he probably had forty pounds on him. That was nothing. The reach was the same.

They circled each other, Kovalenko trying to psych him out with a few test punches Mike didn't fall for. When he came at him, Mike was ready, fist wrapping itself in Kovalenko's jersey. Because their arms were around the same length, it worked out that he could use the good old push and pull: tugging Kovalenko in and slamming him in the face with his knuckles, pushing him back while he was off-balance. Kovalenko cursed in a language that sounded almost like Russian but wasn't like the Russian Mike had picked up from Netty.

"Shut up, little bitch," Mike said to him, in Russian, which depending on your point of view was either a success or complete failure. Kovalenko snapped another curse Mike couldn't understand and lunged forward to try and grab him around the chest. There was a struggle and somehow, despite the fight strap, Kovalenko managed to get the jersey up over his head. That was fine. Better to lose the jersey and fight on in pads. Mike twisted out of it, and he could hear the crowd yelling, and as Kovalenko came back at him, Mike caught him in the face with a right hook and he dropped down.

The linesmen stepped in to separate them, and Mike shook out his aching right hand and wiped some blood away from his eyes with his left hand and skated toward the penalty box, listening to the crowd screaming, *"ASSHOLE! ASSHOLE!"* at him. It didn't really bother him much anymore, although it had bothered the hell out of him when he was still playing in the amateurs and had had expectations about, like, not being called an asshole by thousands of people in one night. Before he'd accepted that was his role. As he sat in the box and waited for someone to hand him a spare jersey, he caught himself on the Jumbotron and waved at the camera, lifted two of his fingers in a salute.

The crowd seemed to take it as a personal insult and booed loudly.

Ringing in the new year the same way he'd started the old one.

They won the game in a resounding 5–1. Bee's entire line had scored, and Mike had gotten two assists, which seemed like a better omen than getting booed by fucking Nashville.

Even though he'd said he wasn't going to go out, and even though they had a game the next day, he had forgotten Netty's intense love of going over the top for every American holiday. And in fact, generally, that Netty was implacable. "Misha, you can't stay in hotel on New Year's Eve. You *cannot*."

"I could, though," Mike started.

"You cannot," Reed cut him off. "The pathological fun-haver-in-chief has spoken."

“Pathological?” Lindy asked. “You been doing crosswords or something, Reedsy?”

“Maybe,” Reed allowed, grinning. “You know I’m only half-fluent in English, after all; gotta shore up on the big words. But come on, Sato, you’re coming out with everyone.”

So Mike went out. He checked his phone before he did, but Danny hadn’t texted him after their initial brief conversation before the games, and he wasn’t really expecting it. It was just New Year’s Eve, and it didn’t matter if he wasn’t spending it with Danny, didn’t matter if he wasn’t talking to him. Whatever, not like he cared.

By the time he found Bee and Mäkelä in the midst of the crowd at the saloon—what kind of normal bar called itself a saloon heading into 2023?—he was pretty drunk, thanks to Netty shoving shot after shot into his hand. It wasn’t a particularly good kind of drunk, at least not for New Year’s. He wasn’t feeling like he wanted to fight someone, but he did feel like he felt two years after he’d gotten drafted and realized he wasn’t getting out of the minors anytime soon. It was that kind of night, it seemed. But he was out, so he was going to have to make the best of it.

He wound up on a bench in between Bee and Mäkelä, both of their arms slung over his shoulders, which was weird but comfortable. He was listing a little to the side, head tucked against Bee’s shoulder, while she stroked her hand through his hair, which he hadn’t cut recently. It was at the length where it started developing waves. It was the length Danny liked. Her hands were soothing, but it reminded him of Danny doing the same thing only a week before. And Mike was horrified to realize that tears were like, prickling at the corner of his eyes. What the *fuck*.

"Michael?" Bee asked. She was drunk too, but she only had to worry about herself. Mäkelä was a stable mountain of a man and had definitely never been healthy scratched from a game for missing morning skate. "Are you okay?"

He buried his face into her shoulder again and said, "Uhhh. No. Sorry. I mean—yes. No. I'm just—I got a lot of shit going on."

"Hey," Bee said, "let's go outside. Sakari, we'll be right back, mussukka."

Mäkelä just patted her on the knee and said, "I'll be here."

Mike followed her outside. It was chilly in Nashville in the winter, especially this late, but he wasn't feeling the cold. Under Bee's judgmental gaze Mike bummed a cigarette from a guy smoking by the door, because he felt like he was going to need it. He inhaled, deeply, his hands shaking as they walked away from a place where the guy could easily hear them. Bee was rubbing warmth into her hands, and he looked up at her, his heart constricting in his chest.

"Bee, I want you to know I love you, okay? I really do."

"I love you too, Michael," she responded, confusion wrinkling her forehead. But she didn't press him. There was a reason he did. Love her.

He was pacing now, even though he knew objectively it was going to be fine and that if anyone was going to react in a way that wouldn't make him regret it, it was Bee. Even knowing that he felt like he was going to puke and he knew he probably looked just as bad. It wasn't alcohol. Bee looked as calm and composed as she always did, although she was swaying gently in place, waiting for him to go on. In the distance, someone was screaming *Happy New Year* over and over again even though midnight was still a little way off, and they could hear the crackle of homegrown fireworks a few blocks away.

"Michael, you know you can tell me anything, right? I trusted you when that connard was making my life miserable and trying to bully me off of the team. You were the *only* one I trusted, because I knew you wouldn't do anything I wasn't ready for you to do. I knew you *understood.* I hope you can trust me to do that now."

Mike thought about their rookie year, about the way the Cons' second-overall pick had spent most of the season sneaking into Bee's hotel room to trash it, or breaking her equipment whenever he had a chance, whispering all kinds of vile, racist shit in her ear. Bee had taken it stoically, the same way she'd always taken it when a teammate decided he didn't like being shown up by a woman, when he felt he had to put her in his place. Eventually, it had been too much to bear. And she'd trusted Mike first, confided in him, because he knew exactly how it felt, had faced it down exactly the same way. Together, they'd come up with a plan to handle him: with some hidden cameras and the assistance of Mäkelä and Reed, they'd pieced together a slideshow that made some very interesting viewing during a video review day.

And in the end, Hill had been the one shipped out of town, and Bee was still standing and so was Mike.

Bee was still standing, watching him with her warm brown eyes. Mike took another deep breath.

"Okay, so, uh, I'm going to tell you like. Two or three things at once. Just let me finish, okay?"

Bee nodded.

"So first, um, I'm, I'm gay. And uh, second, I'm, uh, I guess I'm like…kind of…seeing someone?"

Whatever response he was expecting, Bee didn't make it. Instead of words she barreled into him, threw her arms around his neck, and almost knocked him off his feet because neither of them had the best balance at that moment. He dropped the cigarette so she wouldn't fucking light her own shirt on fire.

"I'm not done," he managed to mumble into her shoulder, even though her arms were wrapped around him so tightly he could hear his ribs creaking.

"I know, but I'm happy for you, and I wanted to do it."

Mike's eyes were burning and it was definitely the cold. His heart was beating too fast, and he couldn't make it slow. "Happy for me?"

"*Yes,* mon frère, for telling me, but mostly because you deserve someone in your life, and I know whoever it is will be—"

"So, uh, about that…"

Bee put a few inches of space between them, but didn't release him, and he didn't pull away. A shadow ghosted across her face, an immediate frown. "Michael, is this why you've been so upset recently? *Who do I have to punch?*"

"God, Bee, I do love you," he said, and buried his face in her shoulder again. Affectionate and embarrassed. "You don't have to punch anyone."

"Are you sure? I will, if he's hurt your feelings."

"It's not like that," Mike said, his fingers smoothing over the back of her jacket before he disentangled himself. He really wished he had that fucking cigarette. But he'd told her, and the world hadn't ended. His hands were shaking and he folded his arms over his chest, hands tucked in his armpits, to hide it. "It's, uh—please don't fucking laugh at me."

"I would *never*."

"He, uh, plays hockey too, and it's not really my place to—uh. You know. Say anything about him. But yeah, he plays too."

Bee's eyes widened, noticeably, but she did not laugh. "Michael…"

"It's, um. It started in the summer, and he's really, actually." Mike swallowed hard. "He's really fucking great, actually."

She wasn't saying anything and he couldn't look her in the eye, because he didn't want to see what her expression looked like. This was new territory and even though the world hadn't ended yet that didn't mean he wasn't still expecting it to.

"I really—I really—he's great," he repeated, finally, and then it was like once he started talking, the words kept coming and he couldn't stop them. "He's helped me so fucking much, Bee. The drills I had you doing with me? The improvement I've had? Actually getting minutes? That was all him. He was the first person to like—the first person to see my potential. I mean, I know you saw it, but he's the first person to actually try to get it through my thick fucking skull that I could be better—that I *should* be better—"

"So why are you…?" Bee asked, voice careful, almost gentle.

Mike was pacing again. Jesus, he wished he still had that cigarette. "He's—he's got a lot of stuff of his own going on. He, uh, he's in pain all the time, I think, and he drinks like—a lot. He missed a practice and got scratched the other day and he won't—he doesn't—I think he knows it's a problem but he won't *do* anything about it, and I just don't want him to—"

"Hey, Michael," Bee said, and gathered him back up into one of those bear hugs again.

He was not crying, but he was definitely wasted and his eyes were burning and he was overwhelmed with feelings. What kinds of feelings, he didn't even fucking know, but it was like his head was going to explode. Or his chest. Or all of him at once. What the fuck, how did people deal with this all of the time? If he felt like this all of the time he'd probably like, man, he didn't even know. Spend most of it screaming incoherently or something. It wasn't even necessarily in a bad way, even though his brain kept howling, *what the fuck, what the fuck* at him.

"Shit, Bee. I'm a goddamn fucking mess."

"I think you are doing pretty well considering. Better than I was doing at this point with Sakari. At least you've never had to buy an emergency plane ticket like I did."

"I'd do it if I had to," Mike said, and was surprised to find it was true.

"So it's like that, eh?"

"I—yeah. I guess it is, yeah."

"So what are you going to do? About—your man?"

"I don't know. I really don't know. I don't know if

there's anything I can do. But Jesus, I've been keeping this shit inside for years. I haven't *ever* been able to say it. Goddamn, Bee."

"Thank you for trusting me, Michael."

"Mon frère," he said, after a moment.

"'My brother.'"

"I know."

"Toton."

"I *know*." He was smiling now.

"Tabarnak, I think we both need a drink after that."

"Hell yes."

Bee leaned over and, impulsively, kissed him on the cheek. "You'll figure it out, Michael."

"I don't know about that."

"You will. I know you. You will."

She hooked her arm through his and took him back into the bar.

CHAPTER FIVE

January

After the disastrous game and conversation with Mike, Danny really did try to cut back on his drinking. He made it three days without anything at all, although he still had to take the Percs to deal with his fucked-up hip and knee and he felt weird and shaky at the end of it. He managed to get a lot of shit done in those three days. He had an uncomfortable meeting with Coach where Danny had had to trot out all the old lines he always trotted out. Yes, he'd made a mistake, no, he didn't have a problem, no, he didn't think he needed to go to rehab.

The thing was, even if he had been ready to do it, there was no reason to trust that he wouldn't get fucked over somehow by agreeing to go. He'd seen it happen to colleagues of his, guys who had legitimately needed help, wanted help, and promptly found themselves traded or on waivers afterward. It wouldn't have been such a big fucking deal to Danny, at least years ago, but when he only had two years left on a league-minimum contract, he couldn't risk *anything*. So he'd lied his fucking ass off, hated himself while he was doing it, and got the fuck out of there as soon as possible.

"You've been doing a good job with the younger guys," Coach had said. "Girard especially really looks up to you, and he listens to you in a way he doesn't listen to our coaching staff. And that's another reason I didn't scratch you for more than one game. But you need to get your shit together, ASAP. You hear me, Garcia?"

"Yes, Coach."

It was hard not to drink, though, on a hockey team where the primary bonding activities consisted of skating and drinking, and they were coming up on New Year's Eve. It was hard not to drink whenever Danny thought about Mike, and how Mike probably had no idea why the fuck Danny wasn't talking to him as often as he usually did, and the guilt was both overwhelming and self-feeding. The worse he felt the more he avoided him, which made him feel worse, which made him want to drink.

hey, Mike texted him before they were both due to head out onto the ice, call me at midnight?

I'll be an hour behind you, but I can try.

ok.

I'm sorry. It's been busy here.

ok.

They beat Minnesota, 6–3, and Danny let Gears and Landry drag him out. Things with Landry had been awkward since the on-ice incident, but at least he appeared to be trying to mend fences. He hadn't said anything and he'd sat next to Danny on the bus to and from the hotel, steadfastly playing a phone game and not saying anything. In practice, he'd gone back to chirping Danny the way he'd always done, no malice in it, just a faint hesitation.

So Danny went, and Danny got drunk, even though he hadn't really meant to. It was almost a relief, the warmth that it brought him, the comfort of it. He checked his phone. It was almost eleven o'clock, which meant that it was almost midnight in Nashville.

Danny said, "Gears, save my seat," and went outside.

It was freezing, but not cold enough to kill his phone, so he found a quiet corner of the street to make the call.

Mike picked up on the third ring, although it was hard to hear him over the background noise. "Hey!" he said, voice warm and slurred, and Danny thought about the night he'd called wasted with his fucked-up mouth and all of the things he told Danny he'd let him do and felt a sharp pang of wanting. He could hear Mike mumbling something away from the speaker, the words lost in the background din, the sounds of people yelling wordlessly.

Danny waited, patiently, slumped a little against the wall.

"Hey," Mike said, after a minute. "Hey, Danny. *Danny.* Hi."

"Hey, babe," Danny said, more easily than he felt. "Happy New Year."

"Happy—Jesus, I miss you."

"I—Mike…"

"What? Too honest?"

"No, I… I miss you too."

"So come on, Danny, why haven't you *called* me?" Mike sounded so plaintive and so goddamn young that Danny fucking hated himself.

"I've been—"

"Busy. Yeah. I know."

"No. Ashamed. I've been ashamed."

"Babe…" Maybe it was the alcohol, but Mike's low, rough voice was so goddamn warm Danny could almost feel it on his skin, like he'd felt Mike's fingers for days after he'd landed back in Pittsburgh. "You don't gotta be, okay? Not with me. I was worried, I'm still worried, but like—don't be ashamed, I, you're, I fucking…" Danny waited, unsure where he was going with this, but evidently whatever it'd been, he couldn't get there.

Mike laughed, suddenly, and then said, resigned, "Too many confessions for one night, dude, and *I'm* not drunk enough."

"How do you mean?"

"New year, new me, right? So I told Bee about me. I said it, out loud, Danny, I actually said it."

"Yeah?"

"She was, she was…it was good. I still can't fucking believe I did it, but she—nothing's changed. I mean, it's changed. But not in a bad way. But the point I'm tryna make, the *point*, is, Danny, Danny, you don't have to be embarrassed around me, okay? Jesus. All right. While I'm sharing my fucking *feelings* tonight, fuck. Okay, here goes: I really like you. Like, I really, *really* like you. Like I haven't hated you for…months and months."

"Mike—"

"Yeah, I know, I'll still fuckin' smash your face in if you make fun of me for it, okay?"

"God, Mike. You're something else."

"One of a fuckin' kind, right?"

Danny was smiling, despite himself, in the dark. Because it was true. Because he really was, and because Danny, like a fool, was head over heels for him. "You are. Jesus, Mike. Wish we could've been in the same place for this. So I could kiss you at midnight."

"Don't worry," Mike said, voice intense with the kind of dumb, expansive bravado that had drawn Danny to him in the first place. "I'll make it up to you next time I see you."

"Yeah?"

"Yeah, I fucking promise. Next time I'll fuck you until *you* cry, how's that sound?"

"It—it sounds good. Really good." Danny let his head fall back against the wall. Hit it with a *thunk*. He felt strange: he knew exactly how big a step it had been for Mike to do this, to say these things, to tell Morin, but he felt the more Mike grew into his own skin, the more comfortable he got on the ice, the less he'd need Danny. Things would come to an end soon, and that was the way it should be, even if it was going to hurt. "You had a big night, babe."

"It's weird," Mike was saying, and Danny could almost see the dopey grin he probably had on his face, "It was all good shit, mostly, but I kind of feel like I want to just fucking like—scream, you know? How the fuck do people process all of this shit like all the time?"

I drink, Danny thought, but what he said was, "You could probably scream if you wanted to. It's New Year's, no one would care."

"Hah, that's all I fucking need, getting arrested for, like, causing a public disturbance or something—oh, hey, that's the New Year, I think. Hey. I *miss* you. I wish you were fucking here, Danny. I fucking do."

I love you, Danny thought, but what he said was, "Wish I was there too, kid. Hey, Happy New Year. Go have fun with your friends, all right? I'll catch up with you tomorrow."

"Danny…"

"Yeah?"

"Danny, take it easy tonight, okay? I'll see you."

He wanted to say it. He really wanted to say it. "G'night, Mike."

He stood out there staring at his phone, the image he had saved as Mike's contact photo. He'd taken it in Philly. It was Mike, shirtless in bed, muscles straining as he tried to wriggle away, his hands over his face like he was trying to ward off the camera. He was laughing. You couldn't see his eyes, just his mouth, parted, grinning. Danny had been sitting on his hips, pinning him down. You couldn't see that, either. The picture faded and the phone locked.

Danny took a deep breath and went back into the bar.

"Yo, Garcia," Landry said, waving him over and sliding a spare beer over to him, "where were you?"

"Phone," Danny said, sliding back into the seat he'd vacated and wrapping his hand around the cold glass.

"Who was it, your *boyfriend*?"

It was a mocking chirp, because of course it was. But Danny thought about Mike. His excited, drunken rambling. *I said it out loud, Danny.* Thought about the way Mike looked waking up in the morning next to him, thought about a lot of shit in that brief second. *Hey, I* miss *you.*

"Yeah, it was," he said, and drank.

"You're—you're kidding."

Danny looked at him with that flat, dead-eyed look that made people squirm, and said nothing.

Landry stared back. He opened and closed his mouth. He was having a kind of face journey, from disbelief to horror to something Danny couldn't entirely categorize. "You're *not* kidding."

"No."

"Oh," Landry said, and looked down at his drink. They sat there in silence for a couple of uncomfortable seconds. Danny took another drink while Landry just looked at his hands. This could go any number of ways and Danny wasn't sure how it *was* going to go. "Your—boyfriend. Okay. Right. So, uh…how's he doing, then?"

"Drunk."

Landry made a noise that was more of a snort than a laugh, exhaled sharply, and said, "I think he's got the right idea. 'Nother round, old man? I could fucking use one."

"Why not? Happy fuckin' New Year, Lands."

All things said, it could have gone worse.

New year, new me. New year, new me. New year—

Mike was busy in January, between drills and games and travel. He didn't mind. It was good to be busy, and things with Danny seemed to be mostly back to normal in that he was his usual self. And even if that didn't exactly make Mike feel great about things, at least they were talking.

The team was flying out to Los Angeles that night,

so he'd packed already. And Bee was going to be playing in the All-Star game again, so Mike had started making plans to go watch it in Vegas and thinking about asking Danny to come out too, because no one had games that weekend.

He was checking out hotels when his mom called, which was unusual. They didn't talk often because no one in the family was good at talking about feelings. It had probably been like that since they'd immigrated to California, like, five generations ago, and it had only gotten worse since as each generation of Sato kids had assimilated further and further and somehow managed to disappoint their parents in new and exciting ways. When he did speak to them it was mostly quick and to the point, coordinating visits, or like, telling them about injuries and stuff. He couldn't remember the last time they'd called just to talk. So when the phone rang, he felt…nervous.

"Mom?"

"Hello, Michael."

"Um—hey, Mom…uh. What's up? How are you?"

"We're fine, I was calling to see whether you knew where we should sit at your hockey game tomorrow."

"You—what?" His parents hadn't come to a game in as long as he could remember. Oh, they'd spent the money on him, no problem. But even in mites, they'd dumped him on teammate carpools, grudgingly driven him to games when they hadn't been able to do that, and completely gave up once he moved fifteen hours away to a billet and they'd seen the way he'd had to learn to play. There was a reason he'd gone through the WHL import draft and tried to get as far away from home as possible. "Why?"

“We wanted to see a game,” she said, like he was an idiot. “And you’re playing in Los Angeles, so we thought we’d come.”

Talking to his mom usually made him feel like an idiot, not through any fault of her own, but because his mom was a genius, extremely terrifying, and usually about four steps ahead of him in any given conversation. It just highlighted how dumb Mike was in general, being around his family.

“But you’ve…never really *wanted* to see me play before. Uh…why now?”

“Don’t be ridiculous. That’s not the case at all.”

“But Mom, I think you came to like. Three juniors games. One Grizzlies game? You guys don’t even like sports.”

“Michael,” Sylvia Sato said patiently. “We’re not sports people, that’s true. But we didn’t avoid coming to your games because we were bored.”

“So…why not?”

“Two reasons: first, we didn’t think you’d be playing this long, so there was no point in investing the effort to learn the game.”

“Jesus, Mom.”

“Second, we didn’t think you were playing with your full heart, and we didn’t want to encourage that kind of behavior. But it seems that something has changed this year, and we’d like to support you.”

“*What the fuck*, Mom?”

“Michael, don’t curse at me.”

“You thought I wasn’t—trying?”

“It didn’t appear that way, Michael. We always knew you were capable of more. Both your father and I are pleased you’re finally showing it.”

"Sit wherever you fucking want to," Mike said, and hung up.

He wished he had time to go to the gym, or that Danny was here, because he really felt like getting punched in the face. It was the better alternative to what he felt now by at least a mile. He walked back and forth in the apartment and thought about calling Danny, except Danny was probably on a plane right now too. He thought about picking a fight with the biggest fucking guy on the ice his first shift in Los Angeles. He thought about the way it had been years of this, but they were still his parents and he still loved them so much. He thought about a lot of things.

He thought about telling Bee the shit he'd been carrying in his chest for years and how much better he'd felt after it. Maybe there was something to be said for actually telling people shit?

He couldn't call his mom back, though. She would eviscerate him politely, and he would deserve it.

Instead, he flipped open his phone and typed, Mom, I'm sorry I cursed at you. I was ALWAYS playing with everything I had. I just didn't know I could do better. Hockey's my life. It's all I ever wanted to do. I know I'm not successful like Natalie or Bryan or Samantha, but I'm trying and I always have been.

As he got onto the bus to go to the airport, his phone vibrated.

Michael, I'm sorry that I misinterpreted things. Your father and I haven't always understood your path, but we'll try to be better in the future. I'm looking forward to watching you play tonight.

Mike stared at the phone for a long time and wondered, not for the first time, how the *fuck* people did this shit every day. It didn't fix anything, but it was something. Maybe.

"You okay, buddy?" Singer asked, as he made his way down the aisle to where Reed was waiting in the back.

"Yeah," Mike said, and caught himself smiling, like a fucking weirdo. "I'm actually pretty good."

Singer pressed his knuckles against Mike's skull and dug them in, the briefest of seconds. "That's what I like to hear."

"Ugh," Mike said, texted Danny, you'd be proud of me I think, then decided he was going to take a nap because being a mature fucking adult was exhausting and passed out in self-defense.

Mike wasn't actually sure how he was going to handle playing a game, knowing his parents would be out in the crowd. Everyone else was used to it: some of the guys on the team had parents whose full-time jobs seemed to be coming to games. Everyone else's parents at least came to the ones within driving distance.

They'd come to see him, only the third time they'd ever made the trip, when he was playing on the Harriers. It had been over winter break. Neither Dad, at high school, nor Mom, at college, had work the next day, so they'd flown up to Portland for a home game. Mike had been sixteen. He'd gotten his knuckle tattoos the year before and Mom had looked like she was going to pass out when she noticed them. He'd gotten more tattoos that year but he'd hidden them. That had worked, but the game itself was a complete disaster.

He'd gotten into a fight with a kid who'd laid a dirty hit on the Harriers' captain, gotten his nose broken, KO'd the guy he'd been fighting, and gotten a game misconduct. His parents had still been in the stands when he limped his way into the dressing room.

Mom and Dad had just looked at him afterward, the kind of look that said, *we're so disappointed in you*, and Mom had said, "We didn't let you come to Portland for this," and Mike hadn't known if she'd meant the fighting, or the tattoos, or the shit he was doing late at night when his billet parents were asleep, which hopefully she didn't know about.

Mike had tried to explain to them that you couldn't just do that to the captain, that his job was to make sure the other team knew that even if the refs missed the call, but it was like when Mom tried to explain physics to him. Words were being spoken, but they meant nothing.

They hadn't come to another after that.

"You're going to be fine, Michael," Bee said, after the pregame soccer match.

He only half heard her. "I can't fight. I really can't fight today."

"You never *have* to fight."

"I mean—sometimes I do. I just—Jesus, Bee, if I fight today, they're never going to come to a game again."

"Well, don't fight, Michael. You're not playing the same kind of game you were then; you don't have to."

"I know, I'm just…fuckin' worried, bud."

"I promise you; you'll be fine. And if someone has to fight, I'll do it for you."

"You would?"

"Anything for you, mon chum."

Mike didn't know what to say, so he hugged her, impulsively, something he didn't often do. Her initial surprise gave way almost immediately to hugging him back. It was just nice. But he felt that displacement, off-balance. He had always been tense, turned inward, and now he was like…well, there was like a lot of fucking character growth going on this year, is all he was saying, and he had some growing pains to work out.

Once he was actually out on the ice, it was easier. His parents might have been in the stands, but Bee was on the ice with him and Danny was probably watching at home. He could do it. Mike was playing with Lindy on the second pair that night, which his parents wouldn't understand, but which made it easier to play a more technical game. He was up against a better caliber of player, and he had to watch it.

These days, he spent a lot of his time on the ice just moving the puck. But moving it productively. Watching his old games, it was painful how fucking sloppy he'd been. Turnovers and icing all over the place. All of the times he'd panicked and just yeeted the puck over the glass. Constant drilling in skating and puck handling had paid off, though, and he usually either got the passes directly to the forwards, or close enough that they could keep it moving out of the neutral zone. Sometimes he'd join the rush and pinch, but Mike still felt nervous about that, like he knew he had the capability to play more offensively, but he hadn't quite gotten the confidence to do it yet.

His parents were watching.

They wouldn't know the difference, but he would.

The Blades played decent hockey, clean, for the most

part. He didn't fight but he was playing his goddamn ass off. By the end of the second period he was sweating heavily, his legs a little shaky. They were tied 2–2; Singer and Netty had scored, and the bench was the usual chaos of a close game where there was still all the time in the world to lose it.

Mike looked up and saw himself on the Jumbotron, chewing on his mouthguard. He'd been scowling before realizing he was on camera, but when he did, he popped it back in and mouthed, *hi, Mom*, and waved. There was a smattering of laughter from the stands, and Mike felt fucking weird again. He was used to getting booed; he wasn't used to that.

And then in the third period, with two minutes left in the game and the score still tied, it happened.

Netty took a stupid penalty and skated, spitting, to the box. Coach had been trying Mike out on PK more often, so he was on the ice when the Blades pulled their goalie to try to take advantage of the situation. He kind of felt like he was going to puke, because if he fucked this up, he was going to feel really fucking responsible for the loss.

Mike didn't mind getting knocked around, and he was certainly getting knocked around by the Blades' forwards as he tried to block them from scoring chances. It didn't quite work and this was one of those times he wished he had anything close to Danny's size. Mäkelä excelled in those chaotic battles, though, his body twisting and flopping as he grabbed for the puck and sent it back into play, right to Mike, who had left the scrum to Lindy and was wide open.

He took a quick assessment. Sally and Andy were covered and Lindy was too close to the net. With a burst of speed, Mike rushed the puck forward. It took the Blades a second to realize what had happened, but by then it was too late; Mike was already over the red line, brain screaming, *careful with your skates, careful with your fucking skates.*

He had three options. He could pass to Sally, still behind him, and let him handle it. He could let one of the Blades' forwards catch up with him, which was going to happen if he didn't make up his mind goddamn soon, because they were probably faster than him. Or he could do something he never would have been able to do last year because he wouldn't have even had the puck here last year.

Mike pulled the stick back to his shoulder, swung it down.

The slapshot was a stupid showy move, because the windup needed took forever and you didn't usually have that time; he almost never made them, never had. He was never going to be able to get the kind of power that a guy who was six and a half feet tall could manage, but Mike was still surprisingly strong, and sometimes, when no one was watching, he'd just line 'em up in practice and let them fly. It was muscle memory at this point, slapping the ice behind the puck, bending the stick as it hit and rolling his wrists.

He almost didn't realize it had actually gone into the empty net until he heard the goal horn and Sally and Lindy had practically boarded him cellying and Bee was screaming loud enough from the bench that he could hear her over the racket.

Mike sat out the rest of the game, his heart thumping in his chest, knocking against his ribs. He downed an entire bottle of water but still felt like he was maybe having a heart attack. It wasn't the kind of game that actually mattered, or at least it wouldn't have mattered to anyone else, but he'd won it in one of the showiest fuckin' ways possible, and he felt, like, whatever else happened, at least he'd shown his parents what he was capable of doing.

Really, what he wanted to do was talk to Danny, see what he thought about the risk Mike had taken, what he could have improved. He wouldn't be able to do that until later. He still had to do the postgame, shower, and see his parents before they went back to Gardena.

Mike was used to his team being good about shit, but he certainly wasn't fucking used to dudes on the other team telling him it had been a good shot or being complimentary about anything, really, but they were doing it, as they all filed off of the ice. Even if it was grudging, he almost felt a little drunk. He mumbled his way through the postgame interviews and said something like, *well, you're always just trying to get the puck in the net*, because like...really that explained everything.

His parents were waiting outside of the visitors' dressing room, and Mike's chest clenched again, because they were both wearing his jersey. Number 13. He'd bought them after it was clear that he wasn't getting traded again, but he hadn't actually ever expected Mom and Dad to wear them. It looked fucking weird, actually, because Mom was always wearing severe buttoned shirts and blazers, and Dad always looked like he'd rolled off the set of *Mr. Rogers*, and it *felt* weird. It was good, but uncomfortable, like they were making fun of him somehow.

Mike took a deep breath and went to hug both of

them, arms slung over both of their shoulders briefly. It was always awkward; both of them were about four inches shorter than he was, and slim. He sometimes felt like if he showed them physical affection he'd accidentally crush them, or they would accidentally eviscerate him with their sharp bony edges.

"You guys didn't have to come" was the first thing he could think of to say.

"We're glad we did," Dad said. "That was quite a goal, Michael."

"Uhh…thanks… I mean, I don't usually manage stuff like that, but it was cool you could see it."

"Do you have to chew on your mouthguard that way?" Mom asked. "I worry about your teeth…"

Mike thought about the fight last year when he'd knocked out Danny's front tooth and said, "You don't have to. I don't get hit in the face that much anymore."

Mom looked pained when he said that, and for a moment he could almost convince himself it was because she was worried about him and not because she thought less of him for fighting. "I'm glad to hear that, Michael."

He showed them around the locker room, giving them a brief rundown of what he had to do to get ready for the games, what he had to do after them, and introducing them to anyone from the team who still remained. No one embarrassed him that much, all of the guys were mostly just thrilled to be able to tell his parents how much he'd improved and how they picked a good day to attend, but Netty noogied him in the head and said, "I thought Misha emerge fully formed and angry," grinning as he did it, and Mom looked like she might murder him.

Bee, on the other hand, hugged Mom and then Dad warmly, so warmly that both of them looked a little surprised. “Michael is one of my favorite people,” she told both of them, laying on the Quebecois charm, “mon frère d’armes, if you will. It’s an honor to meet both of you, madame, monsieur.”

Both of his parents looked at each other, at Mike, and at Bee again. “It’s an honor to meet you too, Beatrice—”

“Bee, please—”

All in all, the whole thing could have gone worse. Mom and Dad didn’t stay that long, because they were old and he had a curfew to make, but when he walked them out to Figueroa Street, both of them hugged him again.

“I’m glad we could meet your friends,” Dad said, after he pulled away. “They seem like a good team.”

“I, uh, I’m really happy to be playing here,” Mike mumbled. It was one thing to talk about feelings with Danny but another thing entirely to do it in front of his parents. The whole night felt surreal, like a dream. Any minute he’d wake up in the penalty box and discover he’d taken a nasty hit to the head, in like, 2018 or something, and everything that had happened to him since then was some kind of brain damage.

He watched them walk away until they vanished in the crowd.

On the way back to the hotel, he texted Danny.

hey, wyd?

Danny didn’t answer, and Mike frowned at his phone. It was only eight thirty in Pittsburgh, and the Hornets weren’t playing. He hated fucking worrying, he hated knowing what Danny was probably doing, and he hated not being there to distract him. It was the only sour note on the rest of the night.

As he was getting into the cold hotel bed, his phone beeped; Danny was FaceTiming him.

When he answered, Mike searched his face to see if he was drunk, but as usual he couldn't tell. Danny looked the way he always did: tired and stupid handsome and Mike's mouth felt a little dry when he said, "Hey."

Danny smiled, slow and wide, and said, "That was a beautiful fuckin' goal, babe."

Mike dug his teeth into his lower lip, thought about all of the things he wanted to say, and settling for something safe, drawled, "Yeah? How're you gonna congratulate me?" And he focused on the way Danny's eyes went dark and intent and tried to put the rest of it out of his head.

Phone sex, it turned out, was easier than talking about feelings. But it still felt bad, avoiding the things he wanted to say. Who fucking knew?

Danny's January ground by interminably. He was exhausted and his body was giving out on him, both because he had an iron grip on what he was drinking and when he was drinking it and that in itself was wearying, but also because he was working with the rookies to get them into playoff shape, and he was still playing his usual minutes and taking his usual abuse on the ice.

The biggest change had been Landry's attitude. The kid hadn't toned down his asshole routine when it came to opposing players, but Danny had been gratified to note that any chirps were based on individual characteristics and not the kind of language that had almost brought them to blows. Landry hadn't asked about Mike again, but he hadn't said anything to anyone else either. Danny would take it. If that's what it took to teach the kid a fucking lesson, it was worth the risk of telling someone who couldn't handle it.

A few weeks in, he called his parents on his off day, before he went to the gym. It was anticlimactic in a way, because he'd built it up so much in his head. But one morning he just knew that he'd have to do it. He'd woken up with a weird buzzing under his skin, like the physical personification of his knowledge that everything was going to go to shit this year. Like the sense of impending doom he always felt had worked its way to the surface, finally.

He did it early in the morning, before he would be too tired and before he could justify drinking, before they would be exhausted from a day at the diner. Ma picked up almost immediately, and she cried throughout the whole conversation, while he told her he was fine, tried to reassure her that he really *was* fine, mentioned he was seeing someone, a really nice guy actually, they'd like him a lot. That his health was fine. He actually lost count the number of times he said, *I'm fine, Ma, I'm fine*, knowing Pa was listening in the background, not saying anything, just absorbing Danny's voice.

"*Lo siento*, Mama," Danny said, over and over again, but there were only so many times you could say *I'm sorry* before that didn't mean anything either. They certainly knew that, but they loved him, so they let him do it anyway.

"Don't be a stranger this time, *mijo*," Pa said, finally.

"I won't," Danny lied.

When they were satisfied, or at least, when they

stopped asking him questions like lawyers with a recalcitrant witness, he finally hung up. He really missed them. He was really fucked up; he had really fucked things up. He stood there for a minute, shaking, and decided that he was going to bend his morning rule because he sure as fuck deserved one after that. So Danny got drunk, and then he went to the gym.

Mike texted while he was between sets, im gonna be at the allstar game for bee will you come? make it worth yr while. After a second, he added an eggplant emoji.

Michael, what the fuck?

uh, the eggplant is a dick, dude, bc im gonna to give you the eggplant slash dick

One, how old do you think I AM, and two, is that really fucking necessary?

old as balls, and yes

…

lmao just fuckin with you dude. but seriously. will you?

I don't know, Mike, it's a long weekend and we're playing that Monday.

cmon i miss you AND i owe you. pleeeease danny im ASKING and that's yr thing right?

Danny stared at his phone. He was sweating from the workout, from the fact that he was still kind of trashed, and he'd never tried combining the two before. He was starting the *checking off new lows* list, he supposed, and it felt like giving up. Mike sure as fucking hell deserved better than that, but even though Danny knew that, knew it in his bones, he also just really missed Mike. He was only human, and he had no self-control.

Okay, I'll come.

😌

You want me to make the arrangements or?

already reserved a room. you can stay with me, i'll send you the info

Oh yeah?

uhhh duh, dude. ok i gotta get to morning skate. if you bitch out on me ill FIND you and u'll be sorry

Jesus, Mike.

😉

He booked tickets to Vegas shortly after the text messages with Mike, and up until the day he was actually boarding the plane, Danny thought about skipping out. Some of the other Hornets would be there. Lévesque was a perennial fixture, unless he was injured, and it was going to be strange, balancing hanging out with the guys and trying to see Mike in secret.

At least they'd be in the same position, since Mike was there for Bee.

They were mostly going to have to do their own things and bow out early. That was going to be easier said than done, because the All-Star Game was usually a shitshow anyway, let alone in Vegas, a city that catered to everyone's worst impulses. Danny, who was only a man and not a particularly strong man, included himself in that. He was going to have to just find Mike early, hope they could slip away, and leave it at that.

He and Lévesque were on cordial enough terms these days, but Danny didn't feel the need to cheer him on or anything. The dude certainly had accomplished enough without Danny's encouragement before they'd played together and would probably accomplish even more after Danny had been forced into retirement. So while he sat in the box with Gears and Landry and Artyomov, he was mostly looking out at the crowd in the futile thought that maybe, somehow, he'd be able to pick Mike's face out of thousands of people.

Part of him almost felt like he could do it, like Mike was some kind of magnetic north, like his body would just orient itself toward him wherever he happened to be.

He made it through the skills competition day without getting too drunk. Morin cleaned up, same as she had last year, and he thought again that it must be nice to be able to have a body that responded the way you needed it to. It was an uncharitable thought, but Danny felt scourged by that raw combination of melancholy and need by the time Mike texted him, can u get away?

Yes. Please.

see you at the hotel. theres a key at the front desk for u but...idk if you looked, i picked a really nice place for you

Danny's chest was doing the thing where it constricted until it ached. You didn't have to, Mike.

i wanted to you fuckin idiot. see you in 20ish? make sure you get the key or i think i gotta come down for you

That was the other strange thing about Vegas. Things that were ostensibly next to each other still took longer than they seemed like they should to reach. He walked for about fifteen minutes, his small backpack of shit slung over his shoulder, to the hotel Mike had picked. As soon as he saw it, combined with the fact that he'd need a key to even get in the elevator, Danny immediately realized that it was a *gesture*.

It was one of those places that Danny knew would have you picked up from the airport, one of those places he never stayed on principle because it just didn't seem worth it. Checking in might've embarrassed him, once upon a time when he was a rookie and hated the way people looked at him sometimes. Now he didn't even give a fuck, beyond the faint sense of unease of using his own name. You had to trust the discretion of places like this, and he didn't like doing that.

It was worth it, though, when he finally got out of the damn elevator and into the ridiculous fucking room Mike had reserved. The first thing he saw were Mike's beat-up Doc Martens tossed carelessly next to the door, because Mike always took his shoes off inside, even in hotel rooms. It was a reminder how out of place both of them were in such a fancy fucking place. He looked up. The room was a two-story loft suite, and it was completely ridiculous. Everything was modern and shiny and opulent in a way that didn't feel homey at all. Even after all of these years he'd never really gotten used to staying in these kinds of places.

Mike had been lying on the couch, still wearing his Morin jersey and skinny jeans, his legs hooked over the armrest. His feet, also tattooed, were bare, and Danny thought about the last time, in Philly, when he'd run his finger down the side of them and told Mike, *no, you have to stay still*, when his whole body had jerked in response. Mike was reading a book, which was also out of place, but when the door opened he rolled off of the couch and to his feet, grinning this hopeful, awkward smile. Danny had never been so glad to see anyone probably in his entire life.

"You *really* didn't have to do this."

Mike ran his hand over his head, which was buzzed back down to the skull again. "Yeah, but I wanted to." He was still smiling, lopsided and a little goofy. It was a side of him Danny would never have expected when they'd first met, but he was starting to see more and more often, and it killed him a little. "C'mon, Danny, we never get to even see each other, and I thought—I don't know, I thought it would be fun. The view's killer, anyway, and we can get room service."

"Hey," Danny said, "come here."

It said something that Mike didn't even hesitate anymore. He crossed the room and fit into Danny's arms like it was the easiest thing in the world, like he'd been waiting for it. Went up on his tiptoes for the kiss, slow and thorough, like he wanted to reacquaint himself with Danny's mouth, his hands soft at the sides of Danny's face. Danny relaxed into it until Mike, the little shit, bit him on the lower lip, sudden and sharp, and Danny's hand slid up, on reflex, to wrap itself around Mike's throat.

Mike tested his grip, twisting his head a little. There wasn't much give, and his voice was strained when he said, "You know, I like this, but I wanna—I told you I wanted to make *you* cry this time."

Danny, who could feel Mike's throat moving against his palm when he talked, bit his lip and didn't answer. Mike's hand came up and his thumb stroked along the outside of Danny's hand, still gripping his throat, and Danny shivered. He knew what Mike wanted.

He was thirty-five years old and he liked sex. He had, without bragging, had a respectable amount of it with both men and women during his lifetime, he knew what he liked, and he wasn't ashamed of that. He maybe had some wires crossed when it came to pain, but that wasn't anything too unusual given his profession. But Danny was used to keeping control of the situation. Even the first night Mike had fucked him, he'd had the situation in hand. The need for control… sure, it was hot, and it had ancillary uses, like nudging Mike in the right direction and getting him to vocalize things he needed.

But when it came down to it, at the heart of things, Danny was fucking terrified of not having it, because of what that might mean and what he might reveal. Someone like Mike, someone brave and open and giving, just let everything go like it was easy, and it was fucking heady to be on the other end of it. Danny didn't have that capability.

Or he hadn't had that capability. He didn't know if he could—

"Mike…"

Mike, with Danny's hand still bruising his throat, smiled. His voice was quiet, rough, like he was sharing a secret, even though they were alone in the room. "I want this. I'm asking for it. Will you?"

Sometimes, with Mike, it was easy to let things happen, easy to be swept up by the fact that Danny loved him and would give him anything he wanted. But this would be a conscious choice or even, more accurately, a struggle. Mike was watching him, and his expression was so… Danny could feel something in his chest break under it.

"All right," he said, and his mouth was desert dry. He let go of Mike's throat. "I'm at your mercy."

"Who said anything about mercy, dude?" Mike was grinning at him in a way that made Danny's skin go hot. "C'mon, Danny, strip 'em."

It took him a minute to process the order—Jesus, Mike really had meant it—but he did it. Unzipped the hoodie first, pulled off his sweater, started to undo his belt. Mike stared at him the whole time, a hungry look that made it easier, somehow.

"Jesus, Danny, you are so—*fucking*—hot—"

He was naked, now, and Mike was still fully clothed. Danny felt off-kilter, uncomfortable with the unfamiliar power imbalance, and the fact that the windows along the far wall of the room were huge and completely uncovered, even if they were on the twenty-ninth floor. But his dick, apparently, was into it. Mike didn't touch it, though, just stepped forward and traced his hand over Danny's chest, down his torso, his abdomen.

"I think about you naked like all the fucking time," Mike said, almost like he didn't realize he was saying it, and Danny, whose natural inclination was to make a cutting remark, couldn't, frozen under Mike's regard, his admiration. "And like—how strong you are, how you could do whatever you wanted to me but you—you're letting me—"

"Mike—"

"Hey," Mike said, that shit-eating grin on his face again, "why don't we go over to the window, huh?"

Danny dug his teeth into his lower lip, but he went over to the window, and Mike followed him and said, "Okay, but you can't touch me until I let you, and you can't come until I tell you."

"Mike..."

"Sucks when it's you, huh? Don't like the tables turned?"

"I—I don't usually—"

"I know you don't, babe, but it's—I'll make it good for you. I promise. Do you trust me?"

He thought about it, barely a second, before he knew. "I—I do." The problem was that he didn't entirely trust himself.

It turned out that Mike was a little demon who'd been taking notes. Danny, standing in front of the window, felt horribly, awfully exposed as Mike got down on his knees in front of him, stared up at him almost reverently. And then he was biting his lip when Mike took Danny's dick in his hand and stroked it, palm rough and dry. Even fully clothed he looked almost pornographic, the way his lips were parted, his face flushed. Danny could *see* just in his eyes how much he wanted this, and it was overwhelming.

He made a noise when Mike went down on him, the wet heat of his mouth, the way his hands smoothed themselves over Danny's thighs, tracing the lines of muscle. He could feel the give at the back of Mike's mouth, tight around him. He fought the urge to thrust forward, because he knew Mike wanted him to stay still, but it was almost too much. Danny closed his eyes, trying to regain control, and Mike pulled away. "Nuh-uh, dude. Keep 'em open."

Danny didn't know where to look. Looking down at Mike was overwhelming, Mike's hands and mouth were overwhelming, but it was somehow worse to look straight ahead at the lights of Vegas sparkling below them. It didn't help that Mike was fucking teasing him, alternating between sucking him off enthusiastically and exploring the depths of Danny's self-control with sly fingers on the sensitive skin of his inner thighs, his balls, just barely skirting the rim of his ass. He dug his teeth into his lower lip and bit down another groan, his legs shaking.

It had been almost a month since Danny had gotten off anywhere except his own hand, and Mike was taking full advantage. He would bring Danny right up to the edge before pulling back and lurching to his feet to kiss him sloppily, enthusiastically, his mouth a little salty. It felt like it went on forever. Danny was losing track of time. He could feel everything: the warmth of Mike's lips, the way Mike's jersey and jeans felt rubbing against his overheated skin. When he looked down, he'd left a damp streak across Mike's torso, and he realized how hard he was breathing, how ragged, how the sweat was beading his temples.

"Mike—"

"I'm not done with you. Stay—stay right there. Stay still."

Danny had a good idea of where this was going when Mike knelt behind him, but he still wasn't exactly prepared for the way it felt, how difficult it was to stay on his feet when Mike's tongue was torturing him, when he was already trembling on the edge of losing control.

Mike stopped. "Hey," he said, his voice scratchy and rough. He sounded so fucking *smug* that Danny wanted to smack him in the face. But they weren't doing that today. "I told you that you can't come yet."

"I—I know, I'm fucking—"

Mike didn't answer, just went back to eating him out, torturously slow and methodical, and Danny lost both language and the little semblance of self-control he had. He didn't even want to think about what he would have looked like if someone was looking in the window. A gasping, moaning mess of a man, barely on his feet, his hands flickering at his sides because he had to *move* but didn't know what to do with them, his head thrown back. Finally, Mike let up to take a breath, and Danny's legs folded in on themselves, and before he could do anything about it, he found himself crumpled on the floor.

"Damn," Mike said, crawling into his lap and pressing wet, biting kisses into Danny's neck. "Danny, *Jesus*."

Danny was flushed red with painful arousal and embarrassment at the way his hips canted up into it, chasing the friction of Mike's jeans against his overheated skin. At the way Mike pushed him back down to prevent it. At the way his entire body was trembling and desperate even as he tried to rein himself back under control.

He reached for Mike, who slapped his hand away. "I told you, you can't touch me until I let you."

Danny didn't say anything, couldn't bring himself to say *please*, even though he wanted it so fucking badly. It was torture, how exposed and raw he felt, with Mike in his lap still fully clothed. "You're a fucking terror." His voice was thin and strained, and he was kind of shocked by how messed up it sounded.

"Learned from the best, dude. Hey, let's take this upstairs, huh?"

Mike slid out of his lap, and when Danny stood to make the long, naked walk, slapped him on the ass. Danny whirled around, on instinct, but caught himself, fists clenched. Mike smiled, slow and hot and full of promise, and said, "That's it, babe," and some icy thing in Danny's chest broke away.

Once they were in the bedroom, Mike walked Danny toward the bed, set his hand against Danny's sweaty chest and shoved him backward, hard enough that he lost his balance, tipped onto the blankets. And Mike finally, *finally* stripped off the rest of his clothes and Danny forgot to breathe for a second, staring at the now-familiar lines of his body, the tattoos that he had finally memorized and dreamed about sometimes, the lean muscle and whipcord strength of him.

Mike was on his knees between Danny's legs. "You good?"

"I want to *come*."

"Eventually."

"Jesus, Mike."

Mike didn't say anything, just pressed his mouth against Danny's hip and sucked a hickey into it, the sharp pain lancing through him, and he hissed. It went on like that, Mike torturing him with his mouth and his hands, getting him close, so close, and then taking his hands away. His whole body was on fire and all he could think about was release. He could feel it, balls tight, toes curling.

Sudden agony; the side of his face. Mike had slapped him, and Danny's entire body rolled in a shudder of pleasure.

"Not until I tell you."

"You haven't—" Danny gasped for air. "You haven't even fucked me yet."

"I know. Do you want me to?"

"Yes."

"Okay, Danny," Mike said, flashing one of those unfairly impish smiles. "You only had to ask."

"Fuck you," Danny started to say, but it came out more like *fuuu-ah*, because Mike slapped him again. This time, he just groaned.

By the time Mike had found the lube and condoms Danny was almost frantic, still holding himself back, probably looking like a crazy person. He felt like a crazy person. His body was a livewire, every inch of him primed and sensitive when Mike touched him, shivering. Mike didn't look much better. The longer they went, the wider his eyes were, the more Danny couldn't stop staring at his mouth, parted and damp. He was—he was something else. He was beautiful.

Danny was going to die and he was going to die unfulfilled and happy for it.

They were both silent when Mike slid into him, slow and inexorable, until he had bottomed out inside. An uncomfortable stretch at first as Danny panted, shuddered, getting used to the feeling. He couldn't stop staring up at Mike, the way his eyes slipped shut when he did it, the way the muscles in his shoulders flexed as he held himself above Danny. *Move, move, move, I need you to move*, Danny thought, but Mike just stayed there, so frustratingly still except for the tremble in his arms that betrayed this wasn't easy for him either.

When he did move, finally, it was so slow, so steady, that Danny almost cried. It was torture, it wasn't what he wanted, what he needed, and his body moved on instinct, hips thrusting up to try to move things along. Mike's eyes snapped open. His palm cracked against Danny's cheek, once on the left side of the face, once on the right.

Danny whimpered. Fucking whimpered.

"You're really bad at following directions, dude," Mike gasped.

"I'm—I'm sorry—"

"Fuck, Danny…"

Mike started to fuck him again, that same steady pace, almost, almost—it wasn't what he needed, but his body was already primed and trembling on the edge of an orgasm, felt like it had been forever, and the friction of Mike's steady, deep thrusts was going to drag it out of him against his will. Danny could hear himself, gasping, could feel a burning sensation at the corners of his eyes, screwed shut, could feel the way his dick had somehow gotten harder, the way his balls had drawn themselves up.

"You're not—*allowed*—" Mike managed, like it

was torturing him to keep that pace just as much as it tortured Danny.

"I *know*, I'm *trying*..." When he opened his eyes, he saw Mike was watching him, and the look in his eyes scourged him. Another chip in the ice. "Mike... please..."

"Please?"

"Please, please, I need—"

"Yeah?"

"God, please, fuck me, fuck me, *harder*, I can't—"

"Oh, god," Mike breathed, and slammed down into him at exactly the right angle, the one he'd been chasing. Pleasure sparked along his spine and he felt the breath catch in his throat, his eyes closed, as Mike fucked him the way he had demanded it. It felt so fucking good that it was actually painful. He'd been on the edge for so long that every drag of Mike's dick, every press of his hands against Danny's wrists, every time his teeth dug into Danny's shoulder, felt like a scourge, like barbed wire against his skin.

He needed. He needed release.

Mike stilled, and Danny's arms strained under his hands. "Wha—what? Mike—"

"You were—gonna—you can't—"

"When—"

"Not yet—"

He wasn't sure how he withstood it, but he did. At least for a time. Every time he felt it coming, Mike would either slow or stop, even though it looked like it was a struggle for him too. It was... Danny couldn't ever remember feeling like this during sex, this ripped open, this raw. He was pretty sure that the noises he was making were inhuman, were horribly embarrassing, but Mike was relentless, determined to make them both suffer, and Danny couldn't even spare the energy for humiliation because he was trying so hard not to come.

Finally he couldn't hold himself back any longer, and he was begging, incoherent, a mess of words and sounds that barely made any sense. It was like something had broken inside of him. And then, to his horror he *was* actually crying, the hot tears leaking out of the corners of his eyes, and he couldn't even wipe them away, couldn't even hide, because of Mike's relentless hands. Mike's face, twisted with the pain of holding himself back and that awful tenderness that destroyed Danny just as much as the denial of release.

"Okay, babe," Mike gasped, "whenever, whenever you fuckin' *want*," and ground down into him, and that was the end.

Danny woke up later to find that Mike had cleaned him off and was back in bed next to him, his hands folded over his chest and staring up at the ceiling. The clock said three a.m.

"Hey," Mike said, his voice rough. "You okay?"

"I'm fine," Danny said, even though he wasn't at all.

Mike propped himself up on his elbow and looked down at him. "You sure? You were pretty—out of it for a bit, there."

Danny licked his lip, tender and raw where he'd bitten through it. "Uhh. I don't, uhh…usually…let anyone do things like this. To me."

"I know you don't. Thank you." Mike's voice was soft.

"Huh?"

"For—for letting me do that. For trusting me. It was—fuck, Danny, the *best*. You know you're amazing, right?"

"Fuck off," he mumbled, embarrassed, and Mike flopped back down into the covers and shoved himself under Danny's arm.

"I'm fucked up, dude. I gotta sleep. But I just—you're okay?"

"Fine," Danny said. Strangely, he felt…not fine, exactly. Different. Like Mike had shown him things that he hadn't known were possible. Not like. He had. But Danny didn't know what to do with that. "I—let's go to sleep, babe."

"Mm," Mike agreed, already halfway there.

Danny stayed awake for a long time after that, thinking.

CHAPTER SIX

February

The rest of the All-Star weekend hadn't been anywhere near as eventful as that first night, but even after Danny had recovered, he still felt off. He'd hidden it well enough. They'd hung out with their teammates separately, and come back to the hotel and fucked desperately, Danny like he had to regain something he'd lost, and Mike like Mike always did.

It had been hard to leave Mike that Sunday, but Danny had done it. He'd flown home to Pittsburgh and he'd made the promise to himself that he was going to be better, that he was going to do better, but even with the distractions of games and exercise and Buddy and FaceTiming with Mike, Danny had to admit to himself that he was not being better. That the lack of control had extended to other aspects of his life.

He hadn't missed practice again but he felt like shit almost all of the time.

By the time February rolled around, Danny felt like every time he was at home alone was a disaster waiting to happen. He knew what he was going to do when he got there, and he felt like shit about it. He felt like he was going to crawl out of his skin half of the time, but he couldn't do anything about it. Every time he tried, he ended up caving.

It was one thing to feel so goddamn miserable and deal with it and another thing entirely to know that you couldn't talk about it.

He couldn't talk to Mike because Mike would worry about him more than he already did, and Danny didn't want to lose him. He couldn't, even though he knew he was going to anyway. He couldn't talk to Araceli, because she'd pity him, or try to fix him, or worse, tell their parents. He couldn't talk to Gears or Landry because both of them were kids and he was the one who gave *them* advice. He couldn't talk to Coach, because he didn't want to get traded or screw up the twilight of his career.

On a freezing night in February, he sat on his porch in just a hoodie and jeans, smoking a cigarette because it was that or he was going to go back inside and pour himself another drink or take another pill and he was already on the other side of what he considered a safe limit. It was quiet on his street, which was the usual way of the neighborhood. Also, it was almost midnight, and Danny was alone with the urge to go back inside and do exactly that, and he thought, *maybe if I was dead, I wouldn't be so fucking tired all the goddamn time.*

Danny exhaled. He had had thoughts like that before, fleeting, but never so clearly formed in his mind.

Thinking about it had never seemed like a relief before.

It was like the more he got to know and then had to leave Mike, the more he was alone, the more the yawning void in his chest grew wider. Like it would consume him. That was the only way he could characterize something he knew was probably depression. He just didn't feel like he could call it that, because it was his fault he felt that way, not something his brain had done to him. His inability to control himself with alcohol and pills. His inability to stop the black moods that swept him when he was alone.

He took out his phone and scrolled through the list of contacts, mostly guys he didn't talk to much anymore. It was hard when you got traded. Some friendships continued, but sometimes it was easier not to keep them up, easier not to see your friends succeeding where you'd failed. Danny had always been content to let things drift. But that also meant…well, here he was, on the porch of an empty house in February, as miserable as he'd ever been, completely alone.

He stopped on the M's. Andrew Martin had been an assistant coach on Danny's first team. He'd been the guy who worked with the defensemen, had been a d-man himself during his playing career, and it had been Marty's guidance that had gotten him back on his feet after the broken hip. Marty had been the reason he still had a career in the league at all.

They'd always had a good relationship. Marty appreciated how hard Danny worked, worried about how much he pushed himself, and had been crushed when Chicago had traded him. He'd been like a second dad away from home for Danny, his voice weirdly soothing, his gap-toothed smile comforting.

They'd kept in touch on and off throughout the years, Marty checking in on him every time he'd gone to a new team, every time an injury made the news.

Marty had been around the block too, but with more success: he was now the head coach on the Jersey Scouts and even though they hadn't made it to or past the first round of the playoffs in a few years, Marty was still beloved in Newark just because that was the kind of guy he was.

It was a stretch, but maybe he'd understand.

Marty didn't pick up right away, but he answered before it went to voice mail, which Danny hadn't been expecting given the hour and because he was in his early sixties. His voice was a little sleepy. "Danny?"

"Hey, Marty," Danny said, "sorry to uhh…sorry to call you so late," and stopped. He sounded a little drunk. He didn't know what to say.

"Is—everything okay?"

Danny was silent for what felt like a long time but wasn't even a minute. His back was cold and clammy with sweat. "Uh…no, Marty. Everything's pretty shit, actually, and I—I don't know what to do."

"Hang on one sec, Danny. Stay on with me, all right?" He heard Marty getting up, murmuring something, probably to his wife, and then silence, as he walked. "Okay, just had to get out of the bedroom."

"I didn't mean to, I'm sorry. I didn't mean to wake you or Julie up."

"It's fine, it's fine. You know I told you when you got traded that you could call me anytime, and I meant it. Talk to me, buddy."

"It's not easy to do that."

"Talk to me in hypotheticals if you gotta, but Danny, if you called me at one in the morning, there's something going on."

"Uh… Marty…if one of your guys had…was maybe,

uh, having an issue with, with drugs and…alcohol… like…bad shit…what would you tell him to do?"

"I'd tell him to take the time he needed to get himself cleaned up," Marty said, without hesitation. "That I'd help him find the resources he needed to do that, that I'd support him through whatever steps he needed to take. And that we'd be here for him when he got back. It's like any other injury. It needs to be healed. That's what I'd tell him, Danny."

"Do you think that's—the normal reaction? In the league?"

"I'll be honest with you, I don't know. It should be. But also, I don't think—well, if I was talking to someone on another team whose policies I didn't know, I'd tell him not to worry about it, because your health comes fucking first, and even if things go to shit after, hockey ain't worth that."

"It is. It is worth it."

"Danny, it's fucking *not*."

"I—hypothetically, the guy we're talking about—Marty, the problem—the problem is he doesn't have a life outside of hockey. I don't have anything after that." He swallowed, hard, because he had never said it aloud, but that was the problem, that was the thing he feared. That was the crux of it. "I only have two seasons left, and after that, I got nothing. I retire and what the fuck am I good for? I won't even be forty years old and what the fuck am I gonna have in my life? What's the fucking point of going on…?"

"Danny, it might seem like that, but that's not fuckin' true. You're one of the best guys I ever coached, and you're only thirty-five, you've got your whole goddamn life ahead of you. It might take you some time to figure out the direction you wanna take it, but—"

"I don't *want* to do anything else. I don't—I don't know *how*."

"Buddy, it's scary as fucking hell when you gotta retire, I can tell you that from firsthand experience. And I'm not saying you gotta retire; I don't know what's going on. But that doesn't mean it's a *bad* thing, and that doesn't mean you can't be happy doing something else, and it doesn't mean you won't find benefits from doing it. Retiring probably saved my marriage, for one thing."

"But how do you know what you want to *do*?"

"I can't tell you that, bud. I know you'd make a fantastic coach, for one. But you could do anything you wanted to do. You're smart, and you're hardworking, and you got a damn good heart. You don't have to know right away. I'd trust you to figure it out."

Danny looked down at his feet. He felt like he should be crying, but there was nothing behind his eyes. "Marty… I don't fucking deserve that. I don't fucking deserve any of that. I'm—I'm a piece of shit, Marty, I'm a lying piece of shit, and I don't know how much longer I can, uh, I can do this, I'm kind of losing my fucking, my fucking mind."

"You sure as fuck do deserve that. Look, Danny. I don't know what kind of trouble you got yourself into, but I'll tell you what you deserve. You deserve a chance to get your shit together, and you deserve a team that will let you do that, and you *deserve* to be happy and healthy."

Marty couldn't see him, of course, but Danny caught

himself shaking his head anyway. "So what—what should I do?"

"If you're asking me? Without details, and based on the way you sound tonight, bud? At least a sixty-day inpatient and outpatient afterward. And then we'd go from there."

Jesus, he must have sounded worse than he thought. "Marty…"

"Danny, buddy, I love you, okay? You're like a son to me, even if you call me about as often as my actual children do. If I can do anything to make this easier for you, you let me fucking *know*."

"I—I'll think about it. Marty…thanks for…thanks for listening. And uh, please don't, please don't worry about me."

"Danny, you fuckin' idiot, I worry about all of my guys, all the time. But I trust you to do the right thing, okay? To do the right thing for yourself."

Danny thought, *you shouldn't*, but what he said was, "Sorry to wake you up, old man. Go back to sleep." He sat up for a long time after that, because he couldn't follow his own goddamn advice.

It didn't get any easier.

The All-Star Game had been like one of Mike's top five experiences that didn't involve actually playing hockey, and it was probably almost number one on the list. It was actually difficult to think of something that had topped it, with the exception of Danny visiting over Christmas. He didn't really want to think too much about the fact that most of the best memories he had involved Danny, especially considering that Danny had been doing that thing recently where his eyes looked so fucking sad but he wouldn't talk about it no matter how much Mike tried to pry.

He alternated between reliving a pretty baller fantasy—fucking Danny in front of a huge open window in a five-star hotel—and worrying about Danny after they hung up at night. It was bad enough that Mike, who hated thinking about things for too long, had actually started doing research. He'd read a few Players' Tribune articles about depression and substance abuse, freaked himself the fuck out, and ended up spending an hour reading forum posts about alcoholism.

What did you do, though, when you thought your boyfriend had a problem, and he probably knew he had a problem, but he was just determined to pretend that everything was fine because he was too fucking proud to ask for help?

On one of the few nights that Bee was home, he worked up the balls to ask her about it again. Mike made them both bison burgers and a quinoa salad, and it wasn't the best-tasting food in the world, but it was edible, which was more than he could say about anything Bee had ever cooked for him. They were sitting on the couch, his legs propped up on the coffee table, her legs in his lap, when he glanced sideways at her.

"You're thinking about something," she said. It wasn't a question.

"Yeah, so, uh…it's, uh, my…boyfriend." Like, that's what Danny was, but it still felt weird to say it out loud. Bee just looked at him, because she was smart enough to know it wasn't something good but understanding enough not to press him until he was ready. Mike exhaled. "The shit I told you at New Year's? It's not getting any better."

"Is he okay? Are *you* unhappy?"

"Unhappy? I mean—only with that. Everything else, he's really…" He knew he probably had a goofy smile on his face, the kind of expression that just happened against his will whenever he talked, or really even thought about Danny. "But I just…the fuck do you *do* when someone doesn't wanna get help, Bee?"

"I don't know if there's anything you can do. I wouldn't know, though. The only other hockey players I really know outside of the team are my brothers, and they're perfect."

Her voice was sour enough that Mike almost laughed, because fuck, did he know that feeling. "I just hate watching it," he said. It was the first time he'd said that aloud either. He did hate it, especially now, when he wasn't there to chase the bleakness from Danny's eyes.

Bee frowned at him. "You could suggest that he talk to the players' association and player assistance but… if he doesn't think he has a problem…"

"I think he knows; the problem is he doesn't wanna do anything about it. It just fucking *sucks*."

Bee patted him on the leg, but she was frowning too. "I worry about you, Michael."

"*I'm* fine. I'm like—legit better than I've ever been. I just wish he was too."

Sometimes, he wondered whether Bee had put two and two together. She was smart, but sometimes she was oblivious, like the fact that she hadn't realized she was in love with Mäkelä for almost an entire year. They'd been watching other teams' games together for long enough that it wasn't completely out of the question to watch Danny's together, even though he had to school his reactions. It was hard, because Mike thought he could, like, see Danny's play coming apart, a little bit. He was slower, and sometimes when the camera swept over him on the bench, regardless of whether he'd been fighting, he looked like he was in pain, and Mike had to clench his goddamn fists.

But Bee was barely home anymore, so that was… fine. It was quiet and lonely, but it didn't matter, because he was working so hard in practice, and FaceTiming Danny when he could at night, and looking forward to the next time they'd be in the same city.

The home crowds were always most intense when they played the Hornets, and even more so now that they were regularly jostling for first and second place in the division. The Cons had won last time, so the fans were happy, but the Hornets had something to prove. Mike just felt on edge because it was the first time he'd be playing Danny since he'd worked on his game, and it was almost like he was in fucking elementary school again, trying to get the teacher's attention but always getting the answer wrong.

That had been before he'd given up and started getting into fights, anyway.

The dressing room before the game reflected some of the tension. Mike looked around at his teammates. Netty was joking with Sally, or at least Netty was joking and Sally was giving him murder-eyes. Singer and Reed were already dressed by their stalls, heads together, going over some kind of complicated play, Reed making expansive gestures with his hands. Mäkelä had an AirPod in, blissfully jamming out to some kind of weird Finnish metal (or folk music, it was anyone's best guess). Bee was sitting next to him with the other bud in her ear, frowning at whatever she heard.

Mike was seized with affection for all of them, even though none of them really knew him, except Bee. And even though they didn't, they still treated him like he belonged.

Once he hit the ice, he was just focused on the game. Slowly, he'd been starting to play closer to the crease, switching it up with Lindy depending on who had joined the rush. Graham was still out with a head injury and Mike had somehow failed his way upward into an almost permanent second pairing with Lindy. Parsons had grumbled about it, and Kelly had grumbled about it, but Coach had just shrugged and said, "Sato earned it."

Mike had kept that one close, but texted Danny about it afterward. Danny had written back, that's my boy, and Mike had felt a weird, confused flush down his chest, reading the words. He tried not to think about it now.

The first period went by quickly, especially because he was agonizing over whether he should fight Danny or not. People almost expected it, you could hear the gasp in the crowd whenever they were on the ice together, but he hadn't had the heart to hit him. He tried to just pay attention to the puck, to keep it moving, to run interference when Lévesque or Artyomov (he still could not entirely believe that he was putting up minutes against *either* of them, in his wildest fucking dreams he wouldn't have expected that) came too close to Mäkelä's crease.

It was difficult when his eyes dragged toward Danny against his will, when he was acutely aware of wherever he happened to be on the ice. When he knew Danny was watching him too. He was trying to play clean, but then when Mike was battling along the boards against Landry, finally got his stick on the puck, someone slammed into him from behind, knocked him into the glass and right down onto the ice.

Danny.

Mike was up on his skates almost immediately, even though his entire body ached. Danny looked at him and dropped his gloves, and Mike, who realized that this was the first time Danny had ever tried to fight him, dropped them too. They circled each other and Mike searched his face, trying to gauge how this was going to go. Danny just looked tired. There was none of the humor behind his eyes that there usually was. Like he didn't want to do it but had gotten tired of waiting for Mike to go for him.

For a second, he felt really guilty, but then Danny punched him in the face, and he got his shit together.

It wasn't like Mike was holding back, but he was aware of the differences fighting, like, now, and fighting before. He really was trying not to hit Danny too hard in the head, to leave his helmet on, to mostly aim for the sturdier parts of his body. Of course, that meant he had lost any advantage he had, because Danny had reach and weight on him.

He didn't even really care when Danny's fist slammed him in the side where his pads didn't cover and knocked the breath right out of him, didn't even really care when a sort of messy wrestling move landed him flat on his ass on the ice with the crushing weight of Danny's body on top of him.

Like…you know, it hurt, but also, he kind of had an aborted boner.

"Dude," he wheezed, as the linesmen pulled Danny off of him, "we still doing this? Even now?"

"Got a reputation to uphold," Danny said, and knocked his helmet gently against Mike's.

He knew it was an affectionate gesture, but it got Danny an additional two minutes in the box.

It was a shitshow of a game. Mike actually ended up fighting Danny again and, with the game misconduct, was forced to sit out the rest of the game with just under ten minutes to go. The final score was 6–5, with Reed taking the game-winning goal in overtime. Afterward, Mike was in the process of stripping off his pads before he got cornered by reporters. Of course they had questions about the fights, they always did.

"Uhh…you know, I guess we just have a thing," he said, exhausted and grumpy and hating the fact that he was being kept here.

"A thing?" the woman—she was from Pittsburgh; he couldn't remember her name—repeated.

"Yeah, you know. I break his face, he breaks mine. It's like a tradition at this point."

She looked delighted, and Mike took the moment to make his escape. The Hornets weren't playing the next day, but Danny had asked for an exception to return on a commercial flight instead of the chartered plane. He hadn't told Mike how he'd managed it, but Mike wasn't sure if he wanted to know. Usually that kind of stuff was only allowed for family and that seemed… uncomfortable, at least, the sort of thing Mike didn't know how to ask.

Did you tell them I'm family? Like. What.

Danny was already naked by the time Mike made it down to the hotel. *Hey, what's wrong*, Mike tried to say, but Danny pushed him up against the door and kissed him so thoroughly that it was impossible to get the words out. Then he completely forgot about the words he had queued up in his head because, well, Danny was naked, and they only had so much time.

Afterward, Mike rolled on top of him and pinned his arms down. Danny looked up at him, exhausted and still a little sweaty, one eyebrow up. He had an entire line of hickeys on his collarbone, one for each time he'd punched Mike during the fights, and he'd gotten them in before Danny shoved him down into the mattress again, but Mike couldn't even feel smug about it.

"What's *up* with you, dude?" he demanded.

Danny twisted his wrists to see if he could break Mike's grip, but Mike just held on harder, and eventually Danny surrendered. "Mike. If you couldn't play hockey, what would you do?"

Mike blinked. "If I couldn't play hockey?"

"Yeah. If you could do something else."

Mike let go of Danny's wrists but didn't roll off of him. He traced the muscle of Danny's chest, scratched his fingers through the soft curly hair there. "I never thought about it."

"Yeah," Danny said, and sounded, like, resigned.

"I mean… I'm not really sure. I'm not good at much that's not hockey."

"What are you talking about?"

This wasn't how Mike thought the night was going to end. His body still felt relaxed and loose and like he could just fucking roll his muscles like a lazy cat. But there was something going on in this conversation that he couldn't quite follow. Like they'd started talking about one thing and now Danny's focus was on him for something completely different, and he felt blindsided, a little.

"I'm not like, you know. Smart or anything."

"The fuck do you mean you're not?"

Mike shrugged. This wasn't a great conversation to have, like, at any time, but particularly when you should've been either enjoying the afterglow or gearing up to go again. "You know. All of my siblings have advanced degrees and shit. I barely finished my GED. I only managed it because Mom said she'd make me stop playing if I didn't."

"That doesn't mean shit."

"Dude, it's cool. I know what I'm capable of doing."

Danny, whatever weird mood he'd been in earlier, seemed to have softened a little. His hand was stroking a line down Mike's thigh. "I don't think you do, babe."

"Well, I mean, I almost didn't graduate high school and I didn't go to college, so."

"You *could* do it."

"But I don't—what—Danny, where the fuck is this coming from?"

Danny stared up at him with this weird look, like if he thought the things hard enough at Mike, he'd be able to read between the lines. Even though Mike had just been telling him he was kind of dumb. "Just think about it, okay? You're pretty young. You *are* smart, and I think you could, you know. Get a degree if you wanted to. You already turned your game around in sort of a record amount of time, I just think you shouldn't sell yourself short."

"But...hockey's one thing and college is...? I don't think it's really, like. The same. I don't think that's something I could do."

"Tell me you'll think about it," Danny said, and that soft, commanding tone was so similar to his sex voice that Mike shuddered on instinct, his brain shorting out a little.

But Danny was kissing him again, and Mike let it go.

Danny thought a lot about that conversation after he went home. Of course Mike hadn't thought about what he was going to do after hockey. Danny certainly hadn't. But Mike was a decade younger than he was, and his body wasn't a fucked-up death trap. It hadn't been too late for him to change his game and maybe when he was nearing the end of his career, he wouldn't feel like Danny felt now. Maybe that was something else Danny could do for him, before Mike decided shit was too much trouble to hang around for.

He didn't bring it up again, though, because every time Mike seemed to suspect that he was going to, he'd change the subject and wouldn't look Danny in the eye for the rest of the call. That was fine: they both had shit they didn't want to talk about.

Danny went to the gym, he went home, he played with Buddy. He took pills, he drank, he got on planes and flew across the country. He played hockey, he took punches, and he doled out punches.

He drank.

And he drank.

And he drank.

Somehow, without meaning to, being with Mike had just yanked the seal off of a decade of bad memories. He was dreaming about the accident again, and he hadn't dreamed about it in years. Getting fucked up helped with that, but not entirely. Sometimes it just brought it back in more vivid relief.

Maybe it was just that Mike reminded him so much of himself when he'd been younger. Maybe it was just that watching Mike fixing his game and letting himself be as fucking amazing as Danny'd always known he was just served as a reminder of his own failures. Maybe it was just that Mike had become another crutch, a comfort Danny didn't deserve.

Something had broken in Vegas and he couldn't put it back together. Wasn't sure if he wanted to.

There were two games left that he'd play against Mike before the season ended. One on the twenty-third and one in the middle of March. He thought about it a lot, on the road.

In Toronto, Gears cornered him before he could get into his hotel room. Usually easygoing and a little shy, he looked unusually determined. He had his hands shoved into his hoodie pockets.

"What's up, kid?" Danny asked.

"Can we talk?"

"Uh…yes? You okay?"

"Can we talk in your room?" Gears was chewing on his lower lip, unable to look him in the eye.

Danny had a bad feeling about it. But he had a lot of bad feelings about a lot of things, and if he'd given in to every bad feeling, he probably wouldn't be around anymore. "Sure," he said, more easily than he felt.

Gears followed him in, watched while Danny sat down in the desk chair and turned it around to face him. Gears didn't sit. He stared at Danny, twenty years old and incredibly, awkwardly brave, and Danny stared back at him.

"So Lands and I have been talking," Gears said finally.

"Gears—" Danny started, because he knew where this was going.

"No! Shut up, dude, hear me out. Seriously."

"It's not—"

"Lands and I have been talking, and we want you to like…dude, you *gotta* do something about this."

"I don't know what you're talking about."

"Sure you fucking don't," Gears said, bitterly. "You've been a fucking mess at practice, dude. We can tell, even if no one else said anything to you yet. We've been watching you when the team goes out. We're fucking *worried* about you."

"You don't have to be worried about me." The words were easy to say; he'd said them in some form or another, over and over, for a decade. "Nothing's wrong."

"Nothing's *wrong*? Dude."

"Nothing's wrong," Danny repeated. If he said it enough, maybe Gears would listen.

"It's just, buddy, you're like our dad. I had a rough-as-fuck rookie year and you've really helped me. With my game and, you know, just feeling like part of the team? Like I deserved to be here? Same for Lands. You're important to us, dude, okay? I don't wanna see you like this. I dunno what's going on, but you look fucking miserable, and at this rate, Coach is gonna notice."

"I've already talked to him. It's just my hip again. But it's fine. I'm working with the trainers."

Gears looked at him like Danny had just slipped a knife between his ribs. "I thought you had more respect for me than that."

"Gears—"

"No. It's cool. It's fine. I'm not gonna—we just wanted you to know we're here for you, all right? But it's okay. You don't want that."

"Gears, it's just—you're really fucking young, and you don't understand."

"You want to *try* me? Or Lands? Or fucking *anyone*? Your boyfriend? I'm sure he fucking cares if you're drinking yourself stupid, dude."

It was strange. There was no reason his ears should be ringing like that, but he felt like he'd just been boxed hard around them. So Landry and Gears *had* been talking about more than his drinking. "That's a low fucking blow, Girard."

"Yeah, well. We're fucking worried about you. Like. It sucks. And *you* suck. Okay, fine. You don't wanna hear it, I can't do anything else about that. I'm fucking out, man."

Both of them avoided him for the rest of the week. Danny understood exactly why and gave them their space. He was surprised to find that he missed their stupid banter and shoving each other and the small periods of joy that brought him. He was so used to things ending, having to leave a team or having people leave him, that it was unexpected to feel like this.

It all came back to Mike.

"Dude, you look really sad today," Mike said to him on one of their video calls. "What's up?"

Mike was in a hotel room in Calgary, sprawled on the bed in front of the computer. The beginnings of a black eye were starting to bloom on his face, and he had two stitches in his cheek. Danny didn't have to ask who'd hit him because he'd watched the game. One of the Calgary forwards, Graves, had started something

Mike had finished. He'd gotten stitched up, come out of the penalty box, and went right back to the game.

Danny hesitated. The conversation with Gears still felt raw. He couldn't…he didn't want Mike to look at him that way. "I—can we talk about it in person? The next time I see you?"

Mike didn't answer right away. He looked at Danny, carefully, with the kind of intense scrutiny that he'd always had. Without the anger. Danny was struck again by how much Mike had grown this year, how grateful he was to have been able to see it and allowed to have been part of it. That was raw, too.

"Sure," Mike said, finally. "But seriously, dude, are you good?"

"I'm an old fucking idiot, but I'm fine. Hey, I gotta go. I'll see you this weekend."

"Yeah."

Danny caught a brief glimpse of Mike's mouth, turned down at the corner, before he hastily ended the call.

The game came around soon enough. Danny knew he was making this a bridge too far, but he had to get through it, knew what was coming during it and after it, and he wasn't going to make it if he wasn't at least a little insulated from life. He got a little drunk before the game. Not too much. Just enough that when he and Mike inevitably met in the neutral zone and the gloves came off, he could barely feel it. Just enough that he was able to get through the postgame interviews without wanting to rip off the heads of the reporters. Just enough that he was able to get back to the hotel to wait for Mike.

It didn't take him long. He was wearing his usual

winter uniform, which usually drove Danny nuts. It was a hoodie under a leather jacket, which just seemed inefficient, especially considering he never zipped the stupid jacket. But today it was just a Mike thing.

"Hey," Mike said, frowning up at him. "You seemed off during the game. Are you okay?"

"Yeah. I—yeah, I'm fine. But we—can we talk?"

He could see the emotion flicker over Mike's face before he was able to hide it. Something like fear. "Yeah, sure."

Danny made his way back to the bed, and sat down on it, a little gingerly, watched Mike shuck his jacket and jeans and shoes, waited for him to crawl into the bed after him. Danny looked down, at the spot on his thigh where Mike's hand was splayed next to Danny's clenched fist. His heart was beating so fucking fast it almost felt like it was going to burst under its own power, a machine pushed past its limits. Sweat drenched his back.

"Danny..."

"It's—sorry. I've never really been able to—talk about this. But I think I gotta talk about it."

Mike didn't say anything, but his thumb rubbed a circle on Danny's thigh, rough and warm.

"I—okay. You've read it. You know what happened to me."

"I haven't heard it from you."

A wheezing noise, not quite a laugh. "*No one's* heard it from me. Not even Celi. Not even my Ma and Pa." He took a breath. "I was twenty-one, and it was my second season with Chicago. I was playing really well. I wasn't, I wasn't drafted high, but I was, really working on my game. The assistant coach there, Marty, was really… It was…"

Mike shifted around and pushed himself high up enough on the mountain of hotel bed pillows that he could get an arm over Danny's shoulders, and for some reason that gesture almost broke him. Mike was always that way. An asshole on the ice; clumsily kind at home. Danny didn't deserve it.

"We were playing the Royal, and we were up by one, and I'd had a fight with Bourque earlier in the game, and there were only ten minutes left in the third and—and I'd already passed the puck. It was gone. But he, uh. He hit me anyway while I was rushing to follow it. And it was at a really high speed, and I wasn't fucking expecting it at all, because fuck, I didn't even have the puck. He hit me. Really hard, and, uh—I fell at a bad angle. I could feel it. And then one of my teammates tripped too and uh—"

Mike's arm was tight around his shoulders and Danny, for a moment, turned his head into Mike's hoodie. He couldn't bring himself to actually look at his face.

"It was like, I could see everything as it was happening, clearly, like you wouldn't even think because everything moves so fast, but I couldn't *do anything* to stop it. And it hurt so fucking bad. And I was just telling myself, don't scream, don't scream, get up. Get up. You're fine. You're fine. I tried to get up. I couldn't get up. It hurt too much and my leg—my leg wasn't really working right. My whole side felt like it was on fire. I tried for like a solid thirty seconds to stand and to, to not scream, to get up, just—get *up*—until the trainer forced me back down on the ice and made me wait for—for the stretcher."

"Jesus, Danny," Mike said, head resting on top of Danny's, voice muffled by his hair.

He took a deep breath. "It was. It was pretty awful. I, uh, broke my femur and my hip. Needed surgery for both of them. The worst part was the recovery. It was so fucking long… I was so bored, and so frustrated, and my body just wasn't doing what I needed it to do. I just wanted to be back on the ice. I was young and I'd been having such a good season and I had my whole *career* waiting and I thought I could handle it. I pushed myself too hard and fucked up the hip again. Ended up needing an additional—if I could go back in time and fucking—"

"Hey. Hey, none of that. Dude, you didn't *know* what would happen."

"I did know. The doctors, the trainers. All of them told me exactly what I had to do, and I was a tough guy, right? I wanted to get back out on the ice. So I lied about it and went back out too fast and—it's just been—I've never been able to skate the same. Since that. Since then." He couldn't pull his face away from Mike's chest, because he couldn't deal with fucking *pity.*

"You've played for like *over a decade* since then, dude. That's pretty fucking impressive."

"Never the kind of game I know I could play. Never the kind of game *you* can play, babe."

"Hey, fuck that. Whatever I have, it's 'cause of you, all right? So fuck off with that. Oh, Jesus, Danny, I'm sorry, I didn't mean—"

He was laughing, muffled by Mike's hoodie. "No. Don't apologize. I didn't—I haven't been able to fucking talk about this to anyone before. I dream about it sometimes. But I've never…"

"Thank you. For telling me. For trusting me? Danny, you're fucking amazing that you've like, been doing everything you do. I don't think *I* could have done that."

"Well, I hope you never have to find out. I just—I loved hockey so much. I love hockey so much. I didn't know what else I *could* do. So I've just had to go on."

"Is that why you…?"

"I mean…everything hurts, at this point. It wasn't just those two injuries. They were the worst, but I've lost count of the number of concussions I've had and just played through. Those aren't the only bones I've broken. It's been… I don't think I'd trade it for the fucking world, if I could go back and do it again, but Mike, I'm held together by spite and fucking Crazy Glue at this point."

Mike's hands were smoothing down his hair, a sweaty mess like the rest of him. Mike didn't seem to mind. "Well, as long as it's working. You're not fucking going anywhere, okay?"

"Hah. Okay."

Mike pulled back enough, just enough, so that Danny could see he was glaring. There was a tension in his body, in the straining muscles. "Fucking promise me, asshole. You're not *going* anywhere."

He thought about laughing it off. Or making some kind of a joke about how Mike was really good at sweet talk. But that was exactly what it was. "I promise. Asshole."

"Good," Mike said, and relaxed again, let Danny lean into him. "Hey. Uh, you know? Let's not fuck tonight, all right? Maybe we could just like…watch a movie and chill or something."

"I—yeah. Mike. Thank you. I…this wasn't easy."

"I know, Danny. Hey. I got you, all right?"

Strangely, Danny almost believed it. He let Mike pick something out and settled in for the long haul. But he only made it halfway through whatever superhero movie was playing before drifting off.

He didn't dream.

Mike woke up early to the sound of Danny's phone alarm. He was too warm, kind of sweaty, and wrapped up in Danny's arms.

"Don't your like…fuckin' arms fall asleep?" he rasped. "Lemme go."

"It's not too bad," Danny mumbled back, voice thick with sleep. He opened his eyes and smiled, and Mike's stomach and chest had that swooping feeling he was unused to and didn't know if he liked. But they were there.

Danny didn't even seem to mind Mike's gross morning breath when he leaned in for a kiss. They both had flights to catch, though, so he wasn't trying to stay in bed, even though it was warm and stupid comfortable, and Danny was doing his level best to make him forget the schedule.

But eventually, he managed it. Mike pulled on his jeans and shirt and hoodie, eyeing Danny nervously. It had been, like, kind of a big conversation last night, and every time he thought about the fact that he was the only person Danny had ever told about it, his chest felt like it was going to burst. It was like being sad, for Danny, but happy, because he'd at least started talking, and he wanted to talk to *Mike*.

The feelings shit was weird, man.

By the time Danny had gotten his bag together and they were ready to say goodbye at the door, Mike was thinking about all of the things he wanted to say, but every time he tried, he had this weird lump in his throat and the words wouldn't come out. He ended up kind of ramming himself into Danny, half a hug, half a head-butt. Danny didn't seem to mind, just ran his hand over Mike's freshly shaved head and down his neck, a strangely comforting gesture considering how last night had went.

"Leaving fucking sucks," he mumbled into Danny's chest.

"Sure does, bud," Danny said, and pulled away with a sigh. "All right. We gotta go, or we aren't gonna go."

Mike went first, because they couldn't even leave together, and he kind of felt like…pretty shitty about it.

Correction: the feelings shit was *really* fucking weird.

Mike felt sometimes like he was going through that period when he was sixteen again, when he'd finally hit his growth spurt and shot up five inches in six months. His whole body had ached. It was like that, except with like…his brain, and understanding things. It was like having a constant headache. Usually he didn't think about things at all if he could help it. But now, he thought about things all the time, and he couldn't make the thoughts stop. He thought about his feelings, and other people's feelings. It was exhausting, and he really didn't know how people did it *all* the time. He tried to go about his business like usual, but mostly it was hard.

He thought about Danny all the time, even when he tried to keep it confined to their calls or texts, which were admittedly a lot. He thought about Danny when he was hanging out with Bee, when he was making himself dinner, when he was at morning skate, sometimes when he was on the ice fighting someone. He thought about Danny getting injured and Danny pushing himself too hard and making it worse—because what a fucking Danny thing to do, honestly—and Danny grinding along for a decade hurting *all* the time because he loved hockey too much to quit.

One weekend afternoon after morning skate, he was at the boxing gym again. It still made him feel better when people punched him, although to make Coach less anxious about the whole thing, he had started wearing protective gear. Even with some cushioning on his head, it was usually a good way to clear his head. He was in the ring with Arjun Sharma again, a guy who probably weighed about the same as Mike but had two inches on him, trading punches, when he had a realization.

It was such a blindside hit that he actually froze in place, and it was a good thing he had given in to Coach's demands, because Sharma punched him right in the side of the head.

"Dude, what the hell?" Sharma said. "I wouldn't have hit you like that; you just froze."

"Uhhh…" Mike's ears were ringing, a little, because the headgear cushioned some of the blow but not all of it. "Sorry. I just—had a thought."

"You had a *thought*?"

"Yeah, you know, like…never mind."

Sharma was looking at him across the ring like he had lost his mind. He probably could have phrased that better. It sounded like he never had thoughts, which wasn't true. He had them almost constantly, much to his dismay.

Mike mumbled, "I have to go," ducked out of the ring, and headed straight for the gym's changing area.

He sat down on one of the benches and frowned. Like, now it was pretty obvious, but it really had hit him like a sledgehammer to the side of the head, or more accurately, like Sharma's right hook to the side of his head. Danny was so obsessed with the idea of Mike going back to school because he didn't want *Mike* to end up in his mid-thirties without options, feeling like the world was ending. Because Danny felt like he didn't have options and like the world was ending.

"Why the fuck don't *you* go back to school, then?" Mike said aloud, before he could stop himself.

"What?" some random dude in the corner responded, looking up from his gym bag. "I have a master's degree."

"Not *you*, I don't fucking care about your master's degree."

Danny wanted him to go back to school because Danny wanted to save him, or something stupid like that, even though Mike had never had more than a few concussions in his whole career and the only thing he'd ever broken was his nose, and his ribs, and his hand, once. But why would Danny bring it up now? Because he was worried about his injuries, or his drinking, or whatever was going on more now? Was there something he hadn't told Mike?

Mike went home and instead of taking a nap before the game, he spent some time googling shit like, *late college entrance requirements* and *online degree don't have time for classes* and then, *community college*. He got overwhelmed pretty quickly, because almost all of the online programs were degree dependent, and at places that didn't sound like he'd really want to go anyway, and the only thing he could really remember about high school was that he'd hated every minute of it. He hadn't ever been good at anything except hockey. Picking a major right out of the gate would have been like trying to buy sticks without testing them first and just letting the equipment guys do it for you. You'd end up out on the ice with something with the wrong length and the wrong flex.

He wanted to text Danny and tell him, *you're wrong about me, I could never do this, I* can *never do this*, but Danny was dealing with enough shit of his own, so he kept that thought to himself, and instead texted Bee, if i wasnt a hockey player what do u think id be good at instead, and immediately regretted it when she called him instead of answering.

She didn't sound like herself. If it was anyone except Bee, he would have said panicked. But Bee didn't get panicked. "Are you okay? Are you injured? Are you quitting?"

"No! It was a hypothetical q—I was just asking."

"Okay, good." He could almost picture her glare. "Tabarnak, you scared the *shit* out of me, Michael."

"It's just someone asked me that the other day and I just can't think of what I'd do. I thought, uh, maybe you'd know what I'm good at."

Bee was silent for a long moment, and said, "I don't know what I'd do either. I can't picture us doing anything else."

"We're gonna get old eventually. I just…don't know what else I'd do."

"I don't like thinking about it. *You* shouldn't think about it."

"So you don't know either?"

"I'm sorry, Michael. I just always assumed I would worry about it when it happened."

"Right. Thanks, Bee."

"It's *my* whole life and *your* whole life, and that's not a bad thing, okay?"

Mike thought about Danny and said, "I dunno, Bee, sometimes I think it can be. But thanks for hearing me out, buddy."

"I'm sorry I couldn't help."

There were a lot of things Bee could help him with, but this wasn't it. And he couldn't ask Danny. Mike took a deep breath and shelved thoughts of college for now. Maybe, one day, in the future he would give it a try, if only to make Danny happy. But for now there were a million other things on his mind.

After all, he had time.

IV.
SPRING

CHAPTER SEVEN

March

Danny felt more and more that he was running out of time. He was paying more attention to his body, which was a blessing and a curse. It was a blessing because he would maybe be able to drag it through the playoffs and take the time to recover over the summer, but it was a curse because every minute he was aware of just how much pain he had to ignore or numb to get through the games. It was likely they were going to make a deep run, too. They were sitting at the top of the division, with the Cons at number two.

Heading into the middle of March, Danny made a promise to himself that he was going to limit the Percs to only what was strictly necessary and to monitor his drinking until after the playoffs, when he'd figure out what his next move would be. He apologized to Gears, but things still weren't quite the same there.

"You really hurt his feelings," Landry said, on the ice during practice one day as they stretched. Stretching was always a bitch for Danny; it was necessary to avoid further injury, but his body didn't move like it used to, couldn't hold the poses as long as the young guys could.

Danny said nothing, because it was true, and he didn't like it.

"I mean...you shouldn't have lied to him like that."

Danny counted to ten and thought about how it was really unfair that, like cats, baby hockey players always attached themselves to you when you least wanted them around. Instead, he said, "It was wrong."

Landry looked sideways at him. "Yeah? You gonna tell *him* that?"

His hands were clenched around his stick. "Last I checked, he didn't want to talk."

"Maybe try again. We're heading into the playoffs. Like. We should be cool, you know?"

"Land—"

"Look, dude, I'm not gonna lecture you or anything, but what Gears said, it's true. Okay? Like you kinda kicked my ass when I needed it. So I'm gonna kick yours, if I have to."

"Thanks," Danny said, mouth dry, because he couldn't think of anything else to say.

"We're *gonna* win the Cup this year. And you're gonna be part of it. And it's gonna be just fucking fine, okay?"

Danny looked down at his skates, and thought about the relentless, dumb optimism of children, and said, "Sure."

March came and March progressed. Mike knew they were definitely going to the playoffs, it was just a matter of whether they came first, or whether the Hornets did. They were still battling for number one in the division, and it was extremely close. The Monument were in third, and it was mathematically impossible for them to improve. It didn't matter: either way, Mike wouldn't play Danny in the first round, but he felt that familiar sense of jumpy nerves in his stomach when he thought about playing Danny in the playoffs anyway.

It had felt like dying last year when they hadn't made it past the first round, and they hadn't even ended up playing the Hornets. It sucked to watch Boston win, but it would suck even more to watch Pittsburgh take the Cup, even if he'd be happy for Danny. He tried not to think about it and tried to focus on going about his normal routine, as much as that was possible when you were nearing the end of the season and your body was starting to eat itself.

He was spotting Bee at the gym, watching her bench 200 pounds. Her muscles were straining, but even though he had his hands curled under the bar ready to help her, she just grunted and pushed through the last rep on her last set, then lay there on the bench sweating.

"Nice," Mike told her.

"Thank you, Michael," Bee said, but she was frowning.

"You okay?"

"Yes, I… I just wanted to tell you I don't know whether I'm going to be around much this summer either."

Mike, remembering the depression summer that had led to Danny blowing him in an alley, said, "Uh… really?"

"I'm sorry, Michael. I met Sakari's parents last summer, and it's really time for him to meet mine, and we won't have much time, between that and training."

"It's cool. I get it, it's important."

"I'm going to miss you."

Mike watched as she sat up, then went to add more weight for his turn. "I'll miss you too, Bee. But it's cool. Seriously, don't worry about me."

Bee patted him on the cheek. Her calloused hands were sweaty and warm on his skin. "I always worry about you."

"Well, you don't have to," Mike said firmly, before sliding onto the bench.

Later that night, he watched the Hornets playing Nashville. Danny rode the bench a lot, but when he was on the ice, he looked almost like his old self: playing carefully, precisely, in the defensive zone. Mike thought about Danny and the long summer ahead of him without Bee, and about Mäkelä meeting Bee's parents. Thought about meeting Celi and Chris. Thought about a lot of things. He'd talked about it with Danny, briefly, after the holidays. That saying stuff to their families was okay, especially since Mike had already met some of Danny's.

He hadn't wanted to say anything to his own family, because, well. There were a lot of reasons. But the more he thought about the long summer alone and the more he thought about Danny, and how maybe a change of scenery would be good for him, the idea coalesced. It made him kind of nauseous thinking about it.

Still, despite the lurch of his stomach, Mike opened Gmail on his phone and composed an email to his mother, because even though he knew he had to do it, he couldn't quite bring himself to call.

He wrote, hey mom. if i came home this summer, could i bring someone with me?

Mike sent the email before he could talk himself out

of doing it, and then went back to watching the game so he wouldn't drive himself insane waiting. It was only about five minutes later that the banner notification popped up and he took a deep breath.

Of course anyone you're dating is welcome in our home, Mom had written back. That's always been the case, even though you haven't felt comfortable doing it before now. May I ask her name?

Mike could feel the beads of sweat, like, prickling on his forehead, but he typed, his name is danny, felt like he was going to vomit, and hit send. He put the phone down in between the couch cushions, where he couldn't see it or check it, and went back to watching the game. The Hornets were losing to Columbus, but Danny hadn't fought anyone, so that was fine.

He was still sweating, twitchy and nervous, but he just sat there and didn't go to get a drink or anything. Mike had felt much more self-conscious about what and why he was drinking since Danny, and even though it kinda sucked to like, have to deal with emotions all of the time, he was starting to get used to being uncomfortable. It was pretty fucking weird, but that was life now.

The Hornets lost, 4–2, and Mike pulled the phone out of the cushions again.

Of course Danny is welcome in our home, she had written. Do you have ideas about dates yet?

It almost felt like someone else's fingers typing, well idk how the playoffs are gonna go so. i'll keep you posted. thanks, mom.

He had thought, once when he was younger and angrier, or maybe just younger and sadder, that doing this would be momentous, some big thing. Instead, he got up, went to make himself dinner, and the minutes just kept ticking on by like nothing had happened. He didn't tell Danny he'd asked, because Danny had enough on his shoulders at the moment, but when he checked his phone before he went to bed, Mom had written, I love you, Michael.

Mike didn't know how to answer that or what to do with it. Instead, he starred and archived the email, and got into bed to stare at the ceiling for a long time before he could sleep.

CHAPTER EIGHT

April

The Hornets finished first in the division and were going to play Carolina in the first round. The Cons had finished second and were set to play the Monument. It wouldn't be until after those games that Danny would know if he would face Mike in the playoffs. Ultimately it didn't matter, whether he would or he wouldn't. He'd have to get through them all the same.

Danny took stock of all of the places his body was likely to give out during the series at some point. The knee was bad and throbbed at night. His hip ached. The shoulder he'd dislocated more often than the other one was going to be an issue. And the low-level headache he always had was still there, unless he was keeping current on the Percs.

"I'm a mess, Buddy," he told the cat.

Buddy had gotten over his initial rage whenever Danny came near him, and had turned into kind of a lap cat. Or a chest cat, more accurately, because that was his favorite perch. He was lying there now, purring his scratchy, rusty purr, and opened one eye when

Danny spoke. Like he knew what Danny was saying but didn't have any advice for him.

"It's okay. I don't know either."

Buddy still didn't have answers for him.

The actual games started before he felt ready. They had home ice advantage in Pittsburgh, but that didn't make much of a difference to Danny. The crowds were there for Lévesque and Artyomov, never for him. In the locker room before they were due to head out, Danny sat in silence; his eyes closed. This would be his second-to-last playoffs if he made it through next year, and the thought was a strange one. Every year he did this, chasing a trophy he'd never won, something ultimately meaningless if he did win. He'd destroyed his body for it. Sometimes it even seemed worth it.

"You all right, old man?" Gears asked.

"Just getting my head together."

Gears looked at him again, one of those long, searching looks. "You good?"

"Gears, I've been playing in the league for fifteen years. I've seen a few playoffs."

"Yeah, but…you know."

"You don't have to worry about me, bud. I'm good."

"We're cool, though?"

"Always were."

Gears held out his hand to fist-bump, and Danny humored him. Gears' awkward, hesitant smile broke his heart a little. "Okay, cool. 'Cause I feel like we got it in the bag this year, dude."

"You and Landry… Be careful, that kind of optimism's catching."

His chest clenched a little when he skated out onto the ice for the introductions and the national anthem;

the smoke and lights and music still choked him up a little, even now, even after long years of doing this. This was that kind of ineffable magic that made the whole thing worth it. But then they were playing, and he only had time to think about that.

There was a reason the Oaks had made it into the playoffs as wildcards. They'd shuffled their lineup around during the season, brought in a new coach to try to end their playoff drought, and it had mostly worked. They still weren't the kind of threat that the Cons would be. Danny was mostly on the ice with the fourth-line forwards and for penalty kill, where he was able to use his size and tendency to stay in the defensive zone to the team's advantage.

It really wasn't any kind of contest. The Oaks might have improved, but the Hornets ran over them like a steamroller, a 5–0 shutout the first game. Danny had gotten three points from primary and secondary assists, so that was something. He'd fought once, but he hadn't been hurt too badly. The Oaks forward who'd tried it wasn't big enough to really get a punch in once Danny got him at arm's length and he hadn't had anywhere near Mike's tenacity.

Afterward, he stood in the cryobath for longer than he should have and limped his way out of the stadium to his car. It was going to be a three-Perc night if he was going to play the next few games.

"Killing it, dude," Mike said, on the video call later.

"Eh, I did all right."

"Three points ain't nothing to sneeze at, *Danny*."

Danny had already caught up with the Cons' game; they'd won too, 3–1. Their coach seemed to be experimenting with the lines and pairings, and Mike had been on the ice with Bee's line often enough to put up an assist on her goal. He'd played really fucking well, like the combination of Danny's push and the Cons' coaches actually working with him had changed him into an entirely different player. He even looked different on the call, excited and smiling as he described the plays and the one fight he'd been forced into.

"And—what are you staring at, dude?" Mike demanded.

"You look really good, Mike. I mean—on the ice, now. Happy."

Mike looked back at him, steady, a little wary. "I am. Danny—*you've* made me really happy. Like being able to do all of this. I wouldn't have been able to do it without you."

"You would have, buddy."

"No, I wouldn't. I didn't—anyway, whatever, that doesn't fucking matter. Anyway, uh, I'm gonna go home this summer for a bit, I think."

Danny's stomach sank, almost reflexively. He hadn't thought about what he'd do over the summer—he had been staying in Pittsburgh, but the sneaky back parts of his mind had been thinking *maybe, maybe you could spend some time in Philadelphia, see Celi and Josie...* "Oh."

"Would you come too? For some of it? I asked my mom…she said it would be fine."

"Sure," Danny said, his voice as steady as he could make it. His eyes burned.

Mike was grinning again, goofy and relieved, and said, "Cool, cool, cool. I haven't made concrete plans yet 'cause, like, I'm planning to make it to the finals this year, you know?"

He was so fucking young and full of bravado and Danny swallowed the lump in his throat. "Not if you don't make it past the second round, buddy."

"Fuck you," Mike said, but he was grinning, still, and Danny thought about saying it, again, the way he always did when they had to leave or when the calls ended, but instead, he stuck to shit-talking, because that was easy, and comfortable, and in the end it meant the same thing.

The playoffs this year felt different than they did last year. Last year Mike had been riding high on the nerves of actually *making* it to the playoffs in his first real season when the Cons hadn't done it in so long, but he was still barely getting any minutes, and then everything was completely ruined when they lost in the first round and it had been a bitter defeat. This year was different. Bee had her head screwed on straight, Mäkelä was on fire, and the top line was scoring like there was nothing in their way.

Mike felt like he had some small contributions to make. He was coming off of a career high of fourteen goals and thirty-two assists, and he still couldn't quite believe that he wasn't going to wake up and realize he'd been dreaming the entire time. He'd gone into the first round feeling in his bones that they were going to win the Cup, *could* win the Cup, because if you didn't go in believing it, how was that ever gonna happen?

It didn't seem like the first round was going to do anything to dissuade those thoughts. They won at home twice, won on the road, lost at home, and then won the series in DC. Mike was on the ice for the game-winning goal, scored by Reed, and he was enveloped in the messy celly afterward, thinking, *I'm so fucking lucky, what the fuck, I need to call Danny and tell him about this.*

In the postgame interviews Mike realized he was smiling more than he usually was when one of the reporters asked him about it.

"Uhhh, it's just really good to like…you know, last year was the first year we'd made it to the playoffs in five seasons, and we got knocked out in the first round. I think it kinda speaks for itself, bro."

The Hornets had easily won their series. Four games to nothing. Mike almost felt sorry for the Oaks, because he knew how *that* felt, but he was too busy feeling nervous about the fact that he'd be playing against Danny again. He wanted to win this so fucking badly, but he had some misgivings. For one, he didn't want to be responsible for injuring Danny and he didn't want to have to keep fighting. He never thought he'd actually think that sentence, let alone say it, so he kept it to his goddamn self.

CHAPTER NINE

May

The second round wasn't any easier on Danny than the first. Playoffs were always like that: you were amped up on adrenaline even while your body was eating itself from the inside out because you were run the fuck down after an eighty-something-game season. It was worse the older he got, although he grimly suited up for every game and went out there like nothing had changed. It was mostly sheer willpower that did it, willpower and the fact that he barely did anything except come home, drink, and pass out on the couch. The mountain of take-out containers in the trash can was growing, but he didn't have the motivation to throw them out. At this rate his sheets were probably about to get up off of the bed and walk away under their own power.

They had home ice advantage in Pittsburgh for the second round too, and he thought about inviting Mike to crash at his place instead of the hotel. He didn't do it, because it was both too risky in the general sense, and too dangerous to let Mike see how he was living these days. Also because he was superstitious enough that he didn't want to fuck during the playoffs and he knew that would've been a lot more difficult if Mike had actually been there.

Still, it was good being home with Buddy, at least. A little easier to fall asleep at night in his own bed rather than a hotel.

The first game went by quickly. He wasn't on the ice with Mike at all, which was the strange consequence of being the lowest man on the defense organizational chart while Mike was almost always second pair now. That was almost a relief, because he didn't want to fight if he didn't have to. The Hornets lost, 3–2 in OT, and the disgruntled noises of the crowd stayed with him all that night.

They only texted when they got home, both too exhausted to call. The last thing Mike wrote was, hey, hang in there, ok? i got a lot of shit i need to show u in gardena this summer.

The Hornets won the next two games, which Danny mostly remembered in flashes because he was so fucking tired, he was practically sleep-playing. Mäkelä pulled with a lower body injury in the first of the two, Morin skating anxiously around the bench during the brief time-out while they got him off the ice. Gears had his first playoff goal and let Danny pick him up off the ice and whirl him around, grinning like an idiot the entire time. Mike scored, too, but Danny couldn't celebrate with him. It was a strange feeling, trying to control his face on the bench, when part of him cursed the scoreboard and part of him wanted to be on his feet yelling.

The Cons won the next game and tied the series at 2–2, and then the Hornets took the lead again. The night before they were due to play the sixth game, Mike FaceTimed Danny from his apartment, and Danny looked him over again. He had a black eye and a raw abrasion on his chin, and he seemed more solemn than he had the last few calls.

"If we don't win tomorrow, we're out of the running."

"I know."

"I'm gonna be so fucking pissed."

"It's okay. You can drink your sorrows away and try again next year."

Mike slanted a gaze from the corner of his eye at him, the kind of look that cut Danny right down to the bone. He was sitting in bed, just in his boxers, body hunched over as he stared at Danny on the computer screen. "I haven't really been drinking that much recently. And it's funny, you know? Things have just seemed. Clearer."

Danny didn't want to know where this was going, so he changed the subject. "And you never know. We could fuck it up too."

"Yeah," Mike said, although he didn't sound particularly confident about it. "You know, I looked at college shit the other day."

"Yeah?"

"Yeah, it's…a lot, dude. I think I could maybe get into community college, but when am I ever gonna have the fucking time?"

"You could always do online classes and transfer later on. There are a ton of options."

"Why don't *you* go back?"

"I'm too old, buddy."

"Danny, you're like, not even out of your mid-thirties."

"Oh, thanks."

"You're not *old*."

"Old enough. Look, Mike, we should both try to sleep. Big day tomorrow."

"Yeah, I'm gonna kick your ass, old man."

"Looking forward to it, babe."

"Night, Danny."

"Night, Mike. See you on the ice."

It took him a long time to fall asleep, or at least, it did until he got out of bed and poured himself another drink. He didn't want things to be clearer. He slept after that, if not exactly easier.

Mike suited up for the game prepared to play his fucking heart out. It was different without Mäkelä, who'd seen them through every single playoffs for the last seven years. Sokolov—Socks, their backup goalie—was fine, but he wasn't Mäkelä, and just having him there was a reminder that Mäkelä had a long summer of rehab ahead of him. Bee had taken it surprisingly well. Or at least, she was worried as fuck, but ever the consummate professional, she'd shoved any emotion down beneath the mask.

"He's going to be okay," she'd told Mike after it happened.

"Are *you* okay?"

"I'm fine. We have games to win and being upset about this is not going to win them."

"Bee…you know you scare me a little, sometimes?"

She'd actually cracked a smile at that, the barest tilt of her mouth upward. "Someone's got to keep you in line, or you'd be insufferable."

The first period was a disaster. The Cons were slow getting a start on it, and Artyomov put one in the net only four minutes into the period. They battled to a draw for the rest of the first, Mike doing extra duty fighting along the boards in the defensive zone and carrying it out for clearer passes into the neutral zone. The second period was equally rough, a trench battle of attrition without a change to the scoreboard. He was frustrated, and he could tell Reed was frustrated, uncharacteristically on edge and seething.

It didn't help that Danny had shoulder-checked Singer into the boards. Mike knew it wasn't on purpose, although Reed sure as hell didn't seem to realize. Reed, who never fought, was actually trying to drop gloves with him. Mike pushed himself to skate between them, yelling at Reed as he did, "Hey, hey, stop that, are you fucking stupid, Reedsy?"

Danny looked exhausted, so Mike gave him that fight, let him basically wrestle Mike to the ice while he pretended to put in a good old college try. It wasn't his best moment, but it wasn't Danny's either. At least Danny wouldn't hurt Reed worse than Reed was prepared to be hurt, and Reed wouldn't hurt Danny out of some misguided attempt at protecting Singer.

"Thanks," Danny said, as the linesmen pulled them apart.

Mike patted him on the arm. "No problem."

He was still in the penalty box when Landry scored the second goal, and he knew from then on that it was probably over.

It was a somber mood in the locker room once the game ended. It had been heartbreaking last year and it was equally heartbreaking this year. Singer's head drooped as he stood before the team, Reed at his side.

"You all played your hearts out this year," he said,

his mouth a terse line. Singer always took the losses harder than anyone, and the rest of them took it hard. "Unfortunately, the Hornets did too. I'm very proud of everyone here. You all stepped up, and you all improved. Next year we'll be even better. Thanks."

Mike sat in his stall for a long time. It had felt bad last year, but it felt worse this year, because he'd felt like he'd been really *trying*, and it still wasn't quite good enough. Sure, there was next season, but that never made losing feel any better. Everyone just looked fucking depressed. Reed was on the verge of tears—he knew the fight had led to the loss—and Sally, calm as always, looked like he might've been plotting Artyomov's murder. Netty tried to spark up some interest in going out to party their sorrows away, but it seemed that most of the team was in Mike's boat: he just wanted to go home and sleep for fifty years.

Even though Danny's team had knocked him out of the playoffs, it made Mike feel a little better, almost instantly, to hear his voice later that night.

"Sorry, babe," was the first thing Danny said.

"It's okay," Mike mumbled. "Someone's gotta lose, and this time it was our turn."

"You'll get there next year."

"Yeah, yeah. Look, do me one favor, okay, Danny?"

"What?"

"Just win the Cup, okay? If you had to knock us out at least take it to the fucking *end*."

"I'll do my level best, Mike."

"Okay. Seriously, though. I'm serious."

"I know," Danny said, the corner of his mouth tipped up in the barest of smiles.

"How are you feeling? Everything holding together?"

“Yeah,” Danny said, stretching his arm experimentally. “Shoulder’s a little stiff, knee’s a little achy, but nothing I can’t handle.”

“Just be careful. Tampa’s got a few guys who’re like—it’s a legal hit, *technically*.”

“Aw, Mike, are you worried about me?”

“’Course I fucking am! I just—Danny, I—I care about you a lot, okay?”

“Mike…”

Danny actually sounded a little choked up, and Mike felt the panic that always came with talking about his emotions too much lancing through his stomach. It was like a heart attack but also like you were going to completely shit yourself. That’s what emotions felt like sometimes. It was too close to saying things you couldn’t come back from, not if the other person didn’t feel the same way.

“I mean, don’t let it go to your head, you stupid asshole, okay? I just want you around for, like, the summer.”

“Okay,” Danny said, but he was smiling again, and Mike found himself smiling reflexively back.

“Now,” Mike said, clearing his throat, “let’s talk about the Tampa guys you’re gonna be up against. I think Cameron is gonna be a problem, he’s like basically your size, but he’s younger—”

Tampa played the kind of hockey Danny used to play at the beginning of his career, before stacking injuries caught up with him. Fast, brutal, and tough. The first game was a slugfest in more ways than one, a grind with no score until the third period, and a finish in OT. Danny had to fight Cameron once, after he tried to level Artyomov, and as he was getting punched in the face, he was thinking about the talk he'd had with Mike last night and the irony of it.

"I told you!" Mike said on the phone later.

"I know, bud, you were right."

"That *fucker.*" His face was almost comically exaggerated in its frustration. "I wish I could've been on the ice with you. I would've kicked his *ass.*"

"I mean, I did okay," Danny said mildly.

"I know, but you shouldn't have to. You should just have to worry about winning, not young guys trying to fucking like—"

"Babe, you do realize what you're saying, right?"

Mike's ears turned bright red, and Danny could see it even in the dim light of Mike's bedroom. "That was—that was before I got to know you."

"I'm just teasing you."

"I *know*, but—look, I'm really—I'm really sorry about how things started. I've been—"

"It's okay. Mike, seriously, it's fine."

"I just don't—"

"It's *okay.*"

Mike looked troubled, like he wanted to go on, but he let Danny change the subject.

The next day Danny knew he was going to have a hard time with it. He woke up sore and bruised, moving slow as fuck to get out of the hotel bed and into the shower. As he brushed his teeth, he thought he was going to need a *long*-ass summer to recover if he was going to make it through next year. The thought, for the first time, held nothing. He couldn't feel any positivity toward it, only dread, even though he knew he was going to keep the inexorable march to the finish line going.

He texted his parents and Celi back. They'd both sent congratulations and their worries about the upcoming games. It was a lot. There were anywhere from four to seven games in the conference finals, and the same in the Cup finals. Danny had never made it that far before, even when his health had been better.

Gears came up to him to fist-bump before they went out onto the ice. "You good?" he asked Danny. It had become a ritual of its own.

Danny, whose skin was tingling a little because he'd taken some Percs to get through the game after a rough practice skate, said, "I'm good, little buddy. Seriously, don't worry about me."

It was a different story on the ice. Danny's knee buckled every time he pushed it skating, but luckily, he wasn't putting out too many minutes. Gears was playing his ass off in their zone, getting his stick in lanes and using perfect body positioning to take away the best angles, and Danny was thrilled for him, and for Landry, who had a current career high in playoff points. Danny didn't have much, but he was still skating, and that was good for something. Every minute he was on the ice meant he was closer to a summer where he could just try to rebuild his body, somehow.

In the second period he was on the ice a little more than he had been in the first, due solely to the fact that the Hornets kept taking stupid penalties and he was killing penalties. Danny didn't mind battling it out around the boards, but he really didn't want Tampa to tie it up, could *not* let them poke it past while he was distracted, and as he was making a rush for the puck, he didn't see Cameron until he ran straight into a hip check, and was airborne.

Bee had taken the loss harder than Mike did, but it cheered her up to watch the rest of the games together. Even when they'd been knocked out of the playoffs, she liked to analyze the competition and offer her thoughts. Sometimes Mike thought it would be better for her if she had *any* hobbies outside of hockey, even if she liked to go fishing or golfing during the summer, the boring shit hockey players usually did that Mike couldn't stand. But if she had, she wouldn't have been Bee.

Mäkelä was crashing at their apartment so he wouldn't have to go up and down the stairs at his own condo. He watched too, stretched out on the chaise lounge of the couch while Bee and Mike were shoved into the other end.

The second game was pretty rough watching; the first game had gone all the way to OT and the second game seemed to be a minor or major penalty almost every time Mike looked up. That meant Danny was on the ice more than he should have been, and Mike's stomach dipped, nervous every time he noticed him. He tried not to let on exactly how nervous he was, because of course Bee and Mäkelä didn't *know*, but he felt kind of sick every time he saw how Danny was skating, every time Mike knew how much he was hurting.

And then Cameron hip-checked Danny, Danny's body went flying, and the crowd in Tampa roared. Mike stopped breathing. Danny's back hit the boards and his head smacked down into the ice and he lay in a heap, not moving. The Hornets on the ice lunged at Cameron and it took a second after the whistle blew for the linesmen to separate everyone. Cameron stood there, helmet askew and face bloody, saying something to the linesman.

"Get up," Mike said, before he could stop himself, feeling like he was going to puke, "get up, get up, get up."

Danny wasn't moving. It was only a few seconds, but they felt like forever.

"Get up," Mike said to the television. His voice sounded funny.

"Michael," Bee said, staring at him, "are you—"

She had probably figured it out, but Mike couldn't care. He was on the edge of the couch, his fists clenched, watching as Danny hauled himself to his feet and skated off the ice without anyone helping him. That was a good sign, but Jesus fucking Christ, that hit had been brutal, and his head had smacked the ice so hard, and at such a bad angle. He had been *out*.

Mike finally exhaled once the camera moved away from Danny, although the announcers were talking about it, going through Danny's extensive list of injuries that should have been career ending, and Mike thought that he'd like to go to Tampa Bay and strangle both of them.

"Mike," Mäkelä said. "Are you okay?"

Mike thought about it for a second. "No, I'm really not."

"Do you…want to talk about it?" Bee asked, hesitant.

He had his head in his hands now. "You know how I told you earlier—*Danny's* my—my boyfriend, Bee. The one I was telling you about. He really…he really *can't* take hits like that…"

"Oh, Michael," Bee said, and he let her pull him toward her. Bee was a big woman, and her arms were really fucking strong, and it was weird, but it felt good to be muscled into a hug from which you couldn't escape even if you'd really wanted to. Behind her, Mäkelä had sat up straight, though his eyes were intense and his face was as stoic as ever.

It was like everything from the whole season was hitting him at once: how much he cared about Danny and how Danny was slowly killing himself and how fucking *Cameron* could have killed him there. It wasn't like he was crying, exactly, because Mike didn't do that, but he could hear the way his breathing sounded, high and ragged, scratchy in his throat. He stayed there until the announcers started talking about Danny again.

"It looks like Garcia is back on the bench, folks, and he's been cleared to keep playing—"

"What?" Mike said, pulling himself out of Bee's arms.

"What?" she repeated. "That's *crazy*, he was clearly unconscious."

"He's really stubborn. It's. Jesus, I hope he didn't fucking *lie* to them," Mike said, even though he knew that was exactly what Danny had done. "Excuse me, I gotta—"

He grabbed his phone. WHAT R U DOING, he texted Danny. DONT PLAY YOU IDIOT

Bee and Mäkelä grimly watched the TV. Danny was back on the ice, but Mike couldn't bear to look. He had probably sent at least ten increasingly crazed texts, which he knew Danny wouldn't be able to read because his phone was in the dressing room. Neither Bee nor Mäkelä said anything to him, although Bee kept her hand on his shoulder the whole time. He was grateful they weren't trying to talk because he didn't know what he was going to say. All he could do was stare at the TV and clench his fists and hope that Danny wasn't going to fucking *die*.

The worst part was that as Mike watched, he could tell that Danny wasn't skating the way he normally did. It wasn't even the injury, he just missed things he usually would have caught or looked aggressive going after the puck in a situation when normally he wouldn't. Mike wouldn't have been able to see it if he hadn't spent so much time studying Danny's games, but it was like watching a different person wearing his body, and Mike didn't fucking like it at all.

Finally, the game ended—the Hornets won—and Danny hadn't taken any other hits. Mike gave it two hours, sweating the whole time, and then went into his bedroom to make the call.

"Hello?" Danny said when he answered. He was in his hotel room, alone, and he looked awful, with two bruised eyes and hollows in his cheeks. He even *sounded* bad. Groggy and in pain.

"Danny! What the hell were you—are you *okay*—what the *fuck*—"

"I'm fine, Mike," Danny mumbled. "I'm good to skate. The trainers said so."

"How the *fuck* are you good to skate? I saw your head hit the ice, and I saw you—that didn't even *look* like you out there."

Danny paused, for a long time, and then he said, "I don't remember talking to the trainers. I don't remember going back out on the ice."

Mike couldn't even say anything at first. The breath just came out of his lungs like he'd been punched. He listened to Danny breathing on the other end of the line, almost comforted that it was like, proof that he was still alive. "Dude, that's concussion shit. That's *bad* concussion shit."

"I know."

"Why the fuck are you—"

"Look, Mike, you wouldn't fucking understand. This is—this is one of my last years where I'm going to have this chance. The last year, this entire—what I've done to myself has a chance of paying off. I have to be out there. I have to do this for the team."

"No you *don't*! You don't have to do anything! The team will fucking understand if you can't play because you have a *concussion*!"

"I have to—"

"Fuck this! What about your—talk to Bee, for fuck's sake, if you won't listen to me."

"Mike—"

But Mike was already dragging the computer back out into the living room and slamming it down on the coffee table. "Bee! Would you fucking tell him it's *crazy* to try to play with a concussion?"

Bee, however surprised she may have been, was immediately up to the task. Her serious face was intent on Danny's image as she said, "Mr. Garcia, please listen to Michael."

"*Mister*—it's just Danny, Jesus."

"You are not helping your team by playing this way," she said sternly.

"Look—thank you for—can you put Mike back on, please?"

Bee handed the computer over and Mike stared at Danny's exhausted, worn-out, injured face, like if he looked intently enough, he could change Danny's mind.

He hated how fucking small his voice sounded when he said, "Danny, *please*."

"Look, babe," Danny said. "I have to. I'm sorry. Look, I have to go," and he ended the call.

Mike was left sitting there, with Bee and Mäkelä staring at him. This wasn't exactly how he'd wanted this to go, but he was too worried for Danny to care about being embarrassed. "What the *fuck* do I do, Bee? He can't play. He's going to, like—get serious brain damage, or post-concussion syndrome, or something. He's going to fucking kill himself."

"You have to do something to convince him," Bee agreed. "Something to stop him."

"I do not think you can do it from here," Mäkelä cut in.

"From here," Mike repeated. "I can't do it *from here*."

"Michael—" Bee said, almost like a warning.

"No! Danny is—Danny's like. He's worth taking that goddamn chance, for fuck's sake. I'm going to—hang on, I gotta call his sister and I gotta get to the airport, sorry, I can't—"

Danny was well aware that what he was doing was fucking stupid, but that didn't mean he was going to make a different choice. He'd been through enough concussions to know that this was a bad one. He wasn't sure how blacked-out Danny had managed to talk his way through the preliminary examination, but by this point in his career, he knew what to say to get back out on the ice, and he'd intentionally thrown off the baseline evals when he'd gone through them the first season he'd played with the Hornets. So it wasn't surprising he'd managed to do it even with his brain disconnected. That didn't mean he felt any better, physically.

He slept most of the plane ride back to Pittsburgh, and he threw up once in the plane bathroom, flushing the toilet at the same time to mask the sound of his retching. His head ached and he felt dizzy whenever he walked. It was hard to respond to simple questions, and sometimes he'd see double when he moved his head too fast. But he was determined to stay on the ice anyway, because at this rate, he wasn't going to make it to the next season.

He took a cab home from the airport and hauled his bags up the stairs to the house and walked right to the couch. Gingerly settled himself down, and sort of just…passed out.

He woke up an interminable amount of time later, groggy and disoriented, to the sound of the doorbell ringing furiously. The noise was awful, slicing right through his skull, and at first, he lay there hoping whoever it was would go away. This turned out to be wishful thinking, because the bell kept ringing, and his headache was pounding in the back of his skull.

He'd missed two calls from Marty. He'd get to those later.

Danny stood up, shedding Buddy off of his shoulder as he did, and limped for the front door, intending to curse out whichever neighbor had been determined to torture him that way. It took him a minute to coordinate his hands to get the door unlocked, but when he did, he slammed it open.

Mike was standing on the porch. His hair was still at its playoffs length and he was wearing clothes wrinkled like he'd slept in them. He looked exhausted.

"...what the fuck?" Danny said finally.

Mike stared back at him, arms crossed over his chest. "Let me in."

Danny hesitated. It was stupid. Of course he should let Mike in. But he knew what was coming next if he did and he wasn't sure if he was ready for it.

"Please," Mike said, and the look on his face cut right through Danny the same way the doorbell had.

He opened the door.

Mike threw himself at Danny, wrapping his arms around him. His balance was bad enough that it almost knocked him over, but he managed to hold himself steady. Hugged Mike back. It felt good. It felt so good. He'd missed it. It was grounding. Not just a warm body next to his, but *Mike*, every stubborn inch of him.

"I'm gonna say some stuff to you," Mike mumbled into Danny's chest. "Let me talk."

"Mike—"

"No! Don't interrupt me. You fucking owe me this much, okay?"

Danny, his mouth dry, let Mike walk him backward until his legs hit the couch.

"Sit."

He did.

Mike got down on his knees on the floor, in between the bracket of Danny's legs. His hands rested on Danny's thighs. It was a position he'd been in before, but there was nothing sexual about this, it was just Mike staring up at him with an expression that Danny couldn't look at for too long. Like the sun, it hurt.

"Look. I know I'm not fucking good at talking about feelings. And I know you're not any fucking good at listening to anyone. But I can't let you go out there and play again. It's too dangerous, you could permanently injure yourself, Danny, you could fucking *die*. Hockey's not worth that."

"Mike, it is worth it, and I have to."

"Are you seriously going to do that to me?"

"I—" Danny faltered. He hadn't thought about it in any sense except the damage he was going to do to himself. The damage he'd always done to himself and accepted as part of his life. Part of his personality.

That had been his entire value to any team he'd been on since that first injury, his ability to take damage and keep going even when it hurt. That was Danny: dependable, solid, a guy who gave 110% even when his body couldn't physically keep up with him.

"Look," Mike said again. His teeth worried his lower lip and his eyes were bright with tears that hadn't fallen yet, and he looked so unlike his usual self that Danny wanted to reach out and pull him off of his knees, tell him that no matter what happened, things were going to be fine. "Please, Danny. I love you, okay? I love you, you stubborn *asshole*, and if you kill yourself out on the ice, I'm—I don't know what I'd do, but please, don't fucking make me find out, okay?"

"I'm not—you—what?"

"I love you," Mike said, like he was angry about it. Maybe he was just angry at Danny. He'd pushed himself off of his knees and climbed into Danny's lap, his hands smoothing out Danny's hair, his shirt. "I love you so fucking much—"

"You shouldn't, Mike. You really shouldn't."

"Well, I fucking *do*, all right?"

"Mike—"

"I really fucking *love* you. Don't play tomorrow. Tell your coach you need to get your head looked at again. Let me take care of you. *Please.* I'm not asking, I'm begging, dude."

The ice in his chest, the thing that had begun cracking that day in Vegas and probably even before, shattered. He took a deep, heaving breath. "I—Mike, I don't know what I'm going to do if I don't play. If I have to retire. What's going to be left of me."

Mike tucked his head into the space between Danny's chin and his chest, one of those affectionate gestures that casually murdered him. "We'll figure it out together, dude. You're not gonna, like, be *alone* for this, okay? I promise. You have your family, and you have me. And I'm not going anywhere."

"Mike, I—" He could hear his voice, thick with unshed tears, with the weight of years of not letting himself rely on anyone else. The weight of years of disappointments and quiet houses. And here was Mike, who'd fallen into his life by accident; Mike, who it was hard to imagine not having in it anymore. Here was Mike, asking him to take care of himself, for no other reason than because he loved Danny. His hands were tangled in Mike's hair, an anchor. The weight of his body, a comfort. "Okay. I'll… I'll make the call."

Mike's arms around him were crushing. *"Thank you."*

"And I—I love you, too."

Mike pulled away, and even though his eyes were still too bright, he was grinning. "Of course you do, dude. I'm fucking awesome."

Danny laughed, unsteadily, and somehow so relieved. “Arrogant little shit.”

“Same thing, babe,” Mike said, and leaned forward to kiss him, carefully, so fucking gently that Danny’s eyes were burning again before he pulled away. “Come on. Make that call, and I’ll get you something to eat.”

V.

SUMMER

CHAPTER TEN

June

The first thing Mike had thought when Danny had let him in—besides his genuine worry for Danny—was that Danny's house was fucking depressing. It wasn't that it was a disaster, exactly. It was partially renovated, but the parts that hadn't been fixed had seen better days. And he was worse than any hockey player Mike had seen about buying furniture. There was the couch and the TV, a kitchen table, and his bed, but that was about it. There was almost no decoration. Mike thought about Danny living in that miserable fucking house all alone, except for Buddy, and his heart kind of clenched.

He wrestled Danny upstairs and into bed that first night, and texted Bee, we're good.

I love you, Michael, she'd written back. You're very brave.

stfu, he wrote back, then sent her a picture of Buddy, who still viewed Mike as a threat and hissed and puffed himself up every time Mike came near.

That thing is horrifying.

that's what i said!

Okay, okay. Go see to your man.

thx, bee. tell mäkelä thx too.

Danny had called the Hornets' coach, gotten checked out again, and had been diagnosed with a stage three concussion. Luckily, there were a couple days in between games, so the worst of the puking and dizziness was over by the time the Hornets were playing again.

It wasn't like things were better: he was still worried as fuck about Danny on a number of levels, both health-wise and drinking-wise. At least he was here to help out. It had been kind of eye-opening how easy it was to just slot into life at Danny's, the morning routine of helping him get dressed and out the door to doctor's appointments or making him breakfast and dinner. He still didn't really know what to do with himself, so he did shit like order groceries online so Danny would have something to eat besides, like, expired eggs and alcohol, and poked around the house for small things he could clean or fix. It wasn't like he ever enjoyed sitting doing nothing, and Danny's house had plenty of shit that needed fixing.

And he watched at home while the Hornets played their third and fourth games and Danny sat in the press box in the CEC and San Jose. They won the third game, putting the series at 2–1, lost the fourth, 2–2, and went back down to San Jose for the fifth game, which put the Hornets ahead at 3–2. There wasn't really a reason for Danny to go, but he was determined to be there in the event that the team did win and determined to be there if they lost. He'd told Mike, *It's Gears' first playoffs, I have to be there*, and that, at least, Mike had understood.

Each time Danny left, Mike stayed at the house in Pittsburgh, checking in on him in the evening.

"You know, you really shouldn't like…be drinking with a concussion, dude," he said, as Danny was packing up his bags to come back to Pittsburgh for what was hopefully the final game.

"I know," Danny said, and didn't make any other excuses.

"I wish you wouldn't."

"I know."

"Danny—"

"Can we talk about it in the offseason, babe?"

"Sure," Mike said, unhappily.

"Hey—Mike," Danny said, not *exactly* trying to change the subject but close enough that Mike felt kind of suspicious about it at first. "Celi and Chris normally have tickets to the last game, but Josie's got a bad cold, so Chris is staying in the hotel room with her. Would you want to sit with Celi for the game?"

"Sure. If that's what you want."

"I'd really like you to be there. If we win it."

Mike ran his hand through his hair, which he really needed to fucking shave again. It was weird, having it that long. "You will," he told Danny. "Just don't—just be careful if you do."

When he hung up the call, Mike wondered how long this was going to be tenable, watching Danny slowly killing himself, even if he wasn't like, being flashy about doing it on the ice. It was, like, kind of life-changing to admit that he loved Danny, was *in love* with Danny—but it was another thing to just do nothing while Danny did everything he could to kill himself slowly. He put it out of his head for now, because there wasn't much he could do at the moment.

But after the playoffs, they'd see.

And maybe he'd look into the school thing more seriously.

Both of them had some shit to work out. But it could wait.

Danny had finally called Marty back from a cab to the stadium, and he still felt kind of shell-shocked by the conversation. Marty had been calling to check in on him like he always did when Danny got benched with an injury, but he'd also been calling to offer him a job. One of Marty's assistant coaches had quit suddenly in the offseason, and Marty wanted Danny to take the job, contingent on completing a stint in rehab.

Danny had hesitated. "Can I think about it, Marty?"

"Sure, bud. I told our GM you probably wouldn't be able to make up your mind until after the playoffs are over. But get back to me soon, because I gotta make some moves."

"Marty...do you really think this is a smart idea? Do you really think this is something I could *do*?"

"If you get healthy, Danny? You're gonna be perfect."

Danny didn't quite know if he believed it, but he didn't have much of a choice. It was rattling around in the back of his head as he sat in the press box waiting for the game to begin. It was an opportunity to keep hockey in his life, to do the kind of work he'd found most satisfying this last year: helping Mike reach his potential, helping Landry grow the fuck up, gaining Gears' friendship and trust, before he'd ruined that too. But it would require doing something he still couldn't quite accept as necessary.

It rattled around in the back of his head while his team played. They were on fire, like the injuries they'd taken over the course of the playoffs had only galvanized them further, made them want it more. It was still hard to focus on the play, because his head felt fuzzy and a little confused. But he did his best. It was almost anticlimactic, in a way, because up in the press box, he wasn't able to be there on the bench to participate. He cheered, reservedly, so he didn't move his head too much, when the guys tied up the score. Cheered again when they pushed it ahead by one, groaned when San Jose tied it up again. In the last two minutes of the third period, San Jose pulled their goalie, and Gears, trying to clear the puck from the blue line, watched it fly past the two defenders and hit the back of the net.

The seconds ticked down until the time ran out and then the ice erupted in screaming, and Danny missed some of the celebrations because he was heading down onto the ice to join it, buffeted by hugs from teammates who really should've remembered the concussion thing but were too excited to care.

Gears skated up to him then, a huge smile on his face, and Danny said, "You won it for us, bud," and Gears' entire face went bright red with embarrassed pleasure.

"I mean, so did everyone, so did you—"

"And *you* scored the game winner on *the* Cup game," Danny said, patting him on the back. "I'm really proud of you."

He looked up on the Jumbotron and saw Celi, tears

streaming down her face, clutching Mike's arm while he patted her reassuringly on the back, and felt almost poleaxed with how important Mike was to him. How much he wanted him to stay. All of this time he'd been worried about Mike leaving once he realized all the shit that was wrong with Danny, with his life, but they were things that were within Danny's control—if he accepted the help he'd been offered. The opportunities people who loved him had made sure to extend to him.

"You okay, dude?" Gears asked.

"I—have to make a phone call—"

"You *what*? *Now?*"

Danny took out his phone, right there on the ice, and called Marty back. It was hard to hear over all of the screaming.

"Danny, what the fuck are you doing, bud?" Marty yelled. "You have a Stanley Cup to hoist!"

"I'll get to that in a minute," Danny said, impatient. "But I want you to know I'll do it. I'll take the job. And I'll go to rehab."

"Buddy, you do *not* know how happy you've made me."

"I dunno, man, I'm feeling pretty fuckin' hopeful myself. Okay, I gotta go, the Cup—it's my turn."

"Go get 'em, kid."

And so Danny walked out onto the ice, and with Gears' and Gray's help, lifted the Cup over his head, and it was a pretty fucking great feeling. But even better was knowing that Mike was in the crowd, watching, and would be there when he went home.

Danny couldn't wait to tell him everything.

BURYING THE HATCHET:
THE UNLIKELY FRIENDSHIP
OF RIVAL ENFORCERS

Posted: August 13, 2023-4:59 PM
Sophia Dawsey | @sophiamdawsey |
sophia.dawsey@postgazette.com

When you think of Danny Garcia and Mike Sato, the first thing that probably comes to mind is their bitter, violent rivalry. Playing for teams with a fifty-year history of hatred, the two defensemen started off on the wrong foot in Sato's first game, and things only got worse from there. They now, officially, hold the record for most fights between two players in league history.

I was intrigued by their narrative after seeing a picture of Sato attending Garcia's Cup Day, reached out to both men to discuss, and was pleasantly surprised when they agreed.

We met for the interview at Garcia's parents' restaurant, a charming neighborhood diner that has been a Detroit staple since the 1930s. Garcia, who retired at the end of the season following a serious concussion, looked relaxed and healthy. Sato, a menace on the best of days, seemed fidgety and on edge.

The conversation opened discussing the history of enforcers and their role in the league. Both men believe that the league is transitioning away from players whose only purpose is to fight.

"That's why I had to change my game," Sato says. "And that's why Danny, you know, kind of saved my career."

"You saved your own career," Garcia interrupts.

"You pushed me in the right direction."

This kind of dynamic continues throughout the interview. Both of them alternately argue and look to each other for reassurance, and Sato, who I've rarely seen smiling, smiles often when he catches Garcia's eye.

I ask whether Garcia could describe the beginning of their unusual friendship.

Garcia thinks for a moment and looks sideways at Sato. "You know, when you meet a guy who plays a similar game to yours, you'll always have things in common. He's really just coming into his prime and I was ending my career, but we've had a lot of the same experiences. A lot of things to talk about."

I point out that they still fought on the ice. Frequently and violently, in fact.

"Well," Garcia says, "that's the job, isn't it?"

Sato shifts uncomfortably, and I notice that his hand is freshly tattooed. He is covered from head to toe in black ink, but the new design on his hand depicts two playing cards, an ace of spades, in black, and a king of hearts, in red.

"Can you explain the significance of this, Mike?"

"No," he says, but after meeting Garcia's eyes, looks

back at me, and amends, "It's his number. Twenty-one." When asked why he had chosen that design, Sato shrugs. "He's my best friend. Everything I have in my career now is thanks to him. Seemed right."

The feelings are just as strong on Garcia's side. When asked about his future plans, he discloses that he has recently completed a sixty-day inpatient rehab and will be starting as an assistant coach in New Jersey prior to the season's beginning.

"He's going to be really good," Sato says, firmly. "New Jersey's very lucky to have him."

"Mike—" Garcia attempts to interrupt.

"They *are*."

Garcia is a big man, but a thoughtful one. His face is nothing but serious when he says, "Mike says I saved his career, but really, he saved my life."

Sato, normally argumentative, does not say anything. Instead, he turns red.

"Can you explain a little further?" I inquire.

Garcia nods. "My last season—I was not in a good place. I wasn't making good decisions, and I was drinking too much; taking pills to numb the pain. I don't think I would have had the courage to ask for help if Mike hadn't been there to give me a push."

"Danny—"

"It's true."

Sato looks down at his hands, and half smiles.

Sato himself is coming off of a career year and is looking forward to next season. When asked about his plans, he responds, "Really the goal now is just to win the Cup. We've got the talent for it and our group has been together a few years now to build chemistry. I believe we can do it."

"We're going to give you a run for your money," Garcia responds, smiling, "but I believe in you."

It would seem that no matter how close the friendship, some element of rivalry remains. After the interview's conclusion, Garcia introduces me to his parents, and we speak about Garcia and Sato for some time, off the record.

It is touching to know that no matter the team or personal rivalries, players in this league can make human connections at a higher level and support each other through tough times.

I will be keeping an eye on both Sato and Garcia in the 2022–2023 season.

Listen to the full interview here.

* * * * *

ACKNOWLEDGMENTS

There are a number of people without whom this book couldn't have been published, and I would like to thank you individually:

Deidre Knight, my agent; your advice, guidance, and firm belief in my writing have been invaluable through this process.

The entire team at Carina—Stephanie Doig but especially Mackenzie Walton, my editor; your patience, eye for seeding a story arc, and careful attention to everything from depth charts to Mike's hair length have made this a much better book than it was when I submitted it. Thank you, also, to Stefanie Molina for a thoughtful and thorough sensitivity read.

Cait, for reading this book and its siblings as I wrote them one email at a time way back in 2018. Your reactions and your thoughts kept me going even when I floundered and without your initial enthusiasm, I don't think this book would be finished today. I appreciate each and every one of your "Mer Web says—"

Jo, for always being so excited to talk stories. You have made writing so much fun for me this year and that has been such a gift. I always looked forward to seeing you in the Gdoc, even if you should have been sleeping.

My server buds, for making me laugh on a daily basis and entertaining my ridiculous ideas and entertaining me with your own.

Cait Nary and KD Casey, for your patience, kindness, and willingness to give advice to a newbie without my being able to provide anything in return. I hope one day I can pay this forward.

Shevaun and Laura for always being there even when I disappeared for long stretches of time to work on my stories or because life was too much. You are both so kind and talented and I owe you the world for putting up with me.

And above all, thank you to my family—all of you—for always believing in me even though I told you you're never allowed to read my books.

(Mom, I will never forgive you for making me a Flyers fan.)

Turn the page to read an excerpt from *Delay of Game* by Ari Baran, the next book in the Penalty Box series.

CHAPTER ONE

July

Zachary Reed had a lot of obsessive thoughts about the captain of his hockey team, but one of the few G-rated ones was: *I need to win Nate a Cup.*

It was probably his least fun obsessive thought, but also the one he had the most. Or almost the most. It had come to him in his second season with the Cons and hadn't gone away.

If anything it had actually gotten worse the longer he knew Nate Singer.

He'd ended up thinking about it until it festered, and now here he was in Tulum, drunk off his ass at the pool of an all-inclusive resort with four of his tier one bros and a bunch of extremely hot strangers wearing next to nothing, and all he could think was: *I need to win Nate a Cup, how am I gonna win Nate a Cup, what will Nate's face look like when I win him a Cup?*

He wondered how it would feel to know that Nate knew that Zach had done it for *him.*

Like: Nate wanted to win, obviously. You didn't wear a C for a major league hockey team by not caring about winning. But he was noble about it. He had all kinds of ideas about the *team's* legacy and what the city deserved. Zach just wanted to make his best bro cry tears of joy, no matter how many people he had to flatten against the boards on the way.

Zach just wanted to give Nate something no one had ever given him before.

He shouldn't be thinking about this.

He was on vacation with the tier one bros, and vacation time with those dudes was all about drinking and dancing really badly and fucking their way through wherever they happened to be. Occasionally, in the past, hooking up with Jammer, who was at the very top tier of tier one bros. Blowing off steam and *not* thinking about hockey for at least a week or two and then crawling, feeling like the living dead, back to the airport to return to real life and training. Refreshed, recharged, whatever happened there stayed there.

Jammer handed him a Modelo Negra. "Dude… you've got that look on your face."

"I'm *thinking*."

"Since when do you do that?"

Zach didn't bother answering him. The pool was saltwater, painted so that the water looked like the crystal blue of the ocean when the light reflected through it. A deeply tanned girl in a barely-there string bikini jumped into the pool and emerged, glistening, to the surface. Jammer watched her intently. As she turned and flipped her hair, spraying droplets everywhere, she saw them looking and smiled; Jammer whistled. He still played for the Royal and was one of the few dudes from the team that Zach still saw on a regular basis. He was a connoisseur of women of all sorts, but he smiled a little ruefully now after looking from the woman to Zach and back.

"She's into *you*, bro."

Zach waved him away. It wasn't like hot people being into him was anything unusual. Generally, he was usually pretty enthusiastic about that. But today, it was just a distraction. "I told you, dude, I'm thinking. I've gotta like… I've gotta win Nate a Cup, you know? I've gotta just *do it*, man."

Jammer's sudden laughter startled him, even though it wasn't that loud over the noise of everyone else screaming and *whoo*ing. He laughed until he wheezed and coughed, and then said, "*Bro.* Oh, bro, you got it bad."

"How do you think I should do it?" Zach said, ignoring him. Not only was Jammer not helping, Zach couldn't let the idea go. And besides, he didn't have *anything* bad. In fact, he was excellent and had never been better. Unlike Jammer, who was content to sit here drinking and ogling pool-goers, Zach was being responsible and thinking about the future.

So really, he was great.

Fantastic.

The best.

He struggled into a sitting position. He was aware he probably looked insane. His hair had gotten long over the summer and he had it up in a miniature topknot, but he was drunk and disheveled enough that the overall effect was less hipster, more hobo. He knew he had that manic intensity you could only get when you were completely fucked up, but he couldn't do anything about that.

He felt slightly insane.

His skin felt hot and tight and uncomfortable, and it wasn't entirely due to the sun.

"Jammer, I gotta do it, I gotta get it for him, this is gonna be the year, but like...should I fight more? What about in the dressing room, should I like, step it up with the rooks? Bro, I gotta do *something*, we were so close last year. You should've seen his *face* when we lost, I can't let him go through that again..."

Jammer stopped laughing and started staring at him like he'd grown another head. "Who are you and what've you done with my Reedsy?"

Zach stared at the pool. The girl was smiling at them again. He thought about how much time he was wasting here in Mexico, when he could be at home, helping Nate achieve his dreams. Zach was gripped with the sudden need to see him, like, right now, even though he couldn't tell Nate about his grand ambitions. It wouldn't be until Nate handed him the Cup on the ice that he'd be able to say, *I did this for you, this was all for you.*

He staggered to his feet. "Bro, I gotta... I gotta go."

"What? Go *where*? Are you gonna puke or something?"

"I'm gonna... I gotta go back to Philly, like, right now, bro. I gotta change my flights. I gotta go, I gotta go."

"Wait a minute, Reeds—"

But Zach was already half running, half staggering to their suite, and he didn't hear whatever else Jammer had to say to him.

Nate walked briskly down the half block it took to get to his parents' house. As always, he greeted them with a new bottle of wine that they would end up storing in the basement and never using. As always, he let his mother hug him and plant an awkwardly wet kiss on his cheek. As always, his father clapped him on the back. His parents lived pretty much around the corner from him; the developers had started building new townhomes nearby, he had jumped at the chance to buy property close to them. It had its downsides, of course, but it was still by design.

The downsides became evident later on, after they'd sat down for dinner.

"You look like you're a million miles away, kid," his father said, from across the table. Dad was a big man, although he'd lost a couple of inches as he'd aged. Nate was taller than him for the first time he could remember, and the experience was disconcerting. His parents had been older when they'd had him, and it was weird being reminded that they were aging in *real* ways.

"I'm just thinking." Nate pushed the meat and potatoes around on his plate with the mismatched cutlery his mom put out when company wasn't there. Coming home always felt like this, on the defensive in case his parents were worrying about him again. It was funny: they were so fucking proud of him, but they also still talked to him like he was the shy, anxious teenager they had dragged to a therapist's office. Who'd refused to talk at all.

Nate had a lot of responsibilities resting on his shoulders. When the season ended those responsibilities, technically, evaporated. At least for a time. Once everyone packed up their lockers and went home to their respective states and provinces and countries, Nate was left alone in Philadelphia, the way he always was. The beginning of the offseason was a familiar routine. Rehab the injuries he inevitably played through by the end of the year. Take a couple of weeks to try to gain back some of the weight he'd lost. Start working out in the gym before eventually getting back on the ice. He usually spent some time at his parents' house, because they never got to see him as often as they would have liked during the season, and because he was a dutiful son.

None of those things helped him feel any better about the season ending. None of those things actually made him feel any kind of hope about the next season on the horizon, but he did them anyway, because that's what was expected of him.

"About what?" Mom asked, bringing another serving dish out of the kitchen.

It was always like this, too: too much food, too many things he shouldn't be eating, even though he did need to pack on some pounds before training seriously started. "The summer. Next season. If the front office is going to make any trades at the draft, or whether they're going to let us try again as a group next season. You know. The usual."

He hated talking about this shit with them: they didn't understand why he got like this in the offseason. They never had. It wasn't worth trying to explain either, because that just made it worse. They *wanted* to get it. But their jobs were so straightforward, with success measured in making a bus route on time or hitting your quotas at the shipyard. Not that either of his parents worked easy jobs. They'd labored hard to put food on the table when he was younger, to pay for his hockey fees and equipment. To make sure he was doing what he loved to do.

It just wasn't the same. He made more money now

than they'd probably made in their entire working careers, and it didn't matter, because when it came down to it, he was a failure. He looked down at the brisket Mom had probably been cooking since earlier that afternoon and pushed at it with his fork again.

"Have you heard from Rachel at all?" Mom asked abruptly.

"What? No, why would she—why would you even ask?"

"I just worry that you're lonely, honey. And I thought maybe… I don't know. Maybe she would have missed you too."

Nate could feel his face flushing, hot and red. Rachel was his ex-fiancée; they'd been together since high school. She had been planning their life together almost since that time. That hadn't stopped her from abruptly dumping him two seasons ago, right around when they were supposed to have started planning the wedding.

His parents still held out hope they would get back together because on paper, everything about Rachel was perfect. She was smart, she was ambitious and she was *beautiful*. She was Jewish. She had grown up on the Main Line and had those Main Line manners, the kind of girl who'd gone to Camp Ramah in the summers. But when her parents moved into the city when she was in high school, she had met Nate and had never looked back.

"I'm not lonely," he said. His mouth felt stuffed full of cotton balls. "I have Zach. I mean, I have the team and Zach. And Bee, I mean, and the rest of the guys. I'm really busy."

It was stupid, that his mind immediately jumped to Zach, when Mom was talking about *romance*. But

Zach was the person in his life: the biggest and most important person in his life. Pretty much the only person he felt completely comfortable around.

"But don't you want to be able to come *home* to someone?" Mom asked, patting Dad on the hand. "When I came home from a rough night driving the 3, it helped to have your dad here to vent to."

"It's the last thing on my mind right now," Nate said. It wasn't a lie, exactly. He hated lying to his parents. It was easier just to omit things, the same way he'd done his whole life. To retreat into silence and let their well-meaning worry wash over him. It was the same reason he kept coming back, dutiful and uncomfortable and awkward, even though he knew how the conversations would end.

"Okay," Mom said. "But just so you know, if you want to, we started paying membership dues at B'nai Abraham again, so we could always..."

"Mom! I don't have *time*." Nate exhaled. "Look, I'm sorry. I didn't mean to snap at you, I really didn't. I just have—uh, a lot on my mind. Could we please—could we please talk about something else?"

"Sure," Dad said, skeptical.

It was a quiet rest of the dinner. Nate's hands and back felt clammy and sweaty as he kept his mouth shut during it. The only comfort was knowing what he'd planned next. He just had to make it through another few hours.

The Penalty Box series is available wherever books are sold, including Harlequin.com.